THE
EMPIRE
OF
DREAMS

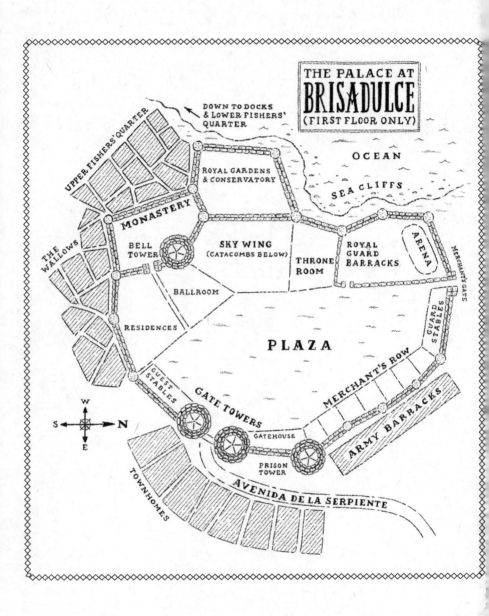

THE
EMPIRE
OF
DREAMS

RAE·CARSON

GREENWILLOW BOOKS

An Imprint of HarperCollins *Publishers*

The Empire of Dreams
Text copyright © 2020 by Rae Carson

The text of this book is set in 11-point Bell MT.
Book design by Paul Zakris

Library of Congress Cataloging-in-Publication Data

Names: Carson, Rae, author.
Title: The empire of dreams / Rae Carson.
Description: First edition. | New York, NY :
Greenwillow Books, an imprint of HarperCollinsPublishers, [2020] |
Audience: Ages 13 up. | Audience: Grades 7-9. |
Summary: "After unearthing a conspiracy at court, Red Sparkle Stone, the foundling orphan Empress Elisa has taken under her wing, dares to become a recruit for the Royal Guard—something no woman has done before"—Provided by publisher.
Identifiers: LCCN 2019060234 |
ISBN 9780062691903 (hardback) | ISBN 9780062691927 (ebook)
Subjects: CYAC: Fantasy. | Kings, queens, rulers, etc. —Fiction. |
Sex role—Fiction. | Foundlings—Fiction.
Classification: LCC PZ7.C2423 Emp 2020 | DDC [Fic]—dc23
LC record available at https://lccn.loc.gov/2019060234)

20 21 22 23 24 PC/LSCH 10 9 8 7 6 5 4 3 2 1
First Edition

GREENWILLOW BOOKS

For every reader who wrote me a letter, emailed,
or messaged me on social media to demand that I tell Red's story.
You made this book happen.
Thank you.

1

Then

THE little girl's memories began in a dark cellar.

She huddled there, knees to chest, fingertips digging into the earthen floor. She liked the feel of it, the coolness, the slight sting as grit separated skin from nails. The earth had always called to her, and she had always answered. Her mamá despaired of her ever having clean hands.

She would have stayed forever if she could, there in the cool dark, smelling the baskets of turnips and hanging braids of garlic, digging with her fingertips. Because it was better than being *up there*, with the banging and the screaming, which she was definitely not listening to but instead digging and digging and digging. Maybe she could dig a tunnel to the other side of the world, or at least a hole so deep she could disappear for real.

She thought hard about the other side of the world. What it must be like. Everyone said it was hotter than a fire pit in summer, with a sea of sand that stretched as far as the eye could see. She'd love to see something like that, she truly would.

The girl imagined it so hard that she did a wonderful job of not listening to *up there* for a very long time. Until she realized she had to pee.

The outhouse was up the ladder, out the door, and off to the right of the hut she shared with her mamá. She was not to leave the cellar. Mamá had specifically said to hide, to be silent, to not cry, no matter what happened. *No matter what happens.* But she was a big girl now, and big girls did not pee in their drawers.

The girl pressed her knees tighter together. It would be over soon. The noises would stop; the trapdoor would open. Light would pour down, and Mamá's hand would reach into the darkness to lift her out.

Something banged against the floor directly overhead. She looked up, startled, as dust fluttered down and peppered her eyes. The girl did not whimper, or even gasp. She blinked against the dirt, blinked and blinked until her cheeks ran with tears. But she would not cry out, and she would not pee. *"Put on your big-girl face,"* Mamá had said.

"Where is it?" someone yelled. A man, with as monstrous a voice as she'd ever heard.

Someone responded, and though she couldn't make out the pleading words, she'd know her mamá's tone and cadence no matter what.

"How much must I destroy before you tell me?" the monster said.

Whatever reply her mamá made was drowned out by a great crash. Something large had been knocked to the floor. The table maybe. Then came the kettle, clanging against the

RAE·CARSON

stone hearth, and the girl stopped digging to put her hands over her ears.

The crashing and pounding went on and on, raining dust onto her head as she cowered in the dark. She pressed her palms to her ears, hard, hard, harder, until her skull hurt.

Silence came, as sudden as a blow.

The girl dared to remove her hands and lift her head, and it seemed that her heart pounding into the strange new quiet was as loud as a scream, and surely if the monster was still *up there*, he could hear it too.

Boot steps traversed the floor above, slow and deliberate. Her mamá said one word, clear and bold: "Please."

The *thunk* that came was not so loud as before, but there was a wetness to it that made a bit of pee blossom warm in the girl's drawers. She clenched tight—clenched her legs, her breath, her soul—and prayed for the monster to go away.

Instead, he continued to sift through all the things that belonged to them, and the girl knew they were in ruins, even without seeing. The table, which they had painted together with vines and flowers. The clay vase on the mantel. The iron spit and the spice rack above it, hanging with dried lavender. The cupboard with the missing drawer where the girl kept Rosita, her straw doll. The rope bed with feather ticking that she and Mamá shared.

The monster was searching for something, even though she couldn't imagine what. She and Mamá barely had enough food to eat, much less a treasure worth searching for.

The boot steps ceased. Light peeked through the slats above

her head. The monster had pulled up the braid rug that covered the door to the cellar.

No, no, no, no, the girl prayed. Mamá was always praying. Praying for more food, praying her toothache would get better, praying Horteño the blacksmith would leave her alone. The prayers never seemed to work, but the girl didn't know what else to do.

A hinge squealed as the monster found the iron ring and gave it a yank.

No, please, no.

Light poured down the ladder, and the girl had been in the dark for so long that it hurt her eyes.

"Ah, there you are," said the monster.

A tiny whimper bled from her lips.

"Why don't you come up?" he asked reasonably.

She shook her head fiercely.

An arm reached for her, draped in the finest, palest linen she'd ever seen. Fingers curled, beckoning her. They were long and slender like spider legs, with skin as white as a cloud.

He said, "I won't hurt you." His accent marked him as Invierno as surely as his pale skin, with words that sounded half swallowed before being reluctantly shoved from his mouth.

"I have to pee," she whispered. The pressure in her belly was awful, and she wriggled her bottom to keep everything inside.

"Let's take care of that, shall we? Climb up, and you can go to the outhouse."

The girl was not stupid. But she couldn't stay in this dark

hole forever. If she refused, the monster would come down after her anyway.

"All right," she whispered, and she rose to her feet. She wiped her dirty hands on her shirt and smoothed back her hair. Her arms quivered as she reached for the ladder rungs and began to pull herself up.

She was slow about it, thinking, thinking, thinking what to do. No one in the village would come to help, not even if she screamed. It was winter, so if she managed to escape, she'd have to find a warm place to hide. Maybe the monster truly meant her no harm, but she remembered the wet *thunk* and its ensuing silence, and she knew that possibility for a fancy.

Too soon, she reached the top rung. Her head peeked above the floor, and sure enough, the cottage was in shambles. Near the hearth, sticking out from beneath a pile of splintered wood, was a dark, slender arm ending in calloused fingertips. A smear of blood coated the back of Mamá's limp hand.

Something changed inside her. It was like a twist at the base of her skull, a little snake of sadness and hate and rage—all combined with a desperate determination that should have died with her mamá but instead would be with her always.

So the girl's decision about what to do was easy: She would die fighting as hard as she could.

She clambered onto the floor, gained her feet, and faced the monster.

He was tall, maybe the tallest person she'd ever seen, with eyes like deepwater ice and near-white hair that fell loosely to his waist. An amulet hung from his neck, a small iron cage housing a shiny blue gemstone.

She barely kept her gasp in check. The monster wasn't just an Invierno; he was an animagus, one of their rare sorcerers who could use his sparkling stone to burn her to the ground, or even hold her in place so she couldn't move at all. She'd seen a few Inviernos in their village before, but never an animagus.

"Well," he said, looking her up and down with his cold, cold eyes. "Aren't you a disgusting little creature."

And somehow she knew he wasn't talking about the dirt under her nails or the hole in the left knee of her trousers or the tiny pee stain at her crotch, but rather her very own self.

A busted table leg with a jagged end lay beside Mamá's hand. Maybe she could reach it before he burned her. Looking the monster straight in the eyes, she said, "May I use the outhouse now?"

"If you answer a few questions first, then yes, of course."

She blinked. She'd expected him to say no. "All right."

"Let's start with . . . who is your father?"

The girl pressed her knees together. It was easier to hold it standing up, but she couldn't last much longer. "Don't know."

"Don't lie to me."

"Are *you* my papá?" she asked, peering closer. Mamá had described him as tall and pale, with hair like falling water. And that's all she'd ever said.

"Don't be ridiculous," said the monster, and the girl felt a relief so huge it almost loosed her bladder.

Then his frozen eyes narrowed. "But it was someone like me, yes?"

The girl said nothing.

"How old are you?"

This part is fuzzy in the girl's memory. Did she hold up six fingers? Seven?

Whatever it was, she absolutely remembers the monster peering at her strangely and saying, "You have an old soul."

She glared. "I'm *precocious.*"

He stepped forward, quick like an asp, into the very air she was breathing. But she did not back away.

The monster said, "Tell me what happened to your anima-lapis."

The girl had no idea what that meant, though it sounded like the Lengua Classica, which she did not speak and did not care to. She shrugged.

The blow came so fast she barely noted it, except suddenly she was on the floor, blackness edging her vision, wet warmth spilling into her drawers. Pain came next, exploding through her cheekbone and her shoulder where she fell. Though she hadn't eaten all day, her belly threatened to toss something up. She blinked and blinked, trying to see straight, as her heartbeat pounded like thunder in her face.

A shape materialized on the floor at her nose: a limp hand.

"I'm sorry, Mamá, I'm sorry," the girl whispered to the hand. "I peed myself."

The monster grabbed the girl's braid and yanked her head

backward. He crouched beside her, his moist breath hot in her ear. "Tell me where it is," he whispered.

Tears streamed down her cheeks. "I don't know what animal apples is," she said. "For true."

"Anima-lapis," he said, with a tug on her braid. "It would look like this." He grabbed his amulet and shoved it in her face. The gemstone winked at her from inside its iron cage.

She shook her head, or maybe she just thought she did. Everything was spinning so badly. "I don't . . . I've never . . ."

She'd never seen a sparkle stone until today. Horteño the blacksmith had told her about them. The stones were magical, beautiful, rare. Only animagi were born with them, though she wasn't sure how a baby could be born with a stone. She'd seen quite a few babies in her short life, and they were messy and soft and loud; not stone-like at all.

He released her braid, and her head clunked against the floor.

Run, she told herself. But her vision was hazy, and her limbs wouldn't obey. Maybe in a minute or so. She just needed to blink a little, catch her breath.

Before she could collect herself, he flipped her neatly onto her back and yanked up her shirt.

She tried to cover herself, but he batted her hands away and bent over her stomach to examine something there. A light finger traced the edge of her navel. It was almost a caress.

"Hmmm," the monster said.

The girl squirmed, but he had her pinned.

"Maybe," he said, softly to himself. "Maybe."

RAE·CARSON

In a way, it was worse than getting hit, having his soft finger glide across her bare belly. It sent shivers all through her and made bile rise in her throat. She wanted to cover her skin so badly. Wash it. Reclaim it.

"All right, let's go," the monster said, gaining his feet and yanking her up with him. "We have a long journey ahead of us."

She pushed her shirt down as fast as she could, wobbling on her feet. Her pee-soaked pants already chafed the skin of her inner thighs. "Are you going to kill me now?" she asked. She needed a weapon. The meat knife would be perfect, but there was no way she'd find it in all this rubble.

"Not yet," he said with a shrug. "If we find your lapis, you might be with us for a very, very long time."

Being with him a very, very long time was probably a very, very bad thing. But it also meant she might live long enough to escape.

She said, "You should look in the cellar. Mamá keeps things there." She didn't look him in the eye when she said it, because she was terrible at tricking people, and he'd surely read her intentions on her face.

A long moment passed. If the monster was smart, he'd tie her up and explore the cellar himself, and she couldn't let that happen.

So she added, "Mamá has a secret place down there. I can show you."

That decided him. "You go first. I'll be right behind you." The sparkle stone dangling at his chest began to glow, and its anger stirred deep in her soul. It made her insides fuzzy and hot. The monster was preparing to use his awful magic.

The girl moved fast, practically throwing herself into the hole. She was still dizzy from the blow to her head, so her foot missed the first rung and she slid halfway down before catching herself with a grip that made the skin of her palms scream. She dropped the rest of the way and landed on her wet bottom.

The cellar felt cool and comforting and familiar, and it gave her strength. As the ladder creaked with the monster's descent, she launched herself into the dark corner where Mamá kept a shelf for dry goods—nearly empty of food this late in the year, but the skinning knife should still be there.

"Girl, show yourself," the monster ordered. He had reached the floor of the cellar, but he wasn't used to the dark like she was.

"Over here," she said, her fingers closing around the knife handle.

He approached cautiously, the light from his sparkling gem casting a bluish glow against the stone walls. His hair seemed especially white in the magical light, his eyes especially icy.

"Where is the secret place?" he said. He was so tall he had to crouch to avoid the hanging garlic braids.

The girl hadn't thought beyond getting the knife, the handle of which was already slick in her damp palm, hidden behind her back. She hesitated.

"Girl?"

She couldn't think what to say or do next.

His amulet brightened. A stream of light burst toward the

floor, crashed into a burlap bag. The smell of burned stew filled the air as flames licked at the sack, warming her cheeks.

"You burned the turnips," she whispered, staring. Magic had been done, for true. Right before her eyes.

"It takes great power to burn turnips," he said. "They contain so much moisture. Show me the secret place."

"It's . . ." The girl got an idea. "It's here. Behind this. I'm not big enough to move it."

The monster stepped forward. He eyed the shelves. Four rickety wooden slats, one of which was damp and half rotted away. They used to be nice shelves, Mamá had told her, before the rot set in.

"There's a hole in the wall where Mamá keeps her special things," she said. "But you have to move the shelf."

He stared down at her. The knife held behind her back was like a beacon, throbbing in her hand. Maybe she should elaborate on the lie before he noticed. What special thing would her mamá hide away? Something precious. Something frightening . . .

Mamá would have sold anything precious. She would have protected her daughter from anything frightening. So the girl was left to stare back at the monster, unable to think of a single thing.

"Have you seen what's inside?" the monster asked.

"No," the girl whispered, more certain than ever that he would see through her. "Mamá said I was too little." Her voice wavered. Her hand hiding the knife shook.

Her fear made the monster smile. "Then let's see for

ourselves, shall we?" He turned his back to her and reached for the shelf.

With a grunt and a heave, he lifted it slightly and pivoted it away, then let it drop with a big *thunk*. He stared at the revealed wall for a moment. His voice was darker than dark when he said, "I don't see anything. There's nothing—"

The girl pretended the monster was a pig at the butcher. With all her might, she plunged the knife into his flank.

And just like a stuck pig, he squealed. Blue-white light shot away from his amulet, a panic flare that exploded against the shelves, collapsing them and setting the remains on fire.

The girl recoiled, tears and smoke blurring her eyes. She had just done a bad, bad thing. No whipping in the world would make up for it. And yet she didn't feel sorry.

The monster babbled and cursed in a language she didn't understand. He swatted at the knife in him while the flames ate the shelves and spread to the sack of cornmeal.

She should flee. She knew she should. But the monster's flailing hand managed to bump the knife handle just so, and it slid out a ways. Blood drenched his beautiful robe, but the knife was barely sticking in him now. The girl had not killed him *enough*.

She darted in. Grabbed the knife handle. Yanked it out.

And plunged it right back in.

It scraped bone this time; she felt that scrape down to the roots of her teeth. He spun around to face her, but his knees buckled and he fell back against the wall. The knife point thrust out of his abdomen, making a tent of his lovely, bloodstained robe.

RAE·CARSON

"You . . ." he gasped. "Disgusting half-breed." His back scraped the wall as he slid to the floor.

His amulet was still glowing, its heat creating an ever-widening circle of char on his robe. "You rotting piece of . . ."

The sorcerer's head lolled against his chest. Fire spread around them; its heat seared the girl's face. She didn't have much time.

Yet she hesitated. Maybe she still hadn't quite killed the monster. If so, he would burn alive in the next few minutes.

Shimmering blood formed a pool around him. Its edges lapped the base of the collapsed shelf, now a bonfire. The blood sizzled, and a scent like cooked meat filled the air. She knew exactly what she was smelling, but she hadn't eaten all day and she couldn't stop her belly's instinctive rumble or keep saliva from drenching her tongue.

Her hands flew to her nose and mouth, and she backed away from the glowing conflagration, the monster's cooking body, and the final scraps of Mamá's winter stores.

Her back banged against the ladder. She whirled, reached for the rungs, and yanked herself up as fast as she could.

She had to flee. No one who sassed an animagus—much less attacked and killed one—got away with it. She'd get no help from the village; she and Mamá were barely tolerated as it was. She had to pack as much as she could, as fast as she could, and get far, far away.

It meant leaving Mamá's body behind. Their tiny cottage. The vegetable garden. All the things she loved. The *only* things she loved.

She stared at her mamá's limp hand, unable to move. Smoke curled up through the planks of the floor. Her lungs and throat were starting to sting.

"Run, my sky," she imagined her mother saying. *"You know how much I want you to live, yes?"*

Well, she had wanted her mamá to live too. Grief swelled inside her, until it exploded into a single gut-wrenching sob.

But that was all she allowed herself. She wiped frantically at her eyes to clear them of tears and stiffened her cheeks and put on her big-girl face.

The girl ran to the door, pressed her ear to the wood, and listened: the muffled stomp of a hoof pawing at snow, the jangle of a bridle, someone barking an order in that language she didn't understand. The animagus's people were just outside. She would have to sneak out the back.

Quieter than a mouse, she stretched up on tiptoes, fingered the iron door hook, and slipped it into its eye, latching the door. It wouldn't hold long if someone tried to force their way in—the door was old and splintered—but it might buy her a few seconds.

She grabbed her ragged cloak from its peg by the door and whipped it over her shoulders. Her fingers fumbled as she tied it at the neck. Mamá's cloak hung beside the door too; the girl wasted a precious moment staring. Mamá would never wear it again.

But it would serve as a blanket. Sometimes, on the coldest nights of the year, Mamá had pulled the cloak from its peg and draped it over them on the bed. They'd spent many days'

RAE·CARSON

worth of hours cuddled together beneath that cloak.

She grabbed it and bunched it up, then shoved it into the basket they used for gathering herbs.

"Cloak, fire, and food," Mamá had told her. *"Remember that, if you ever need to flee."*

The girl's feet twitched to run, but her mamá was right; she wouldn't last long without food. Leftover stew was spilled and soaking into the floor, half covered in detritus from their destroyed furniture. Salt pork was stored in the cellar, but smoke bubbled out of the trapdoor and flames licked the top of the ladder—she dared not go back there. Maybe the cheese wheel? A gift from the blacksmith, which they'd been saving for Deliverance Day. It was around here somewhere. . . .

She searched feverishly, heart pounding and lungs burning, as smoke continued to rise through the floor planking. No cheese anywhere to be seen. Maybe it was buried under the rubble.

Being very careful to *not look* at her mamá's limp hand, the girl tried to nudge aside the fallen table with her leg. It scraped loudly against the floor but hardly moved at all.

Someone rattled the door, trying to enter.

The girl froze.

It rattled again as the girl whimpered, her feet melded to the warming floor. The rattling turned into pounding. The door strained against the latch.

Run, my sky.

She hefted the herb basket that was heavy with her mamá's cloak and fled past the hearth and the pile of ruined, smoking furniture, toward their hut's single tiny window. It wasn't a real window with fancy glass, but rather a large shutter that swung upward, which they would prop open during the summer months to invite the cooling mountain breeze.

The girl unlatched the window. Behind her, pounding sounded again, along with a flurry of angry words, as she cracked the shutter open and peeked outside. Icy air hit her face.

No one was behind the house. Just an empty chicken coop and a tiny garden, all blanketed with snow.

She hooked one leg over the sill and was about to draw up the other when something caught her eye. The tinderbox, on the floor by her feet. It must have fallen from the mantel and slid across the planking. It was almost like her mamá had left it for her. A parting gift. *Cloak, fire, and food.*

The girl reached down and grabbed the tinderbox, shoved it into her herb basket beside the cloak, and slipped through the window.

Her boots crunched in day-old snow. She guided the window shutter so that it closed without a sound. She took a deep breath of clean, smokeless air, gathered her basket close, and sprinted for the trees.

Each footstep was a cacophony of sound, and her every muscle tensed, waiting to feel searing, sorcerous fire at her back.

But nothing came. She reached the trees and dashed behind a thick trunk, pausing to catch her breath and to peek behind her.

The tiny hut she'd shared with Mamá was barely a lump in the snowy meadow. Smoke curled up from the roof. The animagus's people had probably broken through the door by now.

Beside the hut was the smaller lump of the chicken coop, and for once she was glad they'd had to eat or sell all their chickens. She didn't have to worry about them burning alive.

Everything was blanketed with white, glittering slightly in the weak winter sunshine. And against it all was a line of shadows, sized like the feet of a little girl, a perfect trail for anyone to follow from the house to the place where she stood.

They would give chase the moment they realized she wasn't inside. The girl couldn't outrun people on horseback. But maybe she could outthink them. *"Use your head,"* Mamá always said.

For all she knew, the animagus's entourage was made up of horrible sorcerers just like him, the most powerful people in all the world. But if they knew anything about hunting, they would have surrounded the hut right away. Never leave your quarry a good escape. All the mountain folk knew that.

The cold was already seeping into her boots, and her urine-soaked pants were growing icy. The girl's gaze lingered on her home for a final, mournful moment. Then she turned and fled into the forest.

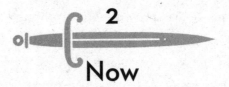

2
Now

I don't know how old I am. Sixteen or seventeen, is everyone's guess. Rosario insists I'm younger, but I don't feel young at all. Today, in any case, I'm going to acquire a birthday. Well, an adoption day, but everyone says we'll celebrate my adoption like a proper birthday every year from now on. Which sounds nice.

I mean, I'm grateful. I really am.

But I would be just as grateful if Elisa and Hector were fishermen on the coast instead of the empress and prince consort. What I want is a quiet, personal ceremony; what I'm getting is political theater.

Lady Mara fusses with my hair. She doesn't have to; she's first lady-in-waiting to the empress and a secret lieutenant in the imperial web of spies, and she can do whatever she damn well pleases. When I tell her as much, she says, "Today, it pleases me to help you with your hair."

"Well, in that case, thank you."

"Red, are you sure you want to cover it up?" she asks,

finishing off a braid that starts at my right temple and winds around to the back of my head. "I think your white streak is quite lovely."

"I want it covered," I assure her. "Black as night."

She frowns, but she complies, reaching for the clay pot on the dressing table. The dye inside is made of crushed walnut shells and kohl, and it costs more than half my monthly allowance.

Most of my hair is still dark from the previous treatment, but my mark shows clearly at the roots above my left temple, a blot of shimmering brightness against my otherwise black hair. If I were to ever let it grow out, it would be a ribbon of white flowing all the way to my waist.

Mara works carefully, spreading the dye with a tiny paintbrush that allows her to avoid my scalp as much as possible. Too much dye on my skin will cause an itchy, burning rash, which is why I sometimes let the roots grow out a little.

"You know," Mara says as she works, "I have a mark too. I know what it's like."

She's referring to the obvious scar on her eyelid, received in a beating from her long-dead father. It pulls that eye downward at the outside corner, making her seem perpetually sad.

"It's not the same," I tell her. "No one sees your scar and thinks, *Vile magic.*"

The paintbrush freezes. "Who said that to you?"

Lady Malka whispered it to her husband once when I passed. It was a false whisper, loud enough for me to hear. And of course there are strange looks every single day, even from the servants. But I've learned the hard way that letting someone jump to my defense just makes life at court harder for me.

"No one," I say. "It's nothing."

Mara glares at me. "You're the worst liar I know. If you ever decide to tell me who it was, I'll have their head."

"That's what I'm afraid of."

Still frowning, Mara gets back to work. A breeze flutters the gauzy curtains of my open balcony. Birds chirrup from the lush flower garden below. The lavender scent of my morning bath lingers in the air. This used to be the queen's suite, before Elisa became empress and moved herself and her husband into the larger monarch's wing next door. I've occupied these rooms as the empress's ward for seven years now, and still I can hardly believe that such luxury is mine.

The curtain separating the tiled bathing area from my bedroom is whisked aside. "Wed?" says a tiny voice.

Princess Ximena rushes in, still in her sleeping gown, bare feet slapping the tile floor. At four years old, she's an artisan when it comes to escaping her nurses and guards.

"Good morning, Mena," I say.

She plants her fists at her hips and peers up into my face. Her large, dark eyes are slightly crossed, and surrounded by the long lashes of her mother. Her round face and stubborn chin are framed by the wild, curling hair of her father.

She looks nothing at all like her namesake. The first Ximena was a thickset, gray-haired woman, a specially trained guardian who eventually gave her life to save the empress.

"Papá says today will make us sistews," the princess says.

"Yes."

"Will you come live in the nuwsewy?"

"Probably not."

Her eyes widen with hurt.

Before I can explain that I'm a little old for the nursery, Mara says, "Maybe Red can spend the night with you once in a while." She dabs the brush into the dye. "As a special treat to you both."

Ximena considers this. "I s'pose," she says, then reaches up with her arms.

Smiling, I grab the little girl and lift her into my lap. "Mena, I hope you understand that I already love you like a sister."

The princess gives me a look that could wither the freshest fruit. "I know *that*."

"Be still, both of you," Mara says, "or this dye is going everywhere."

I'm like a statue, but the princess has no patience for stillness, and she starts fingering the neck ribbon of my dressing gown.

Again Mara pauses. "Red, what's wrong?"

"Nothing." It comes out too fast, too brusque.

"Nervous?" she prods. "You're not usually one for nervousness, but . . ." She gifts me with a soft smile. "This is a *very* big day."

When I woke this morning, I told myself that I would maintain my composure no matter what, *no matter what*, but Mara wields empathy like a weapon. The understanding in her face undoes me; my cheeks grow hot and tears prick at my eyes.

I whisper, "I've worked for this ever since I was a little girl. All those years . . . everything I've learned . . . and finally, today . . ."

"Ah. I see." Mara applies a final brushstroke to the roots of my hair. Then she reaches down for Ximena and lifts her from my lap. "Go get some breakfast, Mena," she says. "Take one of the Royal Guards with you—no sneaking away, yes? When you're done, I'll help dress you for the ceremony."

"All wight," the princess says. Then she wags a finger at me. "Don't be late, Wed!"

"I'll be right on time, I promise." I watch as she disappears behind the curtain.

After the girl is out of earshot, Mara says, "You had that dream again, didn't you?"

"Yes."

In my dream I was running through snow, my feet icy with cold. The hunger in my belly was like a raptor clawing at my gut. I remember wind cutting my cheeks and felled branches cutting my feet and a clear sense of needing to move fast, fast, faster, but I was going nowhere, just *away*. There was no safe place for me. My dream self knew I would run forever, all alone.

"You *have* worked hard," Mara says. She's dabbing powder on my face now, which tickles my nostrils and almost makes me sneeze. "I've never seen anyone work harder. The hours of study, the dancing lessons, the travel tour . . . you impressed everyone who was watching. Exactly as hoped."

This isn't what I want to hear.

"Red?"

RAE·CARSON

I don't want to hear about my hard work. Or that I'm half Invierno. Or that my adoption will begin to change the cultural and political landscape of our empire, opening hearts and minds to the possibility of long-term peace between our people.

Mara says, "Your adoption will begin to change the cultural—"

I hold up a hand. "I know."

"No, you need to understand. This is the culmination of reforms that Elisa and Hector have been working on for *years*. Joya d'Arena is so easily bogged down by tradition, but when the court accepts you as an heir—"

"I *know*, Mara. It's just . . ." Shame clogs my throat. It's embarrassing and weak of me—when I've been working so hard the past few years to appear strong—but what I want to hear is that Empress Elisa and Prince Consort Hector *love* me. That I'm part of their family, no matter what.

Maybe that makes me a stupid, pitiful child, but I did have that dream again, and I just want to feel like I've finally run home.

Mara dabs rouge onto my lips and says, "There's something you're not telling me, but I won't pry. I'll just say that we have every reason to believe the day will go exactly as planned, and after it does, you will be a princess of the empire and third in line for the throne." She stands back to admire her handiwork. "Not bad for a foundling girl with slave marks on her feet."

I force a smile. "Not bad." Mara has always been frank about what I am. Other people think it's polite to pretend away uncomfortable things—the magic mark in my hair, the faded slave tattoos on my feet, my undeniable paternity. It never occurs to them that because those things are part of me, they're pretending *me* away.

"Time to don the monstrosity," she says.

I rise from the stool. "It's only for a few hours, right?"

Mara smiles in sympathy.

The monstrosity is my ceremonial adoption gown. It's a horror of ivory silk, to make my skin appear more traditionally dark and to mute the golden color of my eyes. The sleeves explode with ruffles the size of the Hinder Mountains, a fashion that is apparently all the rage in the vassal kingdom of Orovalle. Worst of all is the train that will stretch behind me, roughly the length of the Joyan coastline, during my formal procession down the aisle.

Everything about the monstrosity has been carefully engineered to make me seem both royal and blandly pleasant. The train and fine silk confer status. The color and ruffles wash away every part of me that might intimidate or dismay.

Mara holds it out so I can step into it, then she shimmies it up over my waist and lifts the billowing sleeves over my shoulders.

"Deep breath," she says, and I comply. "Now let it all out."

I push the air from my lungs, making my torso as small as possible so Mara can quickly lace the back.

"There!" she says, standing aside.

The corset is snug, but comfortable enough. I've always been slight, and tying everything too tight might make me appear smaller, weaker. "What do you think?" I prod.

Mara's lips twitch. "You look like a vanilla scone with sugar icing."

"So . . . perfect?"

"Exactly the look we're going for. Definitely younger."

Which is good, because Empress Elisa, my soon-to-be-mother, is probably only about ten years older than I am, and the Quorum felt that making me look younger might put the court at ease.

"You're as ready as you'll ever be," Mara says. "I'm going to chase down the princess. There's still time; if you want, you can go to the monastery to prepare your heart with prayer—"

"You know I don't believe all that," I snap, harder than I mean to.

Her face softens. "I know, Red. But this is a religious country, and for appearances' sake . . ." Her voice trails off at the look on my face, and she looses an exaggerated sigh. "I don't know how Elisa thinks she's going to make a politician out of you. You have no patience for dissembling."

I plunk down on the bed, not caring that this will wrinkle my overwrought train. "I'm wearing the monstrosity, aren't I?"

"A more than acceptable compromise, if you ask me."

A knock sounds at the door, and Mara rushes over, hand to the dagger at her belt. I tense and clench my fist. It's not that we're in any danger; it's just that I and everyone I know and love—Mara, Hector, Elisa, Rosario, Belén—have been through so much that peril is a constant, comfortable companion, and we are prepared to welcome it always.

"It's me," comes a muffled voice through the door, and Mara swings it open.

"Good morning, Highness," she says to Prince Rosario, my soon-to-be stepbrother and my best friend.

"Mara," the prince says, striding inside. When he sees me, he stops short—and doubles over laughing.

The fifteen-year-old heir to the Joyan Empire is as tall, slender, and strong as a palm, with dark eyes full of mischief and lips always on the verge of smirking. He's the object of many a young court lady's dreams, and depending on which day you ask, either the bane or the pride of his stepmother's existence.

"It's not *that* funny," I say with a mock glare.

"Oh, yes it is, little sister." He straightens the vest of his ceremonial garb and pretends to dab tears from his cheek. Then he raises one eyebrow and gives my gown a thorough study. "It's even worse than you described."

"It's pretty awful," Mara agrees. "I'm going to make sure Mena didn't slip by the Guards again. I'll be there for the procession, Red, cheering you on."

"Thank you."

After she leaves, Rosario settles beside me on the bed so that we are shoulder to shoulder. "I think it's perfect," he says.

"You do?"

"We match," he says, indicating his suit. He wears off-white trimmed in gold, with all the medals and seals of his station pinned to his chest. "Besides," he continues, "once you wear that thing in public, everyone will finally understand the truth: You *are* younger than I am."

"It's good to have ambition, *little brother.*"

It's been a mock argument between us ever since that day, almost eight years ago, when Elisa brought me home from the mountains and introduced me to her seven-year-old prince—who immediately declared himself in charge.

"You're wearing the Queen's Star," I say, indicating the golden star with an inset ruby hanging from his lapel.

He grimaces. "The seneschal is going to announce it. The Quorum thinks it's best to remind everyone that I'm a *hero*"— he sneers out the word—"as I walk you down the aisle."

"I'm sorry." The Battle of Brisadulce took place a year before I became a member of court. But Rosario and Elisa have told me all about it, so I know the Queen's Star is one of Rosario's greatest treasures. He hates having it used as a commodity, as though it cheapens his accomplishment along with all the tragedy of that day.

"Anyway, I brought you something," he says, reaching into a pocket. "Since this will be the first actual birthday you cele-brate, it seems right that someone should give it to you."

"Oh?" I peer at the object in his hand, but he holds it tight, not yet ready to reveal it.

"Every royal child receives this on their first birthday, you see. It's a long tradition, and you should be part of it."

"Well, that's very thoughtful of—"

He opens his hand and exposes a slender stem of marble topped with a golden ball. It looks like a tiny dagger, or maybe a letter opener, but with rounded edges and a jeweled hilt.

Rosario gives it a gentle shake, which causes it to jangle softly. Either the hilt or the golden ball is hollow.

"I . . . what is it?"

Rosario's grin is like the sun spilling over the sea. "It's a baby rattle. For my baby sister."

I consider pretending to be offended, but a giggle escapes before I can stop it.

"And look!" he says, "When your baby teeth finally grow in you can bite, like this." He pantomimes biting down on the rattle. "Gold is very soft, you know. We'll polish out the tooth marks every few months. Any jeweler here in Brisadulce can do it for you."

"Well." I grab the rattle and give it a shake. "Let it never be said that I don't follow the traditions of my adopted country!" I hold it up to the light, which sheens against the golden ball. This tiny bauble is worth more than everything I owned during the first decade of my life all put together.

"I'm not funning you," Rosario says, more solemn now. "Well, not entirely. A jewel rattle really is a traditional gift among the nobility, and if you look there"—he points—"you can see a clasp. Flick that, and the rattle will open. Inside are a few tiny gemstones. Nothing much, but enough to help if you're ever in trouble. The baby-rattle tradition honors a child's first birthday, but it's meant to be an inheritance too. So . . . welcome to the family, I guess?"

I give the rattle another shake. "I don't care what everyone says. You're actually very sweet." I lean over and give his cheek a peck with my lips. "Thanks, little brother."

RAE·CARSON

We chat for a while about nothing in particular, in the way of easy friends with nothing to prove, waiting for the monastery bells to ring the hour. Even though I'm expecting the sound, when the bells finally peal, I startle hard, my heart jumping into my throat as my whole body jolts.

Rosario gives me an understanding look. "That was a bad one," he says calmly.

I nod, even as I close my eyes a moment to focus on my breathing. Everything in me wants to flee or lash out at someone, even though it makes no sense. I'm home. Surrounded by people I love. It was just bells ringing.

Rosario stands, reaching for my hand. "Ready? Or do you need more time?"

I allow him to yank me up.

"Good. Our Royal Guard contingent is just outside the door."

Once I'm a princess, I'm not to venture anywhere without them.

He squeezes my hand. "You get used to having them around, I promise." He lets go and reaches for the door, saying, "They're good company. Completely loyal to Elisa and the family, not to mention the greatest warriors in the empire. I sleep easier, thanks to them."

Sleep. The prince knows how bad I am at it, just like he knows how easily I startle.

Rosario opens the door to my suite, and sure enough, four Royal Guardsmen stand outside, wearing the flowing red capes and shining steel of ceremonial armor. One steps forward, striking his chest with a fist. "Your Highnesses," he acknowledges.

"Fernando, it's a little premature to address me that way," I tell him with a smile. One of the things I've learned while training for court these last few years is how to appear serene even when my heart is racing and my legs are twitching to run.

Fernando grins back. He has a weathered face, an easy smile, and forearms like tree trunks. He's Elisa's best archer—maybe the best in the empire—and he has always been kind to me. "Just practicing," he says. "Ready? The empress, her family, and the Quorum of Five are already in place."

"Lady Mara?"

"Rushing Princess Ximena to the audience hall. I understand there was a minor pomegranate jam incident, but the crisis seems to have been averted."

I take Rosario's proffered elbow. "Let's go," I say, in a voice I don't quite recognize as my own.

The double doors leading to the audience hall have never seemed so massive. Noise filters through them—the buzz of conversation, a lively band of vihuelas, the click of heeled boots on tile. Nearly a thousand people are gathered on the other side of those doors, all come to watch my adoption ceremony.

The seneschal stands ready to open them, flanked by two palace guards armed with long ceremonial spears. He's been at court my whole life, growing smaller and grayer with age, though his booming voice remains as magnificent as ever.

"Ready, my dear?" he says, with such a look of pity that I'm suddenly suspicious.

"I . . ." Maybe Mara cinched my bodice too tightly after all. How can I be expected to breathe in such a thing?

Rosario's hand squeezes my elbow. "It's going to be fine," he whispers.

I inhale deeply through my nose, relax my neck and shoulders, ground myself to the earth. It's a trick Hector taught me, a way to find my "fighting calm." *Harsh winds, rough seas, still hearts*, he always says.

But I must have said it aloud, because the Royal Guardsmen whisper their motto right back at me, "Harsh winds, rough seas, still hearts."

I glance at Fernando, who gives me a quiet nod. It fills me with confidence. With light. "All right. Yes. I'm ready."

The doors open outward, releasing a gust of body-warmed air. The palace guards tap the butts of their spears to the ground, once, twice. A hush falls over the audience. As one, heads turn to stare.

"Lady Red Sparkle Stone!" the seneschal booms, and I wince to hear my ridiculous name echoing over the heads of a thousand people. "Handmaiden to Her Imperial Majesty Empress Lucero-Elisa né Riqueza de Vega! Candidate for imperial adoption!"

Two Royal Guardsmen sweep inside before us, hands to their scabbards. The remaining two, including Fernando, will remain at our backs. It's all highly choreographed—the crown prince as my escort, the Royal Guard contingent, the monstrous adoption gown—to send a message to everyone watching that I'm already royalty, and worthy of such things.

"His Imperial Highness Prince Rosario né Fleurendi de Vega!" the seneschal continues. "Crown Prince and heir to the united kingdoms of Basajuan, Orovalle, and Joya d'Arena! Conde of the Southern Reaches, youngest recipient in our great empire's history of the Queen's Star for acts of gallantry and intrepidity in circumstances of extreme danger!"

The vihuelas begin playing a stately interpretation of the "Entrada Triunfal." Our procession moves forward, and the throng parts to make way, revealing a deep purple carpet that runs the length of the audience hall, ending at a large dais. The dais is occupied by familiar faces—Prince Consort Hector, his daughter Princess Ximena, Lady Mara, and the Quorum lords, all arrayed around Empress Elisa herself on her giant throne.

Hector is solemn as always, but his eyes twinkle as though he's trying to resist winking. Elisa, however, is perfectly imperial, straight-backed and proud, her face grave. Her smile, when it comes, is slow and deliberate, as if reminding everyone of the magnitude of today's ceremony.

But even her measured smile is beautiful, and it's surrounded by the most glorious black hair I've ever seen. She wears a gown of silver blue with cobalt trim and a necklace of sapphires. Her imperial crown is made of shattered Godstones, a symbol of her unique power, and they catch the light of the chandeliers just so. She has always been generously plump, but her rigid posture reveals a waist thickened by two pregnancies—and another on the way.

RAE·CARSON

Her current pregnancy is supposed to be a secret. I glance around, wondering if anyone is noticing.

Standing next to the royal family—*my* family—is Songbird, the Invierno ambassador, who has been attempting to negotiate a new trade and cultural exchange treaty. He wears fabrics that match those of the wealthiest members of the court, a symbol of the ties that already exist between our people, woven in elaborately patterned colors that complement his unnatural height and his pale skin without drawing extra attention to them. His retinue is similarly attired, emphasizing the commonalities between us instead of the differences. The attempt to fit in doesn't succeed; an empty space surrounds his party, as if they are bearers of a contagious disease. The ambassador's large, thoughtful eyes linger on me, curious but not rude.

But the light of Elisa's smile draws my attention back to her, pulls me down the aisle. The "Entrada" crescendos. Nobles twist in place to follow my journey with their eyes. I'm supposed to be here, doing exactly this; I know I am. But my ruffles are ridiculous, stretching the length of the receiving hall. Light from the chandeliers washes my skin to nothing. Everything feels off. Wrong. Like I'm a hawk dressed up to look like a camel.

Rosario's attention is pulled toward the right, and I follow his gaze. It's Lady Carilla, a girl about my age, with blushed round cheeks and huge dark eyes that gaze at the prince in rapt, unwavering attention. I resist the urge to smile.

Someone murmurs off to the left. The slightest sound, but

jarring nonetheless. I glance over—it's Lady Malka, speaking to a companion behind a gloved hand.

Her hand lowers, revealing full lips turned up into something too nasty to be a smile.

Rosario's fingers on my elbow tighten.

Straight ahead, Elisa's face falters. Hector reaches down and grabs her hand.

The air is taut and heavy—how did I not notice it before? Eyes are wide with anticipation. With sure knowledge. I pass a tall, reed-thin man wearing a green silk stole, who glares at me with fire in his eyes. His hate is such a palpable thing that I nearly stumble.

As quietly as I can, I dare to whisper, "Something is wrong."

"Just keep walking," Rosario whispers back.

Is it my mark? Maybe the dye didn't take. Maybe it's shining as white as a cloud for everyone to see. Or perhaps my train ripped, or it picked up something unspeakable on the journey through the palace that now drags in its wake.

We reach the dais. The vihuelas cease, and a hush descends. I hear the tiny *pop* of a candle bubbling in the chandelier above my head.

Father Nicandro, head priest of the Monastery-at-Brisadulce, hobbles forward. He holds a copy of the *Scriptura Sancta* in one arthritic hand, a sparkling tiara in the other. He closes his eyes and intones a blessing in the Lengua Classica, and I should focus on his words, soak up this moment, but all I can think is that something is wrong, wrong, wrong.

Nicandro closes his blessing, and the room mutters "Selah"

in unison. He steps aside and is quickly replaced by Conde Astón of Ciénega del Sur, a man of middle height, broad shoulders, and almost inconceivable wealth. More important, he is the elected speaker of the Chamber of Condes, one of the three governing bodies of our empire. Which makes him the most powerful person in this great hall aside from Elisa herself.

In a loud, clear voice, he says, "Her Imperial Majesty Empress Elisa and His Imperial Highness Prince Consort Hector have petitioned the chamber to adopt the candidate before you, and assume all rights and duties with respect to the child."

I'm hardly a "child." It must be formal wording, set forth in the *Articles of the Empire*, when Elisa agreed to relinquish some of the powers held by the crown in exchange for unanimous ratification of her new peace treaty. I remember Ratification Day well. I ate my first coconut scone.

"The candidate," Conde Astón continues, "named Lady Red Sparkle Stone, was purchased by our empress as a slave from an innkeeper in the free villages and immediately emancipated. According to testimony, the child then played an integral role in securing our victory in the Battle of Basajuan. She has remained a member of court in the years since, bringing no shame or dishonor to herself nor to her warden, the empress. Her natural parentage is unknown, though she is presumed through physical examination by the Imperial Physician Enzo to be half Invierno, and therefore infertile. Her age is estimated at seventeen years."

He pauses, letting everything sink in. None of this is new

information to the court, and I'm not sure why it was necessary to state it aloud. Maybe he's trying to humiliate me. It won't work. I'm not ashamed of my past or of what I am. It's nothing I can help; why be ashamed?

"Is there anyone," the conde says, "who will vouch for the moral character of the imperial adoption candidate?"

Three people will vouch, all carefully arranged in advance. Still, I hold my breath and wait.

Conde Tristán steps forward on the dais until he stands parallel to Elisa's throne. He's a member of the Quorum of Five, and the most delicately beautiful man I've ever seen. He's also one of Elisa's dearest friends.

"By my word and honor, I vouch for the candidate!" Tristán says.

"By my word and honor, I vouch for the candidate!" comes a voice from the crowd. The mayor of Brisadulce, no doubt. I don't know him well, but he owes Elisa a favor.

A pause stretches into awkward silence. Rosario is stiff in the space beside me, and I force my gaze to remain steady, not to look desperately around for help. The next person to vouch was supposed to be Captain Bolivar of the Royal Guard. That is the tradition: a member of the court, a member of the commons, a member of the military. But now that I think of it, I don't remember seeing Captain Bolivar at all during our procession.

Elisa and Hector exchange a worried glance.

Suddenly, a voice booms in my ear. "By my word and honor, I vouch for the candidate!" It's Rosario, coming to my rescue. I give him a quick look of gratitude.

Conde Astón hesitates a moment. "Prince Rosario is not yet an adult, and as a member of the royal family he should not—"

Elisa stands.

"All hear, all hear," the seneschal booms. "Her Imperial Majesty addresses this royal chamber."

The Conde presses his mouth closed, and for the first time I see a crack in his composure as he shifts his feet uncomfortably.

Elisa says, "If anyone would deny Crown Prince Rosario as a member of this court, or reject his right to speak in this chamber, let them do so now, before all assembled."

Silence stretches over the audience hall like the string drawn on an assassin's bow.

Elisa likes to boast that even her enemies love Rosario. He's the son of their former king, after all. For many, he's the exemplar of everything they want in a ruler—someone born to their nation, from the highest possible rank of their nobility, a hero in the old war against the Inviernos, a man.

No one speaks. The bowstring of silence relaxes without firing a single shot.

"Let the ceremony continue," Elisa says, and she takes her seat.

"Let the ceremony continue!" the seneschal says.

Conde Astón can't keep the disappointment from his voice. "Very well. The candidate has been vouched for thrice by members of this distinguished assemblage. We shall now move to ratify. All in favor of the adoption of Lady Red Sparkle Stone to the imperial line, with all the rights, privileges, and duties thereof, up to and including full inheritance according to legal succession, please raise your hand and say 'Aye.'"

I don't dare turn around to look, but a chorus of *aye*s hits my back. Maybe I imagine that the vote is not as full-bodied and enthusiastic as we'd hoped. Then I see Elisa's narrowed eyes, and I'm forced to conclude that I am not imagining it.

Princess Mena presses against her father's leg, her chubby fingers clutching as much fabric of his pants as she can manage. Her brow knits as she looks back and forth between me and the speaker of the chamber.

My upper lip has grown damp.

Finally the speaker allows himself the barest beginning of a smile. He says, "All against, raise your hand and say 'Nay.'"

The *nay*s hit me loud and fierce, like a thunderclap.

Members of the audience begin to titter with amusement. Conde Astón gazes steadily at me, looking like a cat that just found a bowl of cream. His eyes remain fixed on my face as he announces, "The imperial petition is *denied*."

Princess Mena's huge brown eyes fill with tears.

The ground is opening beneath me. Were it not for Rosario's hand on my elbow, the earth would suck me into darkness and swallow me whole. Maybe I want it to.

The amused tittering at my back has become a buzz of excited conversation. I don't dare turn to face them all. I can't.

"God will judge!" someone yells.

"Burn the Treaty of Basajuan!" yells another.

The audience hall becomes chaos. Everyone mills about, either trying to escape the press of bodies or get a better look.

The empress appears furious. Beside her, Prince Hector comforts his daughter, but his right hand is at his scabbard and calculation whirls in his eyes. No one saw this coming. Most especially me.

"Red, let's get you to safety," says a voice in my ear. It's Rosario, reminding me of all my royal training. I'm a target now. A failed princess. Every member of court who only pretended kindness to me because of my eventual position is now free to be openly hostile.

The Royal Guards close formation around me, both protecting me and conferring a modicum of remaining status—a small mercy.

Empress Elisa stands from her throne, hands clasped, face serene. Her gaze fixed on me, she lifts her chin ever so slightly in the direction of the side door. I'm to follow her.

"Court is adjourned!" booms Conde Astón unnecessarily, and his announcement barely penetrates the din.

Rosario's hand is almost painful on my elbow, and the Royal Guards press so tight I can hardly breathe as I'm herded around the dais, through the door, and away, *away* from the imperial court that has just rejected me.

3

Then

IF Horteño the blacksmith, or the wise woman, or any of the other children were forced to flee through the woods pursued by enemies, they would choose to flee toward the village. Toward other people. Toward safety.

But the village would not be safe for the girl.

She and Mamá lived on the outskirts, as far from everyone else as they could. They went to the village only on market day, to trade chickens or eggs, herbs they'd gathered, or firewood they'd cut for the things they needed—meat, thread, chicken feed.

The girl was little, but she wasn't stupid. So she understood that when people spat on her mamá and called her a whore and gave them the worst prices ... that somehow it was all *her* fault. She was the girl with strange golden eyes and skin blanched the color of fever.

"They mostly tolerate you," her mamá had said once, "and they will so long as you're a little girl."

"I'm not stupid!" the girl had snapped. Because "mostly tolerate" was just a polite way to say "hate."

So even though the village beckoned with cozy snow-covered rooftops and familiar faces and pine-sharp smoke curling up from hot chimneys, the girl ran in the opposite direction, toward the mountain peaks and the tree line. It would be colder, harsher, hard to travel, impossible to find food . . . but it wouldn't be hateful.

Besides, she had an idea.

A month ago, she'd chanced upon a tree squirrel, a particularly bold fellow who hadn't run away from her. She was hungry. They were short on supplies. So she'd picked up a rock and threw it at the squirrel as hard as she could.

The rock hit the rodent square in the head, leaving a gash where one eye used to be, but not hard enough to kill it. The squirrel careened away, dizzy and concussed, crashing into trees, barreling through underbrush as it fled.

The girl remembered the sick feeling in her tummy. She never, ever would have thrown a rock at the poor creature just to hurt it. But it had been so close, and she had been so hungry.

So she'd torn after, following the clear trail through the snow. The squirrel would tire eventually. She would find it and put it out of its misery. Or maybe bandage up its head. After it was warm and fed, it would understand that the girl was really a good friend who had just made a terrible mistake.

The squirrel tracks had led to a granite face, polished clean by wind, sparkling in the winter sunshine. And that was where the prints disappeared. She had no way to tell where the squirrel had gone, and she never saw it again.

The girl had to be like the squirrel. If she could reach the smooth granite slopes where snow never caught hold, the sorcerer's people would lose her trail.

She was smart. Mamá always said so. Even Yara the herb woman, who hated her, always called her "wise for her years." So she set off with firm determination in the direction she was fairly sure was east, toward the windward side of the mountains.

She didn't get far before she heard someone yell. The voice sounded far away, but it was hard to judge in these mountains; sometimes a distant sound turned out to be as close as a whisper in the ear. The girl broke into a run.

Running through snow was one of the hardest things in the world, especially if you were little, with little feet and little legs, and a very awkward basket filled with a heavy cloak. She fell to her knees three times before she realized it was faster to just walk.

The voices sounded again, closer. She couldn't help herself—she was too scared and her legs wanted to run too badly, and she gave in, tripping and wading her way up the snowy slope. But no matter how hard she tried, no matter how many times she ordered her legs to go faster, they refused. They felt like porridge. Useless, wobbly things that could barely hold up her body.

The monster's people were catching up to her. Their hands would be on her, a knife in her kidney, long before she could reach the granite slopes. She had to think of something else. But thinking was *hard*. Her vision was blurry now, her breath so loud in her own ears. The pit of hunger in her tummy was

RAE·CARSON

dragging her down, down, down, making her stumble in the snow. Her feet were so cold she could hardly feel them.

She spied a huge slate-colored boulder jutting out of the snow. Beside it was a pine tree, thick with white-laden branches. The girl had climbed plenty of trees. They were familiar. Safe. She plunged toward the boulder.

Its surface was slick and icy cold, and her feet slid down as much as they pushed her up, and she wasted precious seconds scrambling to the top. From there, it was an easy reach to a sturdy pine branch. She hoisted the basket's handle to her shoulder, grabbed the branch with both hands, and lifted one leg and hooked it around.

She'd done it a hundred times before—swung the dangling leg to provide momentum enough to propel her to the top of the branch. But she was hungry and cold, and the heavy basket yanked at her shoulder, and she couldn't quite manage it. She tried again. And again. The third time, one of her hands slipped on the slick branch. Her basket swung wildly against her back, and all of its contents spilled out, crashed to the boulder below, then slid off the rock to plunk down into the snow.

"No!" the girl cried out, before she remembered that hiding from someone meant being very, very quiet.

Maybe she should leave all those things behind. Jump from the tree and take off again. Without a basket full of heavy things, she could go faster. Maybe even run for real.

But she needed that cloak and that tinderbox. *Cloak, fire, and food.*

More voices. A horse neighing.

Panic leaped in her throat. The girl released the branch and fell hard against the boulder, bruising her hip. She half climbed, half slid to the ground, gathered up the cloak and tinderbox as fast as she could. Her hip didn't want to move, but she forced herself to stumble forward, away from the traitor tree, even as she stuffed her precious items back into the basket.

Snow began to fall, lightly at first.

Ahead was a break in the trees. Maybe. It was hard to see. Everything blurred, and the sun had disappeared behind furious black clouds. The girl wiped at her eyes, and wetness smeared the back of her hand, turning instantly chilly. Tears. But she was not crying, she wasn't; it was just the angry wind, making her eyes water.

Blinking rapidly, she pushed through the snow toward the place where the trees seemed to part. Not much farther.

Someone yelled. She didn't recognize the words, but she knew that excited tone. They seemed very close. The girl dared to look over her shoulder, but she saw no one.

The snow came harder, and gusts of wind snatched up powder from yesterday's storm, swirled it into little eddies, whipped it around her ankles. She imagined the flurries were like white monster claws, grabbing for her legs, threatening to pull her down.

She reached the edge of the trees and almost sobbed in relief. They opened onto a granite face that sloped upward, curving toward the summit like a giant upside-down bowl of stone. She'd slipped on granite many times. It would not be easy to get across, especially while her hip hurt so badly and snow was swirling everywhere.

The land transitioned from snow-covered forest to stark stone in the space of a single step. Up here, away from the trees, the wind whipped even harder. A fold of cloak separated from the rest and hung out of the basket, flapping against her back, but she was too scared to slow down even the smallest bit to shove it back in place.

The slope grew steep, and she used a hand to steady herself. Her toes kept slipping, losing their purchase on the rock face. Her hip screamed in agony. The snow fell harder. Between that and the wind tears, she couldn't see where she was going. Just up, up, up, keep going up, don't stop no matter what, *no matter what.*

Before her mind could register that she had crested some kind of rise, her momentum carried her right over and suddenly she was grappling, scraping knees, sliding faster and faster.

Her fingertips found a tiny ledge; it was just enough to slow her descent and pivot her around, but the weight of her legs was too much and her fingers slipped away, leaving some skin behind.

She plummeted, picking up speed like water through a chute, and just as she was thinking, *Sorry, Mamá, I tried not to die,* her feet impacted ground with a bone-numbing force that shivered up her spine and gave her neck a crack. She collapsed to her knees. The basket spilled to the ground beside her, but by some miracle, nothing fell out.

The girl was in a ravine. No, more like a granite crevice. The wind didn't blow so hard here, and the ground felt squishy, filled with an accumulation of dirt and gravel and pine needles and even a bit of snow. The squishy ground had saved her life.

Her first attempt to gain her feet failed; her hip was locking up, and sharp pain in her neck made it hard to move her head.

But ahead, up the slope of the crevice, was a dark spot where the walls of granite closed in. A cave maybe, or at least a depression, that would protect her from the falling snow and from prying eyes. A hiding place. A safe place.

She used her good leg as much as possible to gain her feet. Her cheeks were icy with tears and her heart was like a rug beater against her throat as she pushed forward, toward the inviting murk.

It *was* a cave! The wind instantly quieted as darkness pulled over her head like a blanket. It wasn't very deep. She could barely stand up straight, and an old pile of dry scat hugged the wall near the entrance. Something had used this as a den once, probably one of the big mountain cats. Now it was her den. Her secret place.

With her back to the wall, she slid to the ground. Her belly hurt almost as much as her hip, from terrible emptiness, but there was nothing she could do about that. Not until the monster's men were long gone.

She huddled against the cave wall, tired beyond all understanding, but she wasn't sleepy. So she didn't understand why her vision was going black, why the world was disappearing.

The girl fought to stay conscious. Something important troubled her thoughts as she pulled the cloak from the basket. There was something Mamá would have wanted her to do before she slept. She would remember it any moment, if she could just keep herself from falling. . . .

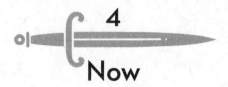

4
Now

THE Quorum of Five council chamber lies in the very center of the palace, in a sacred space centuries old. It's low ceilinged and windowless, with walls made of bulging river rock and thick mortar, draped on all sides by tapestries displaying the sigils of the major countships. Flames flicker from sconces set into the mortar between tapestries. On the floor is a low table, made of a single oaken slab with remnants of bark still clinging to the edges. It's surrounded by red velvet sitting cushions.

The meeting room is hot, airless, and utterly quiet. Elisa is speaking to Hector as we enter. "Did you see Ariña? Standing beside Lady Malka. Looking smug."

"Why *did* we give her a pardon?" Hector says, his voice so taut with quiet fury it scares me.

"We didn't. The chamber of condes did. It's been the better part of a decade. Her friends assured us that she regrets opposing me, that she suffered enough in exile. If she weren't Queen Cosmé's sister, I'd—"

The double doors thunk shut, and the bolt slides home. I feel safer than I have in weeks.

It's like being in a cave.

Elisa plops onto one of the cushions. Little Mena crawls into her lap, and the empress absently strokes her daughter's hair. "So," Elisa begins. "What went wrong?"

Hector's fist crashes to the table, which is the kind of thing that usually startles me, but at the moment I think it's impossible for me to be any more tense or alert to danger. "We had the votes. *We had them.*" He looks around at everyone, his face grave. "We were betrayed. What happened to Captain Bolivar? He was supposed to vouch."

Lord-Commander Dante of the Royal Guard speaks in a quiet voice that is more menacing than any shout. "He'd better be dead, because that is the only excuse I will accept. My best men are searching for him—or his body—right now."

"Oh, no, not Bolivar," Mara says. "He was such a good man."

"We'll find him," Elisa says. "Maybe he yet lives, and has a good explanation."

The room is crowded with bodies, and growing even hotter. The Quorum is here: the empress, Lord-Commander Dante, the General, and two of the empire's highest-ranking condes, Tristán and Juan-Carlos. The five of them usually meet here alone, but with the addition of me, Rosario, Hector, Mara, and the princess, there's barely room for everyone to sit.

And they're all looking at me.

"I . . . I'm sorry. I don't know what I did wrong—"

"Nothing!" Rosario practically yells. "You did nothing wrong!"

"Red, don't apologize," Elisa says.

Conde Tristán puts a hand on my shoulder. "You did everything you were supposed to do. Like Hector said, we were betrayed."

Suddenly all eyes move to Conde Juan-Carlos. It's a reflexive thing. His predecessor was a traitor who nearly plunged our nation into a civil war.

Juan-Carlos's eyes narrow. "I am not my father," he says in a tight voice. He's young for his station, only a few years older than I am, and his face seems perpetually on the verge of a frown.

No one responds. Hector and the General exchange a meaningful glance.

"I have voted with the Quorum every time since taking office," Juan-Carlos continues, "in gratitude for my family retaining its rights and holdings. You can't possibly still doubt my loyalty."

Everyone shifts uncomfortably. I get the feeling they've had this conversation many times behind closed doors.

At last Elisa says, "I do not doubt your loyalty," and I can't be the only person who notices that she refrains from saying "We."

"We'll figure out what happened," Lady Mara jumps in, before anyone can point out the obvious. "The spymaster is seeing to it personally. I expect we'll hear a knock on the door any moment."

"In the meantime, we need a plan," says Conde Tristán. "I hate to say this aloud, but I worry for Red's safety."

RAE·CARSON

The General has been quiet until now. He leans forward, elbows on the table, and says, "Our enemies would be well advised to carry out an assassination now, while we appear weak."

The safe, cave-like feeling dribbles away.

"They have to consider that we will regroup and try again, maybe next year. They'll want to put a stop to any future adoption while sentiment is low." The General is an older man with gray hair and a deep squint pinching a narrow nose. He refused the spectacles Doctor Enzo offered, calling them "modernistic and untrustworthy," though it would be a mistake to think him unprogressive. I clearly remember his acceptance speech eight years before, when he publicly declared that the young Empress Elisa had one of the finest military minds he'd ever encountered.

Elisa sighs. "Overturning a rejected petition would require a two-thirds majority vote. I don't see us getting two-thirds, even in the best of circumstances."

"For now, Red could accompany us on our state visit to Orovalle," Hector says.

"That might be best," Elisa says. "Most of the Royal Guard will be escorting us. And I'm sure once we tell Queen Alodia about our situation, she'll be glad to assign extra protection from her own guard, which is formidable."

Conde Tristán is tapping the table with his forefinger. "I wonder," he says. "Perhaps your schedule was a factor here, with your state trip coming so soon after the adoption ceremony. Whoever engineered this vote knew you would not be around to deal with the repercussions."

Elisa's brow furrows. Mena squirms out of her lap—the empress's absent stroking had become a little too fierce—and plops down beside Hector instead. "That could mean," Elisa says, her hand drifting to her belly of its own accord, "that news of my pregnancy has leaked. They know the real reason for this trip."

Tristán nods. "And that you would never cancel it, no matter what happened. You absolutely *must* be in Orovalle to give birth."

In a more forgiving climate, he means. Surrounded by midwives familiar with the difficult births experienced by the women of Elisa's family.

Hector reaches across his daughter for Elisa's hand and holds tight. The gesture happens mostly under the table, but we all see it. A muscle in Hector's jaw twitches.

They lost their first child in a difficult birth. A son. He suffocated, the umbilical cord wrapped around his neck, before Doctor Enzo could extract him from Elisa's womb. Three years later, the empress almost bled to death giving birth to Princess Ximena. I was surprised—we all were—when Elisa and Hector decided to try one last time.

A knock sounds. Hector leaps to his feet. He and Tristán close ranks before the table to protect everyone else, their hands shifting to their scabbards. Lord-Commander Dante moves to answer. With a nod to Hector and Tristán, he rotates the bolt and swings it aside.

A man strides in, small in stature and nondescript. I don't recognize him, but no one shows alarm as he makes his way over to Mara and bends to whisper something in her ear. She asks him a question—so quietly I can't hear. He nods, whispers back at length, and then he leaves as silently as he came, without so much as a word or gesture to anyone else.

After the bolt is fastened once again, Conde Juan-Carlos says, "The spymaster's messenger?"

Mara nods. "Our spy web was only able to make quick surface inquiries," she explains. "But from what we know so far, a rumor has been spreading the past week about our girl." Mara gives me a smile that is equal measures fondness and sadness.

"Well?" Elisa prompts.

"Apparently Red was overheard saying that religion is a comforting myth. Something about a soothing balm to the hurting masses."

Oh, god.

"And that God belongs in children's stories, not policy."

All eyes are on me again. The skin of my face suddenly burns hot. Were I fully Invierno, my cheeks would be flaming red.

"That does sound like you," Hector says to me.

"I . . . " No use denying it. "I did say that. To one of my tutors." The words almost catch in my throat. I messed everything up. All that hard work, and it was tossed away with a few careless words. "I'm so sorry."

"Stop apologizing!" Elisa snaps. Then, to Mara, "That can't be all of it. Many people in this country are not that devout. Nothing about her being half Invierno?"

"Nothing so far. That anyone will admit to, anyway," Mara

says. "But yes, there is another factor. As you suspected, your pregnancy is no longer a secret. So the pressure to produce an heir through adoption was greatly diminished, your past difficulties notwithstanding."

"So, news of the pregnancy, coupled with rumors of Red's atheism, made her a disqualified candidate," says Conde Juan-Carlos. Do I imagine that his voice holds a hint of satisfaction?

"We can try again next year," Tristán says. "Shore up support. We'll think of a way to get that two-thirds majority."

"The girl will have to prove herself," the General says. "Prove her patriotism."

"She has proven herself enough," Elisa says. "She has *been* proving herself, over and over since the day we found her in that village."

"Not to the people in that audience chamber, apparently," the General says.

Hector is shaking his head. "A two-thirds majority is impossible. Too many want to return to the past, even if it's a past in ruins."

"We'll figure it out later," Tristán says.

"Yes," Hector says. "For now, we need to keep her safe."

"She'll be safest with you, on the road to Orovalle," Lord-Commander Dante says. "A few Guards will stay behind to protect Prince Rosario and oversee the annual recruitment, but most of my best men will be traveling in state."

"It's settled, then," Conde Tristán says. "Red will pack up and leave with—"

I clear my throat. "Maybe . . . that is . . . do *I* get a say in any of this?"

Elisa appears horrified. "Oh, my sky, we were talking right over your head, weren't we? I used to hate it when everyone did that to me."

"Your thoughts on this are most welcome," Hector assures me.

I'm not sure what my thoughts are, except that I hate failing. I hate that everyone is disappointed. And running away doesn't feel right. As a little girl, I ran a lot. Too much. In my nightmares, I'm still running, still scared.

Elisa is searching my face. Mara gives me an encouraging nod. It's so hot is this room I can hardly breathe. I don't know how Elisa can stand it.

"Red?" Rosario prompts.

Finally I say, "I'm done running. It's time to stand my ground."

As soon as the words leave my mouth, I know they're right. If I keep running, I'll keep being scared. I have to face the next thing, whatever it is.

"Standing one's ground is often the last gasp of a dying defense," the General says.

"Or the first move of a budding offense," I retort.

Elisa smiles.

"What did you have in mind?" Hector says.

"I'm not sure . . . maybe . . ." I glance around the room. Everyone meets my gaze except Lord-Commander Dante, whose sole focus is the door and protecting everyone inside.

That's it. That's what I want.

I say, "Send me to the Guard."

"What?" says Lord Dante, forgetting about the door for a moment.

But Elisa seems thoughtful.

"All royal princes spend a year with the Guard recruits, right?" I say, warming to the idea. "Rosario did. So why should it be any different for me or Princess Ximena? Hector, you've taught me how to defend myself. I know it was just to . . . help me with . . . to stay calm and . . . channel certain tendencies. But I learned. And I've trained with Spymaster Belén, sparred with Rosario. I could probably hold my own."

Hector also appears thoughtful. "Oh, you could hold your own," he says.

"Hector," Elisa says, though she's looking at me. "Has there ever been a woman in the Royal Guard?"

"No!" Lord Dante says.

"Yes," Hector says. "Once. A few years before I joined. She dressed as a boy. Posed as her brother, who had obtained an actual sponsorship. When she was discovered a few weeks later, she was immediately sent home."

"For being a girl," Elisa says.

"For lying," Hector clarifies. "For showing up on recruitment day under false pretenses, with a false identity. It was considered treason. King Nicolao chose not to execute her, I'm glad to say. He just sent her home in disgrace."

"So there's no law forbidding a woman to try for the Guard?"

"None at all."

RAE·CARSON

"Your Imperial Majesty," the lord-commander says, "tradition is a powerful thing, and I don't—"

"The safest place for me," I interrupt, "aside from being with the main contingent in Orovalle, would be here, with the remaining Guard."

"Red could do it," Rosario says. "You've all seen how seriously she's taken her training these last few years. *All* of her training."

"We could spread the rumor that it's a punishment," I say. "For failing so utterly. That as a consequence for betraying the crown with my monstrous beliefs, I must redeem myself and devote my life to defending it." The words sound bitter, even to me. My beliefs should not be considered monstrous. It's not like they hurt anybody.

"This year's class is going to be particularly talented," Conde Juan-Carlos says. "My younger brother will stand for recruitment. Some promising young men are transferring from the army recruits. And I hear that Queen Cosmé of Basajuan is sending a few lads with potential, as a show of fealty to the empire."

"Even better," I tell him. "No one will be able to say I made the cut only because it was an uncompetitive year."

"Captain Bolivar will not go easy on you just because you're a girl," the lord-commander says.

"I would not expect him to."

"If Captain Bolivar is still . . . here," Rosario points out.

Everyone in the room pauses to consider. I wish I could hear what they're thinking. Rosario fiddles with the fringe of his cushion. Mena squirms in Hector's lap.

Lord Dante is the first to break the silence. "I still advise that we don't jump into this plan too hastily. There may not be a law against it, per se, but—"

"Lord-Commander Dante," the empress says in a voice I recognize. She's about to pull rank. "Is it my Guard, or is it *my Guard*?"

The commander ducks his head. "Now and always, Your Majesty."

"You are one of my most trusted friends," the empress continues. "More like family. When Hector resigned his post, it gave us great confidence and pleasure to appoint you in his place. I know you will do the right thing and protect the crown's interests in *every* possible capacity."

"Of course, Your Majesty. May I speak freely, Majesty?"

"Always."

"Lady Red is an exceptional candidate for the Royal Guard; I have no doubt about that. And being a woman does not disqualify her in any way. I only meant to say that some will not see things so clearly. If she takes to the sand, her first year will be challenging in ways I can only imagine."

"I want to do it," I say.

"I won't be there to protect you," he says, finally addressing me directly. "I'll be in Orovalle with the empress for months. Maybe a year. Hector won't be here. The empress won't be here. We have no idea where Bolivar is. You'll be on your own."

"I'll be here," Rosario says.

"Every recruit leaves home," I say. "Gives up everything."

"Almost everything," Hector clarifies.

"Right. Except three items. Anyway, everyone is alone when they come to the palace on recruitment day. That's the point, right? We belong to the crown now. Our lives for Elisa's. So I don't need special treatment. I'll succeed or fail on the same terms as everyone else."

The river rock walls and the thick oak door are meant to deter eavesdropping, but they make a silence feel heavy, as though it's pressing in.

Princess Mena whispers something in Hector's ear.

"I think," Hector whispers back, "that if Red can't be your sister, she still wants an excuse to see you every day. Like Guardsman Fernando does."

"Good idea," Ximena says gravely.

Tristán says, "All right, I like this plan. I think it would discourage any assassination attempts. Red is simply not a target anymore, as a mere Guard recruit. Not to mention the fact that the Guard barracks are nearly impossible to penetrate."

"Red will still be a target," Mara says. "Just for different reasons. For being a woman with the audacity to try for the Guard, for instance. Trust me on that." She and Elisa exchange a knowing glance.

"I'm happy to begin spreading the rumor that this is a punishment, as Red suggested," Conde Juan-Carlos says. "I promise to be appropriately smug. It should be very convincing, coming from the bitter son of the disgraced traitor, yes?"

"I expect so, Juan-Carlos," Elisa says. "Thank you. It's safer for her if everyone believes her dishonored." The empress shakes her head ruefully. "The first woman in the Royal Guard! I don't know why I didn't think of it before. Of course women should be in my Guard. And if you're sure you can do this, Red, I'll sponsor your petition for recruitment myself. That guarantees a spot in the sand."

"This is what you want?" Mara asks me.

"I'm sure I want to try." And I am. I've never been more convinced of the rightness of anything, not since that day eight years ago when Elisa bought me and took me away.

The empress smiles. "Then we have a plan."

"We have a plan," Hector echoes.

"Red, be careful," Mara warns. "We *did* have the votes for your adoption, less than a week ago. This was a major coup, to spread those rumors so quickly and convince everyone to change their votes. Whoever did it is still out there, Bolivar is still missing, and the empress's entourage won't be around to investigate."

"I understand."

We all mill about for a short while as I endure half-hearted congratulations, a kiss on the cheek from Mara, hugs from Tristán and Elisa. No one does a good job masking their disappointment at my failed adoption, or their desire to leave the hot Quorum chamber, but at the last second, Hector yanks me aside.

"Red," he says. "You might be the most qualified candidate in the sand this year."

He's so solemn that I'm not sure it's a compliment. "Er . . . thank you?"

"Some recruits, those from especially privileged families,

delay revealing the full extent of their skills and training."

I chew on this a moment. "To keep from showing off, you mean. To keep from making early enemies."

He nods. "Others go in hard and fast to establish a pecking order as quickly as possible. I've seen both strategies succeed and fail."

"So your advice is . . . ?"

"No advice. Just information. I trust you to make the right decision for yourself."

Something about that chokes me up a little, and I find myself swallowing hard.

"And one more thing. The Royal Guard may be the most elite fighting force in the empire, filled with the best men I've ever known. But it's still a large group of men, with all the bad tendencies that large groups of men seem to develop. Especially the new, untried recruits. I made several reforms when I was in charge, work that Lord Dante has continued. But neither of us will be there to reinforce those changes."

"You're saying it will be a dangerous place for me because I'm a woman."

"Yes. But I hope not too dangerous for you to handle, so long as you remain alert."

"I'm always alert."

His weathered face is handsome and hard, but once in a while a softness overtakes it. When he looks at his wife and daughter, for instance. And sometimes, when he looks at me.

The prince consort's hand comes up to cup my cheek. "You can do this, Red. You are brave like Rosario. Smart like Elisa.

Loyal like me. You're the best of all of us, my sky, and *you can do this.*"

"I can do this," I whisper back.

It's the deepest, coolest time of night. I'm lying on my vast canopied bed, the door to my balcony left open to invite the breeze. A slight glow filters through the sheer, fluttering curtains, for the night bloomers in the garden below have opened their petals wide, showing off their luminescing stamens to the night sky. The air smells of cinnamon, thanks to the mug of duerma leaf tea on my bedside table, which was supposed to help me sleep.

But I'm terrible at sleeping, and not even duerma leaf tea can help me tonight.

Beside the mug, the candle on my bedside table has become a puddle of wax, and only the tiniest flame remains. In a few hours, I'll leave this luxurious bedroom suite for cold, austere barracks. Elisa and Hector and everyone I love will leave me behind.

It's my choice, I tell myself. I want them to. I'm a different girl than I used to be. I can handle being alone, and I've slept in worse places than barracks.

The candle flame sputters out, drowning in its own mess. I grab a pillow, yank the bedspread off, and toss it all into the corner on the floor. I make a nest of everything, snug against the wall, and hunker down. Sleepily, bedspread pulled up to my shoulders, I trace the ceramic border that rims the floor of my chamber. In daylight, the tiles are soft yellow with painted blue flowers, but tonight, in the near dark, they are merely something slick and cool for me to focus on.

I'm finally, finally drifting to sleep when a knock sounds at my door.

Lord-Commander Dante stationed several Guards outside, so whoever has knocked is someone they've chosen to let pass. I'm unalarmed as I rise, pad barefoot across the room, and open the door.

It's Rosario, his hair mussed, a sheepish grin on his face.

A flash of movement draws me partly into the corridor, and I glimpse a fast-walking figure in a dressing gown, just before she turns the corner and disappears.

"Was that Lady Carilla?" I ask, making no effort to hide my amusement. "Were the two of you . . . together?"

Rosario pushes inside. "No."

"Well, maybe you should be. At the adoption ceremony, she couldn't take her eyes off you. She's nice. I like Carilla."

Rosario closes the door and latches it. "It's not like that between us."

"Then what's it like, little brother?"

The prince opens his mouth to retort, but changes his mind when he sees all my bedding tossed in the corner. "Sleeping on the floor again?"

I shrug. "Rosario, why are you here? The monastery rang the third hour."

He plunks down on my bed. "Couldn't sleep. Figured you might be up too."

I plop down beside him. "What's keeping *you* awake?"

He pulls his knees to his chest and rests his chin on top of them. "Captain Bolivar. Still missing. I trained with him. I . . ."

"He was the captain in charge during the year you spent with the Guard."

"Yes. But not just that. I can't stop thinking about him . . . Red, what if it wasn't an accident? What if he was purposely kept away from that audience hall?"

The crickets have fallen silent, and tree frogs are taking up the chorus in their place. Their chirrupy, bell-like sound is something I've always found pleasant. It means dawn is not far off.

"I think," I begin carefully, "that if Bolivar was purposely disposed of, it speaks to a wider plot. A possible coup."

"Exactly. And with Elisa and Hector leaving, who do you think is the next, most likely target?"

Oh. Understanding lands like a rock in my gut. "You are."

"I am. And if that adoption had gone through, you would be too. I'm glad you're going to the Guard."

The prince is frightened for his life. No wonder he can't sleep. "What does Elisa think about all this? Surely you've shared your suspicions with her. Maybe you should go with her to Orovalle."

"She says I'll be well guarded. She also says that we must not consolidate targets. The entire royal family should not be on the road at the same time. And she wants me to stay behind and treat with the Invierno ambassador. To 'practice my diplomacy.'"

"That sounds like Elisa."

"Pragmatic to a fault," he agrees. "I hate that she's right. Since becoming the ruler of Joya d'Arena, she's had six attempts on her life. And those are just the ones we know about. She's always a target. By splitting up, we take some pressure off each other."

"So what are you going to do about it?"

The prince takes a deep breath. It's too dim to see his features clearly, but I can hear the frown in his voice when he says, "I'm going to keep my head down. Sleep in a different bed every night. One of my Guards will prepare all my food. I may spend some time training in the Guard hideout beneath the Wallows."

"I think all that sounds wise."

After a long pause, he says, "Red, is this what being emperor will be like? Always wondering if the next corner hides an assassin? If my next scone is full of poison? I don't think I can live like that."

And I don't think I have an answer for him. We sit together in silence. Then the monastery bells ring the fourth hour, and it's like an explosion in my chest. I startle so hard that I bite my tongue.

Rosario waits in patient silence as I breathe deep to settle my heartbeat, in through my nose and out through my mouth, just like Hector taught me. With the metal tang of blood in my mouth comes clarity. I do have an answer for Rosario.

"I've been afraid my whole life," I say. "I don't remember everything that happened to me, but my body certainly remembers how to be afraid. Hector calls it the soldier sickness. He says he's seen it a lot, especially lately, since the war."

Rosario knocks my shoulder with his own, giving me a gentle shove. "I know how you are. What I don't understand is . . . how can you live with it?"

"When I figure it out, I'll let you know."

Rosario snorts. "I thought you were going to say something wise and inspiring."

"No. Just . . . you're not alone. I understand what it's like to be afraid, and I don't blame you for it one bit."

He leans his head on my shoulder, and his soft hair tickles my cheek. "Thanks, little sister."

"No problem, little brother. You can sleep here if you want. I've got the floor."

RAE·CARSON

5

Then

WHEN the girl woke, it was to the wavering, flashing orange of torches against the night.

They provided just enough light that she could make out the shape of a huge snowdrift blocking half the entrance to her den. She froze, more still than a rabbit with a hawk overhead.

The girl was colder than cold, like her very bones were made of icicles, and her lips felt puffy in her face. Though she had obviously slept all day and into the night, she wanted nothing more than to close her eyes and return to oblivion.

Her mamá had taught her about cold sickness. Your bones like ice. Your eyes so heavy with the need to sleep they're like rocks in your eye sockets. Your lips that swell to cracking.

It meant she needed to get warm—quick, before she was dead.

That was it, the thing she was trying to remember before she blacked out. Her mamá would have wanted her to build a fire. The tinderbox was still in the basket, barely a stretch away. But she couldn't chance moving with the torches so close.

Voices drifted toward her, muffled by snow and stone. That language again, with the funny syllables and singsong cadence. The language of monsters. She hardly dared to breathe.

They were above her, maybe right over her head, peering into the ravine. If they climbed down, they'd see her little den. But the ravine was thick with snow now. It probably didn't look like much. You had to be born to these mountains to understand how tricky things were in winter, like how ledges and overhangs were smaller than they seemed and you'd better watch your step or else, and how crevices were always deeper, with sharp branches and hard boulders and maybe even tiny cozy dens hidden beneath the snow.

Being so still for so long was awful. It made her think and feel things she didn't want to think and feel. Like how cold she was. How hungry. How tired. How alone. And oh, she missed her mamá so much it was an actual pain in her belly, far worse than the cramp of days-old hunger.

The monsters talked in their funny language for a long time. Daylight began to turn the walls of her den to murky gray. Their footsteps dislodged snow, which tumbled down from above, pattering onto her snowdrift. That snowdrift had probably saved her life, blocking out the worst of the wind.

A hawk squealed. Wind whistled against the granite slopes, and more snow floated down. It occurred to the girl, distantly, that she couldn't feel her toes.

Suddenly it was brilliant daylight, and a sliver of blinding brightness angled right into her eyes. Maybe she had blacked out again. She didn't remember falling asleep, but the voices were gone and the sun was high.

Still, she waited a moment, listening.

Nothing. No funny language, no footsteps, just the ever-present wind and the chatter of mountain jays, who would never be so joyous if the monsters were still around.

Carefully, slowly, she reached for her basket. Her fingers were clumsy and thick and she dropped her tinderbox twice before bringing it to her lap.

Now, for kindling. Detritus covered the floor—some pine needles, a few small sticks, the dried cat droppings.

She gathered it all into a little pile. It wouldn't burn long, but maybe it would be enough to stave off the cold sickness.

The girl fumbled with her tinderbox. It was wooden with a hinged lid, and it took several tries to get it open. Everything inside was intact: a firesteel with a small handle, a flat piece of uneven flint, some dry grass tinder.

She left the tinder alone; she had plenty in her den, and she might need it later. She lifted firesteel and flint from the box and struck them—at an angle, just like Mamá had taught her.

Pain blossomed in her knuckle. She popped it into her mouth and sucked. The girl had scraped a good chunk of skin off, with no spark to show for it.

She tried again. And again. On the fourth try, she got a decent spark, but it landed in the dirt and fizzled away. The girl leaned closer to her little pile and aimed. This time, the spark landed on some dry pine needles. They crackled and grayed and she held her breath—until she remembered that she was supposed to blow oh-so-gently to fan it into flame.

She did, just like she had practiced with Mamá, and the pine needles caught for true. A beautiful, bright flame licked at them, then hungrily leaped for the tiny sticks, and finally for the cat droppings.

Warmth flooded her cheeks and fingers, which all began to itch. The girl was so relieved she almost cried.

But the fire was burning itself out too quickly. It wouldn't last long enough for her to get warm, not really. There were probably more branches outside, under the snow, but she didn't dare go out there. What if the monsters were still nearby?

The girl glanced around her tiny den. She spied another branch, a small pile of pine needles, collected in a crack. Still not enough.

Then her eyes settled on the basket. It was big, made of willow. Sitting on the ground, it rose past her knees. It could hold a month's worth of herbs, a week's worth of chicken feed, an entire cloak with a tinderbox.

Her lower lip trembled. She caressed the handle with her forefinger. Mamá had woven this basket herself. They'd collected the willow shoots together along the creek. One of their bundles had dried a beautiful reddish brown, which Mamá had used to make a lovely stripe just under the basket lip.

You know how much I want you to live, yes?

She burned the basket.

Hours later, thirst drove her outside. The sun was high overhead. Melting water sheened down the walls of her crevice. She tried to lick the stone, but found it was easier to just grab handfuls of snow. The cold made her tongue itch, and each handful was barely a few drops in her mouth once it melted. Her lips and gums drank up the water almost before it could reach her throat.

She ate so much snow she thought she might burst.

She rummaged around the ground outside and found a few branches, which she took back inside her den. She brushed snow from them as best she could, but when she placed them over the flame they crackled and popped and hissed with melting water. The girl was grateful when they caught and burned.

Now, for food. Eating snow had at least given her tummy something to do for a while. She was still dizzy, still weak, and for some reason the thirst in her belly was worsening. She shivered. And then she shivered some more. Not even the fire was making her feel warmer.

She stared out the entrance to her den at the steep crevice walls. She'd have to climb out somehow. The walls were slick with meltwater, and her hip still hurt something awful. Still, she had to try.

The girl gave herself a little while longer, to drink more snowmelt water—which was not slaking her thirst at all—to absorb the warmth of the fire, to gather her courage.

She had no basket to carry the cloak, so she put it on, working the bone hook through the clasp. It was so huge that it would drag behind her, maybe even trip her if she wasn't careful.

The girl shoved her tinderbox down her shirt and stepped into the cold sunshine. She stared at the granite walls.

There was no way up. No cracks, no ledges, absolutely nothing to hold on to. Just slick gray stone covered with water that would freeze into sheets as soon as the sun was no longer directly above.

A rustling sounded just ahead, where a stunted manzanita shrub clung to a bit of soil at the bottom of the crevice. Her eyes roved the shrub hungrily, but it was too early in winter for edible manzanita blooms to appear. Maybe she could chew on a branch, give her mouth something to do, trick it into thinking she was eating. She stepped forward.

A snowshoe rabbit burst from the shrub, a flash of white with only a few patches of summer brown left in its fur. The girl tore after it.

Her cloak caught in detritus and she nearly tripped, but she kept going. A rabbit! A rabbit would feed her for two days. Maybe the crevice would dead end. The critter would have nowhere to go and she could catch it and—

The crevice hooked right and broke apart, spilling her onto a snowy meadow. The rabbit tracks bounded across the snow, and she followed—across a frozen creek, around a clutch of young pines, down a slope. And straight into a wall of thorny bushes she could not penetrate. The rabbit was gone.

A little whimper escaped her lips. Dizziness made her sway, and the girl allowed herself to crumble into the snow.

It had been stupid to chase a rabbit. She couldn't catch a rabbit on foot in fresh powder snow even if she was rested and well-fed. She was a foolish little girl, just like the blacksmith always said.

At least she'd found her way out of the crevice.

An icy blast hit her cheeks. Blackness roiled overhead, and wind whipped the tree branches into angry, punishing paddles. Another storm was coming.

She glanced around in a panic. She had forgotten to track her journey. *"Pay attention to where you're going,"* Mamá always said. *"Or you'll get lost."*

The girl spied her footprints, and relief filled her. She could follow her own trail back to the cave. The girl forced herself to her feet.

Her hip throbbed in agony. Her stomach was a pit of raw pain. Snow swirled; she tracked it dizzily as it dipped and swooped in the air, until she realized that she had forgotten to keep walking.

Keep walking, keep walking. The snowfall thickened. It gathered in small drifts against the trees, filled the dips in the land. The footprints she followed began to soften and blur. Soon she couldn't see them at all. She had no way to retrace her steps.

Nothing looked familiar. She'd torn after that rabbit so fast that she hadn't paid attention to anything else. She was truly, hopelessly lost.

"You're a smart girl," her mamá always said. *"Think, my sky."*

She reached for a nearby pine branch and in one swift motion, stripped a handful of pine needles, which she shoved into her mouth. Chewing pine needles would keep the whites of her eyes from turning yellow and make her teeth stay in her mouth. Or so Yara the herb woman had told her. She just had to be careful not to swallow, no matter how angrily her tummy demanded it.

With the sharp tang came a brief clarity: She had to find her village. People there were hateful, sure, but asking for help would be better than starving or freezing to death. But which direction should she go?

She had no idea. She was too little to decide such an important thing. Too scared, too hungry, too dizzy.

The pine needles were pulp in her mouth now. She wanted to swallow them more than anything, but she knew they would give her belly a bad pain. She forced herself to spit them out.

The girl stood there in the pine grove for too long, trying to make herself move, unable to take a single step, much less think. Tears pooled in her eyes and froze on their way down her cheeks. *I'm not smart, Mamá, I'm not smart at all, you were wrong about me.*

Minutes passed. Her eyelids grew heavy. She was supposed to be thinking about something. Something important. Maybe she would just sit down in the soft snow.

A mountain jay cawed, and it startled her. She saw a flash of dark blue wings trimmed in black. It drew her forward.

The jay flitted from branch to branch, cawing as it went. Such a pretty little thing, so full of life and energy, able to gobble up distances with a hop and flap. The bird made it look easy.

The girl wanted to be a bird. She would spread her wings and fly far away. It would be effortless, so different from this icy trudging. Actually, the trudging wasn't so bad anymore. She couldn't really feel her feet. She wasn't even sure if she was moving or not.

Of their own accord, her arms came up to shoulder height. She flapped them experimentally. Did she imagine that her feet lifted off the ground a little?

"You have always been my sweet sky," Mamá said in her ear. *"Now, fly!"*

The girl lunged forward, wings flapping. She had a vague memory of struggling before, but everything was painless now, easy. She flapped all the way down the icy slope.

The girl's feet met air. Her heart leaped into her throat as she fell from the cliff's edge, flapping, flapping, flapping.

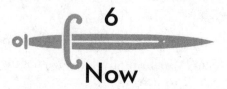

6
Now

ON the dawn of the empress's departure, a ribbon of clouds along the eastern horizon masks the rising sun, keeping the air cool and dim. The city's earliest risers are already awake; the scent of warm yeast permeates everything as palace bakers set out their bread for the day, and distant ship bells herald departures into coastal fishing waters.

The giant carriage house is bustling as I enter. Stable hands check and double-check traces, horses kick up their knees with impatience, and Royal Guardsmen load supplies onto pack camels. Five carriages are ready to go, all lined up. Dead center of the procession is the royal carriage itself, rich with mahogany and gilded scrollwork, littered with plush cushions, windowed to let in the breeze. Elisa will ride in it one-fifth of the time. For safety, she'll rotate carriages regularly, and only a handful of Guards will know where she is at any given moment.

The empress herself stands before the carriage, dressed in simple traveling clothes, her long hair wrapped around her head in a crown of braids. She's giving last-minute instructions to one of her Guards, but when she sees me, she smiles and waves me over.

"Did you choose three items to take with you to the Guard?" she asks with forced cheer.

"Yes. It was an easier choice than I thought."

Recruits who aren't princes give up everything else, Rosario reminded me this morning before leaving my chamber. *Title, property, loyalty to anyone other than Elisa—for the privilege of joining.* Which sounded funny at the time. I'm already loyal to Elisa. I hold no title or property aside from her indulgence anyway. I'm giving up nothing.

You're giving up a luxurious life as the empress's ward, Rosario said candidly, and I'm not quite sure how I feel about that yet.

"Good," Elisa says. "That's good."

We stare at each other. I shift awkwardly on my feet. Neither of us has ever been disposed to offer up what we're feeling.

"Do you . . . need anything? From me?" she asks.

"No. I'm fine. I just came to say goodbye." We are of equal height, and I can't escape her dark gaze. I should be taller, being half Invierno, but Doctor Enzo says a rough start in life made it hard for me to grow.

The empress gives me a look I can't read and says softly, "You never ask for anything, do you, Red?"

"I . . . don't want to be a bother."

I'm almost certain her answering glare is mocking. "Ask me for something," she orders. "Right now. Anything. It's an imperial command."

I glare right back. "I ask that you have a safe journey and take good care of yourself and that baby."

Her lips twitch. "A nimble deflection," she says. "But don't think I'll let this go. I'll ask you again when I return, so consider hard."

I'm not sure what to say to that.

"Your Majesty, we are loaded and ready," calls one of her Guards.

"I have to go," Elisa says. Her hand comes up to stroke my hair. "Be well, Red. I'm so proud you're taking to the sand today."

Moments later, she is bundled into her carriage, and Lord-Commander Dante gives the order. Wheels creak, camels grumble, and footsteps march forward in a steady one-two. I linger, watching as the procession files out of the carriage house and into the gloomy dawn.

I exit the dark arched corridor and enter the arena. The morning sun is still low, the arena cloaked in shadow, the air crisp with residual night. I'm the first to arrive, and I stand in the sand all alone, dwarfed by the stone walls around me.

This will be my last moment alone for a very long time.

I'm dressed like a desert nomad, in a loose linen shirt, a leather utility belt, and comfortable pants that tuck into my camel-hair boots. I've cut my black hair short, and without the extra length, it curls slightly at my temples and nape.

I carry my three chosen items. All recruits are allowed exactly three possessions from their previous lives, and mine are sure to provoke mockery and scorn. But they are precious to me, and I will have them, no matter what.

The training arena is a massive oval, two hands' deep in sand. Opposite the iron portcullis where I entered are straw practice dummies and archery targets. Beside the targets is a weapons rack, filled mostly with wooden swords and daggers, but also a few steel weapons. Blunted, I hope.

I've attended my share of recruitment days, and every year the Guard comes up with a creative way to test the new recruits' mettle. During Hector's year, recruits were given the ridiculous task of washing the entire arena with scrub brushes and dirty water. The recruits never see weapons on the first day. It means they're breaking with tradition this year. I can't help but wonder if it's because of me.

I don't wait long. Three young men enter, dressed exactly alike, their own items in hand. They're older than I am, taller and stronger. Probably the army recruits Juan-Carlos mentioned, with two years of formal training already.

They look me up and down, not bothering to mask their surprise. One smirks openly. I don't know if Juan-Carlos has gotten the word out yet about my "punishment," so I'm not sure what these young men are seeing—the failed princess from a few days ago, or merely a girl daring to take to the sand.

I'm half tempted to step over and introduce myself, like it's a perfectly normal day and I've every right to be here. I'm not sure why I hesitate.

Another boy enters through the portcullis. He's half a head shorter than I am and barely fourteen years old, with chub still in his cheeks and huge brown eyes surrounded by luxurious black lashes. He holds a beautiful folded blanket in his arms, dark blue with a black wave pattern and a lavish fringe.

He startles to a stop when he sees a girl in the arena, but then a shy smile overtakes his face, and he heads my way with deliberation. His blanket bulges, attesting to other, hidden items.

"Morning," he says.

"Morning," I answer, more than a little grateful to be acknowledged politely. "Beautiful blanket."

"Thank you! Mamá made it for me." He looks up at the brightening sky. "It's a good day for some mean-spirited hazing, yes?"

I bark a laugh. "Is that what's going to happen?"

"Mostly to you and me. You for being a girl. Me for being small but enviably handsome."

"I do see your point. I'm Red. I'd shake your hand, but . . ." I lift my hands, which are gripping my three small items so that they remain hidden.

"Weird name. You'll get double the hazing just for that. I'm Aldo. Nice to meet you, Red."

"Nice to meet you, Aldo."

"Who are those three?" he says, looking toward the young men.

"Former army recruits, I think. They haven't stopped smirking since they saw me."

"Huh. Can you take them in a fight?"

Hector's words come back to me. *Some recruits delay revealing the full extent of their skills and training.*

"Look at them!" I say. "They're huge."

"Yeah, me neither," Aldo says.

Another boy enters, as tall as the army recruits but leaner, with broad shoulders and gangly arms that promise more growth, if not more height. He has quick dark eyes and the most perfectly symmetrical cheekbones I've ever noticed. Seventeen years old, is my guess. He considers the army recruits, then Aldo and me. I see the exact moment he makes his choice. He heads toward the recruits.

Aldo whistles soft and low. "I think I have competition for the Most Handsome medal."

"Sorry. But yes, I think you're right."

Several more boys drift into the arena, dressed like me in the attire of desert nomads. Queen Cosmé's contingent from Basajuan, no doubt. They're the only ones so far who don't noticeably react to seeing a girl in the sand, but they still choose to keep to themselves, avoiding me and Aldo as well as the others.

The sun is rising, and the walls of the arena are turning from ochre dark to milky sandstone. A crowd begins to form around us, some standing on the wall, others sitting with their legs dangling over the edge: palace guards, servants, city watchmen, more than a few nobles. Annual recruitment is always an event. Sometimes even Elisa and Hector attend.

Maybe Rosario will be here, but a quick scan of the growing crowd does not reveal him. Good. We still don't know what happened to Captain Bolivar, and I feel better knowing that Rosario is keeping out of sight.

Everyone on the walls is staring at me. Whispering to each

other about me. Some are laughing. Others appear deadly serious. *Go ahead*, I think. *Get a good look.* I stare back daggers with my eyes.

"You're . . . popular today," Aldo whispers.

"It's you they're looking at," I tell him. "They're overwhelmed by your handsomeness."

"Understandable."

Abruptly, the audience's focus is drawn back toward the portcullis, where another young man strides through, chin held high, shoulders relaxed and easy. He wears loose clothing made of pale blue silk, a popular form of dress among the wealthiest southern nobles. At his back are several other young men, who follow him in formation like baby ducks after their mother. The crowd rumbles with recognition.

I don't know him by sight, but I've no doubt he's a rich conde's son with the best training and tutoring money can buy and an already established contingent of lackeys. A crowd favorite. Everyone expects him to make the final cut, me included.

More enter, until I count exactly thirty-two of us. The iron portcullis slams down, barring us in.

A Royal Guardsman strides toward us, red cloak whipping at his back. His shining ceremonial breastplate reflects blinding flashes of rising sunshine, and I can't help wincing.

"Recruits!" he booms. I don't recognize his face or voice.

"That's not Captain Bolivar," Aldo whispers.

"No."

"Doesn't the captain usually oversee training? God, I'm nervous," he says.

RAE·CARSON

"Line up!" the Guard orders. "From here to here." He indicates an imaginary line with a sweep of his arm. "Orderly and tight. Now!"

We hurry to comply, scurrying around each other like ants after a dropped crumb.

"I said *now*, recruits."

A bit more adjusting and our line is straight, though unevenly spaced. I end up with Aldo on my left, one of the army recruits on my right. The army recruit peers down at me, somehow missing my gaze. It takes a moment for me to realize he's trying to see down my shirt.

I hope I get to spar with him.

"That was clumsy but serviceable," the Guard says. "I'm Sergeant DeLuca. You will address me as sergeant or sir. Now, let's see what riffraff God brought us this year."

Sergeant DeLuca's evaluating gaze sweeps the line. He nods to the silken-clad conde's son with such deference it's almost a bow. He nods again to the Basajuan contingent. His gaze slides right over everyone else, as if they're not worthy of notice. Then it snags on me. A slight smile curves his lips, and I'm reminded of a cat that just sighted a sparrow.

He says, "Never in all my years have I seen a little girl take to the sands."

I stare straight ahead, determined that my face will betray nothing.

"I can't imagine what the empress was thinking, sponsoring you," he says.

And I can't imagine that I've never seen this Guard before,

though I've been at court for eight years. What kind of Royal Guardsman is never allowed into Elisa's chambers? Never watches over her at major functions? Only the lowest in rank, who manages to be just useful enough to keep from being dismissed.

Sergeant DeLuca is not someone I should trust.

Come to think of it, I recognize very few of the Guards in the arena today. Lord-Commander Dante must have left behind everyone who wasn't part of Elisa's inner circle of trust.

They're still Royal Guard, I remind myself. Maybe not the best of them, but smart enough and capable enough to remain members of the most elite fighting force in the world. I'll do well to not underestimate any of them.

"I expect you'll wash out within a week," DeLuca adds. "Maybe even today."

I expect he'll be surprised.

"Why are you smiling?" he demands, leaning in so that his breath is hot in my face.

A direct question, so I must respond. "Just glad to be here, sir."

"We'll see how you feel later. Name?"

As if he doesn't know. "Red."

The army boy beside me chuckles.

"Ah, yes, the half-breed who failed to become a princess. And what three items did you bring with you, *Recruit* Red?" Not Princess Red. Not Lady Red. He's reminding me that I'm no one.

I've been dreading this moment. I open my hands and show him my items.

RAE·CARSON

He peers at my right hand. "What is that?"

"A pot of black dye."

"What for?"

"It has sentimental value."

His eyes narrow; he knows I'm lying. "And this here? This is a baby rattle. Are you going to tell me it has sentimental value too?"

"Naturally."

He grabs the rattle from my left palm and lifts it high for the crowd to see. "Recruit Red is going to protect the empress with a baby rattle!" he says, and a wave of polite laughter sweeps over us.

But the recruits aren't laughing. They're staring at my hand. Because by lifting away the baby rattle, the sergeant revealed my third item: a thumb-sized gemstone of glorious sapphire blue. But it is no mere sapphire.

"Holy God," Aldo says.

A recruit down the line whistles appreciatively.

DeLuca spins back around, my rattle clattering in his hand. His confused look is quickly replaced by shock. "Is that . . . ?"

"A Godstone," I confirm. "A gift from a friend."

The Inviernos would call it an anima-lapis. The most valuable commodity in the world. And Empress Elisa is the only person known to have a collection of them.

The Guard takes a step back.

"It's not going to hurt you," I tell him, which must be the worst possible thing to say, because something hot and angry flits across his face. Like maybe he *hates* me.

Slowly, carefully, he places the baby rattle back into my palm, covering up the Godstone. He says, in a voice so low only my fellow recruits can hear, "She is not here to help you now."

It's a threat, clear as day. I can't let it go.

"She is not, sir. And even if she were, she would not help me. I'm to succeed or fail on my own, like any other recruit."

He blinks. "A pretty speech."

"Thank you, sir."

He dismisses me with a shrug and moves down the line, pausing at each recruit to level mild insults and intimidation. Aldo is too small, even smaller than "the little girl." The boy with quick, dark eyes is the son of a traitor, and DeLuca will be watching him. The army recruit who tried to look down my shirt brought a soft coral blanket with a fringe as one of his three items; the sergeant tells him it's fit for a *real* princess.

If I were Elisa, I'd listen closely to every single one, get to know my fellow recruits, evaluate them silently and begin to strategize. But I'm not Elisa, and DeLuca isn't clever with his slurs, and I find the whole thing tedious.

When he's at the opposite end of the line, I can barely hear him talking, which is a small relief. The sun is starting to beat against my skin. Sweat dampens the nape of my neck.

"You shouldn't have brought a Godstone," Aldo whispers.

He might be right. I should have brought a warm blanket, like Aldo and the army boy did. "Why not?" I whisper back.

"DeLuca has sworn his life and honor to the empress. And you've just proven that you're closer to her than he'll ever be."

"So?"

"You've made him feel bad. And look bad. He'll take it out on you."

"Why is it my job to make him feel good about himself?"

Aldo is silent a moment. "Huh. Good point." He stares at my hand as though the Godstone it holds might grow legs and scuttle away.

"What?" I say. "What's wrong?"

"It's weird thinking how that . . . *thing* . . . used to be lodged in some sorcerer's navel."

Which is why the Inviernos have so many names for it. Life stone, soul spark, umbilical stone, anima-lapis, Godstone. A living material that grows as hard as a gem before falling out at age three or four. But like bones, Godstones last long after the body's death. "Definitely gross," I agree.

"Shut up, you two. You'll get us into trouble," says the army recruit boy.

"I think I'm already in trouble," I tell him, and he surprises me by chuckling.

At last DeLuca finishes his tour of torpid abuses. He centers himself before us, hands clasped behind his back. "As many of you know, Her Imperial Majesty is not in residence. She travels in state to Amalur, the capital of Orovalle. A highly trained and trusted contingent of the Royal Guard was left behind to protect her interests here at home."

I barely choke back a laugh.

The rich conde's son raises his hand.

"Yes, recruit?" says Sergeant DeLuca.

"I expected to see Captain Bolivar here today. Is he not overseeing recruitment this year?"

DeLuca's right eye gives a slight twitch. "The captain is otherwise occupied."

Which is a bold-faced lie. I don't blame him for it; I wouldn't want Elisa's enemies to know that the captain of her Royal Guard is missing either.

DeLuca continues, "Because of our reduced manpower, we'll be training recruits to take on responsibilities as quickly as possible. Those who show themselves loyal and competent will be assigned official Royal Guard duties within the year, starting with watch shifts, commissary, and supply routes. We'll add to these responsibilities as recruits demonstrate potential."

At this, a few boys shift in place, and excited murmurings filter down the line. I understand their eagerness, but uneasiness tickles the back of my neck. It usually takes *years* for the Guard to vet its recruits for loyalty and discretion, even for simple duties like escorting supplies and standing watch. It's the only way to keep Elisa and her family safe.

"I see you're all eager to get started," DeLuca says. "Fine, then. To the weapons rack, ladies!"

I grit my teeth as I follow everyone to the other end of the arena, wondering if DeLuca hates women in general or if it's just me.

"You!" the sergeant says, pointing to the boy who tried to look down my shirt. "Tell me your name again?"

"Pedrón."

"Pick a weapon, Recruit Pedrón."

"Yes, sir." Pedrón obediently sets his pretty coral blanket on the ground and peruses the weapons—swords, daggers, spears, shields, a maul, a longbow, a crossbow, a single-bladed ax, a double-bladed ax. He reaches for the crossbow.

"No projectiles!" DeLuca calls out. "Today we are evaluating your close quarters combat aptitude."

Which is a questionable idea. Many of these boys have had training, for true, but several haven't had a lick. Any good teacher knows that the best way to determine someone's aptitude is to try to teach them something.

The boy selects a wooden longsword. A good choice. He's tall enough to make use of it.

"Now you," DeLuca says, gesturing to Aldo. "Choose your weapon."

"*What?*" I say, before I can think better of it. "Pedrón has four years and a full arm's length on Aldo!"

DeLuca rounds on me, fury in his eyes. "Do you think the empress's enemies give a roach's ass if they're fairly matched or not?"

"I . . . no, of course not."

"Interrupt a training session again, and you're short a ration."

I'm about to protest further, but Aldo catches my eye and gives me the barest nod of his head. "Yes, sir," I say weakly.

Aldo steps to the weapons rack. He chooses two wooden daggers.

"That's two weapons, not one," Sergeant DeLuca says.

Aldo's expression reveals nothing as he returns one of the daggers to the rack.

"Make a circle, everyone!"

We do, and Aldo and Pedrón face each other, wooden weapons brandished.

"The match lasts until first blood—or until I call a halt, understood?"

"Yes, sir!" we all respond.

"We know that not everyone has prior training. Just do your best, and trust in our expertise to evaluate you according to your current skill level." This was one of Hector's reforms, and it's good to hear DeLuca repeat it, even if I don't trust him to follow through. "Understood?"

"Yes, sir!"

"Begin."

Pedrón lunges with his sword, creating a perfect straight line from shoulder to blade tip. It's a pretty bit of choreography, but it's too slow, and Aldo dodges easily.

"Saw that coming from way down south of Ventierra," Aldo taunts.

Pedrón shrugs and gives Aldo a wry smile. Then, quick as a scorpion, he whips the sword around and whacks Aldo in the shoulder with the blunt side.

Aldo yelps as the momentum from the blow spins him, and he tumbles to the ground, landing hard on his stomach.

He groans, clutching the sand with his fingers, like he's trying to get up but can't.

Other recruits lean in, worry marking their faces. Not

worried for Aldo, I'm sure. Worried for themselves. They see this exact punishment and humiliation in their very near futures.

But they didn't see what I did. Aldo exaggerated everything. The flat of Pedrón's blade barely hit him. It was a perfectly executed bit of theater for a boy who wanted out of a mismatch as quickly as possible.

Pedrón steps forward as if to deal a killing blow.

"Halt!" DeLuca calls. "Now help your fellow recruit to his feet," he orders, and Pedrón does as commanded, reaching for Aldo and yanking him up.

Clutching his side, Aldo staggers over to stand beside me.

"Well done," I whisper.

Aldo tries very hard not to grin.

"Recruit Pedrón," DeLuca says, "you have good power and adequate speed for your size, but you can be better. We'll work on that. Recruit Aldo, you have better speed and extraordinary spatial awareness. We'll teach you some *real* fighting skills so you won't have to rely on deception."

My eyes widen. Perhaps DeLuca is not the idiot I took him for. Off to the side, a few other Guards are discussing something quietly among themselves, though their eyes remain on the recruits. Maybe they really are evaluating us.

"Next up, Recruit Iván."

The handsome boy with quick, dark eyes steps forward. The son of a traitor. Which makes him Juan-Carlos's younger brother.

"And Recruit Red."

I'm stepping forward even as Iván says, "I won't fight a girl."

"Don't worry, I'll go easy on you," I tell him.

"It wouldn't be fair," Iván says. "And I don't want to get into the habit of pulling my punches or weakening my blows."

"It's clear you have great respect for women," I say gravely, and Iván gives me a puzzled look, unsure how I just managed to insult him.

DeLuca considers. "Fine," he says.

Weird that he's not pressing the matter. Maybe Iván holds some status with DeLuca, being the brother of a Quorum lord. We're supposed to leave status behind to come here, but such things are never true in practice.

"Any volunteers to fight a girl?" DeLuca calls out.

Several boys appear uncomfortable, looking everywhere but at the sergeant, lest they catch his eye. But there's no shortage of hands raised.

The crowd on the walls is as thick as I've ever seen it. People are leaning forward, eyes wide, chatting excitedly. This is the best spectacle they've seen all year.

"You," the sergeant says, pointing to the rich boy with fine silks. "Recruit Valentino."

Valentino. Where do I know that name?

The rich boy steps forward. "*I* won't pull my punches or soften my blows," he says, heading toward the weapons rack. The look he gives me is not unfriendly.

"Thank you," I tell him, and he smiles.

Valentino moves like a dancer, all grace and power and exquisite control, with not a single wasted movement. He is well trained and fully come into his own body. A man, not a boy.

He chooses the double-bladed ax. It's wooden, like most of the practice weapons, but it's by far the largest and heaviest of them.

"Recruit Red? You must choose a weapon."

I stare at them all, remembering Hector's words. Should I reveal my skills and training or save them for later? Should I look for an easy way out of this match like Aldo did? Valentino seems to be a worthy adversary. Losing to him wouldn't be too humiliating. I'd get a black eye out of it maybe. A bloody nose. And a whole lot of sympathy.

Then again, I just declared my close relationship to the empress with my Godstone. People already hate me for that.

"Recruit Red?" the sergeant prompts.

All eyes are on me, the failed princess. From the crowd, faintly at first, comes a chant: "Choose, choose, choose . . ."

The spear would give me reach. The dagger would complement my speed. The short sword would be a decent compromise between the two.

"Choose, choose, choose."

I reach for the dagger. My hand freezes midair.

"Choose, choose, choose!"

I turn to Valentino, clasping my hands behind my back.

The crowd goes still.

"Recruit Red! Are you refusing to fight?" DeLuca asks.

"No, sir!"

"Then choose a weapon."

"No, sir!"

My opponent's mouth parts slightly, understanding dawning.

Sergeant DeLuca says, "What do you think you're—"

Loud and clear so everyone can hear, I say, "I don't need a weapon."

My declaration somehow fills the space, and the other boys shift away from Valentino and me, enlarging our fighting circle. The arena is deadly quiet.

"I meant it," Valentino says. "I won't soften my blows. Even if you refuse a weapon." As if to emphasize the point, he whirls the ax around, testing its weight and balance. His forearm is corded with muscle, and his ax, though wooden, is hefty enough to break my bones.

I ground my feet to the earth, feeling the warmth of the sand through my boots. I breathe deep through my nose, relax my shoulders. *Harsh winds, rough seas, still hearts.*

Someone in the crowd above us yells, "Olé, Ciénega del Sur!" Ah, that's it. That's where I've heard Valentino's name.

"You're the son of Conde Astón, yes?" I say aloud. "Of Ciénega del Sur." The speaker of the chamber of condes, who so gleefully announced my failed adoption to the entire court. Valentino is his third son, and therefore in little danger of inheriting.

Valentino says, "But we leave all that behind to become Royal Guard, right?"

"Right."

"Are you going to gossip like little girls?" DeLuca says, "Or are you going to fight?"

"You haven't told us to begin," I point out.

"Begin."

Valentino moves so fast it's a blur, slicing at a diagonal as if to cleave me from shoulder to opposite hip.

But I'm faster. A diagonal blow must be dodged at the highest point, and I barely manage it, swiveling to the side so that the ax meets air.

"Nicely done," Valentino says, already back in place.

"You spoke true about not softening your blows," I say. His weapon would have shattered my collarbone if it had landed. Maybe he's trying to kill me.

He grins, casually whirling his weapon. It seems light in his hand, as if it's made of nothing.

His shoulders reveal his next move a split second before the blow comes, and I'm already throwing my head back as the ax blade sings through the air a finger's breadth from my nose.

I've been drilled in this maneuver so many times that I'm not even thinking, just reacting with muscle memory as my dodge becomes a leg sweep. I twist to the side as I fall. My hands hit the sand as my foot arcs out, crashes into Valentino's ankles, knocks them out from under him.

The crowd gasps.

I'm on my feet in an instant, but so is Valentino. He wipes sand from his silk tunic.

"You're fast," he says.

"You too. Almost got me."

"You've had training," he accuses.

"Maybe as much as you."

He whirls his ax again, eyes narrowed. There's nothing more dangerous than an opponent who thinks, Elisa always says.

I have to end this soon, on the off chance that the son of Elisa's most powerful rival really *is* trying to kill me. He's bigger and stronger, and I can't dodge every blow, even with all my training.

Valentino shifts the ax into his right hand only, leaving his left hand free. He's about to try a feint, see if he can trick me into dodging into his blow. It's what I'd do.

He sweeps toward my head with the ax, enticing me to dodge right, but his other shoulder is priming to ambush me with a punch.

I duck down and slightly left, barely missing the ax blade. While his torso twists into his useless swing, I dart forward and slam my elbow into his kidney.

His flank is soft with surprise. My elbow hits harder than I expect, and he crumples to the sand.

Valentino struggles to find his feet, but I dash forward and stomp on his wrist. His fingers release the ax handle. Quick as a blink, I grab the ax and scurry out of reach.

I give the weapon an experimental swing, watching as Valentino manages to get his knees beneath him. The weapon is even heavier than I anticipated.

I advance on him, trying to figure out a way to draw blood and end the match without hurting him too much more, but DeLuca says, "Halt!"

The arena is as still as night. I just defeated a young man

twice my size, disarming him in the process, but no applause or cheering greets me.

"Well," DeLuca says. "I see a bit of Lord-Commander Hector's fighting style in you."

I open my mouth to tell him that Dante is Lord-Commander now, not Hector, who gave up command when his daughter was born. But I think better of correcting him.

Everyone is staring. I go to help Valentino up, the way Pedrón helped Aldo, but he waves me off. DeLuca says nothing. Valentino finally gets to his feet, but he remains bent over.

At last, a single applause sounds. A clap of pity, come too late. I glance around.

It's Iván, Juan-Carlos's brother, the boy who refused to fight a girl. Then Aldo joins him, grinning ear to ear. A few other recruits begin to clap. And finally, distantly, comes a smattering of applause from the audience lining the edges.

But not everyone approves, and the sound fades fast, leaving us in silence once again.

"You still have a lot to learn," DeLuca says, frowning.

"Yes, sir, I do." And it's true. I've spent so much time learning how to defend myself, how to stay alive and survive, that I know little about attacking. It's a weakness that will become obvious to everyone soon enough.

"And Recruit Valentino . . . if the little girl hasn't wounded you too badly, we'll get you started on broadsword training right away."

"I'll be fine," Valentino says through gritted teeth.

DeLuca grunts, and then he moves on, calling on two other recruits to choose their weapons.

I return the ax to the rack and run back to the line. Valentino sidles over to me and Aldo. "That was . . . unexpected," he breathes through his pain.

"Unexpected?" Aldo whispers. "That was *incredible.*"

"I hit you harder than I meant to," I confess.

"I can handle it," he says.

"Were you trying to kill me?" I ask.

The question startles him. "No. I didn't expect DeLuca to let me use the ax. It's too heavy for safe sparring. But then I was committed in front of everyone."

"Huh." I find myself believing him.

"You know . . ." He winces. "This is really starting to hurt."

Two other recruits are called out to face each other, both of them from Basajuan, and both of them named Arturo, which is the most common name in the east. My attention is half on the Arturos, half on Valentino, when I say, "You might piss blood tonight. Drink as much water as you can and try not to exert yourself for a few days. If you can't piss at all, be sure to tell someone. Don't tough it out."

"Whatever you say, Doctor Red."

I look up at his face to find him grinning. "I really am sorry," I tell him.

"I'll get you next time."

"I know you will."

There's a warmth in my cheeks that has nothing to do with sun and sand. I've met two people—Aldo and

Valentino—who have the potential to become friends. Not a bad morning at all.

But then I happen to glance beyond the sparring recruits— who are clumsily swinging their wooden daggers—to Valentino's entourage, the boys who followed him into the arena like ducklings after their beloved mother.

They're staring at me with such pure, icy hatred that a chill shivers down my spine.

7

Then

THE girl woke to pain so bright and hot she could hardly draw breath. It came from her ankle. She tried to wiggle it, but agony shot up her leg and into her hip.

So she lay as still as she could, just trying to breathe. Gradually she became aware of other things: warmth against her cheeks, dancing firelight, straw poking her back, the scents of burning pine and—wonder of wonders—a baking meat pie.

A little whimper escaped her lips. Her stomach turned over hard, and she couldn't tell if she wanted to feast or vomit.

Hunger won out.

"Please," she whispered, almost like a prayer.

A flurry of syllables greeted her, and she almost screamed. It was the monster's language. They had found her.

But a cool hand pressed gently against her forehead. More words followed—soft, kind, feminine.

The girl's heart steadied. Voice wavering, she tried again. "Please. Food?"

"Do you not speak the Lengua Classica?" said the woman's voice, in the girl's own language.

"No." The girl blinked.

Her vision had been slow to clear, but she could see the monster woman now. She was beautiful, maybe the most beautiful creature the girl had ever seen, with delicate, chiseled features, hair that shone reddish brown, and eyes green as grass, shaped like a cat's. How could the woman see with such eyes?

"You must drink first," the woman said. "See how your belly handles it before introducing food."

The mere mention of drink made the girl swallow hard. Her throat was parched and aching, and she suddenly wanted water more than anything in the whole world. The girl remembered her manners and said, "Yes, please, thank you, please, yes."

A hand reached beneath the base of her head and tilted her up. A cup was set against her lips, and cold, perfect, beautiful water slid down her throat.

The cup was pulled away, and the girl tried to chase after it, lunging up from the poking straw mattress. Cool hands held her down.

"More soon," the monster woman said. "Patience, sweet thing."

The girl laid back and tried to have patience.

Something sparkled at the woman's earlobes, something that clinked softly every time she moved—jewelry made of glass, almost like tiny sparkle stones. "I found you in a snowdrift, when I was fetching water," the monster woman said. "You must be from one of the villages to the north. I think you fell off the cliff."

The girl didn't remember falling. Just running and hiding and more running and . . . flying? Or maybe that part had been a dream.

"Your ankle is broken, but I've splinted it, and I expect it to heal perfectly. The snowdrift may have saved your life."

The girl said nothing. The monster woman seemed so kind, but the girl knew better. You couldn't trust monsters. They said perfectly reasonable things and then burned your turnips.

In a trembling voice, the girl asked, "Do you have a sparkle stone? Are you going to burn me?"

The monster woman laughed, and her glass earrings tinkled. "Not all Inviernos are animagi," she said. Her voice turned bitter. "If I were a sorcerer, I wouldn't have to make my living here, in one of the godforsaken free villages." She tipped the cup to the girl's lips once again, and the girl drank greedily.

"So, no," the woman continued. "I don't have an anima-lapis, or a Godstone, as the Joyans sometimes call them. "

Relief flooded the girl. She turned her head toward the hearth. Glass figurines rested on the mantel, shiny and sparkling with firelight—a deer with elaborate antlers, a tiny rabbit, and one that made her gasp with its beauty: a heron lifting into flight, dripping glass water behind it.

Below, a lidded black pot hung from a rotating spit just outside the flames' reach. The best smell she had ever smelled was coming from inside. A potpie, if she didn't miss her guess, filled with bubbling dough and chunks of moist chicken meat.

"Before I give you food," the monster woman said, "you must tell me something."

RAE·CARSON

Saliva filled her mouth. "What?"

"What village are you from? Where are your parents?"

The girl knew better than to tell the monster woman anything, but there was a potpie. "Mamá is dead," she said.

The words dislodged something inside her, something that roiled around in her belly for a moment and then came exploding out of her body in a wracking sob. *Mamá is dead. Mamá is dead.*

"There, there, sweet thing, I'm so sorry to hear. And your village?"

The village she and Mamá had lived outside of had a name, but she couldn't remember it. And she didn't care to. No one there wanted her anyway. She said, through gulping tears, "No village. I'm from nowhere."

"Oh, good," the woman muttered. "That's good."

The girl didn't understand what was good about that, but she could hardly think beyond the potpie scent. It had actual salt in it, she was certain. And oregano.

"You're a pretty thing," the monster woman said. Her soft hand came up to caress the girl's cheek. The girl couldn't help herself; she leaned into this feeling of kindness as tears continued to pour down her cheeks. The woman said, her voice as satiny and exquisite as butterfly wings, "You're not really an Invierno, are you? I couldn't tell at first; you're so pale and skinny. But I see it now. You're a half-breed. A mula."

The girl didn't know what a mula was, but it sounded nice, and she was hungry, so she nodded. Yes, she would be a mula.

The monster woman's smile changed, and the girl thought

of beautiful, bright summer clouds right before they burst with deadly hail.

"We must tattoo your feet," the monster-woman said.

The little girl, whose name was now Mula, had done nothing but sleep and eat for three days. But now the monster woman wanted her to start *contributing*.

"What's a tattoo?" Mula asked.

"A special mark," the woman said. "It's very pretty. Bright blue like the sky."

Mula liked the color blue. It was her second-favorite color, after red. "Like jewelry?" Mula asked.

"Yes, like jewelry. For your feet. You won't be able to walk for a few days while the color sets, but you can't walk on that ankle anyway. I'll find simple tasks for you at first. Can you peel turnips? Mend? Scrub dishes?"

Mula nodded. She was a big girl, and big girls knew how to do all those things.

"Good. That's good."

Mula beamed. She was happy to please the monster woman.

"If you turn out to have clever fingers, I'll teach you about glassmaking. That's what I do, you see. Blow glass and sell it. Mobiles, figurines, ornaments, wind chimes. Do you want to learn how to make glass, Mula?"

"Yes."

"You must address me as 'my lady.' Say 'Yes, my lady.'"

"Yes, my lady."

"Good girl."

RAE·CARSON

The next day, a man came to the hut. The girl called Mula noticed his hands—calloused and cracked, with fingers stained bright blue. He carried a leather satchel, and inside were packets of things, all wrapped in parchment or dried leaves, along with several long pointy tools that looked like writing quills, except so, so much sharper.

The monster woman helped Mula hobble to the table and sit, while the blue-fingered man poured some dark berries from a packet into a gray stone mortar and used a pestle to crush them, adding a bit of liquid that smelled like mead gone sour.

The monster woman instructed Mula to sit with her feet up on the table. It was awkward, and it hurt her healing ankle, but she knew better than to complain.

The mixture in the mortar turned bright blue like the sky. "Azure berries," the man explained cheerfully. "Very rare, very expensive. That's why not everyone can afford to have slaves. The tattoos cost too much."

Mula gave the monster woman a puzzled look. What did he mean by "slaves"?

The man dipped one of the sharp quills into the bright ink.

"Now hold still," the monster woman ordered. "No matter what."

"Heels are very hard to tattoo," the man said. "The skin is so thick. They will need a deep application."

"I understand," the monster woman said. "Whatever it takes."

Mula was still puzzling their words when the man brought the quill tip to her heel, and pure fire shot into her skin. She screamed.

8
Now

EVERYONE takes a turn sparring. The Arturos from Basajuan show some talent, as does the darkly frowning boy Iván. The three army recruits are all brawn and no finesse—Pedrón is definitely the best of them. A few boys demonstrate little to no training, though I know this will not automatically disqualify them, especially the young ones. Everyone will be given a chance to learn.

One boy, though, ends up flat on his back in the sand and is deathly still for several breaths. We all lean forward, some with concern, others with unnerving eagerness. *Get up, get up, get up,* I plead silently, while Aldo whispers, "Is he dead?"

The boy moves, digging furrows in the sand with his heels and groaning. Several Guardsmen rush forward and huddle around, so that all I see are his still-kicking legs. After a moment, they heft him from the sand and carry him from the arena.

"Well," Aldo says. "I guess we have our first wash."

The mood is somber after that, the remaining sparring matches half-hearted.

The sun is high, the skin of my face and arms hot, before everyone is done. Sergeant DeLuca lines us all up again.

"What now?" Aldo whispers.

"No idea."

Sergeant DeLuca steps back and faces us. "It's time to take the oath. Your answers will be binding, so respond only if you are certain."

He allows time for his words to soak in, gazing at each of us in turn. Then he draws his sword and raises it to the sky. His voice booms: "Do you have what it takes to be Royal Guard?"

"Yes, sir!" we answer in unison.

"Will you work harder than you've ever worked, through pain, through pride, through exhaustion, to become something more?"

"Yes, sir!"

"Do you give up everything you own, everything you are, and swear to protect Elisa né Riqueza de Vega, Queen of Joya d'Arena and Empress of the United Joyan Empire, along with her family and her interests—even unto death?"

"YES, SIR!"

I am prepared to speak the real Guard's Oath. It is poetic and powerful, and I have already memorized it. But the true oath will have to wait; we aren't allowed to swear that until we've successfully completed our training and formally joined the Guard.

"Then let me be the first to welcome you to Royal Guard recruitment training," DeLuca finishes. He re-sheathes his sword, slamming it home in his scabbard. He beckons to a

Guard standing near the portcullis, who hurries over.

"Guardsman Bruno will be your nursemaid for the remainder of the day. He'll get you situated with bunks and show you around. You'll obey his orders as though they come from the empress herself, or risk being dismissed. Do you understand?"

"Yes, sir!"

Guardsman Bruno steps forward. He's an intense fellow, with eyebrows like caterpillars hovering over a magnificently broken nose.

Looking down that crooked nose at us, he says, "This way to quarters. Follow in an orderly fashion."

We do as asked. It's such a relief to pass under the portcullis and leave the sun-scorched arena for the cool dark of the barracks. The heat has always been a challenge for me. It will be one of my greatest disadvantages.

"Your face is really red," Aldo says as we file through the stone tunnel toward our quarters.

"She is aptly named," Valentino says.

"You Inviernos," someone says at my back, and I turn to find Iván frowning at me. "With your light skin and light eyes; too soft for this desert. It's a wonder your people were worthy foes for so long."

"I'm *not* an Invierno," I snap.

"You're not Joyan either," he says with a shrug.

"At least I'm not a traitor," I say, which is cruel, but he struck first.

The effect is immediate. Iván's eyes have so much fire I feel like he wants to burn me alive. "I am not my father," he says in a low, dangerous voice. His older brother uttered the exact same words a few days ago in the Quorum chamber.

I round on him and stick a finger in his chest. "I'm not my father either, you ridiculous goat," I say.

He stares down at me, then at my finger, which I quickly remove. Provoking him was foolish. He's twice my height and carries at least as much rage. Everyone around us is silent and still with anticipation, waiting—maybe hoping—for us to come to blows.

I can't back away now. "I'm a loyal Joyan," I say, "and I would protect Eli . . . the empress with my life. Would *you*?"

Guardsman Bruno senses that the recruits are not at his heels and turns around, but he does not call us to task. Maybe he's as curious as everyone else to see what happens.

At last Iván says, "I just said I would, same as everyone." His tone is wary, calculated.

Not exactly a yes, but I say, "Good" and turn away from him.

I'm filled with misgiving as we all hurry to catch up to Bruno, who continues on as though nothing has happened.

We turn left and find ourselves in a squat, windowless chamber, filled with bunked cots. The walls are made of hardened earth, buttressed by massive ceiling beams. Three oil lamps hang from the center beam, providing meager orange light. The room is cool and slightly damp, and it smells faintly of rat feces.

Guardsman Bruno says, "Go claim a bed."

Everyone rushes forward. I dart to the farthest end of the

room and grab the bottom bunk. It would be wiser to sleep near the doorway, allowing myself a quick escape, not to mention fresher air. But I like the way this bunk is tucked into the corner. It feels like a cave.

Beside each bunk is a small chest with two drawers, one drawer for each of us. I place my three precious items in the bottom drawer. I'll have to come up with a better hiding place soon. Hector told me that thieving is rare in the Guard and harshly punished, but I'd rather take precautions.

"Do you mind having me for a bunkmate?" says a voice at my shoulder. It's Aldo.

"Do you snore?"

"I'm not sure. I don't think—"

"I'm glad to have you as a bunkmate."

His grin is sheepish as he drapes his beautiful blanket over the top bunk and stashes his other two items—a gold ring with the crest removed, and a small perfumer's vial—into the drawer above mine. Maybe they're remembrances of home and family. But he's not asking about my items, so I won't ask about his.

Aldo says, "I thought they might put you in a different room, being a girl and all."

I shrug. "It wouldn't be right to give me my own room. I guess I'll get the same treatment as everyone else."

"But how will you get dressed? And . . . er . . . relieve your-self . . ."

"I'll figure it out."

Everyone sorts themselves quickly. I'm glad to see the army

recruits, including Pedrón, the boy who tried to look down my shirt, taking bunks near the doorway. I'll sleep easier with them far away. Valentino is a few bunks down from Aldo and me. Iván tries several times to claim a bunk, only to be rebuffed. No one wants to sleep near the son of a traitor.

Eventually he ends up right across from us, with a bunk all to himself. He claims the bottom, leaving the one above him free. The empty top bunk will be a constant reminder of the boy who washed out this morning. Perhaps, after a few weeks, this chamber will have a lot of empty spaces.

"We should name this section of quarters," Aldo says to me and Iván. "Outcast Territory?"

"The Badlands," I suggest.

"Ostracism Alley," Aldo says with a perfectly straight face.

Iván looks back and forth between us, eyes narrowed, as though he's only mostly sure that we're joking. After too long a pause, he offers, "Traitors' Corner?"

Aldo nods. "I like it."

"Me too," I say. "Traitors' Corner it is."

Something clangs—loud and grating—and I startle hard, nearly banging my head on the top bunk. My heart is racing, my breath coming fast, as my mind works out the fact that someone hit the brass bell hanging from the entrance to our quarters. Just a bell. Nothing to be frightened of.

The chamber has gone silent. My companions were startled too, so my overreaction has gone unnoticed. "I guess that's how they'll wake us every morning," Aldo whispers, and my lungs fill with dread. If he's right, it means I'll be startled awake every morning for the foreseeable future.

"Midday meal is up!" yells Guardsman Bruno. "Form two lines based on bunk order, and follow me to the mess."

I groan. If I'd known our meal line would be based on bunk placement, I might have chosen differently. But Aldo is laughing quietly to himself. "Of course we're last. Of *course* we are."

"I hear the food is terrible," Iván says.

"And I hear we'd better eat it anyway," I say, "because we can't know when we'll eat next."

The mess hall is a twin to our bunk room, except instead of beds the room is filled with tidy rows of long tables and benches. The air is hot and dry, thanks to a bread oven and a massive hearth. Above the mantel, a huge plaque stretches the width of the stone chimney with the Royal Guard motto burn-etched into it: *Harsh winds, rough seas, still hearts.*

Young men are lined up at the hearth, getting sludge ladled into ceramic bowls by a man in a blacksmith's apron. The room goes silent as we enter, and everyone turns to stare at us.

Aldo whispers, "I think those are the second years."

"There are only ten left!" one of the Basajuan recruits whispers back.

Which means more than half washed out. Everyone in our group glances around, no doubt wondering which of us will make it. The second years are assessing us the same way. More than one gaze lands on me.

"Line up behind the second years," Guardsman Bruno commands, and we scurry to obey. One by one, we're given a bowl and spoon, and yellowish slop with brown bits is plopped into our bowls.

"Smells like piss," someone says.

"Is this rat meat?" says another.

We find spots on the benches and sit to eat. I'm surprised to find that several boys want to sit by me, even a few of the second years. I ignore them all, just spoon yellow sludge into my mouth like nothing is happening. It's not that bad; a little salty perhaps, but the sludge is actually cornmeal and the brown bits turn out to be bacon.

"You're eating this stuff as though you *like* it," Aldo points out.

I shrug. "I never turn down a meal."

Pedrón and his fellow army recruits sidle over. They are focused and intent, making me feel like a cornered rabbit. "That move you did," one says. "That leg sweep. Where'd you learn that?"

I blink up at him, wondering how much to reveal. I've always been terrible at hedging. Though, come to think of it, I can't think of a single good reason to be evasive at this point. Everyone already understands my close association with the royal family. Besides, we're supposed to be allies here. *Brothers* in arms. "I had a good teacher," I say. "The best teacher."

"But I haven't seen that move before," he persists. "I mean . . . you landed *on your hands* while sweeping your legs. . . ."

"I haven't seen a move like that since the acrobats visited my mother's hacienda," Aldo says.

"You were like water," says another army recruit. "You were there, and suddenly you weren't."

I set my spoon down. "Look," I say. "It might have escaped your notice, but I'm smaller than most of you."

Two of the army recruits exchange a waggly eyebrowed look. "We noticed that. Among other things."

Others drift toward us, curious about our conversation. I sense bodies at my back, peering over my shoulders, and I resist the urge to visibly squirm.

"I'll never be a strong as most of you, or have the reach," I continue gamely. "So my teacher took stock of my advantages and trained me accordingly. For instance, he noticed my quickness. And that I have good abdominal strength. You think that move was about landing on my hands? It was about having control of my center and knowing where my body is at every second."

"In other words," Pedrón says, "he trained you to fight like a girl."

I glare at him. "If by that you mean he trained me to fight like a small girl who can thrash large men."

"She definitely thrashed me," Valentino says.

I can't believe how good-natured he's being, and I give him a grateful look. "You'll thrash me next time."

Pedrón leans forward, and something about his wide grin gives me a shudder. "There's just one thing I have to know." He pauses, looking around for encouragement.

His companion nudges his shoulder. "Go on, ask her," he says, as though they've discussed whatever this is between themselves already.

"Just out of curiosity, of course," Pedrón says. "You being Invierno and all—"

"I'm not an Invier—"

"Do you have. . . the same. . . parts? As normal girls?" He looks down in the direction of my lap, giving no doubt as to what he means by "parts."

I gape at him, truly at a loss for words.

He presses on. "I mean, you're a hybrid, right? A mula. Infertile. So . . . does that mean you have different parts?"

Rage boils in my gut. My fist clenches, but I stop short of raising it. I look around for allies; why is no one saying anything? Aldo's eyes are wide with shock. Valentino shifts uncomfortably on his feet. Iván seems darkly amused.

But no one comes to my aid. Maybe they're all curious. Maybe they're all obsessed with "parts."

Would it be awkward for me to crawl under the table and die? Instead I let my rage burn through and glare at him until he blinks and turns away.

"Where'd you get that Godstone?" asks one of the second years.

"Is it true you don't believe in God?" asks another.

Suddenly the questions are pounding at me so fast I can hardly keep up.

Have you been inside the empress's private chambers? Have you ever met an animagus? Are you betrothed to anyone? Is it true you like other girls? No, I heard she and Prince Rosario are lovers. How'd you get that funny name? Is it true you used to be a slave?

Their words are a weight, pressing and pressing in until I feel too small to be a real person. I can't help it: My shoulders hunch, my head droops; I coil in on myself until they're no longer the ones making me feel small anymore. I'm doing all the work myself.

"Red, are you all right?"

It's the only question that gets through, and I look up and find Aldo's peering face. His concern is palpable. Hearing my true name is a lifeline.

I unfurl. And I force a smile for the benefit of everyone around me. *When in doubt, smile,* Mara always says. *Men are stupid. Smiling puts them at ease.* "I'm fine," I tell him, and it almost feels like the truth.

The questions keep coming, but I ignore them, shoving slop into my smiling, smiling face. I don't know what the afternoon holds, but all these boys are going to regret harassing me when they had a chance to eat.

I don't wait long before being proved right. Guardsman Bruno calls us to attention. "First years, line up against the wall!"

We do as asked, many leaving their bowls hardly touched. Servants scurry to clear the tables while we mill about, eventually lining up shoulder to shoulder, backs against the stone wall of the mess.

Guardsman Bruno walks down the line, hands clasped behind his back. "We have an opportunity here," he says. "With so many of us gone, our stable is nearly empty. So you are going to clean it. From top to bottom."

Someone groans. The second years look on with obvious amusement.

"Empty the stable completely of straw and hay, scrub the floors and walls, oil the hinges, make repairs to the gates, polish the spare tack, reset the rattraps, and replace the entire area with fresh straw."

"That's going to take all day," someone whispers, too loudly.

"And well into the night," Guardsman Bruno snaps back. "So you'd better get to it. Follow me."

He leads us down a dark corridor, past another bunk room, and into daylight. We've reached the dusty riding arena, which is shared with the palace Guard. The palace itself is at our backs now, a huge edifice rising high to block the worst of the sun's afternoon rays. Before us is a long narrow stable, huddled up against the walls that encircle the palace grounds. Atop the walls, between crenellations, I glimpse the helmets of palace guards as they walk their rounds.

"That's a *lot* of stalls," Aldo says.

"Thirty-six, to be exact," Bruno says. "Be grateful we're not cleaning the army stable. It's even bigger."

Horses peek out over the lower doors of a few stalls, hoping our approach means treats or at least a little exercise, and I'm sorry to disappoint them. The majority of stalls are vacant, just like Bruno said.

To the left is an empty wagon. Leaning against it are several pitchforks.

"Any volunteers to polish tack?" Bruno says. The Arturos raise their hands, and he directs them toward a stable hand for guidance.

"And who wants to muck?"

I raise my hand. I did plenty of mucking when I was a little girl living in the free villages. It's been years, and my memories of that time are foggy, but if I've learned anything, it's that the body remembers.

Bruno indicates that I should grab a pitchfork, along with Aldo, Valentino, and Pedrón. We are to remove all the straw from the empty stalls and dump it in this wagon, which will haul everything away once we're finished.

The wooden handle feels rough in my hands. My calluses are different these days—from gripping a sword or dagger, from the string of a bow, from knitting. I hope they hold true.

"You know," Aldo says as he plunges his pitchfork into a pile of manure, "this Royal Guard thing might be a swindle. Maybe it's just a way for the crown to get free labor."

"That's good, right?" Valentino says. "Keeps our taxes low." He winces as he bends over. Clumps of manure are already sticking to his beautiful blue silks.

"Go easy, Valentino," I say. "Work in the back of the stall where the Guards can't see. We'll cover for you."

"No, we won't," Pedrón says.

"Yes," I say, glaring. "We will. Just like we might cover for you someday."

Pedrón considers this. Then he shrugs and gets to work.

"Thanks, Red," says Valentino.

An hour later, the wagon isn't even half full, and a stable hand comes to check our progress. He's a short fellow with long sideburns and weathered skin, and he sidles so close that

I can smell the horse musk on his skin. I resist the urge to step away and make more space for myself.

"Everything all right?" he asks, and his breath smells like something crawled into his mouth and died screaming. "Any questions?"

"We're fine," Aldo assures him.

"Glad to hear it."

I'm considering whether or not to tell him to back off when I feel his hand at my waist. Of their own accord, my fingers bend, my knuckles aim for his windpipe.

I stop myself just in time. Because he's not taking liberties. He's slipping something into my pocket. Something light. A note, I'd wager, though I don't dare pat my pocket to check just now.

"I'll let Guardsman Bruno know you're all doing a good job," he says, and the stable hand walks off, whistling a merry tune.

"That was weird," Valentino says between pained breaths. He's tossing out one forkful of straw for every three of ours.

"Hector told me they'd be evaluating us," I say. "All the time, no matter what we were doing. So I'm sure that stable hand will report back to Bruno for true." I'm dying to reach into my pocket. The imperial spy network uses pickpockets and sleight of hand to pass messages. Or maybe it's an enemy, and the note contains a threat.

"You know the prince consort well, do you?" Aldo says.

I freeze, pitchfork raised, unsure how much I should say. Once again, I fall back on the truth. "He was going to be my adopted father, remember?"

"Oh. Right. Well, I thought maybe that was all for show."

Pain needles my gut, as though Aldo had sifted through my mind for my worst fears, plucked them out, and stabbed me with them. *It was all for show.*

Valentino says, "My father thought it was a political ploy. To force people to start accepting the Invierno presence in Joya."

"I'm not an Invern—"

"I'll never accept Inviernos," Pedrón says. "Inviernos killed my uncle."

He's not the only person in the capital who feels that way, even if he's the only one who has said it to my face. We are silent a long moment, tossing straw into the wagon, and my own tossing is perhaps a little more violent than necessary. It's a nice, distracting rhythm. Scoop, carry, toss. Scoop, carry, toss.

Valentino is the one to break the silence. He leans against the wall, hand to his side, and breathes heavily. "So, Pedrón. If you disagree with the empress's foreign policy, why did you join the Royal Guard?"

Good question. We all look to Pedrón for his answer.

The army recruit responds without pausing his work. "I do hate her foreign policy, but I like *her* quite a lot. She saved us all. And she's . . . nice." He tosses a huge pile of straw into the wagon, wipes sweat from his forehead with the back of his hand, and plunges the pitchfork into another pile. "I think she's not taking the Invierno threat seriously enough. That's all right. I'll take it seriously for her. Maybe next time an Invierno comes for her, I'll be there."

RAE·CARSON

I say, "So you want to protect Elisa from herself."

"Sort of. I guess." Pedrón grins. "Also, joining the Royal Guard is great way to meet girls. Girls love Royal Guard recruits. Even more than army."

"Gross," I say as Aldo rolls his eyes.

"Little did I know," Pedrón continues unabashed, "that I'd meet some girls on my very first day." He winks at me.

"Girls?" I say. "More than one?"

"You and Aldo," he says.

"Next time we spar," Aldo says, "I'm going to kick your ass."

"If you can reach it, little girl."

Aldo shrugs it off, but his face is stony and he avoids our gazes as he mucks.

"By the way, Red," Pedrón says, "do you want to sneak into my bunk some night?"

"Are you always this disgusting?"

"I promise you'll have a good time."

"I said no!"

"No, you didn't. You said, 'Are you always this disgusting?'"

"You really need to widen your definition of the word 'no.'"

"Well, if you change your mind . . ."

"Let it go, army reject," Valentino says.

Surprisingly, Pedrón doesn't push things further. We fall back into silence, mucking, mucking, mucking until the sun is low. The dinner bell rings. We all look up expectantly.

"Sweet God, I'm so hungry," Pedrón says.

"Keep working," Guardsman Bruno yells. "No chow until the job is done!"

Pedrón groans. My stomach growls, even though I'm one of the few who made sure to get a decent meal.

Once the stable is empty of straw, we sweep it of dust and leavings with whisk brooms. Two second years bring buckets and rags, and we get to work scrubbing the stone floors.

An hour later, a stable hand comes to light all the torches. Crickets sing as we polish the hinges, tighten loose latches, replace all the straw with a fresh load just delivered. My hands are raw, my back aches, and I'll never, ever get the smell of manure out of my hair.

At last Guardsman Bruno takes pity on us. "Get yourselves back to the dining hall. After you eat, you may all use the latrine, then get to bed. Do it fast, because you'll need your sleep for tomorrow."

We rush toward the mess. Valentino lags behind, and I slow down to keep him company.

He says, "I think I need to use the latrine *before* we eat."

"If you sneak in, I'll guard the door."

"Thank you."

And that's exactly what we do. While the others go on ahead, we peel off at the door to the latrine. The room contains a row of holes across a long stone bench. Beside each hole is a bucket of mulch with a scoop, used to tamp down the smell. It's not as disgusting as it could be. This place is kept clean, the latrine regularly emptied, and I find myself pitying whoever has that particular task.

I turn my back while Valentino tends to his needs. After a moment, he taps me on the shoulder.

RAE·CARSON

"Any blood?" I ask.

"None."

"Good sign."

"Are you always so . . . frank?"

"Yes."

"I hear that's an Invierno trait."

Before I can answer, he adds, "Your turn. It's a chance for you to get a little privacy. I'll watch the door."

"Thank you." I rush to comply because in addition to taking care of my needs, this is my chance to read the note in my pocket.

I pull it out while I sit. It's a folded parchment, sealed with a bright blob of red wax, which is stamped with the imperial crest. I break the seal. My heart begins to race when I recognize Rosario's handwriting: characteristically rushed and marred with a few small ink blots.

come to the place we first met
at the second hour
let no one see you
bring Iván

I shove the note back into my pocket, finish my business, and pull up my pants. As Valentino and I rush to catch everyone else, my thoughts are a maelstrom of worry.

When I spoke to Rosario, he was afraid for his life. Has something gone wrong?

The place he and I first met is a hideout located beneath the city district known as the Wallows. The prince mentioned that he might spend some time there. I can reach it through the catacombs, but no one is supposed to know about it. I hate the idea of sharing it with Iván.

We'll have to sneak out of the bunk room and hope everyone is sleeping too soundly to notice. I really picked the wrong bunk. I'll have to traverse the whole room just to get out the door.

Rosario knows I understand this vast palace better than anyone, except maybe Hector and the spymaster. Once I'm in the latrine, I can get us almost all the way to the catacombs using secret passages. So, by ordering us to arrive unseen, the prince fully intends for me to reveal some of the palace's most ancient secrets to Iván.

My muscles burn from working all day, and I need rest more than anything, but I won't dare let myself fall asleep even for a moment, lest I miss the second hour. I'm going to be exhausted tomorrow. If we have any training exercises, I won't be able to perform creditably.

I'll have to worry about that later. Rosario is my friend, and my future emperor, and he might be in trouble. If I could leave right this second, I would.

But if it turns out he's just lonely and frightened, I'm going to whack him upside the head with my baby rattle. No, no, that can't be it. Rosario isn't an idiot, and he's no stranger to peril or intrigue. If he's summoning me, he has a good reason.

In the dining hall, I make a point of sitting next to Iván, which turns out to be easy because no one else wants to. He glares at me when I settle beside him, but says nothing. His knuckles are scraped raw. While I was mucking stalls, he spent the whole day mending the thatch roof and patching mortar in the walls.

When everyone is distracted, I slip the note out of my pocket, just far enough so that he can glimpse the imperial seal.

I whisper, "The prince wants to meet with us tonight. Just you and me. We'll have to sneak out. I'll wake you when it's time to go."

Iván's hand holding his spoon freezes. A dollop of cornmeal falls from the spoon and plops back into the bowl.

Then he nods and continues to shove slop into his mouth, treating me with stony disregard.

9

Then

WEEKS passed. The pain of her tattoos faded. But her ankle was not healing.

The monster woman made her do everything: boil turnips, wash dishes, weed the garden, chop firewood, empty and clean the slop buckets, fetch water from the stream, mend clothing, darn socks, scrape and tan hides, scrub the stone floors.

Mula fell onto her cot every night exhausted, and even though she was given two small meals a day, they weren't enough. Her dreams were filled with running through the forest after quick rabbits and one-eyed squirrels, while the hole in her tummy grew wider and wider. Sometimes she could *see* the hole in her tummy, like the giant eye of a needle. She was a hollow girl, with nothing to her insides at all.

Other times, the one-eyed squirrel would turn around and taunt her, saying things like, "I only have one eye, but at least I have nuts," or "Even *I'm* not as disgusting as a half-breed."

The monster woman worked her so hard because she herself had work to do. Important work, that made her disappear into the glassblowing shed for hours, sometimes all day. And if she came out of that shed and Mula's chores weren't finished, the girl could expect to go to bed without even her meager dinner. Once in a while, if the monster woman was especially disappointed, Mula would get a cuff across the face or a vigorous shaking.

The girl was slow about her chores, it was true, but only because she could hardly walk. She was a big girl, precocious even, and she knew how to do all the tasks given to her. But her body wouldn't do them. Her ankle was still too broken, her belly too empty, her eyes too sleepy, to ever do a good job, the kind of job that would have made Mamá proud.

Mula remembered how, when Horteño the blacksmith broke his leg, he walked around on a crutch for a while. So Mula begged the monster woman for a crutch, even remembering to say, "Please, my lady."

In answer, the monster woman backhanded her, sending her flying into a pile of freshly washed, neatly stacked dishes.

Head pounding, vision blurring, Mula set about cleaning up the mess without another word. Fortunately, only one wooden plate had chipped. If she was lucky, the monster woman wouldn't notice.

After that, Mula stopped asking for things. Instead she watched, and she learned.

She learned that she and the monster woman lived in one of the free villages, which wasn't exactly Joya d'Arena, but not exactly Invierne either, and both Joyans and Inviernos lived there. Once, on her way to market day to trade glass baubles for some winter apples, she stopped in her tracks, right in the middle of the snow. Because only a few paces away was a boy, a few years older, with delicate features, ebony hair, and light eyes the color of molten gold. He was skinny and barefoot in the snow, and every time he took a step, his heels flashed the bright blue of his slave marks.

When he saw her, he winced and turned away in disgust, and something inside her died. She'd been hated her whole life, by everyone except her mother. But there was something particularly awful about being hated by someone just like her, another mule slave. Like maybe she had missed the point all along. Maybe she should be hating herself.

Mula also learned that her mistress, the monster woman, loved ale. At first, the girl merely smelled it on her breath. Later, the monster woman would return to the house with an unsteady gait and words that were too slippery to make sense. Mula realized that instead of working in her shed, she was drinking, drinking, drinking. The day the woman took off her own shoes and sent Mula to the market to trade them for eggs, she knew they were running out of money.

The girl began to consider escape.

She was scared by the prospect of fleeing through the forest in winter, all alone and hungry. But she was scared of the monster woman too. The forest might kill her, for true, but the monster woman might do it gleefully, with hatred in her eyes and drunkenness in her speech. Mula realized she had to choose between scary things, pick which kind of scared was the best kind of scared.

She picked the forest.

But first she had to heal her ankle. So one morning while chopping firewood, she sidled quietly into the woods and poked through the snow and underbrush for a long branch, which she dragged back to the chopping stump. With her ax, she cleared it of offshoots, sized it to her armpit, and used the hood of her mother's cloak to create a cushion on top. There. Now she had her crutch.

That night, Mula held her breath when the monster woman walked in the door and saw what she had made. Would she let her keep it? Would she box Mula's ears?

The woman shrugged, then crumpled onto her cot, already passed out.

Over the next few days, Mula hoarded food. Just tiny squirrel-sized bits of turnip and jerky, a very small pinch from a loaf of bread. She hid it all in the snow, beside the cottage foundation, where the cold temperature would keep it from turning black with mold.

But when she returned to her stash later to add a withered apple, she discovered that mice had found her food and eaten it all, leaving nothing but a tiny bit of shredded turnip.

Mula started over.

She tried hiding food in a little hole in the cottage foundation and covering the opening with stones, but the mice managed to tunnel through.

She buried food in the near-frozen ground, but squirrels dug it up.

She hid some food in a basket beside the hearth, but it rotted, giving off a sour smell that would definitely earn her a cuff if the monster woman noticed.

Finally her eye chanced upon a glass vase on the mantel, one of the few baubles the monster woman hadn't yet sold. It had a wide base and a narrow neck—too narrow for even a tiny mouse—and a slight amber cast that made it sparkle like fire. She took the vase from the mantel, shoved some pine nuts down that narrow neck, and buried it outside in the snow near the outhouse. Gradually she added bread crumbs, bits of jerky, a twig for brushing her teeth.

It was three days before the monster woman noticed that the vase was missing. Mula was prepared. She had thought up a perfect lie and had practiced it and practiced it.

"Where's my vase?" the monster woman said. "It used to be right there. Right there."

"I traded it for ale, my lady," Mula said. "A few days ago. Remember?" The girl waited, trying her best to look innocent. She was terrible at lying. It put a funny feeling in her belly and a flush on her cheeks.

"Oh . . . yes, I suppose I . . ." The monster woman shrugged. She ate some wheat mash, washed it down with some ale, and passed out on her cot.

Mula stood over her a long moment. The monster woman looked so vulnerable. With her face slack, her lips parted, her hand clutching her blanket, she looked . . . soft, almost sweet. As though kindness could have lived inside her.

The girl remembered her mother's skinning knife, the way it had slid into the sorcerer's body like he was nothing, the way it had scraped against his bones.

The next morning, while Mula was chopping a turnip to

RAE·CARSON

make a thin stew base, she held the knife up so that it caught firelight from the hearth. She twisted it this way and that, watching the play of light, wondering if she could do it again. Stab someone. Stab them so bad they died.

Her lower lip started to tremble. If she did it, she'd be hateful for true, deserving of all the nasty looks she got.

After setting the stew to simmer, she put the knife back on the mantel and refused to think about it again.

Three weeks later, her hidden vase was full, and her ankle was healed well enough that she could walk long distances. *Tonight*, she told herself. Tonight, when the monster woman was asleep, she would sneak out of the cottage and flee into the forest. It was a good night for it. Winter was losing its frozen grip on the village. Meltwater tinkled as it dripped from the roof. The earth smelled rich and loamy. Birds were beginning to sing again. This time, she wouldn't be so cold.

Besides, Mula was smarter now, a more grown-up girl than the last time she'd fled. Instead of running aimlessly, she would go west, to the place where sand stretched across the world like a sea, where the weather was warm and no sorcerers lived.

Mula rehearsed it all in her mind. She would wait for the woman to start snoring. She would quietly slip on her shoes, don her mother's now-hoodless cloak, grab the knife from the mantel, and slip out the door. She would sneak to the outhouse and unbury her glass vase full of food scraps. Then she would tiptoe westward, away from the village and into the woods. She'd walk as long and far as her sore ankle would allow. By the time the monster woman woke and discovered her missing, she'd be too far away to find.

The girl spent the day in a state of terrified excitement. Her hands wouldn't stop trembling. Her heart felt like it was going to scamper out of her chest. She dropped the water bucket on her way back from the creek and had to return for a refill. She nicked her forefinger slicing an apple. Their last apple, but Mula hoped that if she stewed it with some sugar and nutmeg, it would put the monster woman in a good mood and help her sleep.

Finally day became night, and the woman came trudging up to the door. She stopped before entering, just stood there quietly on the stoop.

Mula held her breath.

The door creaked open, and Mula knew right away that something was terribly, terribly wrong, because the monster woman's bright blue eyes shimmered with fire, like sparkle stones about to destroy the winter stores.

The girl's legs twitched to run, but the woman stood huge and menacing in the doorway. There was nowhere to go.

The girl squeaked out, "Would you like some apple stew, my lady?"

In response, the monster woman lifted something she was holding in her hand. It gleamed amber in the firelight.

Her glass vase, full of food scraps. Water slipped down the sides and dripped on the floor.

"I found this by the outhouse," the woman said. "Half buried in melting snow."

Mula said nothing. The fire crackled. Outside, a chunk of

snow dislodged from the roof and plopped onto a drift.

"You were going to run away, weren't you?"

"No," the girl whispered.

"You *were,* you lying mule!" The woman was screaming now. "You were going to leave me! After everything I've done for you. How *could* you?"

"I'll stay!" Mula said, and tears spilled down her cheeks. "I promise, I'll stay, I'll stay, I'll st—"

The woman threw the vase at her head; Mula ducked. The vase exploded against the fireplace, a crystal sound that spiked deep into her soul. Bread crumbs and nuts and shimmery glass slivers rained down onto the hearth.

"Come with me." The woman darted forward, grabbed her arm, and dragged her toward the door.

"I need my cloak," Mula pleaded. Her arm hurt. The woman was squeezing way too tight.

"Shut up," the woman snapped.

"You're hurting my arm."

The woman stopped so suddenly that Mula collided with her hip. The monster woman rounded on her and stared down at the girl, gripping so tightly that Mula feared her arm might fall off.

"Your arm?" the woman said. "*Your* arm?"

"Y . . . yes?"

The woman crouched before her and speared the girl with her sparkle-stone eyes. With her free hand, she softly caressed Mula's smarting skin. "Sweet thing," she said, "this is *my* arm."

"I . . . no . . ."

The woman fingered the bit of black hair that had escaped the girl's braid and hung down her forehead. "This is my soft hair," she said, so quietly it was almost a whisper.

Mula tried to grab her braid, reclaim it, but the woman batted her hand away.

The woman's forefinger traced her cheek. "My cheek. My sweet little nose. My chin."

The girl discovered that she couldn't breathe.

The woman's forefinger was so soft on her skin and yet somehow like fire as it traced the line of her neck, swirled down her chest, rested between her not-yet-budded breasts. "Mine. All *mine*. I own you, Mula. I can do whatever I please with you."

Mula remembered her dream, when she had looked down to discover a gaping nothingness where her belly ought to be. Maybe it wasn't a dream. Maybe she was disappearing for true.

The monster woman yanked her out the door. The girl's bare feet squelched in the melting snow. "Where are you taking—"

"We're going to teach you a lesson."

The monster woman dragged her past the glassmaking shed, across the icy creek, around the waterwheel and miller's cottage. They stopped in front of a small one-room house with a large porch and two windows. Whoever lived here must be very rich, to afford two windows.

The monster woman knocked.

The door opened, and out stepped the blue-fingered man,

RAE·CARSON

the one who had tattooed Mula's feet. He wore a leather apron with pockets filled with his strange, sharp tools. He wiped his hands on a rag—also stained blue.

"What do you want?" he grumbled.

"This slave," the monster woman said, shoving Mula forward. "She tried to run away. She needs to be taught a lesson."

"Oh?" The blue-fingered man grinned through his beard.

Mula tried praying. *Please, God, make me disappear for true.*

The man vised her shoulder with one hand and dragged her into his house. With the other hand, he lifted a large iron ladle from its place on the mantel. He studied the ladle a moment, admiring it. It gleamed gray in the firelight.

The door slammed shut behind her.

The girl doesn't remember what happened next.

10
Now

WE'RE all so exhausted that we stumble to our bunks in near silence. Almost everyone is asleep before Guardsman Bruno can blow out the lamps.

One of the army recruits near the door snores loudly, and I'm glad. Maybe it will help me stay awake. Faintly, filtered through stone and mortar, comes the cymbal clash of iron and steel. Perhaps the second years are doing a nighttime training maneuver. No, the direction is all wrong for that. It must be the Guard blacksmith, mending weapons well into the night. Everyone is taking the opportunity to catch up on work while the empress is away.

It means that sneaking around at night would be impossible . . . if I didn't know every corridor and passage so intimately.

The monastery bells ring twelve times. In an hour, I'll wake Iván, allowing us plenty of time to make the journey. I have no idea how I'll keep myself from falling asleep until then. My thighs burn, my shoulders ache, my eyelids are as heavy as millstones, and I want nothing more than to sink into this thin, poking mattress and drift into oblivion.

Thinking of the poking mattress gives me an idea. I slip open the bedside drawer, grab my golden baby rattle, and shove it beneath the middle part of my back. It's extraordinarily painful.

My back is deeply bruised by the time the bells ring once, sharp and startling, and something shoots through my blood that's part relief, part exhilaration. It's one advantage of having the soldier sickness, Hector says. I can be ready to flee or fight faster than just about anyone.

The bunk creaks as I slip off the mattress. I freeze a moment, listening, but no one stirs. I tiptoe to Iván's bed and gently shake him awake.

He lurches up, banging his head against the top bunk. "Ow," he says.

I shush him. "Get your shoes on," I whisper. "Time to go."

"Already on," he says, slipping his booted feet from beneath his blanket and placing them on the floor. "Let's get this over with."

Together we creep toward the entrance to the bunk room. Someone flips over in their bed, muttering, and we go still. One of the recruits is sleeping with his arm hanging over the side of the bed, his knuckles resting on the floor. Next to him, the Arturos from Basajuan have climbed into the same cot together; they sleep with their arms wrapped around each other, one's forehead snugged beneath the other's chin.

When no one stirs, we continue our agonizingly slow

journey, past the snoring army recruit, through the archway, and into the hall glowing with torchlight.

"You have a letter with the imperial seal," Iván whispers. "Surely we can just . . . go wherever we want? Flash that seal to gain entry?"

"The prince's orders are to let no one see us."

He frowns. "How are we supposed to avoid all the patrols?"

"Just follow me. I'm going to move fast, so keep up."

"But where are we—"

"Please stop talking."

The exit from the barracks is sure to have a sentry or two. So instead of leaving that way, I usher Iván into the latrine.

"Is this an elaborate prank to humiliate me?" he whispers. "Lure me into the latrine, ambush—"

I can't have him doubting me the whole way; I don't have *time* for it. I shove Rosario's letter in his face. "Go ahead. Read it."

He does. His mouth forms an O. "That's the prince's writing," he observes.

I say, "I don't care enough about you to devise an elaborate prank, and I have no idea why the prince wants you to come along. But we have orders from our liege, and we must obey. Now will you *please* be quiet and follow me?"

Iván nods, handing the letter back, which I shove into my pocket. He makes a gesture as if to say, "Lead the way."

It occurs to me to ask him how he knows what Rosario's handwriting looks like, but I'd so much rather not talk to him.

Three torches line the back wall, just above the row of

privies. I move toward the one on the right, step up onto the privy seat, and remove the torch.

The empty sconce is brass like the others, but a careful look reveals that it's placed in the stone wall a little differently, jutting out farther, with a more pronounced outline around its mortar setting.

I give the sconce a firm twist to the left.

A section of wall pulls back into darkness and slides silently to the side.

"Holy God," Iván says. "How did you know—"

"Let's go. Hurry!" Still holding the torch, I step into darkness.

I sense Iván at my back. Once we are both well inside, I push down on a brass lever, and the stone door slides closed.

Finally it's safe to whisper. "I'm going to show you a lot of things tonight, Iván. Secret things. And if you tell anyone about them—"

"You'll tattle to your empress?"

I round on him; he towers over me. "No. I'll kill you."

He opens his mouth. Closes it. The torchlight makes hollows of his cheeks. After a moment, a mocking grin spreads across his face. "Do you really think—"

"I'm not being dramatic. Very few know about the passageways I'm going to show you. Even among the Royal Guard, only those in Elisa's inner circle know them all. Her safety depends on keeping it that way. So if you tell anyone, I. Will. Kill. You."

His eyes narrow as if in thought. He'd have beautiful eyes

if they weren't so darkly veiled and quick to anger. He says, "Actually, that sounds fair."

Not the response I was expecting, but I'll take it. "It's safe to whisper in most of these passages," I tell him. "When the stone walls give way to wood, though, we must be quiet like mice."

"Understood."

The passage is narrow and dusty, though not as dusty as it once was. The empress has been keeping these routes in better condition than previous monarchs, and the torchlight reveals lighter patches of fresh mortar, where either Royal Guards or the spymaster's people have completed maintenance. We turn right once, then left, ignoring a branching corridor. The ceiling becomes lower; Iván must duck his head to continue.

"Do you think someone will notice the missing torch in the latrine?" he whispers.

"Maybe, but all torches in the palace are free to use."

"Oh. That's good." After a moment, he adds, "Have you killed anyone before?"

I guide us down a short set of stairs. The walls close in so tight they nearly brush my shoulders. "Yes."

"Who?"

"None of your business."

Our passage ends at a large wooden panel. I slide it aside, revealing a small storage closet. We slip into the closet, shut the panel, and snuff out the torch. Light filters in from the hallway. Chests are stacked shoulder-high against the walls, and a few burlap bags spill into the center, leaving us little room to maneuver. Iván's body invades my space; like me, he smells of manure and sun-warmed straw.

"This is the awkward part," I say to his chest. "We have an open hallway to travel, which will take us to the entrance to the catacombs. There's always a Royal Guard on duty there, and absolutely no way past him. We'll have to walk right up and show him the prince's seal."

"The prince said we shouldn't be seen."

"You have a better idea? Fortunately, the catacomb guard is always someone Elisa trusts completely, so we can count on him to be discreet."

"What about a distraction?"

"The guard will never desert his post. Not for anything. The last one who did that was executed by Luz-Manuel, the former General."

"Whatever is down there must be extremely important."

"Yes. Now hush. I have to listen."

I put my ear to the door of the storage closet and listen for footsteps. Nothing. Quietly, gradually, I crack the door open and peek outside. The corridor is clear.

"Now let's go," I say. "Quickly."

We dart from the storage closet and close the door softly behind us. This corridor is one of the oldest in the palace, made of bulging river rock set into mortar three fingers thick. The cobblestones are worn smooth by centuries of footsteps. Flickering torchlight turns the floor from iron gray to soft orange.

The corridor dead-ends at the entrance to the catacombs, and sure enough, a tall, broad-shouldered man stands guard, dressed in his formal breastplate, armed with both sword and bow.

"Hello, Fernando," I say.

"Lady Red," he acknowledges.

"Just Recruit Red, now. I thought you'd be with Elisa."

He gives me a wry grin. "Alas, a very few of us are stuck here. There's still a prince to protect, you see." Fernando lowers his voice. "I hear you made quite an impression on your first day."

I frown, and Fernando gives me a sympathetic smile. "The prince said to expect you. Hurry inside before someone sees." With that, he opens the door and gestures for us to enter.

Fernando shuts the door behind us. We're in a narrow, dark tunnel, but an orange glow testifies to something ahead.

"Stay close," I order.

"Are you always this bossy and disagreeable?" Iván asks.

"I'm usually laughing and inquisitive. Must be the company."

"Huh. I've heard that Inviernos don't understand sarcasm, but you wield it with ease."

"I'm *Joyan*, you daft dung beetle."

"But your skin . . . those golden eyes . . ."

"Don't confuse my ancestry with my nationality. Joya d'Arena is my home, and I'd give my life for it."

"So you admit you have Invierno blood—" Iván's thought dies on his lips, for we have reached the Hall of Skulls.

It's a cathedral of bones, with archways made of human ribs and walls made of human skulls. Thousands of people must have died to create this space because there are so many bones, layered atop one another, pressing down. In the desert, bones are always white, bleached by the relentless sun. Here, they are as gray as stone.

I hate this place. Rows of votive candles are supposed to create a warm and sacred glow, but it just feels fiery and cruel, a reminder that death is too harsh, too final. Strangely, Elisa loves it here. She says it reminds her that death is an important foundation of her great city, and that something of the dead can last forever.

I guess I want my legacy to be more than a pile of ashen bones.

In the center of it all stands an altar of white marble veined in black. On it are three fresh long-stemmed roses. They are the holy variety, with the sharpest and hardest of thorns, just in case a supplicant wishes to prick a finger and offer a drop of blood in the holy sacrament of pain.

Arched doorways on either side open to dark tombs. "This way." I lead Iván into the third doorway on the right.

Inside are several caskets resting on giant pedestals, each covered in a silken banner. Some of the banners are old and tattered and moth-eaten. One is barely a decade old and in excellent condition.

"Is that . . . ?"

"King Alejandro," I confirm. "Elisa's first husband and Rosario's father."

Iván stares at the casket, unblinking, for the space of several breaths.

"Iván?"

"Rosario always says the sins of the father shall be visited upon the children, from generation to generation."

"That's from the *Scriptura Sancta*," I say. The holy text is full of horrible things like that. It's one of the reasons I could never believe in a god.

"I liked him," Iván says. "The king, I mean. Everyone says he was a weak monarch, an inattentive father. But he was kind to me."

"You met him?"

"When I was very little. Six or seven." I remind myself that Iván's father was a member of the Quorum of Five and a part-time resident of this palace, before he turned traitor and tried to start a civil war. So it makes sense that Iván would have met the royal family at a young age.

"He must have made an impression," I say.

Iván shrugs. "I guess. Where to next, bossy girl?" He's trying to pass it off like it's no big deal, but once again shadows veil his eyes, and he refuses to meet my gaze.

"Over here. There's a small latch beneath the base of the casket. Help me find it? I've never come this way alone before."

Together, we crouch to run our fingers along the base of the pedestal. The floor is gritty here, and slightly damp against my fingertips.

"I've got it," he says. I leap backward to make room as the casket pivots to the side, revealing a deep stairway spiraling down into blackness.

"Holy *God*," Iván says.

"Be very careful. Sometimes these steps are covered in a really gross slime."

"Slime?"

"Algae, maybe? It's very wet, where we're going."

"This is the weirdest night of my life," he mutters to himself.

The stairway leads deep into the earth, and the going is agonizingly slow. I'm always hesitant to place my hand on the wall for balance, lest I risk shoving slime beneath my fingernails. Finally it levels off, and the tunnel opens to an irregular, cave-like chamber. Sand covers the floor, rippled from being underwater at high tide. Barnacles climb the walls to knee height.

"This room gets flooded!" Iván says.

"You figured that out all by yourself?"

"Red," he says, coming to an abrupt halt.

I whirl back around, ready to lay into him for slowing us down.

"Please stop insulting me," he says.

"What?"

"Threatening me. Questioning my intelligence. Calling me a daft dung beetle."

"Don't forget 'ridiculous goat.'"

He sighs. "You're being petty and mean."

I open my mouth, but my protest dies. Hector would be so disappointed in me. *You're a member of court and a favorite of the empress,* he always says. *Your actions have meaning; your words have power.* "You're right. I'm sorry."

"You are?" He seems taken aback.

I'm angry and scared. Scared for Rosario, angry at everyone who voted against my adoption . . . maybe I'm even a little
angry at Hector and Elisa for leaving me here all alone, even
though it was mostly my own idea. It's making me lash out at
Iván, an easy target because of his own questionable parentage.
"I won't do it again."

I turn back around to continue our journey.

"Well, that went better than I expected," he mutters.

"It doesn't mean I like you."

"I would never presume."

The cavern narrows to a tight corridor of rough limestone,
and we squeeze inside.

"I can hardly see a thing," Iván says.

"We're almost there."

Our path ends at a stair, rough-hewn, damp with water, and
aiming steeply upward.

"It smells like fish," Iván observes.

"Yes."

The top of the stair opens onto a high stone plateau. When
Iván's head crests the stair, he gasps.

I know how he feels, because even though I've been to this
secret place dozens of times, my first sight always takes my
breath away.

We're inside an immense cavern, lit by lanterns and torchlight. Spread below us is a small village with thatch-roofed huts
surrounding a massive bonfire. Rope ladders and swinging
bridges connect the village to smaller caves high in the walls,
along with a few additional huts that have found precarious

purchase on plateaus like the one we stand on. Lush vines drip from cracks in the ceiling. A cool night breeze teases the torch flames, so that the light in the cavern is constantly shifting. Something in the limestone walls catches the light just so, causing the entire cavern to glisten.

The underground river curves along the back wall, hugging a small beach area. The river is crystal clear and deceptively smooth, hiding a strong current. This close to the sea, it's a bit brackish, mixing with ocean water during high tide.

Sitting on the beach is a bearded, barefoot man, mending a fishing net. Others are about as well, in spite of the late hour—cooking over the bonfire, sharpening blades, scraping scales from a fish.

"I had no idea this was here," Iván says. "No idea at all. A whole village. Underground."

"Rosario was in hiding here for a long time," I say. Looking him dead in the eye, I add, "During your father's coup of the palace." I'm satisfied by a small wince.

"There are gaps in the ceiling," he says, looking up. "That one ladder leads to . . . where?"

"The Wallows. To a hut with a trapdoor—all under heavy guard. The surrounding yard is a bit porous. During the day, enough light filters down that torches are unnecessary."

"The Wallows is the most dangerous district in Brisadulce."

"Which makes it a good place for a hideout, don't you think? Enough gawking. Let's go find Rosario."

"I see him—right up there."

A quiet shape waits just ahead in the shadows, where a niche has been carved into the stone. He's dressed in drab servants' clothes, not even those of palace servants—but I recognize the stance, the peculiar tenseness, at once. I am afraid for him.

Rosario sees us on the path at the same moment. He steps from the shadow, his shoulders slumping with relief. "Red. Iván. I'm so glad you're here." Before I can respond, he grabs me, hugs me tight, doesn't let go. "Little sister," he says in my ear. "It's been a really long day."

I squeeze him back. "For us too, little brother. Is something wrong? Are you all right?"

Rosario releases me, steps away to clap Iván on the back. "Come with me," he says. "I have to show you something."

He leads us to the very edge of the village, where a hut cozies up to the cavern wall. A curtain embroidered with red sacrament roses covers the doorway. Rosario sweeps the curtain aside and ushers us inside.

An oil lamp hangs from the ceiling, illuminating a round space with a dirt floor. On the floor is a single bed pallet of palm fronds and sheepskin. A man lies there, his back to us. Gray peppers his black hair, along with a fair amount of cavern scree.

"I've brought some friends," Rosario says to the man on the floor.

The man turns over—slowly and painfully—revealing days-old stubble, bloodshot eyes, and a pallor so blanched and sickly I almost don't recognize him. When I do, I gasp.

It's Bolivar, the missing captain. The man who was supposed to speak for me at my adoption ceremony.

"Lady Red," he says, his voice cracked and aching.

RAE·CARSON

"Captain! You look awful."

"That's her way of saying she's really glad to see you," Rosario amends.

The captain's smile is weak. "I know how she is. And who are you?" he says to Iván.

"This is my friend Iván," Rosario says. "He's the younger brother of Lord-Conde Juan-Carlos."

"Ah, yes, the traitor's son."

Iván's face is as cold and lifeless as the grave, and I feel a twinge of something uncomfortable.

Softly I say, "Iván is not his father, apparently."

Iván gives me a quizzical look.

"Of course not," the captain says. "I just . . . this blasted illness has made me tired and . . . uncouth." He closes his eyes a moment and breathes deeply through his nose, as though summoning strength.

"So, what happened?" I ask. "Rosario, are *you* in danger?"

"I'm fine. For now. Have a seat," Rosario orders, and we comply, sitting cross-legged on the dirt floor beside the captain's sleeping pallet. Once we're situated, the prince says, "This is not a natural illness. The captain was *poisoned*."

It's like a punch to the gut. Ramifications hit me from all sides, coming so hard and fast it's hard to sort through them. But one thought crystallizes, clearer than all the others and as sharp as glass.

"This was done so he couldn't speak for me at the ceremony," I say in a choked voice.

"Yes, probably," Rosario says.

"Even though whoever orchestrated this had the votes to stop it."

"They wanted to be doubly certain the adoption would not go through. No one expected me to speak up for you. And the awkwardness of it all . . . I wouldn't be surprised if it swayed a few voters in the end."

Iván leans forward. "Where was the poison administered?" he asks the captain. "Were you in the barracks? The monastery? In your own quarters?"

Good question. We all look to the captain.

"Quarters," the captain says. "I think . . . my tea." He's not up for this conversation. Every response is a major effort.

"His quarters are in the Royal Guard barracks," Rosario says meaningfully. "He does not keep chambers in the palace, like the lord-commander does. And the only way to access his quarters is through the barracks. No one but Royal Guards, the empress, and her family are allowed inside."

Iván and I exchange a startled look.

"You're saying the Guard was infiltrated," I say.

"Yes," Rosario confirms. "We have an assassin among us. That's why I called you here. I need the two of you to find out who it is."

Hearing there's an assassin in the Royal Guard is like hearing that the sun is purple or that camels fly. It takes a moment for my thoughts to catch up to the idea, accept it, and finally, to face it head-on.

I say, "Tell me everything you can about the poison that was used."

"That's as good a place to start as any," says Iván.

"I . . ." Bolivar begins. "Duerma . . . in my tea."

Rosario places a hand on the captain's shoulder. "I'll tell them. You just rest."

Bolivar gives him a grateful look. He pulls his wool blanket up to his shoulders and closes his eyes.

"We think it was sweet dream," Rosario says.

Iván says, "That stuff made from the duerma plant."

"So you've heard of it," Rosario says.

"*I* haven't," I say.

Rosario explains, "It first appeared in Brisadulce a few years ago. Sailors are using it a lot. They say it dulls pain, eases seasickness, aids sleep. And it causes a general sense of euphoria in certain doses."

"We've started seeing it in our countship too," Iván says. "Just this year. A little bit makes you forget your troubles. But too much, and you'll never have any troubles again."

"Everyone has a little duerma leaf once in a while," I say, thinking of the many times Mara put some in my tea to help me sleep. It gives the drink a spicy taste, almost like cinnamon. "But this is different?"

"Definitely different. Much stronger," says Rosario. "With a stronger taste and a stronger scent. Someone figured out how to distill it into a syrup from the duerma berries themselves, using a process that remains a mystery. They also figured out how to make very large quantities. Whoever they are, they're becoming wealthy beyond imagining."

"This doesn't narrow things down at all," I say. "*Anyone*

could have gotten hold of some and given it to Captain Bolivar."

"Anyone in the Guard," Rosario clarifies.

We are silent a long moment, contemplating. The oil lamp sputters, casting odd shadows against the hut's palm thatching. Captain Bolivar startles in his sleep. He wrenches his blanket down, muttering, but does not awaken. Sweat now sheens his brow.

Rosario whispers, "He almost died." I hear his unspoken words too. *He might still die.*

"I'll be honest," Iván says. "I have no idea where to start. Even with most of the Guard traveling with the empress, the group remaining is huge—servants and support staff, the Guards who oversee training, four years' worth of recruits. . . ."

"Rosario, you could order a search of the barracks," I suggest. "See if anyone is in possession of sweet dream poison."

"I've considered it. I just don't have the staff. Think about who Elisa would normally use for such a task."

"The Royal Guard," I say glumly.

"Exactly. If I started searching with my remaining contingent of trusted bodyguards, the assassin would hide the evidence long before they reached him."

Iván asks, "How do we know the assassin isn't traveling with the empress? I mean, Captain Bolivar was poisoned before she left, right?"

"It's possible," the prince says, "but highly, highly unlikely. Everyone accompanying the empress is a trusted longtime confidant. Most have been with us since before the Second Battle of Brisadulce. And why attack the captain? Why not the empress herself? No, it was someone who has access to the Guard barracks—but not to Elisa."

"You think there's something bigger going on here," I say.

"Yes. Well, I'm not sure. If this were an isolated event, I'd think the poisoner was a rival of the captain's. Or it was a prank gone horribly wrong. But the way it coincided with the sabotage of your adoption ceremony . . ." Rosario shakes his head. "It feels like an opening volley. Like it heralds something else. Something worse."

"Maybe it's Red's Invierno blood that has someone so riled up," Iván suggests.

"I'm not an In—"

"You keep saying that," he says. "And I get that you're Joyan in your heart of hearts, but people just don't *see* you like that. Besides, you deny your parentage so stridently, one has to wonder what you're ashamed of."

My fists ball up of their own accord. I'd love nothing more than to give that beautiful face the bloodiest nose. Through clenched teeth I say, "I'm not ashamed of anything about myself."

"Oh? Then why do you hide that white streak in your hair? White like the hair of an animagus, I'm told. A *magic* mark."

I rise to my feet. My fists are thunder, my breath is fire as I advance on him.

"Stop it!" Rosario yells. "Both of you, just stop. Red, sit down."

I turn my fury on Rosario.

A wave of sadness passes across his face. Softly,

commandingly, Rosario says, "Recruit Red, as your prince, I order you to sit down at once."

It's like a slap to the face. In eight years of growing up together, Rosario has never pulled rank on me. Not once.

I make my face blank as I obey. But as I sit, I clasp my hands together in my lap to hide the fact that they're trembling just a little.

The ruckus has roused Captain Bolivar, who peers at us blearily.

"I can't believe you made me do that," Rosario says. "You two are my most trusted friends."

I say, *"Him?"* even as Iván says, *"Her?"*

"I said *stop it*." I've never seen Rosario like this, so frustrated, so angry, so frightened. "I don't know what's going on between you two, but get over it, grow up, and get along."

I open my mouth to insist that Iván started it, but I realize how petulant it will sound and wisely keep quiet. Instead, I stare at the hands clasped in my lap and concentrate on my breathing. I imagine Hector's voice in my head. *In four counts, out four counts.*

When I'm certain I have control of my temper, I address Bolivar as though nothing has happened: "Captain, do you remember who brought your tea?"

"Made it myself," he mumbles.

"So you have your own stash of tea," I clarify.

"Yes."

"Did someone bring you water for it?"

"No. Boiled that myself too."

RAE·CARSON

Iván says, "The captain has quarters to himself, I assume."

"He does," Rosario says.

"With a locking door?" I ask.

"Yes," the captain says.

"So it would not be easy to waltz into your quarters and poison your stash or kettle."

"He told me he took his tea the night before the adoption ceremony," Rosario says. "As is his habit. He started to feel odd as he was readying for bed, suspected poison, and forced himself to vomit. Then he passed out on the floor of the latrine. When he woke, he found himself inside the secret passage; he vaguely remembers dragging himself inside when he was barely conscious."

"That explains why Lord-Commander Dante couldn't find him," I say.

"We suspect he was out cold for more than a day. When he regained consciousness, he stumbled to the catacombs. Fernando helped him reach the village, then sent for me. I brought Doctor Enzo down here to treat him. The doctor says he needs rest and lots of water to flush out the rest of the poison."

"Did the tea taste unusual?" I ask.

"Tasted funny," the captain says. "Spicier, with sediment. Only had a few sips."

"We need to get inside his quarters," Iván says. "Have a look around."

"I agree," I say. "We'll have to be sneaky about it. Recruits aren't allowed anywhere near the officers' quarters."

"We'll figure out a way," Iván assures me.

"I sent a message to Elisa," Rosario says. "Via pigeon. But it will be a few days before her entourage reaches the oasis way station to receive it."

"Good," I say. "She might be in danger too. Or Princess Ximena."

"Hector won't let anything happen to either of them."

"I hope you're right."

Rosario says, "Well, you two have a place to start." He gains his feet with obvious reluctance. "Unfortunately, I must return to my quarters. I have a long day ahead of pretending nothing is wrong."

"Do you have an escort back?" I ask. "Is it safe for you to leave the Wallows?"

"I'm very well protected," he assures me. "And I'll be keeping all my public appearances to a minimum until we figure this out or I receive specific orders from the empress. Besides, I'm brave, remember? Everyone says so." Rosario's tone is self-mocking, and I think of his Queen's Star medal. Perhaps the prince is wondering if he can measure up to the gallantry of his early childhood. *It's easy to be brave when you're a little boy,* he told me once. *You still think the world is ultimately good. That nothing truly bad will happen to you.*

I get to my feet and grasp Rosario's shoulder. I'm staring at Bolivar, his prone form barely breathing, when I say, "*Please* be safe, little brother."

"You too, little sister. Here." He pulls an iron key from his pocket and places it in my palm. "This will get you into Bolivar's quarters."

RAE·CARSON

I close the key into my fist.

"What if we need to contact you?" Iván asks.

"Use the stable hand, the one who slipped the message to you. He's one of the spymaster's people. Now go. If you hurry back, you might be able to get a few hours' sleep. The second day of training is always awful, and I need both of you to perform well."

"We'll do our best," I assure him.

"Do better than your best," Rosario says. "Do you understand what I'm saying? It's the single most important thing right now. *Don't get cut.*"

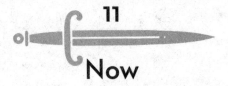

11

Now

IVÁN and I sneak back to the barracks. Our bunk room is silent when we enter, except for some soft snoring. Before letting Iván collapse into his bed, I grab his arm and whisper as quietly as possible, "We should eat dinner together again tomorrow, go over what we might have learned, plan how we're going to get into Bolivar's quarters."

He nods once, then stretches out and closes his eyes.

I'm about to stretch out on my own, but my hands encounter something wet and sticky on the blanket. It smells of rich loam and wet ash, and I almost loose an actual sob.

I know exactly what it is, even in the dark: my hair dye, spilled all over my bed, staining my fingers. Someone noticed I was gone and took the opportunity to vandalize my things.

I rip the blanket from my cot and wad it up so the dye doesn't get anywhere else. Carefully, I slide open the bedside drawer and peer inside. I breathe deeply of relief to discover the dark shapes of my baby rattle and Godstone, still intact. But my pot of dye is in ruins.

On closer look, a tiny bit of ink remains, trapped in the curve of a ceramic shard. Not enough for even one hair treatment. My white streak will start showing within days. In two weeks, it will be a blotch on my forehead. In a few months, a streak all the way to my chin.

Who would do such a thing? Someone who hates me. Someone who wants to hurt me. No, maybe it was just a prank. Not everyone understands how important that dye is to me, what great pains I take to cover the white streak in my hair.

Either way, I've no recourse for acquiring more. I could sell the jewels in my baby rattle, but I'd need time and freedom to leave the barracks during market day. Perhaps Rosario could help me.

Or maybe that would be an abuse of our friendship. He has more important things to worry about. *I* have more important things to worry about. Like whether or not whoever did this realized how long I was gone, whether they saw Iván and me leave, whether they followed us into the latrine.

And figuring out who poisoned Captain Bolivar.

I stretch out on my cot, the blanket wadded up at my feet, Bolivar's key still clutched in my fist. I close my eyes and listen hard for anyone who might be stirring, but I hear nothing except the deep, even breathing of slumber.

More than anything, I need to join my fellow recruits in sleep. Tomorrow, I begin searching for an assassin while facing the notorious second day of training. But even though my limbs are like lead and my eyes burn with dryness, my mind won't stop churning.

In desperation, I slip from my bed and curl up on the floor, my back to the wall. The cold stone is safe and solid, and at last I drift away.

I'm fleeing through the pine forest, barefoot in the snow, chased by a brass bell that won't stop ringing, its crystal clash driving deep into my mind, shattering my thoughts, my sleep. . . .

My eyes fly open, and it's a moment before I orient myself. I'm on the floor, chilled to the bone. My shoulder aches from my odd sleeping angle. A soft-checked face with long-lashed eyes is peering down at me. "Red? You all right?" says Aldo. "Did you fall off the bed?" He reaches for me. "Get up before Guardsman Bruno sees you."

He helps me to my feet. Everyone else is scurrying to don their boots and make up their cots. Across from us, Iván bumps his head on the top bunk in his hurry to situate himself. I hope he's not as tired as I am.

I join them all in the fray, shoving on my boots. I slip the key down my sock along my outer right heel and twist my foot around to test it. It chafes a little, but it's nothing I can't handle.

Next, I flip out my blanket to appear as though I'm making up my cot, but it's really to assess the damage in the light. The woolen fabric is blotched with black dye, which is already drying. So many recruits choose a blanket as one of their three precious items because the standard barracks issue is this cheap, thick, scratchy affair; a boon, in this case, because dye leaked through in only a few places. It's ugly, but salvageable.

RAE·CARSON

"What happened?" Aldo says, tucking in his shirt. "Your blanket . . ."

I shrug it off. "A prank."

"Huh? Who would do—"

I'm saved having to respond when Guardsman Bruno stomps in. "To the dining hall," he booms, "by bunk order. Eat fast. We have a big day."

We line up. As I pass Bruno on the way to the mess, I sneak a glimpse at him. Did Guardsman Bruno poison Captain Bolivar? But my quick glance reveals nothing, save for a stern glare from beneath caterpillar brows.

We are served cornmeal mush again, and no one repeats yesterday's mistake; we all shovel the slop into our mouths and wash it down with water as fast as we can. Within minutes, our bowls are scraped clean and we are marched out of the barracks and into the sand.

The arena has been transformed with obstacles. Near the weapons rack, a long wooden beam is suspended by hanging ropes—I'm guessing we'll have to run across, adjusting for the sway. Beyond that is a giant cedar log that I assume must be rolled over the lumpy sand to a flag marker. Next comes a set of wooden hurdles, staggered at varying heights, followed by a net climb to a high platform. A landing area below the platform is cushioned by a pile of straw. After that, water basins are lined up four wide and ten deep, all filled to the brim. And finally, a wooden barrier juts from the sand, surpassing even the height of the surrounding walls.

The arena walls aren't as thick with onlookers as they were

yesterday, but they still hold a fair-sized audience. News of whatever happens today will be all over the city by nightfall.

News of my humiliation, that is. Even if I'd gotten a full night's sleep, even if the morning was cool and breezy instead of brick-oven hot, I'm not strong enough to roll that log, and I'm not tall enough to get over that barrier. I have no idea how I'll pass this course.

Sergeant DeLuca is inspecting the net climb, checking the rope. Satisfied, he clasps his hands behind his back and turns to face us. He announces, "One of you is about to be cut from training."

A wave of murmurs flows down the line. Aldo whispers, "Who do you think?"

I can't respond. I can hardly breathe. It's me. It has to be me. Whoever vandalized my empty bunk last night must have reported me missing.

DeLuca continues, "At *least* one of you. Maybe more. We'll be watching closely as you traverse the obstacle course. Excellent physical fitness is essential to protecting our empress. Therefore, the recruit who performs the poorest will gather his—or *her*—things and leave the barracks."

The sergeant means to intimidate me by singling me out. Instead, he has filled me with breath and hope. They haven't yet decided who to cut. I still have a small chance.

"We'll be evaluating you based on several factors," the sergeant continues. "Speed, naturally. But also technique and effort. Strength and strategy. And of course teamwork, since you'll be traversing the course in pairs, working together."

I glance down the line, evaluating my fellow recruits. I need to pair up with someone tall, if I'm to have any chance of making it over that barrier. Maybe Valentino. No, he appears even more tired than I feel, with blanched skin and hollow eyes— like he's a ghost of himself. His ducklings mill around him. One pats his shoulder; another says something that makes him laugh. Valentino leans against one of them in a show of weakness that fills me with misgiving. He's smiling, sure, and even chatting with his friends, but he's barely on his feet.

Iván or Pedrón, then. I ready myself to dart over and claim one of them as soon as I'm given leave.

"In order to complete the course," the sergeant says, "both you *and* your assigned partner must complete it. This is the Royal Guard, and we leave no man behind."

"Or woman," Aldo whispers under his breath, but I don't have space in my head to be bothered by that, because the sergeant just said we'd have *assigned* partners, and there's no way he'll pair me with someone who might allow me a chance of success.

"Recruit Red," the sergeant says, as though reading my thoughts. "You will partner with . . . what's that black stuff on your hands?"

"Ink, sir."

"Royal Guard recruits are to be well groomed at all times. Why did you enter the training arena with ink on your hands?"

"Because it wouldn't come off on my pants, sir."

He blinks. "How did this happen?"

"A harmless prank, sir. I'm sure the ink will fade in a few

days." Everyone is staring at my stained hands now, and I fight the urge to hide them behind my back.

"Be sure that it does."

"Yes, sir."

"As I was saying, you will partner with Recruit Aldo."

I try to keep my face blank, even though it feels as though my heart is sinking into my toes. A glance toward Aldo confirms that he is unsuccessful at hiding his own despair. We are the smallest of all the recruits. There's no way we can finish the course together.

Sergeant DeLuca goes down the line, pairing recruits, and there can be no mistake that he's matching strong with strong, weak with weak, tall with tall. We have an uneven number of recruits, so he pairs Pedrón with Guardsman Bruno. At least we know his favorite.

"He's sabotaging us," Aldo whispers.

"For some reason, they need to get rid of some recruits."

"Too many mouths to feed? I heard they're going to assign uniforms today, which is great because I stink. Maybe they're short on uniforms?"

"Maybe." Or maybe Sergeant DeLuca is the assassin, and he wants as few prying eyes as possible while he . . . does whatever it is he's doing.

Two of Valentino's ducklings are up first. They're both tall, broad shouldered, and fit. I anticipate they'll have no trouble at all.

"Watch carefully," I say to Aldo. "We might get an idea how to run the course ourselves."

"My current idea is to pray and hope for a miracle," Aldo says.

"That's never worked for me," I tell him.

DeLuca raises his hand to the sky. The boys stand before him, weight shifted to the balls of their feet, ready to take off.

"Oléeee, Ciénega del Sur!" someone yells from the audience, and the two boys wave merrily in response.

"You can do it, Beto and Juan!" calls Valentino to his friends.

DeLuca's hand sweeps down, and the boys shoot forward, sprinting for the sway beam. They arrive at the same time, and for a split second they knock shoulders trying to climb on. Common sense prevails. One steps back, allowing the other a way forward.

He climbs on; the beam sways wildly. He crouches for a moment, adjusting his balance. Gradually he stands, arms out, and begins to creep forward.

"That's it, Beto! You've got it!" Valentino yells.

When he's halfway across, Juan loses patience and tries to mount the beam himself. It jerks sideways. Beto flails, tumbles to the ground.

A smattering of laughter hits us from the audience.

Beto climbs back on. Juan wisely chooses to wait this time. Slowly—too slowly—Beto makes his way down the beam. When he leaps off, the beam ricochets backward, bumping Juan in the chest hard enough that he plops in the sand.

More laughter does not prevent Juan from leaping to his feet and attacking the beam. He's a little faster than Beto, a little lighter on his feet, and he makes it across in mere seconds while Beto urges his partner onward.

Juan hops off into the sand, and together he and Beto run for the giant cedar log.

Aldo whispers, "We'll do fine on the beam. Better than Beto and Juan."

I think he's right. The next obstacle, though, will be another matter.

Juan and Beto crouch before the log, one at each end, and try to push it over. The log tips forward a tiny bit before rolling right back into place.

"If they're struggling, there's no way *we're* going to budge it," Aldo whispers.

Beto's voice carries over to us: "We have to do this at exactly the same time. On three. Ready? One, two, *three.*"

This time, they coordinate their effort, and the log rolls over once and thumps into the sand.

"Again!" yells Beto. "One, two, three."

Another roll, another thump. They repeat this process seven times, until the log reaches the flag marker. "Well done!" Valentino yells as the boys dash for the hurdles.

The boys' long legs serve them well, and they clear all the hurdles easily, except for the tallest, which they mount using their hands, and then swing their legs over.

"We'll be slower at that one, but we can do it," I tell Aldo.

Beto and Juan reach the net climb. They treat it like it's a ladder, climbing hand over foot, but the net is not entirely taut, and they swing wildly, holding tight to keep from falling.

Beto's foot shoots through and he spends a precious moment untangling himself before continuing. Still, the boys reach the high platform without too much trouble, and leap off into the pile of straw.

Juan is slow to get up, and he limps slightly as they head toward the water basins.

"High knees!" Valentino yells. "Oléeee, Ciénega del Sur!"

I spare a glance toward Sergeant DeLuca. Surely all these displays of countship pride rankle; we're supposed to leave our previous loyalties behind to join the Guard. But I guess being the son of the richest conde in the kingdom still holds sway, because DeLuca does not react in the slightest.

Beto and Juan start to run through the water basins. Each basin is perfectly round, with a diameter the width of a mead barrel. They're lined up four across, which allows both recruits to go at the same time. The edges of the basins reach higher than their knees, and I realize they're deeper than they look because they're partially buried in the sand to hold them in place. The boys are forced to slow down and place each leg carefully in each basin. Water sloshes everywhere, pushing them against the sides, soaking their clothes and even their hair.

When they finally exit the other end, they are both slumped over with the effort, and their legs drag as they push toward the final barrier. Water drains from their clothes and shoes, leaving dark stains in the sand behind them.

They pause a moment to stare up at the barrier. It's made of wooden slats that are perfectly joined, leaving no hand- or footholds. Crossbeams buttress the structure on the other side, but the surface they're staring up at might as well be a sleek, sheer granite cliff. It's almost the height of two fully grown men.

Beto bends over, hands on his knees, and takes a few gasping breaths. Then he straightens, places his back against the wall, and cups his hands before him, indicating that Juan should step in.

Juan places his foot into Beto's hands. The two murmur something to each other. Juan nods once, then springboards up as Beto launches with hands and thighs. Juan's fingertips barely reach the top, grapple with the edge. It seems as though he's going to slip, but Beto pushes on the bottoms of his feet and Juan is able to hook an elbow over, then an armpit, and finally a leg. Soon, he's straddling the wall.

Valentino and the remaining ducklings cheer.

Juan grips the wall with one hand and leans down toward Beto with the other. "Jump," he orders.

Beto jumps, misses.

He takes a few steps back. Then he runs at the wall full speed, launching himself at the last moment toward Juan's waiting hand. They grasp forearms. Beto's body swings against the wall, thumping it once, twice. Veins pop out on Juan's neck as he pulls his friend, one-handed, up, up, up, until finally Beto can grasp the edge of the wall himself.

Beto yanks himself over, and they both land on the other side and raise their hands in victory.

Valentino and his friends whoop and holler. The audience

cheers. Second years rush to reset the obstacle course, carrying buckets of water to refill the basins, rolling the log back into place.

"We're never getting over that wall," Aldo says.

"Maybe, maybe not," I say.

"You have an idea?"

"Not yet."

Next up are the Arturos. This pair is a little shorter than the Ciénega del Sur partners, but they're notably stronger. They struggle with the sway beam but make much quicker work of the rolling log. The wall proves a challenge; it takes them several tries to reach the top, but they do, and then they fall over into the sand, exhausted, while onlookers cheer them on.

Iván goes next, along with a boy from Basajuan whose arms are as thin and bony as flagpoles. Like me, Iván has been paired with someone who gives him little chance of success. But it turns out that Iván is a wonder, because the moment he hits the sway beam, it's obvious that he's fast and agile, in absolute control of his body. The skinny boy also proves light on his feet, and they are across the beam in record time. They roll the log with effort, but they do it—Iván is stronger and more coordinated than I realized, and I remember Hector's words about how some candidates hold back, hesitant to reveal the extent of their skills and training. Iván held back yesterday.

The skinny boy struggles with one of the hurdles, knocking it over twice before Iván runs back, holds the hurdle steady while the boy climbs over. Then they're up the net faster than rats climbing the rigging of a caravel, and through the water basins like they're little more than monsoon puddles.

Iván launches his partner to the top of the wall, who then reaches back to help him over. They topple to the ground on the other side and collapse onto their backs, gasping for air. Theirs is the fastest time yet.

Sergeant DeLuca frowns, but everyone else is cheering—Aldo and I loudest of all.

"That was incredible," I say to Aldo.

"Iván is in better condition than I realized," Aldo says.

"Recruit Red! Recruit Aldo!" the sergeant barks. "You're up."

The arena goes silent. Even our fellow recruits, who have been cheering and clapping all along, offer nothing in the way of encouragement. Everyone expects us to fail. Maybe they're hoping for it.

As I step forward, I feel a hand on my shoulder and turn around. It's Iván. Sweat pours from his forehead, plastering his black hair to his temples, and he's still sucking air. "There's a hollow in the ground beneath the log, about a third of the way down," he says, fast and low. "You can use it to get your hands under the log, give yourself better leverage."

"I . . . Thank you."

"Recruit Red, what's the delay?" yells the sergeant, and I hurry to get into place.

"What are we going to do?" Aldo whispers.

"Our best," I say.

"Not sure that'll be good enough."

Everyone in the arena is silent but rapt. Their anticipation is like a taut sail, full of energy, ready to spring a ship from the harbor. Whether we succeed or fail, the crowd will be entertained.

It sparks an idea. "Let's give everyone a show," I say.

"Huh?"

"We can't do this well. Let's do it *wildly*."

Aldo grins.

Sergeant DeLuca raises his hand, sweeps it downward.

We sprint for the sway beam. "Onto my back!" I yell. Aldo doesn't hesitate. He springs up, arms wrapping my neck while I hook his legs with my elbows. He's not that heavy—I've lifted worse while training with Hector—and I'm able to scramble onto the beam. It sways like an ocean wave, and I'm still a long moment, centering myself. *Harsh winds, rough seas, still hearts.* Aldo obliges me by being stiff and motionless on my back, as easy a burden as possible.

Carefully I make my way across the beam.

"That's it, Red, you can do it!" It's Valentino, and his cheer breaks something loose. Everyone else starts cheering too, even his ducklings. Even the surrounding crowd. It warms me more than I would ever admit aloud.

We reach the end, and I step off, Aldo slipping from my back.

The giant log lies before us.

I slide my hands along its length, looking for the indention Iván mentioned. *There.* A slope in the earth, hidden by the arena's deep layer of sand. I dig down until I'm able to get my whole hand and part of my wrist beneath the log. On the other end, Aldo has dug under the log as best he can.

He looks at me expectantly. "On three?" he says, and I nod. "One, two, *three.*"

We grunt and heave, but nothing happens. The log wobbles slightly but does not budge.

The cheering fades.

Then comes Iván's voice. "You can do it! Try again."

"Try again!" is echoed all around us. I appreciate the sentiment, but this isn't a problem we're going to solve with a good attitude and plucky determination. We are simply not strong enough.

I straighten and stare down at the log in dismay. Failed when we've hardly begun. Maybe we should skip this obstacle and at least complete the others. Which is probably against the rules, but surely it would be better than nothing?

My gaze catches on the weapons rack at the arena's edge. "Aldo! I have an idea!" I sprint toward the rack, and Aldo follows.

"What do you think you're doing?" the sergeant calls. "Get back . . ."

I ignore him, grabbing the same huge wooden ax that Valentino swung at my head just yesterday. "Aldo, grab the strongest, thickest weapon you can—"

"Like this?" Aldo has lifted a broadsword from the rack, one of the few weapons not made of wood.

"Perfect. Let's go." Aldo can barely lift the sword, so he drags it in the sand behind him as we return to the log.

The audience buzzes with speculation about what we're going to do. I expect to hear DeLuca's booming voice, ordering us to desist, but he doesn't even bother to repeat his earlier protest.

I lay the tip of the battle-ax sideways against the sand, and then thrust it beneath the log until it will go no farther. Aldo does the same with his broadsword. I hope that sword is made of quality steel, or this will never work. "On three!" I yell. "One, two, *three*."

We lever our weapons upward, and the log shifts. I strain against my ax. The log shifts a little more. I press my foot against it. Aldo mirrors me on his end, and together we push and heave and kick. The log rolls over and thumps into the sand.

The crowd erupts with cheering.

With our battle-ax and broadsword, we lever the log all the way across. We're slow about it, slower than any team thus far, but eventually our log reaches the flag marker. We drop our weapons, leaving them in the sand.

Aldo and I exchange a quick grin of triumph as we dash for the hurdles. My legs are rubbery, my vision blurry with sweat and exhaustion, but I'm hopeful now. Maybe we can do this.

Several of the hurdles are too tall for us to jump, and we must use our hands to push up and swing our legs over. The last one is too tall for Aldo to do even that, so I make a show of bowing formally, getting down on one knee like a supplicant, and offering my bent knee to him as a stepping stool. Aldo gapes at me a moment, an odd wonder blooming on his face, before he steps onto my proffered knee.

The crowd loves it; several whistle as Aldo hops up and over.

"Any ideas for a wild net climb?" I ask between breaths.

"I practically grew up on a ship," he says breathlessly. "Let me go first."

Aldo launches for the net, lands on all fours, then swings around the edge so that he's hanging underneath.

The crowd looses a collective gasp.

He spiders up the net from below, hands and legs moving so fast he's a blur. As he nears the top, he lowers his legs so that he's hanging. He swings back and forth, back and forth, and once he's picked up enough momentum, he whips his body up and around, landing neatly on the platform.

Valentino yells, "Nice work, Aldo!" as the crowd whoops and hollers.

I follow at an anticlimactic pace, but Aldo grabs the top of the net and pulls it taut, which helps me pick up speed and finish creditably. Together we jump from the platform into the straw pile. Remembering the way Juan limped after his jump, I duck my head and turn my landing into a forward roll, which garners a few cheers.

We dash toward the water basins. Iván and his tall partner were able to run through them by kicking up their knees, but Aldo's legs and mine are far too short for that: The edges of the basins nearly reach my crotch. We step gingerly, lifting each leg high, careful not to scrape our thighs. The water sloshes around, threatening our balance, weighing down our pants and our boots, making each step a torture.

But it's also refreshing and cool. About halfway through, I stop to cup some water with my hands and take a long drink.

Aldo pantomimes bathing by splashing his face and his armpits. The crowd laughs.

The truth is I'm stalling, because I still have no idea how we're going to get over the final barrier.

Aldo and I step from the last basin and drag our dripping selves toward it. My breath is ragged, my hands puckered and raw, as we stare up at the wooden wall in dismay.

"Any ideas?" I ask Aldo.

"My praying seems to have worked so far, so I'm going to keep doing that."

I'm laughing when the idea strikes. "I'll be right back!"

Running through sand is hard enough with good food and sleep, and my ankles and lower legs burn with effort as I sprint back toward the weapons rack.

The longbow is still there, but the arrows are too thin and flimsy for what I have in mind. However, behind the quiver of arrows, almost hidden, is a rusty crossbow, and with it a satchel containing exactly six bolts. They are iron tipped and thick as thumbs. They just might work.

I run back to the barrier and take a good, long look, sizing it up.

I'm no expert with bows and crossbows like Fernando and Mara, but I'm competent. If I take my time and steady my breath, I can put those bolts in the general proximity of where I want them.

"Aldo, step away from the wall," I order, and he complies, already grinning ear to ear.

The first bolt should go about thigh high, enough to be

a large but comfortable step. I load the first bolt. Take aim. Inhale.

I release on exhale, and the bow kicks back against my forearm even as the bolt thuds into the wall, burying itself almost two knuckles deep. I grin at this bit of luck. The wall must be made of pine. If it had been hardwood, the bolt would not have embedded itself so far.

I send five more bolts into the wall, staggering left and right, ever upward.

Aldo places his foot on the first one, testing. "Feels solid!" he says. And with that he launches up, grabs the next bolt, and climbs my makeshift ladder until he reaches the top. He pauses there, straddling the edge, just in case I need help.

But I don't. All the recruits yell encouragement as I shimmy up the wall like it's nothing.

Together, we slip over the side and hang, feet dangling, then allow ourselves to drop into the sand. I collapse, gasping for breath. But Aldo jumps up and bows as though he's accepting laurels. The crowd screams approval.

Aldo helps me to my feet, and we turn to face Sergeant DeLuca.

A hush falls over the arena.

The sergeant regards us, lips pursed, brows knitted. At last he says, "Congratulations, Recruit Aldo and Recruit Red. You've achieved the *slowest* obstacle-course time in the history of Royal Guard training."

The crowd boos, and it takes a moment for me to realize they're not booing Aldo and me but the sergeant.

DeLuca holds up his hand. "However! It was also the most innovative. You've given your trainers much to consider."

With that, he signals that Valentino and one of his ducklings are up next, and Aldo and I move to rejoin our fellow recruits.

On his way to the sway beam, Valentino says, "Nice job, Red!" and gives my back a hard thump.

I respond with a cheery "Good luck!" But a curl of dread is making me queasy. Valentino is listing a little to the left, his gaze unfocused, his skin sallow. Something is deeply wrong; I'm sure of it. Maybe it's his kidney, from when I elbowed him. I resist the urge to call out to him to be careful. Instead, I yell, "Olé, Ciénega del Sur!" because he cheered me on without hesitation, and I owe him one.

"Oléeee!" his ducklings respond.

Valentino and his partner stand before the sway beam, awaiting the sergeant's signal. Iván sidles up to me. His eyes are shadowed, his mouth on the edge of a frown. "Something's wrong with Valentino," he whispers.

"He'll be fine," Aldo says. "I mean, he's the son of the richest conde in the kingdom. Everyone loves him. They can't cut him, no matter what. Right?"

Sergeant DeLuca gives the signal, and Valentino and his partner dash for the sway beam. Valentino's course is wobbly; he lags behind right away.

His partner climbs onto the beam, places his feet just so, spreads out his arms for balance, and gradually pushes up to a standing position.

"Olé, Sancho!" Valentino yells cheerily.

"Is he drunk?" Iván says.

Sancho is nearly to the end of the beam when Valentino reaches it, grasps it, tries to climb on.

His effort makes the beam sway wildly in its rope, and Sancho flails a moment before tumbling off into the sand. He scrambles to his feet, tries to remount, but he can't get good purchase because Valentino is still trying to climb on.

"Valentino!" he yells. "Stop!"

Valentino backs away, looking baffled. Sancho climbs back on, finishes the beam walk, jumps off. "All right, *now* you can go," he says, beckoning to his friend.

Valentino tries again. His foot slips off before he can leverage himself up. He places both hands on the beam and tries again, but the beam recoils, spearing him in the chest and knocking him backward into the sand.

He doesn't move. A breeze blasts through the arena, sending up a dusting of sand, ruffling the beautiful blue silk of Valentino's clothes.

"Come on, get up," I murmur.

"Olé, Valentino!" someone yells. "You can do it!"

But he doesn't budge, and I can't tell if he's breathing or if it's just the wind playing with his tunic. Sancho stands at the end of the sway beam, looking back and forth between Sergeant DeLuca and Valentino, his face gradually shifting from annoyance to concern.

Finally, he can't take it any longer; he rushes over to his friend and falls to his knees in the sand beside him. "Valentino?" he says, shaking his shoulder. "Are you all right? He's not breathing! Somebody help!"

I'm about to dash forward, but DeLuca has sprung to action, along with several other Guardsmen, and they surround him quickly, creating a wall of bodies. Just like they did with the boy yesterday, they lift Valentino from the sand and carry him out of the arena while the rest of us look on in growing horror.

"What *happened*?" I say to no one in particular. "He was fine yesterday. He said there was no blood . . . he said . . ." *What if it's my fault? What if the injury to his kidney was worse than he let on?*

All the recruits are milling about, whispering among themselves. The audience rimming the arena is as silent as a catacomb. Sancho stands alone in the sand, staring at the dark tunnel his friend just disappeared into.

"Is Valentino dead?" Aldo asks.

"I saw his leg move when they were lifting him," Iván says.

"Are you *sure*?" I ask.

"No," Iván says.

Guardsman Bruno calls us to order. "Back in line!" he hollers. "Recruit Sancho, take a break. You'll be running the course with Recruit Pedrón. You two, Luca and Andrés—" He gestures toward the remaining army recruits. "You're up next. We *will* finish this today."

Two by two, everyone attempts the obstacle course. It's easier now. Anyone who struggles with the log roll uses Aldo's and my method of levering it with weapons. Second years try to remove the crossbow bolts from the final barrier, but they are lodged deep and immovable. Everyone climbs them easily.

The course is boring now, the mood somber. The crowd gradually thins until it's gone. No one yells, "Olé!"

The final recruits struggle the most—another small, weak-looking pair who can't budge the log any better than Aldo and I could. They try to lever it, but after being used all morning the wooden ax finally snaps, and the log refuses to budge. They are forced to skip the log roll, and they finish the rest of the course with their shoulders slumped, their faces dejected.

"Well," Aldo says. "We didn't hold the record for slowest time for very long at all."

"I'm glad we weren't the worst? I guess?"

"We might still be cut."

He doesn't need to remind me.

Guardsman Bruno calls us to attention. "You're getting a midday meal today," he says. "Your instructors have work to do, so go eat your grub. We'll fetch you from the dining hall when we're ready for you."

"Instructors?" Aldo whispers. "What instructors? No one has taught us anything yet."

"The first few days are just to get rid of the riffraff," says a voice in my ear. It's Pedrón, stepping in between Aldo and me. "Actual training will start soon."

"How do you know that?" Aldo asks.

"My brother is a third year." Another reason why DeLuca likes him. "Red, I'm going to sit by you in the dining hall, all right?"

"Whatever you say," I tell him, trying not to act surprised. I was hoping to sit next to Iván. I need to talk to him about getting inside Captain Bolivar's quarters. That's assuming neither of us gets cut, of course. "Pedrón, do you know what this work is that Bruno mentioned? Are they deciding who to cut?"

"Oh, definitely. After we eat, they'll call us into the bunk room in small groups to present us with our uniforms. See, they don't want to issue uniforms if you're not going to be here very long; they always wait for the first few recruits to wash out. The empress has a budget, you know."

I'm well aware. Ever since the Year Without a Summer, when crops failed and the coffers never filled, Elisa has had to be circumspect about how she outfits and arms her Royal Guard. It also meant I got a smaller allowance than her ladies-in-waiting, even though I was her official ward.

My mouth begins to water as soon as we enter the dining hall, because I smell yeast and butter and piquant spice. We line up, and instead of yellow slop, we're served black beans seasoned with epazote, roasted peppers, and a chunk of fresh bread glazed with honey.

"Is this a special occasion?" Aldo says. "I was expecting slop."

"It's one of Hector's reforms," I tell him. "We'll get a real meal about twice each week. Tradition was that Guard recruits grew strong and tough through deprivation, but Hector observed that they actually performed better if they were well rested and well fed."

"It's another reason army recruits try to transfer to the Royal Guard, if they show promise," Pedrón says. "Royal Guard recruits are treated better."

Iván says, "That's why they wash out as many as they can

in the first few weeks. Guard training is *expensive.*"

We find seats at the tables. As threatened, Pedrón sits at my left, a little too close for comfort, but I can't move away because I'm hemmed in by Aldo and Iván on the right. Beto sits right across from us. He glares at me over his bowl as he eats.

"You and Juan did really well on the course today," I say, just to make conversation.

A muscle in his jaw twitches, but Beto doesn't respond.

"I hope Valentino is all right," Aldo adds.

Beto slams his spoon down, so hard I startle backward on the bench. "What do either of you care?"

"Huh?" I say, even as I try to calm my heart and steady my breathing.

"You're the one who hurt him."

"I didn't mean . . . Is that why he collapsed? Because I injured him?"

"He took some stuff for the pain," Beto says. "It made him weird."

"What stuff?" I ask.

Beto shrugs. "All I know is he held back with you yesterday, and you went for his kidney like a spiteful bitch, and now he might be dead. He was my *friend.*"

I gape at him. If a *boy* had beaten a larger, armed opponent the way I had, I'd bet my golden baby rattle that Beto wouldn't call him spiteful or a bitch. He'd use words like tough or heroic or brilliant.

"Valentino did not go easy on Red," Iván says. "He lost to her fairly. Anyone could see that."

RAE·CARSON

"Who asked you, traitor?" Beto says. "Son of the Invierno lover. Is that why you're sticking up for Red? You love Inviernos too?"

Iván is deadly silent for the space of several breaths. Then he plunges his spoon back into his beans and continues to eat, ignoring Beto.

"That's right," Beto says. "Back down, you Invierno-loving coward."

"Beto." I set my spoon in my bowl and meet him glare for glare. "It's time for you to find another table."

"Or what? I can sit wherever—"

"Or you'll find out if this spiteful bitch can thrash *another* much larger opponent while unarmed."

His mouth opens, closes. He looks around to see who's watching. Everyone is too busy with their first good meal to care. He sweeps his bowl from the table and stands. "If it turns out that Valentino is dead, or if he's washed out of the Guard because of this, you'll be—"

"Goodbye, Beto."

I watch him walk away, and I don't relax my gaze until he's seated elsewhere and shoving bread into his mouth.

"Is it just me, or was there actual fire coming out of his ears?" Aldo says.

"Watch your back, Red," says Iván. "Valentino is his god. He won't let this go."

"Well, *I'm* not an Invierno lover," Pedrón interjects all of a sudden. "He was just talking about Iván, right? Not me."

Aldo and I exchange a puzzled look.

"What's wrong with loving an Invierno?" I ask. When Pedrón starts to sputter, I add, "I mean, I know they're our former enemy, but Queen Alodia of Orovalle is married to one now."

"Right," says Aldo. "Prince Storm. He was an ally to our empress even before he married her sister."

"Exactly," I say. "Things have changed."

"Not that much, they haven't," Iván says darkly.

We finish our meal in silence. Servants come to clear our dishes. We wait. The monastery bells ring the first hour. Finally Sergeant DeLuca enters the dining hall, several other Guardsmen at his back. He holds a long piece of parchment in his hand.

Aldo takes a deep breath. "Time to find out if we made the cut," he says.

My vision narrows. My muscles tense, as though preparing to flee or fight. But there is nothing for my body to do but wait.

RAE·CARSON

12

Then

THE girl forgot, but the body knew.

The body knew hunger. A constant ache in the pit of the stomach. The desperate pleasure of licking a dirty plate just for the taste of food.

The body knew loneliness. The craving for comfort, the search for any sign of kindness. A smile from a stranger in the market was sustenance for weeks.

The body knew pain, bruise and blood and needle.

The body knew danger. The casual slap, the thunderclap of a sudden blow, the grip with no escape.

The body waited.

The girl forgot. But the body would always remember.

13
Now

DELUCA looks at his parchment and calls out four names: "Recruits Sancho, Itzal, Beto, and Iván. Come with me."

Iván rises from the table, face displaying both incredulity and relief.

"Congratulations, Iván," I say.

He nods acknowledgment, and follows the others from the dining hall.

"No surprises there," Aldo says.

"I didn't expect Iván to be in the first group," I say. "I thought DeLuca hated him."

Aldo shrugs. "Iván is the brother of a Quorum lord. Not to mention pretty enough to make an angel cry."

"I thought maybe it had something to do with him being well trained and in excellent shape."

"That too."

It seems as though we wait forever—though it's probably only a few minutes—before DeLuca returns to claim another group. This time, he calls Pedrón's name, along with the other army recruits, Andrés and Luca, and one of Valentino's remaining ducklings. "Oh, thank God," Pedrón says, rising from the table, and I'm surprised to discover he had anything to worry about. He runs his hand through his short-cropped hair and grins down at me. "See you in there, Red," he says, and I hope he's right.

The next group contains most of the Basajuan contingent, including the taller Arturo. The one after that sweeps up all of Valentino's remaining lackeys, along with the shorter Arturo. My hopes dwindle along with the recruits still seated in the dining hall. Soon only six of us remain, including me, Aldo, the two boys who couldn't complete the log roll, and two others.

DeLuca returns. He pauses a long moment, staring down at us. He's torturing us on purpose.

At last he says, "Recruit Aldo. Recruit Red. Come with me. The rest of you may return home. Her Imperial Majesty thanks you for your service."

Aldo's breath leaves him in a *whoosh*. I stand up so fast I knock my knee against the table. As we hurry after DeLuca, I spare a thought for the boys left behind. I feel terrible for them. And so relieved they were cut instead of me.

We enter the bunk room to a smattering of applause. Everyone is standing at the foot of his bunk, each smartly dressed in a brown vest that laces up over a linen tunic. The vest and tunic fall mid-thigh over black woolen pants and brown leather boots. Everything is cinched up by a leather scabbard, empty until we've earned the right to carry weapons.

"I knew you'd make it, Red," says Pedrón, grinning proudly in his new uniform.

"Your clothes are folded on your bunks," Sergeant DeLuca says. "Please change immediately."

As Aldo and I walk the gauntlet of uniformed recruits to our shared bunk, Beto says, "Yes, Red, change immediately. I promise I won't look." His voice is mocking, his intent clear.

Aldo grabs his new clothes from the top bunk and gets started right away, whipping off filthy pants and shirt. The other recruits whoop and holler, poking fun at his skinny legs. The mockery is undeserved; Aldo may be small, but he's also fit, with muscled thighs and an abdomen like a granite cliff.

He finishes, stands at attention at the end of his bunk.

"What are you waiting for, Red?" taunts Beto.

I look to Sergeant DeLuca. Does he really want me to change in front of everyone? He returns my look with a raised brow.

All right then. I'll make this quick. I'll ignore them all. I'll be fine.

I reach for the tie of my linen shirt. Someone whistles.

"Red," says Iván. "Wait."

He steps forward, stands in front of me with his legs slightly spread and his arms crossed. Aldo joins him, standing shoulder to shoulder with Iván, though a head shorter. Then another boy, whose name I haven't bothered to learn—did DeLuca call him Itzal?—stands beside Aldo. They've created a privacy wall for me.

I swallow a sudden lump in my throat and dart behind

them. I'll have to work as fast as I can, before any of them think better of helping me or DeLuca decides to put a stop to it.

The first thing I do is fish out Bolivar's key and transfer it to the pocket of my new pants.

Everything fits, even the boots. The vest hugs my shape so perfectly it's as if the royal tailor himself sculpted it. The pants and shirt are loose enough for comfortable maneuvering. The boots are stiff, but they'll allow room for my toes to flex once they're broken in. I waste a precious moment marveling at how good this uniform feels to wear. Like it was meant to be mine. Like I'm truly a Royal Guard recruit now.

I tap Iván on the shoulder. "I'm finished. Thank you."

He and the others step aside, and we take our places before our bunks.

DeLuca says, "You have the quartermaster and his staff to thank for your tailored uniforms. His eye for fit is extraordinary, as always. You will demonstrate your gratitude to the quartermaster by keeping your uniforms in good condition at all times. If you do not know how to launder or repair your clothing, you will be taught. Never enter the training arena in the morning with a uniform that is damaged or dirty. You will be given time each evening for laundry and ablutions. Do you understand?"

"Yes, sir!" we respond in unison.

"The next official cuts will be in three days," he says. "Until then, we have work to do. The first two mornings demonstrated a shameful lack of fitness. We'll remedy that immediately."

"Uh-oh," Aldo whispers.

"You will spend the afternoon running the walls."

Several boys groan loudly.

DeLuca says, "Complaining is taken into consideration when determining cuts," and the boys fall immediately silent. "You must complete ten full laps around the palace. If you complete them before the dinner bell, you'll be allowed free time tomorrow evening."

The other boys look glum at this announcement, but I'm secretly thrilled. I may be small and not as strong as the others, but I can run. I've run the walls plenty of times with Hector. Sometimes even with Mara. I love looking out over the eastern rooftops to the swooping desert dunes, and over the western rooftops to the endless azure sea. I love the fresh air and wide-open sky, the solid stone beneath my feet and the cheery hellos I get from palace guards as I pass.

And by finishing well, I'll earn free time tomorrow. Time to find Bolivar's quarters, maybe.

"Any questions?" Sergeant DeLuca asks.

I raise my hand.

"Recruit Red?"

"Do you have word on Valentino?"

"He's very ill. Too ill to return to the Guard. We expect him to make a full recovery eventually, but most of you will likely never see him again."

The duckling contingent, led by Beto, buzzes at this news, and their murmurings are both relieved and angry. I understand how they feel. I'm so glad Valentino is going to be all right, especially glad that I didn't accidentally kill him. Because

I liked him. He was smart and kind and an excellent candidate, and he was maybe about to become my friend.

"Guardsman Bruno will lead you to the walls," DeLuca says. "People will be watching. Do us proud."

And with that, we march in our new uniforms, out of the dark barracks and back into the sunshine.

I finish third.

It was harder than I expected, thanks to these new boots and the fact that I only got a few hours' sleep last night. My breathing was fine and my endurance held. But my feet are covered in blisters—several of them broken—and each step is a stinging agony. I'm not the only one. We're all moving gingerly as we return to the dining hall.

More than half the first years are still out on the walls, struggling to finish, so there are plenty of empty seats. I make a point of sitting beside Iván, who finished fifth. Aldo is not back yet, or Pedrón, though I expect them shortly. The Basajuan boys are all here, though, which is no surprise; the desert nomads spend their days walking and running.

"We can search the captain's quarters tomorrow," I tell Iván in a low voice.

"I think we should find Valentino instead," he says. "See if we can talk to him."

"Why?" I say around a mouthful of food. We're back to eating cornmeal sludge.

"Beto said Valentino took stuff, remember? I want to find out what it was."

"You think it might have been sweet dream. Like the poison given to Bolivar."

Iván nods. "If it is, we need to know who he got it from."

Makes sense. Except . . . "If any of the ducklings have free time tomorrow, they'll probably use it to visit Valentino. They practically worship him."

Iván snorts, which takes me aback because it's almost a laugh. I'm not sure I've heard him laugh before, or even seen him smile. "*Ducklings.* That's appropriate." He takes a bite of sludge, swallows, then says, "You might be right. If Valentino is seeing visitors, it will be hard to get him alone."

"So maybe we investigate the captain's quarters first, and visit Valentino at our next opportunity?"

"Fine. Now let me eat." With that, Iván visibly cuts me off, tilting his shoulder just so. It's not *quite* like he's turning his back on me, but almost.

With a sigh, I slide down the bench to give him a little space, and finish my sludge.

It's full dark. Everyone has finished running the wall, though only some of us earned free time. We were shown to the laundry area—a dungeon with a low arched ceiling, filled with basins and washboards that stink of sweat and lye—and given a brief lesson on how to clean our uniforms. It's astonishing to me that so many of these boys have never in their lives laundered even the tiniest sock.

Afterward, a stray cricket serenaded us as we took turns doing our business in the latrine. Now we're collapsed onto our bunks. Guardsman Bruno has just blown out the oil lamps, and the monastery has rung the tenth hour. I sink into the mattress, exhausted but grateful, Bolivar's key now stuffed down my sock so it doesn't fall out during my sleep. I've passed the first hurdle, survived the first cut. For once, I might fall asleep easy and stay that way.

I drift off, as effortlessly as a cloud in the breeze.

My eyes fly open when a hand presses down on my mouth.

"Unngggh!" I try to speak, but someone holds me fast. Hands are gripping my arms and legs too, pressing tight, relentless. I can't move at all. I can hardly breathe.

"You got Valentino cut," says a voice in my ear. It's Beto. His damp breath is hot and so, so close.

I try to whip my head to the side, but the hand on my face presses down until the slats of my cot dig into my skull. Beto is going to break my neck.

"What's going on?" someone asks blearily, and I can't tell who because blood is rushing past my ears and bile is rising in my throat and there's a pressure in my chest that's familiar and comforting and terrifying all at the same time because it means I'm about to lose control of myself.

"Stay out of it!" growls Beto. "This is none of your business. It's between us and Red." He kisses me on the forehead; his hot, wet lips feel like slugs against my skin. "Isn't that right, little mula?"

Mula.

The pressure in my chest becomes a maelstrom. Tears leak from my eyes.

"Aw, poor Red, are you cry—"

With all my strength, I bite down on the fleshy part of his palm. Beto yelps, lurching backward as wonderful, glorious air fills my lungs.

The others are startled enough to loosen their grip. I fling myself over the side of the cot and onto the floor. I'm on my feet in an instant. "Get her!" Beto yells.

Beds creak as everyone around us wakes. I'm trapped between bunks, my back to the wall, as Beto and two duck-lings approach. In the dark, they are looming shapes, like the shadow monsters from my nightmares.

Hold back, a tiny voice says. *Don't hurt them.* But the mael-strom has me firmly in its grip now, and I'm helpless against it.

A shadow shoulder swings back, priming for the punch. I dodge left, grab his forearm as it sails past, use his own momen-tum to slam his fist into the wall.

He doubles over in pain, cradling his fist. I take the oppor-tunity to grab the back of his head and smash his face against my swiftly rising knee. He shrieks as his nose shatters.

I lift my heel, shove it into his broken face, and send him reeling backward into the arms of his friends.

"Who's next?" I say, advancing. I am fire. I am a thunder-storm. The remaining two shadows start to back away.

Someone grabs me from behind, squeezes my neck, pins my arms to my sides—a fourth person I didn't notice before. The other two shadows see their opportunity and attack, fists flying.

Pain explodes in my abdomen. In my cheekbone. Everything

RAE·CARSON

freezes. The bunk room disappears. Instead, I see blue-stained fingers and iron ladles.

A glass heron sitting on a fireplace mantel, poised to take flight.

Distantly, I know I'm being pummeled. I should defend myself; someone taught me exactly what to do. But I'm helpless, because the blue-stained fingers are coming closer. They hold a vicious-looking quill; no, it's a needle. I'm about to get a tattoo.

"Please," I whisper. "Not again."

Someone screams. Not me. The pressure against my throat lessens.

"Red!" someone yells.

The pain in my cheekbone sharpens to a brutal here and now because I am *Red*. I am Red Sparkle Stone of Joya d'Arena and a Royal Guard recruit, and someone is attacking me.

I raise my leg and slam my heel into my attacker's instep, crunching bones. I whirl on him before he can recover. He reaches feebly for my neck, but I'm faster. I send the heel of my palm up into his chin. His head snaps back and his teeth crunch. He staggers, disoriented, and I fell him with a swift kick to the groin.

I don't bother to watch him writhe on the floor. I turn to discover that the two remaining shadows are grappling with someone else. I reach for the one on the left, grab a handful of hair, and yank backward with all my strength. Hair rips from its roots as his neck kinks backward. I sweep the back of his leg with my foot. He topples; I step aside and let him fall, his head cracking against the edge of the cot.

When I look up, the final shadow is subdued. He sits huddled on the ground, cradling a broken arm. Above him looms my ally, tall with gangly shoulders, but somehow as steady and large as a mountain. It's Iván.

He turns to me. "I think that's all of them."

The maelstrom is slowing. As my heartbeat approaches normal, the pains in my rib and my cheekbone intensify, making it hurt to breathe. My stomach roils, threatening to toss up my cornmeal sludge. Everyone is awake now, their shadowed bodies sitting up in their cots, watching us.

My limbs are shaking. They always shake after the maelstrom leaves.

I say the first thing that comes to mind. "I didn't need your help, Iván."

Iván has a split lip and disheveled hair, but he doesn't seem bad off. As usual, he's frowning at me. "I didn't want to help you."

"You didn't? I mean, good. I don't need saving." Blood drips wet and warm from my nose to my upper lip. I wipe it with my sleeve before remembering that I'll have to wash the blood out of my shirt before morning.

"I know you don't," Iván says.

I give him a perplexed look. "Then why—"

"Red, I don't even *like* you. But what they were doing was wrong. It wasn't about saving you. It was about stopping them."

"Oh." It's the kind of thing Rosario would say. *Bad men need stopping.*

"What's going on here?" It's Guardsman Bruno, standing in the doorway with a torch. Several other Guards are right behind him.

I let my gaze fall to my recent attackers. All four are on the floor. I recognize Sancho in spite of his smashed face; his breathing makes an odd whistling noise. Beto is collapsed against the wall cradling a broken arm; the torch flame casts light on his hands. His cuticles are stained black. He's the one who spilled my hair dye.

Two of the other ducklings are curled up like babies in the cradle—one is still protecting his crotch, the other is blinking oddly while blood seeps from his head wound.

Aldo sits up in his bunk, looking down at me, eyes wide. "I'm sorry I didn't help, Red," he whispers. "I panicked, and . . . I was afraid . . ."

"I was just about to jump in," Pedrón says, trying to look gallant. "I really was. In fact, these boys are lucky I was slow to wake up, or I would have—"

"Shut up, Pedrón," I snap.

"I'll ask one more time," Guardsman Bruno says, his gaze sweeping over the injured boys. "What happened? Who started this?"

I'm not sure what to say. If I blame the ducklings, everyone might hate me even more. If I don't, maybe other boys will think they can get away with the same thing.

In the distance, the latrine cricket chirps and chirps.

"Fine," says Bruno. "Tomorrow morning all of you will run—"

"These recruits started it," Aldo says, gesturing toward Beto. "They attacked Recruit Red while she slept, all four of them at once. They said something about her being Empress Elisa's favorite and then started pummeling her. They attacked a defenseless recruit, Guardsman. It was awful."

I blink up at him. I don't remember that part about being Elisa's favorite. Maybe he's altering the story on purpose, reminding everyone that I was sponsored by the empress herself.

"And you stepped in to help?" Bruno asks, indicating Iván and his busted lip.

Iván remains silent, but Aldo says, "Yes, but she didn't need Iván's help. She took care of them on her own. In fact, they're lucky they didn't get themselves killed. Frankly, anyone who attacks Red is an idiot."

And now Aldo is warning all the other recruits not to come after me.

"Is this true, Recruit Red? Recruit Iván?"

"It's true," I say. "Just like Aldo said. Except that Iván . . ." I hate to admit this, but I'm going to anyway. "Iván handled Beto so I could take care of the others. He really did help."

"I slept through the beginning," says the boy named Itzal. "But the rest was exactly as they said."

A few other boys jump in with "Red is telling the truth" and "In the mess hall, I heard Beto trying to convince the others to attack her" and "Red was just defending herself." I gape at them all. Never, ever did I expect a show of support.

Bruno presses his lips together, considering. "All right, Red

RAE·CARSON

and Iván, go get cleaned up. Red, if you feel like you need to get your wounds tended, I'll give you leave."

"I'll be fine."

To the Guards accompanying him, Bruno says, "Get this trash out of here; these boys are going home."

"So much for Ciénega del Sur," Aldo mutters.

As Iván and I stumble to the laundry dungeon to clean up, I do a quick count in my head. We've lost ten recruits in two days.

The laundry contains three empty basins with paddles for stirring, four smaller buckets with washboards, and two stone benches, all arrayed around a rusty drain in the floor. A wooden shelf displays buckets of lye, rope soap, coral for scraping, and several neatly folded rags in various shades of faded gray. A spigot beside the shelf *drip drip drip*s with water.

"Let me know when you've covered yourself back up," Iván says, turning his back to me.

Quickly, I strip off my vest and shirt, then re-don the vest.

"I'm decent," I say, studying the shirt. A large drop of blood already browns on the collar. A lighter spray patters the right sleeve, and a smear mars the left from when I wiped my nose. My stomach roils as I stare. Aside from the smear, I'm not entirely sure whose blood I'm looking at. "I really hurt those boys," I whisper. *With the skills I'm teaching you comes responsibility*, Hector told me. *You must use them wisely.*

Iván says, "They had it coming."

"But . . . Sancho's face . . ." I can't stop seeing the bloody mess, or hearing the whistle sound of his breathing.

What would Hector think of what I did?

Iván whips off his own vest; blood from his split lip has dribbled down his chest, and the vest will need a thorough soaking. "It was a brutal takedown," he acknowledges, and somehow I know it's a simple observation, not a judgment. "Efficient and deadly. Prince Hector taught you to fight like a street brawler."

I grab a bucket and turn the spigot. Water pours out, unpleasantly cold on my hands, filling the air with a hint of brine. I'm glad to have a task right now, a sensation. Anything to distract me from my still-racing heart and needle pinpricks of firing nerves. It might be a while before I can sleep tonight.

"What works best on blood?" Iván asks. "Lye?"

"Just soak it in cold water. Do it fast before the stain sets."

"Sounds easy enough."

Favoring my injured rib, I sit on a bench and dip my shirt into the bucket, letting it soak for several seconds. Iván follows my lead. "Have you never done laundry before?" I ask him.

"My brother always did the laundry," he said. "We couldn't afford staff for a while after . . . everything. So we divvied up the chores. I was the countship's stable boy for several years."

"Your brother did the laundry?" I say, gaping. "Lord-Conde Juan-Carlos was a *laundry boy*?"

"No, not him. My other brother. The one who died."

"Oh." The blood is already lifting from my sleeve, whirling up in tiny eddies. Or maybe it's the torchlight playing tricks on my eyes.

"He was only twelve."

I have a guess about what happened to Iván's brother: "An Invierno killed him."

"A sniper with a longbow. During the first big battle I remember."

"Is that why you hate Inviernos so much?"

"Among other reasons."

Iván's bucket is trapped between his knees, and he rubs his thumb against his soaking vest, but he seems hardly aware of the action. After a long moment he says, "What about you? Why do you *love* Inviernos so much?"

"I hate them as much as you do. Maybe more. Well, except for a few. They're not all bad, I guess."

"Does that mean you hate yourself?"

I open my mouth to protest, but the words just aren't there. For once, I have nothing to say.

"Fine," he says. "Why do you hate *some* Inviernos so much?"

Maybe this is too personal, too raw, to talk about with someone I don't like or trust, but I've never been good at keeping my thoughts to myself, and the words bubble up before I can stop them. "The first one I met was an animagus. He killed my mother."

"That's . . . how old were you?"

"Six or seven, maybe."

"How did you get away?"

"I killed him right back."

He jerks in his seat, and water sloshes over the side of the bucket. He says, "You killed an animagus."

"Yes."

"When you were a little girl."

"Yes."

"How?"

I've told this only to Hector and Rosario. Why am I telling Iván? "I'm not sure how. I dream about it. Sometimes in the dream, I kill him by pushing him into the fireplace. He falls and hits his head on the mantel. But most of the time, I stab him with a skinning knife. That's how I think it must have happened. The stabbing, I mean. Because that's the memory that makes me . . . I can still smell his blood."

Gently Iván asks, "Was it during a battle too?"

"No. He was looking for something. Something of my father's, I think."

A partial truth. Filtered through the sieve of life and retrospection, my memories tell me the animagus was looking for a Godstone. Like the one hidden in my drawer in the bunk room.

"And before you ask . . ." I hold up a hand to forestall the question forming on his lips. "No, I don't know who my father is, and no, I've never met him, and no, I don't care to."

Iván's lips quirk. "Fair enough. But you've met some Inviernos since then that you didn't hate?"

"Not at first. The next one I met made me her slave and beat me on the regular. Several other Inviernos came to the village I lived in. Sometimes animagi. My next master always needed money; he often sold my blood to them so they could work their magic. I was a good bleeder, he always said."

"That's disgusting."

"Yes."

He holds up his vest; water drips back into the bucket. "Almost clean."

"Iván, don't move."

"What?"

I grab a clean rag from the shelf. "Your lip is dripping blood. Be still, or you'll have to launder your shirt too."

I hold the rag beneath the spigot just enough to dampen it, then gently press it against his mouth.

"Is it as swollen as it feels?" Iván mumbles into the rag.

"You look like a puffer fish."

His grin becomes a wince before it can truly bloom on his face. "It really hurts to smile," he says.

"I'll do you a favor and be perfectly dull. Actually, you should stop talking entirely and let me keep up the pressure, or this will never stop bleeding. Beto got you good."

"I got him better."

"Yes. Now shut up."

"Distract me."

"Huh?"

"Tell me a story to keep me from talking. Like, how you got that white streak in your hair."

I yank the rag away and prime my shoulder to punch him in the nose, but I stop myself. He's not mocking me. He's asking for true. Out of curiosity.

"Fine," I say, reapplying the rag. "But after I tell you, you must truthfully answer a question of mine."

"Deal."

I take a deep breath. "It was Elisa."

"The *empress* gave you that mark?"

"Stop talking! As I'm sure you've heard, she bought me while passing through the free villages toward Invierne. Hector had been taken hostage by an enemy, and she was desperate to get him back. We were in horrible danger the whole time; I know this now. But . . . I was just happy. I'd been bought by a fine lady, you see, and I was given warm clothes and kind words and the same food as everyone else. I thought I was the luckiest girl in the world."

He raises an eyebrow as if to say, "Go on."

"A few days later, we caught up to Elisa's enemy, and we attacked his camp, freed Hector. It all went mostly well. But after the battle, just as we were realizing that one of them had gotten away, he launched from the trees and attacked Elisa. I remember it so clearly . . . she couldn't breathe. There were all these dried leaves in her hair. Her arm was stretched out on the ground, limp, dirt in her nails . . . it made me think of my mother. The last thing I ever saw of her was her hand, sticking out from beneath a pile of rubble, and I . . . Elisa had been so kind to me. . . . It's like I went to another place in my head, and I wasn't me anymore but this *monster. . . .*"

I pause a moment, swallow hard, take a breath. The spigot *drip drip drip*s. Iván's eyes are intent on me, but again there's no judgment there. He's just listening.

"I launched at him. Pounded him with my fists until he let go of Elisa's throat. But I was just a little girl, and he was a fully grown Invierno assassin, so of course he had me flipped over and pinned in seconds. He hit me so hard my sternum caved in."

Iván's brows knit, as he puzzles something out.

"The next thing I knew," I continue, "I was alive and awake on the cold ground, Elisa collapsed on top of me. Turns out, Hector had killed the assassin, then Elisa used the power of her Godstone to heal me. There was a lot of blood on the ground by then, and Elisa was newly come into her power, so the healing was . . . intense."

I dash off the words as if they're no big deal, and I gently peel up a corner of the rag to check Iván's lip. "The bleeding has lessened," I say.

The laundry dungeon is cooler than the barracks, and the chill dimples my arms. It's easy to imagine myself back in the mountains, the air brittle with approaching winter. I don't remember a lot of what happened to me before I met Elisa, but my flesh remembers being cold.

Iván points toward my hairline, to remind me that I haven't quite finished my story.

"The truth is, we don't know for sure how it got there," I tell him. "Mara was the one who noticed it, a little while after Elisa healed me. Just a little blotch above my forehead that gradually grew out with my hair. Father Nicandro is sure it was Elisa's magic, though. Did you know that an animagus's hair grows lighter and lighter with magic use? That's why so many of them have white hair. Anyway, I've always been close to the magic of the earth. I can sense Godstones being used, just like a priest can, or like Elisa's sister Alodia. I mean, I'm no sorcerer, but Father Nicandro thinks that my affinity, combined with an enormous dose of healing power, caused a bit of my hair to turn white."

He doesn't respond for so long that I'm sure I must have offended him somehow. He just stares off into the distance, his dark eyes churning. I pull the rag away and inspect his lip. "The bleeding has stopped. You might want to take a rag to bed with you, though."

He catches my wrist as I'm drawing away. "This assassin. The one who almost killed you. It was Franco, wasn't it?" His grip is a little painful.

I blink. "Yes. Though his Invierno name, his *real* name, was Listen to the Falling Water, for Her Secrets Carve Canyons into Hearts of Stone."

When Iván doesn't respond, I add, "And yes, I realize he's the man who conspired with your father to start a civil war."

"No wonder you hate me."

"I don't ha— I mean, Rosario has ordered us to get along, so I will if you will."

He releases my wrist so fast that I lurch backward. Any semblance of peace between us seems to be gone; his brow is furrowed, his dark eyes churn. "By telling me all that," he says, soft and low, "were you trying to make me feel sorry for you? Do you want me to know how much you've suffered?" His tone is contemptuous, mocking.

"No."

He raises an eyebrow.

"Iván, I was just answering your questions. No one has to

feel sorry for me. Since becoming ward of the empress, I've had such comfort and ease. I had a rough start, sure, and being half Invierno doesn't exactly win me friends, but I'm still the luckiest girl in the world. All those things can be true at once, you know."

Ivan's not looking at me anymore. He pulls his vest from the bucket and wrings it out over the floor drain. "We should get back to the barracks. Get some sleep if we can."

"You still owe me the answer to a question. We had a deal, remember?"

His frown deepens. "Fine. Ask your question."

After assuring myself that the bloodstains are no longer visible, I follow his lead and wring the water from my shirt. "Elisa ruined your father," I tell him, shaking it out flat. "I mean, he deserved it, but she destroyed him utterly, exiled him, gave him over to the Inviernos."

"Is there a point? Just ask your question."

"Your countship has been in disgrace ever since, even though your brother is a Quorum lord. Your coffers are empty. You hate Inviernos, so you can't possibly agree with the treaty Elisa brokered. So my question is this: Why did you join the Royal Guard? Why do you want to protect the person who brought such misery upon you and your family?"

He's silent a long moment, staring at me. I hate staring; it's one of the reasons I cover my mark. One less thing for people to gawk at.

The constant *drip plink* of the spigot echoes around us. I force myself to meet his gaze without flinching, even though my feet are twitching to run, my ears growing warm.

"You're right," he says at last. "The empress ruined my father, and our countship is slow to recover from the devastation."

"Then why—"

"I loved my father. But I hated him too." His slight grin is self-deprecating. "Those things can be true at once, you know."

I'm not sure what to say to that.

"He was the worst person I ever knew," he continues. "And no, I don't feel like telling you about that. But the day the empress stripped him of his title and exiled him was the best day of my life."

I blink. "Huh. Well, in that case I'm glad for you."

"We really should get back to the barracks," he says. "You think our clothes will dry in the next few hours?"

"Hope so." I head toward the doorway, and Iván follows.

"I haven't told anyone that," he says to my back, "about my father, I mean."

Without turning around, I say, "Besides you, only Hector and Rosario know about me killing that animagus."

We enter the hallway and step quietly toward the bunk room. "Meet me after dinner tomorrow," he says. "We'll use our free time to investigate Bolivar's quarters."

"I still have the key," I assure him.

"All this confiding and conspiring," he says. "I hope it doesn't mean we're becoming *friends*."

"Of course not," I snap.

Just before being enveloped by the darkness of the bunk room, I note a hint of a smile edging his swollen lip. I turn my head away before he can see any reaction on mine.

✧ ✧ ✧

I'm prone on my cot, trying to fall back asleep. My stomach is in knots, my lowest right rib feels like shards of glass, and daggers of pain stab my skull in perfect time with my heartbeat.

I reach into the drawer and root around until my hand closes around my Godstone. It's cool and hard, with faceted edges. I bring it to my chest and run my thumb along one edge, back and forth, back and forth. I give a passing thought to the long-dead animagus this stone once belonged to, then I decide I don't care about them.

Just like Elisa showed me, I send my awareness deep into the earth, seeking the magic that lives there, swirling beneath the skin of the world. She taught me this as a meditation—because I refused the comfort of prayer—to help quell the maelstrom that comes when I can't control my fear.

I'm no sorcerer. I can't bend the magic to my will. Which is just as well; I'm afraid what might happen to my hair.

Magic squirms beneath the crust of the earth, Elisa always says, yearning to break free. I don't believe in any god, but the power she speaks of is real. When I reach for it, it tingles along my neck, suffuses me with warmth, connects me to everything. And sometimes, when I'm lucky, the magic speeds the healing of my wounds.

I close my eyes, trying to be mindful of all my body's sensations, like Elisa taught me. Suddenly, everything is too familiar. Lying on a poking straw tick, trying to sleep through unspeakable pain. For a brief moment, I smell damp pinewood smoking on the fire, mixed with the scent of cheap ale on sour breath. But I swallow, and it's gone. A phantom memory. Not even real.

I clutch the Godstone to my chest and firmly remind myself that I'm the luckiest girl in the world.

Hours later, the brass bell is like a cymbal at the base of my skull. I sense everyone scurrying around me, making their bunks, throwing on their boots. My nose feels like it has swollen to twice its size, and my rib gives me a nasty pinch as I swing my legs over the side of the bed and toss my Godstone back into the drawer.

A quick glance toward Iván's bunk reveals that he's already gone, his bed perfectly made. He's likely eating right now.

"You all right, Red?" Aldo asks. An imprint from a blanket wrinkle is pressed into his left cheek.

"Not bad," I tell him with forced cheer. I can handle a swollen nose and a nasty rib pinch. Maybe the Godstone worked a little.

"Don't be too long," he warns. "You need to make a show of looking strong in the sand today, even if you don't feel it."

"Good point."

"I'll save a place for you at the breakfast table."

Aldo, and everyone else, exits the barracks for the mess while I lace my boots. Once they're gone, I change back into my almost-dry shirt and re-don the vest. I stand and gently stretch, testing my muscles. My bruised rib pulls badly, but it's not hampering my motion. I got lucky.

I'm heading toward the doorway when my belly cramps,

deep and low, and I stop in my tracks, swearing loudly.

The spasms herald my monthly courses, coming several days earlier than I planned, probably because of the beating I took last night. If all else goes normally, the cramping means I have exactly one day to procure supplies.

I have no idea who to ask. And if I did, would they think I was asking for special treatment? Maybe no one will notice if some of the laundry room rags go missing.

On the other hand, getting caught stealing is the fastest way to get kicked out of the Guard.

I hurry to the mess hall to down a quick breakfast. I'll have to figure it out later.

14
Now

EVEN though it's early morning, the sun rains pure fire onto my cheeks when I enter the arena, and heat from the sand seeps through the soles of my boots.

The weapons rack has been filled with wooden swords. Before it stands a tall, lithe man with slicked black hair and a waxed mustache that dangles past his chin. He holds his own sword point down in the sand and leans on it in as though it's a walking cane—an unforgivable treatment of such a weapon. The steel of his blade glints in the morning light, revealing script etched near the hilt, though I'm too far away to make out what it says.

Sergeant DeLuca storms into the arena. "Good morning, recruits!"

The mustached swordsman pivots at the sound of the sergeant's voice, revealing that most of his other arm is missing. His sleeve is tied into a knot about halfway past where his elbow would have been.

"Stop gaping and line up!" the sergeant yells.

We scurry to comply.

"Tomorrow and every day thereafter," the sergeant says, "you will line up immediately upon entering the arena without being commanded. Understood?"

"Yes, sir!"

DeLuca walks down the line, hands clasped behind his back. "Today we have a very special guest. Please welcome Swordmaster Santiago."

We applaud obligingly. The name sounds vaguely familiar.

"Master Santiago will begin your lessons in swordcraft. He's one of the finest swordsmen in the empire and an excellent teacher. Though not an official member of the Royal Guard, he has been a trusted associate of the imperial family for over a decade. Master Santiago served as personal bodyguard to the dowager queen at her estate in Puerto Verde until her death a few years ago. Since then, he has been an instructor for private guard corps all over the empire, even serving a six-month post with Brisadulce's own garrison. You will accord him the same respect as any senior member of the Guard and obey his orders as if they come from me or the Lord-Commander himself."

Aldo whispers, "Has the Guard ever brought in an outsider for training before?"

"Never," I whisper back.

Sergeant DeLuca steps aside and gestures toward the swordmaster. "Master Santiago, the class is yours."

"Thank you, Sergeant," says Santiago. He lifts his chin and addresses the recruits. "Each of you claim a practice sword, then return to your place in line."

As one, we rush to the rack and jostle each other to grab a weapon. All the largest swords disappear first. I'm happy to claim a short sword with a thick cross hilt and a nicked wooden blade. Maybe a light weapon will be easier on my aching rib.

After we get back in line, Master Santiago individually directs each of us to new positions until we are in a staggered formation of two lines, all of us standing a full arm's length apart.

"Look around and mark your position," says Santiago. "This is how you will line up for forms and exercises."

I'm in the middle front, with Aldo to my right, Pedrón to my left, and Iván staggered behind us. Itzal is on the far left end, after Luca and Andrés.

Santiago says, "Now grip your sword hilts, and raise your blades to the sky."

We do as asked, raising our wooden weapons. My rib screams in protest.

"Hold them there."

I'm glad I picked a small sword.

Santiago paces before us. "You're holding light practice blades. Children's toys made of pine. Nothing at all like real steel swords. Yet some of you are already struggling. Your shoulders burn. Your wrists tremble. No, don't drop them; keep them raised high."

He weaves through our staggered line, and I watch as he inspects each of us in turn. When he gets to Itzal, he reaches up and adjusts his grip on the hilt, moving the boy's thumb so it wraps toward his fingers.

RAE·CARSON

Santiago steps back to observe us all. His gaze lingers on me. My bruised rib is making each breath a torture, but I refuse to let my blade waver.

"I've never trained a girl before," he says.

"You'll find it uncannily similar to training any other person," I tell him, and now I wish I hadn't spoken, because my words have revealed my ragged breath. Pain makes black spots flit in my vision. Maybe my rib is broken after all.

His eyes narrow. "Are you injured?" he asks.

"Yes."

"Maybe you should rest. Leave the training to the boys."

"No!"

"Are you sure?"

"Yes!"

He smiles. "Good."

Master Santiago lifts his own sword, whips it around as though it's as light as a feather.

Addressing us all, he says, "Most of you are not fit to learn sword work. Don't worry; I will make you fit. For the next few weeks, you will practice forms, and forms only. You will strengthen your shoulders, your arms, even your fingers. You'll perfect your grip. You'll learn to find and keep your center of balance, no matter where your sword is or how you're holding it. Now, follow my lead."

He turns his back to us, dips into a deep right lunge, and extends his sword out, parallel to the ground. "Assume this position!" he yells.

We mimic him, some with more success than others. I

recognize the form; it's called Eastern Wind, and Hector taught it to me long ago. Pain rips my side, but my thigh muscles find the motion easy and natural.

"Now move as I move," the swordmaster says. He slowly, gently transitions through a series of forms—arcs his sword around in Path of the Sun, whips it diagonally downward in Slit the Rope, thrusts it high in Salute the Sky, then brings it down—elbow out, heels together, blade at his nose—in Bulwark. His movements are graceful and efficient, more like that of a dancer than a weapons master.

He turns back around. "How did that feel?" he says.

Beside me, Pedrón is breathing hard. Aldo isn't even breaking a sweat. My rib throbs, and my bruised nose and eye socket are somehow making the sunshine seem like daggers of light in my face. But the forms are familiar to my muscles and so, so much easier than sparring. If we do this for the next two weeks, my injuries might have a chance to heal.

"Again!" Santiago booms. "This time, I will watch."

We move through the forms again—Eastern Wind, Path of the Sun, Slit the Rope, Salute the Sky, Bulwark.

"That was horrific," the swordmaster says. "An assault to my eyes. If you *must* have a reference, watch these two"—with the point of his sword, he indicates Aldo and me—"whose forms are merely dreadful. Now do it again."

My shoulders itch with the sure knowledge that I'm being closely watched as we move through the forms another time.

"What *was* that?" the swordmaster says, striding toward

RAE·CARSON

Pedrón. He waves his amputated arm under the boy's nose. "It's called Salute the Sky, not Pummel the Sky in the Face like a Clumsy Sack. Now do it again."

We do it again. And again. And over and over until my shoulder burns and my thighs ache. Sweat dribbles down my forehead and stings my eyes. A sunburn heats the back of my neck.

Then, the swordmaster orders us to switch hands and start all over again.

"Hardly fair," Pedrón whispers. "Being one-handed himself."

I glare up at him. Injuries like the swordmaster's are common, especially after the war.

As though he overheard the boy, Santiago says, "I know what you are thinking, yes, I do. But if you are injured in the line of duty, for instance"—he waves his arm stump in the air—"by taking a poisoned Invierno arrow to the elbow, your duty does not end. You must still protect our beloved empress, yes? So you will learn to use either hand with skill and confidence, as I once did."

The muscles in my sides are beginning to protest and the sunburn on my neck is fire by the time Santiago calls a halt. "Stop, stop, I can take no more of this misery," he says. "It is clear you are nowhere near ready to learn fighting skills. You will master these forms before I teach you even the simplest block. I expect it will take a month or more. Of course I'll be delighted if you surprise me and master them all sooner, but . . ." He sighs dramatically. "I never bet on such improbable odds."

With that, he releases us back into the care of Sergeant

DeLuca, who thanks him with a deferential nod. Swordmaster Santiago strides from the arena without looking back.

"After the midday meal," says the sergeant to us, "those of you who earned free time may do as you please until the dinner bell. Everyone else will remain in the mess to be assigned some afternoon chores."

Several boys groan.

"You are dismissed," the sergeant says.

Everything about this feels wrong to me—an outsider brought in for training, the classic forms detached from their practical application. But it could just be tiredness and injury whispering to me. We return our wooden swords to the rack and flee the hot arena for the cool barracks.

Today's lunch is an oat mash mixed with shredded coconut and drizzled with honey. It's not exactly a coconut scone, but I'm grateful for it anyway. I find a seat beside Iván.

"To Bolivar's quarters after this?" I whisper, settling on the bench.

He nods, spooning mash into his mouth.

"How'd you like those forms?" I ask, to make conversation.

"Fine. I've done them before, though I was taught a slightly different variation of Slit the Rope."

"Same here. Hector does a more sideways motion. I like the diagonal version just fine, though."

"I've never done *just* forms before," Iván says. "They were always accompanied by actual swordwork."

"It's a little odd," I agree.

A moment later, we are joined by Aldo, then Itzal, then Pedrón and the army recruits.

"You seemed to handle those forms all right," Pedrón says.

I ignore him, taking another bite of oat mash.

"That swordmaster is a hypocrite," Pedrón carries on. "Asking us to learn everything with both hands. I bet he's not even very good."

Pedrón is an ignorant fool. "And I bet he could thrash all you army boys at once, even with only one hand," I say.

"It's in your best interests to become adept with either hand," Iván says. "That way, if you get injured, you can still keep your job."

Pedrón shrugs. "Maybe."

"Go on," says Luca, nudging Pedrón with his elbow. "Ask her."

"Ask me what?" I say, dread filling my gut. I'm fully expecting another question about *parts*—or worse.

Pedrón puts his elbows on the table and leans forward. "See, my boys and me, we spent some time in the army barracks before transferring here. So we've done some sword training. We *are* ready to learn more."

"Master Santiago says we're not," Aldo says.

"That's my point. He won't teach us until we learn those stupid forms. So, will you do it, Red?"

"Do what?"

"Teach us the forms. You and Aldo, I mean. If we practice a little every night, maybe we can get to the fighting stuff faster."

I blink. He's asking for my *help*.

"She's not going to do it," says Andrés. "I told you she wouldn't. She wants us to get cut."

"Of course I'll do it," I say.

"You will?" Pedrón says, a surprised grin forming.

"I can't speak for Aldo, but I'm happy to help anyone who wants it."

"I'm happy to help too," Aldo says.

Pedrón suddenly appears suspicious. "You're not . . . I mean, you don't think that will give us an advantage? We might get picked over you."

I shrug. "The best thing that could happen is that we *all* become such strong candidates that they can't bring themselves to cut *any* of us."

Silence greets me. Then, "Is that even possible?" Pedrón says.

"Why not? They do such a good job of pitting recruits against each other in competition that they've probably never bothered to find out."

Pedrón takes a few bites, chews thoughtfully. "So, can we get started after lunch then?"

"No, sorry," I say pointing to my eye, which is surely bright plum by now. "I got walloped last night, remember? Another night of sleep will set me to rights. So anyone who wants to practice the forms can meet up in the arena tomorrow night during laundry time."

"I'll be there," Pedrón says.

"And me," says Itzal.

"Me too," says Aldo.

Iván remains silent.

"We'll spread the word," says Luca.

We get busy eating, but after a moment, Itzal asks, "Aldo, where did *you* learn the forms? You looked very at ease out there."

Pedrón snorts. "For once."

Aldo says, "Mamá hired a tutor for me."

"I thought you said you were raised on a ship," I say.

"I was."

"Who's your mother?" Pedrón asks.

"No one you've heard of. A merchant."

"A rich merchant, to be able to afford a tutor for classical swordsmanship," Itzal points out.

"She's done well for herself," Aldo says, his voice colored with pride.

"And your father?" Iván asks.

Aldo shrugs. "He wasn't around." He says it offhand, in the most casual tone, but his face is suddenly as blank as I've ever seen it. "He sent money for a while."

"Then he stopped?" Itzal says.

"Then he died."

"Oh."

I give Aldo a sympathetic look. It obviously pains him to talk about his father.

After an awkward silence, Pedrón blurts, "I wish *my* papá had sent money at *any* time in my life! But he was a poor fisherman, always drunk, not a coin to his name."

"Then how did you get into the Guard?" Itzal asks. "Sponsorships cost money."

I say, "The Royal Guard isn't just for rich people anymore."

"Red's right," Pedrón says. "I came in second place at the annual strongman contest. That got me a position with the army recruits. I did well enough there to transfer to the Guard."

"Still," Itzal says, "*most* people who join the Guard are rich. Sons of rich merchants, second and third sons of condes."

"Do you ever talk about anything besides money?" Iván asks.

Itzal considers this. "No," he says. "Just money. My father was a moneylender. I grew up thinking about it, talking about it, wanting more of it. Until the Guard opportunity came up, the thing I wanted most in the world was to become grotesquely rich."

"And now?" Iván prompts.

"I still wouldn't mind becoming grotesquely rich." Everyone snickers, and the attention seems to make Itzal uncomfortable. "What about you, Iván?" he says, to deflect. "What do you want most in the world?"

Iván's eyes narrow, and I imagine his possible answers: *I want my countship to regain its reputation. I want to prove myself to everyone. I want my father to stay far, far away. None of your business.*

He says, "I want to make it through all four years of training and become a Guardsman so everyone will stop questioning my loyalty."

"That's fair," Itzal says. "What about you, Pedrón?"

Pedrón grins. "I want to marry the most beautiful woman in the world and have ten children with her." His grin fades as

RAE·CARSON

he amends, "Well, I'm not sure I want to *have* ten children with her so much as I want to *make* ten children with her."

The other army recruits laugh and clap him on the back like he's just said the cleverest thing in the world.

"Is that all *you* think about?" Itzal challenges.

Pedrón ponders. "No. I'm a deeply layered and complicated person. In addition to getting with beautiful girls, I often think about sword fighting. Oh! And food. I think about food a lot."

I roll my eyes at him.

"What about you, Red?" Pedrón asks. "What do you want most in the world?" He waggles his eyebrows as though hinting at something scandalous.

I open my mouth to tell the truth, like I always do, but the words stick in my throat. It's not that I want to lie; it's that the truth is too precious and heartrending. So I say the second thing that comes to mind. "I want a girlfriend."

Pedrón slams the table with his palm in a gesture of victory. "I told you all she liked girls! That's why she won't visit my bunk."

"No, I just mean I want a friend who's a girl. Someone my age. A few of the girls in the palace have been nice to me, but no one . . . It's hard to be my friend, I guess." The half-Invierno girl with a magic mark in her hair and slave tattoos on her feet isn't exactly in high demand, even if she is a favorite of the empress.

"Well," Pedrón says, "now you have Aldo."

Aldo slams his spoon on the table and is halfway out of his seat, but he stops when I say, loudly, "Pedrón, if you insult someone one more time by calling them a girl, I will gut you."

Everyone looks eagerly to Pedrón for his response. He surprises me by looking sheepish. "I guess now that we have a girl in the Guard, it's not really a good idea."

"It was never a good idea."

"Whatever you say, Red."

"And you." I turn my fury on Aldo. "Stop acting like you've taken a sword to the chest every time someone calls you a girl. It's not an insult. Girls are not cockroaches or rats or horse dung. We are *people*, and it's perfectly *fine* to be one of us, so *stop*."

Aldo blinks up at me, his brown eyes huge.

Pedrón says to me, "You're kind of adorable when you're angry."

I have to leave, and I have to do it right this second or what I did to Sancho is going to seem like a cheek slap. I stand, sweeping up my bowl. "I'm going to take a nap," I say, turning my back on all of them.

"That's not a bad idea," I hear Iván say, and the bench scrapes as several others rise from the table.

Somehow Iván and I have to meet and sneak away from everyone else to investigate Bolivar's quarters. I'm sorting through possibilities as I dump my bowl with the rest of the dirty dishes, and I'm almost out the door when someone tugs on my sleeve. "Red."

It's Aldo, looking like a kicked puppy. "You were right," he says. "I'll stop being an ass every time someone compares me to a girl."

I stare down at him. Is he expecting a pat on the head? A biscuit? Simply for not being an ass?

He says, "Are you mad at me?"

"Yes."

"I said I was sorry!"

"How nice."

He frowns. "I'll prove it to you."

I decide to throw this sad puppy a bone. "I know you will, Aldo. Thank you."

He brightens. "Have a good nap!" he says, and heads for the latrine.

I watch him go, feeling strange, like maybe I've given something up, yielded too much. Aldo is the only person in this place who seems to want to be my friend, and I'm not sure if conceding to him chips away at myself or gives me strength.

"Red."

I jump, startled but not badly. It's Iván this time.

"You still have that key?" he says under his breath.

"I do."

"Then let's go. Quick, before someone sees."

Together we hurry down the hallway in the opposite direction, into the depths of the Royal Guard barracks.

The officers' quarters lie just below the ground floor. I know of a secret passage that would take us directly to the monarch's wing from here, but Rosario would have to give me an imperial edict before I'd reveal it to Iván.

"It smells a lot better here," Iván says.

"Some of the officers' rooms back up against the palace wall and have actual windows," I tell him. "They're high and small, of course, too small for anyone to use them for access."

"I'll never take fresh air for granted again."

Fresh air isn't the only difference between the officers' quarters and the recruit barracks. A plush rug runs the length of the corridor, a woven pattern displaying the de Riqueza seal, trimmed in Royal Guard crimson. Oil lamps light the passage instead of torches. All the door have locks.

By some miracle, Iván and I have this hallway to ourselves. But probably not for long.

"Which room is Bolivar's?" Iván whispers.

"I'm not sure. I've only been to this wing a few times, but I think I can remember the general vicinity of his room . . . I hope."

"Then how will we—"

"We try the key in all the locks. When the key works, it's Bolivar's room, right?"

"That's a terrible idea."

"The worst."

We reach a doorway I think might be the captain's, and I pull the key from my pocket.

"What if this is the wrong room, and someone is in there?" Iván says.

"If that happens, say we're running an errand for Fernando, but we accidentally got the wrong room. Except *you* have to be the one to say it. I'm a terrible liar."

I place the key in the keyhole.

"You think Fernando will back us up?"

"Yes." If this isn't Bolivar's room, it might be Sergeant DeLuca's. Or the quartermaster's. I take a deep breath and try turning the key, but it sticks, and the door does not open. I freeze, listening for sounds on the other side.

Calmly, Iván says, "Try the next one."

We creep down the hall to the neighboring door. This time, the key turns with a soft click.

Iván shoves me inside. He pulls the door shut behind us and locks it so no one can follow.

We're in a small but comfortable room containing a four-poster bed, a wide hearth with an oaken slab mantel, a small mahogany desk with a stool, and several shelves for clothing and personal items. Everything speaks to a tidy mind that prefers comfort and practicality to ostentation.

A single high window lets in air and light, but perhaps not enough light to investigate. I consider lighting the candles on the mantel and desk, but everything is preserved and still, with a layer of dust across the desk and a bit of ash drifted across the floor from the fireplace. Maybe it wouldn't be wise to leave evidence that someone was here recently.

Without a word, Iván starts sorting through the shelves, careful to examine everything while also returning it folded or arranged exactly as he found it. I follow his example and start sifting through the desk drawer.

"Tell me again what we're looking for?" Iván says.

"Honestly, I'm not sure," I say, pushing aside a neat pile of parchment and an inkwell. "Anything. Maybe we'll know it when we see it."

"Or smell it," Iván points out. "Remember, sweet dream supposedly has a spicy scent."

There's nothing of interest in the drawer. I shut it and move to the fireplace. "He thought he might have been poisoned through his tea, right?" I say. A kettle hangs from a swinging iron arm. I lift the top and peer inside, sniffing. Do I imagine that it smells faintly of cinnamon?

"I think our captain may have a taste for sweets," Iván says.

"What do you mean?"

"Look. Do they smell odd to you?"

He thrusts a glass dish toward me. It's filled with small, doughy balls that have been rolled in sugar and grated coconut. I give them an obliging sniff and immediately recoil.

"They've gone sour," I say. "Tamarind candies."

"But there's a lingering spicy smell, yes?"

Reluctantly, I give them another sniff. "You're right. It's faint. The teakettle smells like that too."

"The scent has faded. It's been almost a week."

I stare up at Iván, thinking hard, and it strikes me all of a sudden how very tall he is. I say, "You think Bolivar was poisoned both ways?"

"Makes sense," he says. "Too much would be noticeable, yes? But if the poison is spread out, delivered in smaller doses through multiple foods . . ."

"Then you end up ingesting a lot without even realizing it."

"Exactly." Every time Iván gets to thinking hard, a little crease appears at the corner of his right eye. He returns the dish of rotting candy to the shelf. Then his gaze snaps to mine. He says, "Red."

RAE·CARSON

I raise an eyebrow at him.

"This could happen to *any* of us."

"Why do you say . . . oh. Because the poison is too diluted to taste. We might not even know we were taking it."

"And because the tea and the candy had to come from different sources, right? Whoever is doing this must have their hands in everything. Like supply routes. Or maybe they have total kitchen access."

I sit on Bolivar's writing stool to give my sore rib a break. "Not necessarily. Maybe there's a merchant in the city who sells both tea and tamarind candy in their market stall. Maybe that's where Bolivar got it. We can make some inquiries."

"But if not . . ."

"If not, then you're right. Bolivar probably got both the tea and the candy right here in the barracks."

Iván starts to pace, and it's almost comical the way his long legs force him to turn so often. I'm content to watch him because for some reason his pacing makes the warmth of home fill my chest. Then I realize why: Elisa paces like this, back and forth, staring at the floor, whenever she's mulling a tricky problem.

I miss her. And tiny Ximena. And especially Hector.

Iván comes to a sudden halt, and he spins around to face me. "Where does tamarind come from?"

"Down south. The jungles of Selvarica."

"And duerma leaf tea?"

"East beyond the great sands. It grows in the desert foothills, in shady spots. It's one of Basajuan's biggest exports."

He blinks. "You knew all that off the top of your head."

"I had royal tutors for eight years," I point out.

"All right, Red of the royal education, tell me what all this means."

"I'm not sure what you're getting at."

"If tamarind and duerma leaf tea come from two of the most distant corners of our empire . . ."

"Oh. You're saying there's no way they were poisoned at the source."

"Exactly. They were poisoned after they arrived here in Brisadulce."

I consider this. "I'm not sure that tells us anything we didn't already suspect."

"It tells us that we need to find out where—"

A key rattles in the lock.

I throw myself to the floor and slide under the bed. Iván follows my lead, making a loud *clunk* that I'm certain can be heard all the way to the Wallows.

The door creaks open. Boot steps approach.

There's barely enough room under this bed; I must turn my head sideways to keep it from brushing the slats. My breath fogs the wood plank floor. My injured rib is a dagger in my side.

Iván is taut in the space beside me, his shoulder mashed against mine. His knees poke my thighs; they are slightly bent to prevent his feet from sticking out from under the bed.

The stool scrapes the floor as it's whisked aside. The writing-desk drawer slides open. Someone rustles through the pile of parchment, rummages through quills and ink. The boots move toward the shelves.

I hardly dare breathe as I stare at the boots. They're made of hard leather and tanned a rich brown-red; standard issue Royal Guard. Who could it be? Someone with very large feet and a slight inward pronation. Maybe it's Bolivar himself, recovered and returned home. But no, items from the shelf are being tossed onto the bed. The flap of a cloak suddenly drapes over the side and drags on the floor, obscuring my view of the boots.

Whoever it is searches for something, just like Iván and I did, except without any care for Bolivar's things.

He moves toward the fireplace. Metal squeals against stone as he grabs the poker and prods at the ash pile within. Then comes a loud, frustrated sigh, followed by a long pause.

The boot steps come near the bed.

The cloak disappears, then suddenly becomes a pile on the floor in the corner. A weight plunks down on the mattress, pressing the wooden slat against my ear, smashing my cheek into the floor. I'm staring at two worn boot heels, afraid to move the tiniest bit lest I scrape all the skin from my cheek.

He sits on the bed a long time. Surely he can hear my heartbeat? Iván is as still and silent as death beside me. If my head hurts this badly, Iván's skull must be near to breaking.

At last the bed creaks as the man stands, and I barely hold my gasp in check as I'm overwhelmed with space and air and room to breathe.

He lingers a long moment, turning in place as if to survey

the room one last time. Then he steps out the door and closes it behind him. The key rattles, locking us in.

We listen as his boot steps fade down the corridor outside. Finally Iván scooches out from under the bed, and I follow, brushing off my pants, which picked up some ash and dust from the floor.

"Well," Iván says in a low voice. "That was terrifying."

Standing up straight gives my rib a nasty pinch. "Do you think he knew we were there?"

"I hope not." Iván frowns. "Were you hurt? You're wincing."

"I'm fine. Just need some rest. It seemed like he was looking for something." I glance around. The room is disheveled now, the clothing on the shelves upended, the desk drawer half open, more ash spilling from the fireplace.

"Who was it, do you think?"

"Someone who was issued Royal Guard boots."

"That doesn't narrow it down much," Iván says.

"And someone with a key to Bolivar's quarters," I add.

"That, on the other hand, narrows it down quite a bit more. The quartermaster might have keys to everyone's rooms."

I nod. "Lord-Commander Dante too, but he's away with Elisa right now. Cleaning staff would have access to all these rooms, right? Though I doubt servants wear those boots."

Iván's face turns grave. "Sergeant DeLuca," he says. "The sergeant was left in charge of the barracks. Maybe that means getting a master key."

"DeLuca is already our most obvious suspect," I say. "He had the most to gain from Bolivar's disappearance."

"Exactly. That's how he got placed in charge."

We stare at each other a moment. Iván's face has an intensity about it that I don't dislike.

"This is not proof," I point out.

"No. We need something more."

"Whoever it was had big feet, worn boots, and a slight inward pronation. We should keep an eye out."

Iván's brows lift. "Good observations. Hopefully no one will notice us staring at everyone's feet."

"So what do we do next? Maybe get a message to Rosario and tell him . . . uh, Iván?"

"Red?"

My gaze has moved beyond him, to the shelves and their disarrayed contents. "Where is that dish full of tamarind candies? Didn't you put it right back there?" I point.

Iván whirls. He swiftly clears the shelves of remaining items—a pair of socks, a rolled-up belt, an extra shirt—and tosses them onto the bed.

He says, "It's not here. He must have taken it."

"Getting rid of evidence?"

"Yes, probably. No, wait, let's not jump to a conclusion. Maybe he was just ridding the room of molding candy."

I make a sweeping gesture, indicating the whole chamber. "It's not like whoever it was showed any care for this place."

"True." Iván's lips press together as though in grim thought. Then he says, "I know your rib hurts more than you admit, so let's go back to the bunk room so you can rest. While you do that, I'll find the stable hand and get a message to Rosario."

"I . . . thank you." I must admit, this task of sussing out an assassin would be a lot harder if I had to do it alone. "What will you tell him?"

"The prince needs to know the poison isn't being delivered only through duerma leaf tea—he needs to be testing *all* his food. And I want to ask him about Swordmaster Santiago. Find out what he thinks of the man."

"That's too much for one secret note." I reach into Bolivar's desk and grab quill, inkwell, and parchment. I dip the nib, but my first scratch produces nothing. I lick it and try again and finally get a good flow of ink. "We must keep words to a minimum, in case the note is intercepted." I start scribbling.

"Was that part of your royal education too?"

"Yes."

I blow on the ink to help it dry and show Iván what I've written:

Made small progress on our assignment. When can we meet?—IR

"IR," he says. "Iván and Red?" When I nod, he adds, "I'll get this to the stable hand messenger."

"And the next time we're given free time, I say we track down Valentino and see what he can tell us."

"Agreed. Let's go."

We reach the bunk room without incident. Two of the Basajuan boys are taking the opportunity to rest in their cots. Aldo is back in Traitors' Corner, cross-legged on his top bunk. He is staring at his ring—one of his precious three items—but puts it away when the door bangs shut. He looks up and grins to see me, but his grin falters a little when he notes Iván at my side.

"Where've you been?" he asks, his gaze shifting between us. "I thought you were going to take a nap."

"I am. Had something to take care of first. *Girl* stuff."

"Oh." Aldo's gaze drops back to the cards arrayed on his bed, as though he's trying not to appear hurt.

Iván says, "I have an errand to run, but I'll be back soon. The Ciénega del Sur boys are gone now, but I'd rather take precautions. So, with your permission, Red, I'd like to keep watch while you sleep."

I blink up at him. It's on my lips to tell him I don't need watching over, but what comes out of my mouth is: "Actually, that's a good idea. Thank you."

"I'll be back as soon as I can." And with that, he leaves the bunk room to deliver our note.

"You and Iván seem to be getting friendly," Aldo says cautiously.

I shrug. "Just like you and me, I guess. You know how it is. We denizens of Traitors' Corner have to stick together."

"Sure."

Careful of my wounded rib, I lie on my cot and stretch out. A wave of cramping hits my gut, so sudden and fierce that I gasp.

"Red?" Aldo's head peers down at me over the edge of his bunk. "You all right?"

I'm curled up in a fetal position now, my hand to my pelvis.

My lower back feels as though it's being squeezed in a carpenter's vise.

"Oh," Aldo says. "Your monthly courses."

"Yes," I breathe through the pain. "How did you know?"

"Mamá has a difficult time of it. Sometimes her pains are so bad she can't leave the bed for two days. I used to help her a lot."

"My pains aren't *that* bad. I should be fine after a nap."

"Is there anything I can do?"

"Let me sleep."

His face falls. "Sorry. I'll leave you alone."

"No, wait. Aldo?"

"Yes, Red?" he says eagerly.

"I need rags. I thought about taking some from the laundry, but—" Another wave of cramps takes my breath away.

Aldo jumps from the bed. "I'll handle it. Just sleep."

"Really? I mean . . . thank you."

I reach into the drawer for my Godstone, then I tuck my back against the wall and pull my ink-stained blanket over my shoulders, making my own tiny cave. Distantly, metal clashes on metal—the second years must be practicing in the arena—and I find the sound oddly soothing.

I never nap; I can barely sleep at night, much less during the day. My cramps are ferocious. I was attacked last night in this very bed. But the soldier sickness knows no reason, and somehow, I feel my muscles relaxing. My bones are heavy; my heart beats with perfect, normal steadiness.

I cradle the Godstone to my chest, close my eyes, and sink into my mattress.

RAE·CARSON

✧ ✧ ✧

The brass bell clangs, and I spring from the bed before I'm even half awake. It takes a moment for my mind to catch up to my surroundings: The scent of slightly burned porridge indicates that dinner is ready in the mess. Several recruits returned while I slept, and they hurry to re-don their boots. Aldo is back on the top bunk. Iván is here too, as he promised.

At my questioning look, Iván gives his head a slight shake, and my heart sinks. Does that mean he wasn't able to deliver our message?

"Later," he mouths, eyeing Aldo.

Iván and everyone else heads toward the mess, and I move to pursue, feeling a little queasy. What went wrong? Are we cut off from communicating with Rosario?

Aldo puts a hand on my shoulder. "Wait, Red."

He allows time for the other recruits to trickle away, then he reaches under his mattress and pulls out several long rags and a wad of straw. "The quartermaster didn't have much to spare except this ticking for mattress repairs," Aldo says. "For now, you can wrap it in these strips. Throw the ticking away when you're done, but wash and reuse the strips. Mamá always preferred wool to straw. I'll try to get wool for you later on."

"Aldo," I breathe as he hands the pile over to me. "This is perfect. Thank you so . . . wait, this fabric . . ." It's tightly woven, dyed rich blue with black trim. I've seen gowns at Deliverance Day balls that were made of lesser material. "Is this your blanket? The one your mamá made for you?"

Aldo shrugs. "Like I said, the quartermaster didn't have a

lot to spare. Tight fabrics like this offer the best protection, right?"

I gape at him. This was one of his three items. And he destroyed it for me.

He says. "It's no big deal, for a friend."

"Well, it's a big deal to me."

His grin could light up the whole world. "I'm going to get some dinner. I'll save you a seat."

Quickly, I wrap some straw in the strips he provided and shove the wad into place. It's not the most comfortable solution I've used, but it'll do. I pile the remaining supplies in my drawer, covering up the Godstone, the baby rattle, and the empty dye pot.

We're served overcooked, oversalted porridge for dinner, and I eat every bite. Aldo and I are surrounded by recruits at the table, providing no opportunity for me to discreetly speak with Iván.

After dinner, Guardsman Bruno ushers us all into the arena and commands us to sit. Aldo is practically a burr in my side, and it seems awkward and pointed when I move away from him in order to be close to Iván.

Evening light paints the walls purple pink, and a cool breeze brings the scents of sweet lantana and sharp desert sage. I'm delighted when, instead of conducting physical exercises, Bruno subjects us to a long lecture on the care and maintenance of various weapon types.

I already know all this, so instead of listening, I watch him walk. Back and forth across the sand he goes, hands clasped behind his back, droning on and on. His boots are certainly worn enough to be the ones I spied while stuck beneath Bolivar's bed, but I'm not sure his feet are big enough. Sometimes it seems as though he's walking on the inner arch of his feet, but maybe it's just the uneven sand.

A quick glance over at Iván reveals that he's watching Bruno's feet too.

Finally Bruno's pacing takes him down the line of recruits, far enough away that I dare lean toward Iván and whisper, "What happened?"

"The messenger has disappeared," Iván whispers back.

"What?"

"He hasn't shown up for work in two days. I asked around. The stable master considers his absence to be dereliction of duty, and the stable hand is no longer employed by the Royal Guard."

Questions compete for dominance in my head, but Bruno is heading this way again and I'm forced to fall silent. His voice becomes louder, his words eager and fast, as he catalogs various types of polishing oils and whetstones, noting which ones perform best with which metal alloys.

As soon as Bruno is once again out of whispering earshot, I say, "Do you think someone realized he was a spy?"

"I have no idea. I just know he's not there anymore, and he's not welcome to return."

"Then we're cut off from Rosario."

"We have to figure out another way to contact him."

"It might be days . . ." I'm forced to hush as Bruno passes by.

After a moment, I try again. "It might be days until we have a chance to leave the barracks."

Ivan says, "Then we'll have to sneak out in the middle of the night again."

"No! Every time we do that, we put this whole mission at risk. What if we're caught?"

"It would be worse if Rosario was poisoned because we couldn't warn him."

"The prince is smart. Well informed. He'll know one of his assets is missing, and he'll reestablish contact with us soon. We're no use to him if we get cut."

I look up at Iván to find him frowning deeply. He says, "I disagree. I think—"

"Would you two stop whispering?" says Itzal from his place nearby.

"Go flirt on your own time," says one of the Basajuan recruits.

Bruno is suddenly looming over us all. "Is there a problem here?" he asks.

"No, sir!" Itzal says. "We were just wondering whether Basajuan steel is superior to that of Ciénega del Sur." I send Itzal a grateful look.

Bruno seems pleased by the question. "Both regions produce excellent steel, but the mines of Ciénega del Sur occasionally yield iron ore with too many impurities—something having to do with being near the ocean, I'd wager—which makes it difficult to refine. You can't go wrong with either, but given a choice, I'd take Basajuan."

"Thank you for clarifying, sir," Itzal says.

My mind is a muddle as Bruno finishes his lecture. Iván is right; we need to make sure Rosario knows to be looking for poison in all his food. But I'm right too; if we get caught sneaking around, it could mean instant dismissal from the Guard, which puts our whole assignment at risk. *It's the single most important thing right now*, Rosario said. *Don't get cut.* It was his primary order, the one we must obey above all others.

The spy network is competent and loyal. Rosario will learn of the missing stable hand soon enough, if he hasn't learned of it already. He'll find a way to reestablish contact with us. Iván and I will have to wait and trust our prince.

Guardsman Bruno dismisses us, indicating that we have just enough time to wash up and do laundry before the lamps are snuffed. After everyone is finished, I take a private moment to change out my straw and wash my rags.

It's a good thing I got a nap, because I lie awake a long time, listening to my fellow recruits snore, hoping I've made the right decision to wait and do nothing.

15

Then

THE girl's memories resurfaced in another dark cellar, as she was gathering turnips and dried meat for a stew. The meat was billed as lamb, but she knew it was really dog. And dogmeat stew wasn't too bad, all things considered. The meat bits were a little dry and chewy, but the flavor was fine.

Not that Mula would eat any of it today. The stew was for guests, not slaves. And that was too bad, because Mula had worked through most of the night to clean ash from the bread oven. She was very tired, and very, very hungry.

She worked at an inn now, for a man named Orlín who had bought her from the monster woman over a year ago. Life was better at the inn, even though she worked sunup to sundown. Even though shiny callus rings on her wrists and ankles indicated that she was tied to her cot each night after her work was done.

A good worker, the monster woman had said, as she and Orlín agreed upon a price. *But sometimes she tries to escape.*

Mula knew these things had happened the same way she

knew that the desert became hot in summer—it was assured, incontrovertible knowledge, even though she couldn't place herself there. She didn't actually remember.

When her basket was full, she began pulling herself up the steep stone steps leading to the kitchen. Halfway up, she stopped, gasping.

Because the back of her neck was prickling, and her limbs hummed with energy. It was almost like a song in her blood.

Familiarity grated at her. She had felt this before; she was sure of it. But when? Sometime while she lived with the monster woman? No, it was before that. Mula thought hard.

Flames engulfing a wooden shelf. Smoke making her lungs scream. A sizzling puddle of blood . . .

The basket fell from her hand. Turnips and meat strips spilled, toppled down the stairs, plunked onto the damp dirt floor. She hardly noticed.

Her hands shook, and she couldn't get enough breath. A sorcerer was somewhere in the village. Maybe even here at the inn. And he had a sparkle stone with him.

She had to hide. If an animagus saw her, he would surely burn her. He would know, just by looking at her guilty face, that she had stabbed another animagus once, stabbed him so bad he died.

Mula half ran, half tripped down the steps, ignoring the spilled, dirt-encrusted turnips. She ducked beneath the stair and lodged herself in a tiny space behind a mead barrel. The girl pulled her knees to her chest and held herself in the tightest, smallest ball.

Her skin continued prickling. Her blood continued to sing, making her limbs twitch and her pulse race. She squeezed her eyes tight but couldn't keep the tears from leaking out.

Hours later, the cook found her.

"There you are, you lazy half-breed," he said. He had yellow teeth and foul breath, and arms so skinny a girl would never guess he spent so much time tasting food. He scooted the heavy mead barrel aside and grabbed her by the ear. "Out with you. Gather up the turnips and the meat, scrape off the dirt as best you can, and get yourself up to the kitchen. Do it quickly and I won't tell Orlín you've been shirking."

But the sorcerer was still nearby. She could feel it in her bones. "I . . . can't."

He backhanded her across the face, so hard she crashed against the mead barrel, bruising her spine. She struggled to her feet, put a hand to her stinging cheek.

"Disobey one more time and there'll be a whipping in it for you, and nothing but bread crust for a week. Now get to work."

She bent to retrieve the fallen basket. She grabbed a turnip, wiped it against her sleeve to clean it, and placed it inside.

Satisfied, the cook began to climb the stairs.

"Wait," Mula called out in a trembling voice.

The cook turned.

"Is the bad man up there? Inside the inn?"

"Huh? Oh, you mean the White Hair?"

Mula nodded.

"He's finishing up a bowl of stew. Might stay the night."

The girl froze. Her ears were ringing now. Her face and neck filled with heat.

"Is that why you're shirking? You're afraid of the White Hair?"

"Y . . . yes."

The cook gave her a sympathetic look. "Can't say I blame you. I try to steer clear myself. Better get used to it, though, because war is coming, mark my words. And when the White Hairs march their Invierno army west to Joya d'Arena, we're going to see plenty of them."

Mula gaped at him. An army of monsters led by sorcerers. Something like that could burn down the whole world.

"You're lucky, mule girl," the cook said. "To live here in one of the free villages. We may not have nice roads or fancy castles, and sure, trying to farm these mountain slopes is like coaxing grain from a stone, but at least we're left alone. Better to break your back bettering your own life than to die in some fancy lord's war, hear?"

"Hear," Mula whispered. She wasn't lucky, no matter what the cook said. She had never been lucky.

"Anyway, get back to work. Come up quick with a full basket, and I'll find work for you in the kitchen, out of sight."

"Thank you!"

The cook disappeared up the stairs.

Mula worked fast, gathering turnips and meat strips, wiping them with her clothes, picking out the most stubborn flecks of dirt. Her basket was only half-full when the cook returned. His eyes were wide, and he was breathless.

"Come now," he said gesturing.

The girl couldn't move. Fear rooted her to the earthen floor.

"Now!" he practically shouted. "Leave the basket. Orlín wants you right away."

Mula forced her feet to tackle the stair steps, though it seemed like an invisible force was dragging her back into the cool safety of the cellar. *No, no, not up there.*

"Hurry!" the cook said, and when she was near enough, he grabbed her arm and yanked her the remaining distance.

He held her fast before the hearth, which was bright with long flames. "You're filthy," he said, and he smacked at the dust on her pants and wiped a spot on her cheek with a rag. "That will have to do. Now come."

His grip on her upper arm was iron strong as he dragged her from the kitchen, into the busy common room.

Dining tables were scattered throughout, some long with benches, a few round with stools, all stained from ale and spilled stew. A stone fireplace climbed the wall at one end, with fresh-cut pinewood stacked beside it. Rushes covered the floor, sour with ale and urine, and a single window looked out over the snowy rooftops of the village.

At the long table nearest the hearth sat a group of monster people, and even their thick woolen coats and fur stoles could not disguise their tall slenderness. Their hair was a riot of color—one had black hair, just like a Joyan, another the bright copper of a late sunset, still another had hair of polished chestnut.

The sorcerer sat at the head of the table, slightly apart from the others. His eyes were the deep blue of a high mountain lake. His cloud-white hair was pulled back into a long braid that wrapped around his neck and dangled down his chest. Mula didn't see an amulet there. Maybe it was hidden beneath his fur stole.

Then she saw the staff leaning against the table beside him, made of twisted oak. Embedded in the very top, gripped by sculpted wooden claws, was a bright blue sparkle stone. The girl loosed a single, sharp sob.

Orlín the innkeeper approached, wiping his hands on a rag. His nearly bald head shimmered with sweat. "There you are," he said. "Come with me."

The cook returned to the kitchen as the girl was yanked forward by the innkeeper, toward the sorcerer.

"No," Mula said. "Please! I don't want to go over there. I'll do anything. I'll clean chamber pots for a month. I'll boil all the sheets. I'll—"

"You'll do whatever I tell you, Mula. I own you."

They stopped before the table, and the sorcerer looked up from his bowl of stew. The tingling inside her was ferocious now. She hadn't eaten all day, but maybe she would vomit anyway.

"Thisss is the bleeder?" asked the sorcerer. She hated the way monster people hissed when they spoke the Lengua Plebeya. Like snakes hiding in the grass.

"Yes, my lord," said Orlín.

"She is a mula."

"Yes, my lord."

"Have you bled her before?"

Orlín hesitated. He settled on the truth. "No, my lord. This will be her first time."

The sorcerer grunted. "I guess we'll sssee. Come here, mule girl."

The innkeeper shoved her forward. The sorcerer reached out with his long spider fingers and touched her cheek. His fingers were warm and dry. Bile rose in her throat.

"Sso young," he murmured. He turned to one of his companions. "Needle," he commanded.

His copper-haired companion rummaged around in a pack for a moment, retrieved a leather fold with ties, and set it on the table. He untied it, flipped it open, revealing sewing supplies—needles, thread, a thimble. He pulled out the very largest needle and handed it to the sorcerer, who took it gingerly.

"Give me your finger," the sorcerer said.

If Mula refused an important customer, Orlín would beat her, then make her sleep outside, tied up in the sheep pen. Still, she was slow about lifting her hand.

"Mula, do as the lord commands, hear?" Orlín growled.

"Hear." She lifted her forefinger toward the sorcerer. It hovered in the air before him, fragile and trembling like a baby bird.

The sorcerer grabbed her hand, shoved the needle deep into the flesh of her fingertip. Pain zinged all through her hand and up her arm.

"Now we shall see," the sorcerer said. He angled her hand downward. Blood welled around the needle, which throbbed so badly it felt like her heart had departed her chest and taken up residence in her fingertip.

A single fat drop of crimson slipped down the needle and fell to the floor.

The sorcerer grabbed his staff, closed his eyes, muttered something. The gem in the staff's tip began to glow. The tingling in Mula's limbs became a maelstrom of sensation, like a thousand black flies were buzzing around inside her, trying to break free of her skin.

"Oh," the sorcerer breathed. "Oh, yes. God lovesss your blood, mule girl. Yours in particular."

His lake-water blue eyes flew open. "Look how my animalapis responds! It is ssso eager to do magic." To Orlín he said, "Where did you acquire this creature?"

"From the glassblower. She has a booth in the market, if you want to speak to her."

The sorcerer yanked the needle out of the girl's fingertip. Two large drops of blood followed, splatting onto the stone floor. The sparkle stone flared brighter. Mula was about to see magic done, for true.

But then the sorcerer set the staff against the table and leaned back in his chair. The light in the gemstone faded. Mula remembered how to breathe.

He said, "I'll pay you five coppers for a jar of her blood."

"Seven coppers," said the innkeeper.

The sorcerer frowned. "Six."

"Done."

The sorcerer's red-haired companion removed a glass jar

from his rucksack. It wasn't a large jar; it would barely hold a mugful of ale. "I don't have a hollow needle or a bleeding tube," the sorcerer said to no one in particular. "So we'll have to cut her thumb."

"No . . ." Mula tried to step back, but Orlín was in the way. He grabbed her shoulders and held her fast as the copper-haired man pulled out a dagger and a whetstone. He spat on the stone, rubbed the blade across it. *Swick, swick.* Then he reached forward and slipped the blade's edge across the fleshiest part of Mula's thumb.

Blood welled immediately, and the pain came a split second after. The redheaded man held the jar beneath her thumb and caught the blood as it fell; he had cut deep enough to provide a steady *drip-plop*. The blood slipped down the inside edge of the glass, coating it in thick scarlet. The room began to spin.

"Let her sit," the sorcerer said. "She's going to faint."

They guided her to the bench and she sank onto it gratefully.

"It helps to look away from the blood," the copper-haired man said. "Think about something else."

Mula didn't want to cry in front of all these awful men, but she hardly knew up from down and her life's blood was leaving her body and she had just seen a sparkle stone go bright with power. Her lips trembled; her eyes filled with liquid.

So she thought hard about the other side of the world. What it must be like. She imagined a desert, the sun shining on snowless mountains of orange sand. Warmth blanketing her skin. More sky than a single person ever knew existed. If she got to see the great desert for true, she'd know she was lucky after all.

RAE·CARSON

"There we go," said the copper-haired man. "That wasn't so bad, yes?" He wrapped her finger in a strip of cloth and tied it off. "Put pressure on that for a few minutes until the bleeding stops," he said.

She cradled her thumb in her hand. It throbbed so badly she could hardly stand it.

The red-haired man stoppered the jar and slipped it into the rucksack. The sorcerer counted out six coppers and handed them to Orlín. "You've got a good bleeder here. My countrymen will be coming through soon, and they'll pay you decent money to bleed her so long as you keep her well fed and watered."

Orlín was staring at the coppers in his palm. "I will. Thank you, my lord." To Mula he said, "Go back to the kitchen. Cook needs your help."

The girl was weak and dizzy, distant from her own body, and her thumb throbbed like a drum. But she wanted more than anything to get away from the sorcerer, so she turned and fled, careening into tables and chairs as she went.

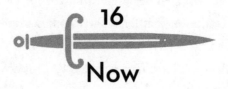

16
Now

ALL day long, at every meal, at every pause in training, Iván insists that we must do something to reach Rosario immediately. He seems certain that I can conjure some secret passageway to take us directly to the prince.

And I keep telling him that we must have patience. Rosario is no fool. He will reach out to us again.

I hope I am right.

By the end of the day, Iván is so frustrated with me, I'm worried that he's going to sneak off to try something stupid on his own.

But as I head to the arena for informal practice, I'm hoping that if he does do something stupid, he will succeed.

Pedrón and the other former army recruits are already in the sand when Aldo and I arrive. We are soon joined by Itzal. Finally Iván comes, looking sullen and worried. I'm both relieved and disappointed.

"Is this everybody?" he asks.

"It appears so," I reply. Only seven recruits in total, but a low number of students makes for a manageable class. The moon is high, and torches are sconced at the entrance to the barracks, casting pools of orange onto the sand. It's plenty enough light to see by. "Let's get started."

Aldo grabs a wooden sword from the rack, and we all follow his lead.

"So, what do we do?" Pedrón says.

Aldo shrugs. I say, "Er . . . I guess we should line up the way Master Santiago showed us?"

Everyone shifts around in the sand until we're in two staggered lines of four and three.

"Now what?" Pedrón says.

Everyone is looking to me for guidance. Little do they know that I've never taught anyone anything before. But I had Hector, and Hector was a great teacher. "Go through the forms Santiago has shown us so far. Keep an eye on Aldo for a reference if you forget what comes next. I'm going to watch you all and see if I can figure out what's made Santiago so surly."

Aldo says, "Let's start with Bulwark!" and he clicks his heels together, striking the pose. Everyone follows his lead, and I weave among them, eyeing their stance, posture, and grip.

"Now Eastern Wind," Aldo says.

The recruits go through them all, holding each pose for several seconds, which allows me to evaluate. Pedrón is all power and no finesse, as though he's trying to pummel the sky to death. Itzal has little body awareness and tends to move in the wrong direction. Iván is near perfect, and I have no idea why he decided to join us.

Once everyone settles back into Bulwark, Pedrón says, "So, can you fix us?"

"Not a chance," I blurt, before I realize this is one of those moments when a lot of good people would choose to tell a harmless lie.

Pedrón tosses his wooden sword in the sand. "What a waste of time."

"Wait!" I say, before Pedrón can storm out of the arena.

He gives me a skeptical look, but he stays.

"You might be able to fix *yourself*, though. Give it a try, all right? I'll tell you what I see, and you decide if I'm worth listening to. One thing's for sure; you can't get worse."

His fellow army recruits snicker, and somehow this softens him instead of making him angry. He bends to retrieve the sword.

I size him up—his brick of a jaw and his rampart shoulders and his bulky, clumsy hands—wondering how to help him. What would Hector say?

"Pedrón, it might help you to think of your sword as a beautiful girl."

He grins. Lifts the blade to his mouth. Kisses it, long and slow.

"Er . . . that's not what I meant."

Iván mutters, "That poor sword."

I try again. "What I *meant* was, you need to treat the sword like an equal partner, not a tool. You need to dance with it, not bludgeon the air to death. Pretend like the two of you belong together."

RAE·CARSON

Pedrón holds the sword out and stares at it. "I don't understand."

"Let me see you Salute the Sky."

He raises his sword in a furious thrust. It lists slightly leftward.

"Now do it again, but slower. Make sure your sword makes a perfect line upward; don't let it tilt to either side."

He tries again, slower this time.

"That's better. Don't fight so hard with it. The stabbing and slashing will come later. For now, think of your sword as a dance partner, not a weapon."

"I hate dancing," he says, lowering his sword to his side.

"And your enemy loves you for it. It makes you easy to kill."

Which is exactly what Hector said to me once, in different circumstances. "Let me show you something. Go back into Salute the Sky."

When he lifts his sword, I swing mine at him, slowly but aimed squarely at his chest.

Immediately, he swings his blade down to block me. The sharp smack of wood rattles my arm.

Pedrón is as startled as I am. "Are you all right?"

"I'm fine! But you see why we learn Salute the Sky. You can defend yourself from that position, but you can also attack. If your form is wrong, your block will miss. If your form is wrong, your attack will fail. And then what?"

He hesitates. "And then I'm dead?"

The other recruits have stopped practicing to watch us. "And then you're dead." I turn to the others. "Every one of these forms is designed to save your life. Every one of them is a way to take advantage of an opening or to counter an attack."

"She's right," Aldo says. "I'll show you. Iván, Eastern Wind."

Iván takes up the proper stance and Aldo swings his sword at him, shouting, "Path of the Sun."

Iván moves into the form and deflects Aldo's blade, so Aldo counters with an attack from the opposite direction. "Slit the Rope!"

Iván's blade slashes downward and sweeps Aldo's sword aside. Aldo is already shouting, "Salute the Sky!"

Iván raises his blade and stands wide-eyed, panting. "What next?"

Aldo whirls his sword around, grinning like a boy receiving his Deliverance Day gift. He *loves* this. He may be smaller than the other boys, but he has an ease and grace with his body that will make him a dangerous opponent in any fight. "What's next is you're ready to attack if I leave myself open, or ready to block my next attack, just like Red said."

I nod to Aldo.

Pedrón says. "Fine, I get it. But once we master these forms, we can get to the fun stuff, right?"

"Pedrón, these forms *are* the fun stuff."

We go through them again, slowly. We'll have to speed them up, but for now, slowing down the movements allows the recruits time to think and adjust and feel their limbs in motion.

Aldo moves them into Slit the Rope, and Itzal swipes the wrong direction, whacking Pedrón's thigh with his wooden blade.

RAE·CARSON

"Ow! What did you do that for?"

"Sorry!"

I step over to Itzal, grab his wrists, and gently guide him through the correct motion. "Like this," I say. "Concentrate on how that feels."

The next time they move through Slit the Rope, Itzal starts to go in the wrong direction but catches himself and corrects. The third time, he gets it right.

At the end of the third pass, everyone looks at me expectantly. They suck air. Andrés is shimmery with sweat.

"You're already getting better," I assure them. "Take a moment to catch your breath, then we'll go through it again."

Pedrón smiles in triumph.

But a strange frisson slips down my spine, like the ghost of an unwelcome thought. I watch the boys as they breathe deep and stretch their shoulders. These exercises shouldn't be difficult. I don't understand why such simple, controlled movements would be so foreign to them.

Itzal gives his sword an experimental swipe, clumsy but almost serviceable.

The earth tilts.

I was in a cellar with a butcher's knife, swiping diagonally at the hanging carcass of a skinned dog. Blood and offal soaked the dirt floor. Footsteps on the floor above set my carcass to swinging. Still, my swipes were perfect, creating flawless cuts of meat for Orlín the innkeeper to sell to customers as beef.

My swipes were perfect because they had to be. Orlín stood beside me, skinning another animal. If I jostled him in the slightest, I'd earn myself a blow to the ear.

I was good at this, making myself as tiny as possible. Aware of every part of my body at all times. I could feel his skin beside mine, a heat aura of dangerous space I would never, ever touch.

"Red?"

I slip back into myself. The warmth of the sand is a grounding force, and I say, without even a hitch, "Let's go again."

I watch them as they follow Aldo's lead through the forms. What must it be like to bludgeon your way through life without a care for anyone else? Some of them can't do the forms well, not because they're inherently clumsy, but because they've never had to control themselves or consider their blundering bodies in relation to someone else's space. The world has always made space for them.

Maybe this is a thing that only happens to boys.

My body is vibrating now, like it always does after a vivid memory. I step into formation and do the next few sets along with the others, needing a release for the sudden surge in my limbs.

A Guardsman enters the arena to snuff the torches. He gives us a long glance before returning to the barracks.

"Training is over for tonight," I say. "Let's get back to the bunk room."

In the morning, a slight burn permeates the muscles in my shoulders and forearms. It reminds me of training with Hector

RAE·CARSON

and Rosario. It's the burn of accomplishment.

Pedrón, Itzal, and the army recruits seem to struggle, though, wincing as they pull on their boots, rising gingerly to their feet.

Aldo and I exchange an amused glance.

In the training arena, Master Santiago puts us through the forms again, this time adding Sandstorm and Sleeping Heron.

After a few sequences, he steps back, appraising us all. One side of his mustache is not as thoroughly waxed as the other; it drifts below his lip with the slight breeze.

"I did not expect to say this," he says, frowning, "but some of you made minor improvements compared to your previous tragedy." He walks over to Pedrón and sticks his mustache in the boy's face. "Did you consume a magical elixir? Sell your soul to an evil trickster?"

"Er . . . no, sir?"

"And you," Master Santiago says, moving toward Itzal. "You have suddenly learned the difference between left and right, like a serviceable three-year-old. How is this possible?"

"Got a good night's sleep, sir."

"I'm so glad to hear it. Since you slept so well, please step forward and lead your fellow recruits in the next set."

Itzal opens his mouth to protest, closes it, glances at me in panic. I give him what I hope is a subtle nod of encouragement.

He forces himself to walk to the front of our formation. Itzal says, "Begin with Bulwark!" and demonstrates with his sword.

Without a reference, Itzal is once again terrible. Gradually, with some correction from Master Santiago and some snickering from the direction of the Basajuan boys, we make it through the entire sequence.

My shoulders tremble with effort by the time Santiago releases us, saying, "Even with your trifling improvements, all my hope dies when I look upon you." He shakes his head in seeming despair and waves a hand at us. "Go. Be gone from my sorrowful eyes, for I can endure no more."

That night, the Arturos and their fellow Basajuaños join our class.

During the next few days, we fall into a routine. Mornings begin abruptly with a clanging brass bell, followed by an uninspiring breakfast, then sword forms with Master Santiago. After lunch comes fitness training, occasionally accompanied by the second years, which consists of log lifting or sprints through the sand or—on one glorious day—drawing various sizes and types of bows. We don't get to shoot anything, but the repetition of pulling back on the string and bending the wood is enough to make my neck and shoulders burn and puts a large blister on my finger.

After dinner, we either do an assigned chore, like cleaning the mess or unloading supplies, or we run the walls.

We're allotted free time before lights-outs for laundry and ablutions, and that's when we head back out to the arena and practice our forms by torchlight. We're getting better. Master Santiago becomes less scathing in his criticism. By the end of the week, he announces that *some* of us are no longer an assault to his eyes, and if *everyone* made such marked

RAE·CARSON

improvement, he might consider beginning our sword training soon. That night, every single first-year recruit joins our class.

I can't be sure whether or not the Godstone is helping, but my rib heals fast.

I'm not the strongest or fittest of the recruits, but I do myself proud, especially with running and forms. I love the burn in my muscles that attests to hard work. I love pushing my body to find out exactly what it can do. I love feeling exhausted and accomplished each night when I finally fall into my bunk.

But as each day passes, and we don't hear from Rosario, Iván grows quieter and darker until his face displays a constant glower. He hardly speaks to me, won't even meet my gaze as we ready for bed in Traitors' Corner. I fear he's right to be angry, that I made a terrible decision and this agonized waiting might get our prince killed.

Finally, one evening as we're eating shredded chicken in a sauce of tomatoes and chilies all scooped up with corn tortillas, Sergeant DeLuca storms into the mess. He wears bright ceremonial armor and a sweeping red cloak.

The room goes silent.

"Two of you have a special assignment tonight," he says.

Several of us exchange puzzled glances.

"The Invierno ambassador is holding a soiree for His Imperial Highness Prince Rosario and several friends. Because it's an intimate affair attended by trusted confidants, our threat assessment is low. Still, the Royal Guard will be in attendance, as always. Since these types of events pose little risk to the imperial family, they are considered training opportunities for Guard recruits."

Itzal leans forward on the bench. Pedrón sits up straighter than a flowering agave. Suddenly, everyone seems to beg the sergeant with their eyes, saying, "Please pick me."

"When assigned to one of these events, you are to observe as silently and unobtrusively as possible. Be alert for any threat. Report anything suspicious to the nearest attending Guard, but do not act. You are to comport yourself with quiet decorum at all times. Do not speak unless spoken to. Do not eat or drink anything set before you. When you return to the barracks, you will say nothing of what you have heard or seen to your fellow recruits, as a test of your ability to be loyal and discreet. Am I clear?"

We respond with a pattering of "Yes, sirs."

Sergeant DeLuca says, "Recruit Iván, Recruit Red, please stand so I can inspect your uniforms."

We do as ordered. All eyes are on us, and the sergeant looks us over carefully, from the tops of our heads all the way down to the toes of our boots. He frowns, peering closer at me. "Recruit Red, I think you have something in your hair."

Suddenly everyone in the room is staring at me. Of its own accord, my hand moves toward my head. Maybe food got stuck somewhere. Maybe someone put something in my hair as a joke. Maybe—

"Oh." The sergeant recoils from me as if startled. "Never mind. It's nothing."

Someone behind me chuckles. I let my hand fall to my side.

I keep my face neutral, my breathing calm, even as sure knowledge sets in: My magic mark is showing again. And I have no dye left for covering it up.

To everyone else, the sergeant says, "Don't worry about being overlooked this time. Plenty of opportunities await, and everyone will get a chance." He gestures for Iván and me to follow him.

As I'm leaving the table, I quickly lean down and say to Aldo, "Can you run the class tonight?"

"Of course. Have fun." His words are cheery, but his gaze is not. The others stare at us with a mix of wonder and envy. Some of them are ogling my hairline.

Iván and I follow Sergeant DeLuca from the barracks. My face feels hot, and I resist the urge to finger my hair for the telltale change in texture that indicates it's growing out a soft, magical white.

I force myself to put it from my mind. We have more important things to worry about tonight, because this is what we've been waiting for. Rosario must have specifically requested Iván and me.

Somehow, tonight, Rosario plans to speak with us. Maybe he'll get us alone. Or perhaps he'll disguise his message in casual table conversation. Iván and I will have to be careful—and alert to the prince's cues.

The sergeant leads us through a series of corridors, past the royal apartments where I used to live, beyond the monastery, into the oldest wing of the palace. This giant, sprawling edifice is more like a small city. It was quilted together over centuries, and it shows in the way the walls change from sandstone to river rock and finally to crumbling adobe that the palace architects despair of ever keeping properly patched. Naturally, this area of deferred maintenance is where the Invierno ambassador and his staff are housed.

Tall double doors of polished mahogany mark the entrance to the ambassador's quarters. An Invierno seneschal stands before them, tall, pale, and lithe, with shining hair the golden brown of sun-kissed wheat fields.

"Good evening, Sergeant," the Invierno says, in the lilt of one who was raised to speak the Lengua Classica.

Iván tenses in the space beside me. I can almost feel heat coming off his skin.

"These two recruits will be attending the prince tonight," DeLuca says. "I'm to deliver them to the Guard in charge."

"This way." The Invierno opens the door and ushers us through a short hallway into a long dining room with a curved ceiling. Blue glass lanterns line the ceiling, casting the walls of the dining room in something like moonlight. A porcelain vase in an alcove overflows with blooms, filling the room with the scents of freesia and lantana.

Several attendees are already seated at the table. Conde Astón of Ciénega del Sur glares at me in challenge as we enter. There can be no doubt that Valentino's father blames me for his son's failure.

Beside him is Lady Jada, the mayor's wife. As usual, her black hair is tied back too severely into a neat chignon. Jada can be frivolous and unintelligent, but Elisa has always valued her kindness and loyalty. Her smile toward me is warm, which I am happy to return.

Next to her is Lady Carilla, who waves at me while grinning brilliantly, and it takes all my discipline to resist waving merrily back. She is short and plump with a small overbite and a weak chin, not nearly as beautiful as the young women Rosario usually spends time with.

Whenever the girls at court have been kind to me, it has always been a ploy to get close to Rosario. I've wondered if Carilla is different, if given time and slightly different circumstances, we might have been friends.

At the head of the table is the prince himself, and he stands as we enter. He is wan, with dark circles under his eyes, but his carriage is strong, his stride confident, as he approaches.

"Thank you, Sergeant," the prince says. "I'll escort these recruits to Guardsman Fernando and make sure they are returned safely to the barracks later tonight."

DeLuca opens his mouth as if to protest, but changes his mind. "Yes, Highness, of course."

"This way." Rosario guides us through a door at the end of the dining room and into a small kitchen. The area is warm with a busy hearth and milling with servants. My mouth waters at the scent of fresh turnip slices soaking in salted lime juice.

Rosario shoves us into a corner behind a shelf of dry storage. "Listen," he whispers once we're out of sight. "Fernando is not here tonight."

"Why not?" I whisper back.

"Then who is your acting Guard?" Iván says.

"You are."

"What?" I whisper, too loudly. "Is Fernando—"

"I'll explain later. For now, just listen. You will stand behind me at either shoulder. Do not let anyone except Carilla approach close enough to touch me. Serving staff have been instructed to hand items to you, and you will in turn place them before me. Understood?"

My heart is ferocious in my chest. Something terrible has happened. "Of course," I say.

"Whatever you need," Iván says.

"I don't expect any trouble tonight," Rosario says. "Truly. But we're going to take precautions anyway. Ambassador Songbird is aware of the situation. He'll be sitting on my right, across from Carilla, as an additional buffer. After dinner, we'll talk more. Now, let's go."

"Rosario, wait." I grab his arm. "Do you have a taster tonight?"

He glares down at my hand grasping his arm, as though I've affronted him. Rosario's mind-set is that of an imperial prince tonight, not a friend. I release him.

"Sorry," I say hurriedly. "But it's important. If you don't have one, I should taste all your food first."

His gaze softens. "I have a taster, thank you. But Red?" He puts his hand on my shoulder and looks me straight in the eye. "Please never, ever taste my food. I can't risk you. You either, Iván. Now let's go."

I stare at Rosario's back as we return with him to the dining room. Does he realize that by becoming Royal Guards, Iván and I will put ourselves at risk every single day?

The ambassador, named Spring Floods Spark Songbird Joy, arrived during the short time we were in the kitchen. He stands tall behind his designated chair, for Invierno custom forbids him from taking a seat until the guest of honor has done so first.

He wears a soft robe of light blue trimmed in dark gray embroidery, and his long copper-gold hair is tied back in a queue. He greets Rosario formally, but when he sees me, he frowns. "Lady Red Sparkle Stone," he says. "I did not expect to see you here."

"I'm just Recruit Red now, Excellency. But it's a pleasure to see you, as always."

Ambassador Songbird cracks a rare smile. "You talk like a true Joyan, saying what you do not mean."

I smile back gamely. "I *am* a true Joyan, Your Excellency."

"And yet these Joyans refused to accept you as their princess." The dining room is suddenly silent, save for the muffled sound of food sizzling in the kitchen. He adds, "I was really hoping they would. It would have been best for everyone."

"That has no bearing on whether or not I'm a true Joyan," I say. "I'm sure you can agree that most Joyans are not princesses."

Someone clears their throat; I've been talking out of place. I'm only a Guard recruit, with specific instructions to comport myself with quiet decorum.

So I take up a posture behind Rosario's right shoulder—head

up, hands behind my back, heels together—which I hope will put an end to anyone addressing me.

"And Lord Iván," the ambassador says. "Excuse me, *Recruit* Iván. I'm equally surprised to see you."

Unlike me, Iván is wise and does not answer, simply stares straight ahead from his post behind the prince's left shoulder.

Though everyone is acquainted, the ambassador formally introduces each attendee and then recites a blessing from the *Scriptura Sancta*. Servants sweep in with the first course—a tomato bisque soup with lobster and scallions. Just as Rosario instructed, a steaming bowl is handed to me first, and even though I know he has a taster in the kitchen, I give the soup a good long sniff for the scent of sweet dream before setting it before him.

"I hear Altapalma had a marvelous tomato harvest this year," Lady Jada observes, spooning up her soup.

"That countship suffered terribly after the Year Without a Summer," Conde Astón observes. "It's good to see the land recovering *finally*."

Rosario's shoulders tense because he knows where this will eventually go; Astón never wastes an opportunity to criticize Elisa.

"The Year Without a Summer was just as devastating to Invierno crops," Ambassador Songbird points out.

"I heard that many Inviernos blame our empress for all that mess," Lady Jada says. "Can you imagine? Women get blamed for everything, I suppose. Even the weather!"

"Well, actually," Conde Astón says, "there's been some

discussion among scholars at the university that our empress was indeed to blame, that she changed the weather patterns that year with her overuse of magic. It altered the delicate spiritual balance of the world."

I barely refrain from rolling my eyes.

"Can magic really change the weather?" Carilla asks in her soft, unassuming voice.

"How should I know?" Conde Astón says. "It's *magic*." He waves his spoon in the air, making a vaguely magical gesture.

"It's physics," Rosario says darkly. "And it was definitely caused by my stepmother. But things would have been worse if she had *not* acted the way she did."

Astón gives the prince an indulgent smile. "I know you've been told that. It's certainly a politically prudent viewpoint."

"It's the truth."

"The prince is correct," says Ambassador Songbird. "Though I would clarify and say it was both magic and physics."

"How do you mean?" Lady Jada asks.

"The empress destroyed several mountains that year using magic, yes? This is historical record."

Others around the table nod.

"This destruction was in many ways irresponsible; it threw enough ash and dust into the air to lower temperatures everywhere during the next growing season." Rosario is about to protest, but the ambassador holds up a hand to dissuade him and adds, "But her actions saved the Invierno capital from the Eyes of God, massive twin volcanoes on the brink of major eruption. Had they been allowed to erupt, the effect would have been tenfold, plunging us into an age of ice."

I remember that year well, the first summer after I came to Brisadulce. It snowed in the desert, making swooping white hills of the sand dunes. It was all anyone talked about.

Astón raises one eyebrow. "So you say."

"So say all the experts at our own universities," Songbird clarifies.

Astón chuckles, giving no doubt as to what he thinks about Invierno "experts."

My heart beats too fast for the mere act of standing behind my prince, and my face is warm. If I were fully Invierno, my cheeks would be bright red by now. This is what it's like to be a Royal Guard. Hearing and seeing everything, doing and saying nothing. No matter how strongly you feel about an issue or event. Even if you were there to witness it.

"I imagine an age of ice would have had far-reaching consequences," Carilla says. "So many plants and animals could not have survived. They might have gone extinct, just like the great luminescing birds of ancient Invierne."

"Lady Carilla is correct," Rosario says. "It would have been catastrophic. My stepmother saved the world that year."

"Let's not get carried away!" Astón says. "It's fashionable to exaggerate the accomplishments of our monarchs, but that usually happens long after their deaths, as their reigns fade to myth and legend."

Rosario raises his chin and says, "As the only Joyan bearer of a Godstone, Elisa is a living legend, the kind who only comes along once every century."

"It's heartwarming to know you have such love and loyalty for her," Astón says.

I wish I could see Rosario's face during this long silence. I imagine him glowering, so I'm surprised when he says, lightly, "Ambassador Songbird, my compliments to your cook. This soup is delicious."

The ambassador inclines his head. "It's an Invierno recipe, modified with Joyan spices. I thought it an appropriate starter for this occasion."

Servants bring a main dish of red snapper on a bed of greens and lime-soaked radish slices, along with roasted peppers stuffed with cheese. My mouth waters. Nothing I've eaten in the last two weeks smells as delicious as this.

As everyone eats, the conversation moves to the increase in wood-based construction projects—which Ambassador Songbird is quick to point out is thanks to new trade pacts with Invierno loggers—and then to the precipitous price drop of Basajuan wool, which Lady Jada believes may affect wardrobe choices for the upcoming Deliverance Gala.

"Do you have a gown picked out for the gala already?" Carilla asks Lady Jada.

"I do!" Jada says. "My designer is piecing it together now. We found an incredible silk, dyed with azure berries. I saw it and simply had to have it."

The mere mention of azure berries used to make my stomach roil, but as the tattoos on my feet have faded, so has my aversion. I admit they produce an incredible shade of silk.

"I can't wait to see it," Carilla says.

"And you? Anything picked out yet?"

Carilla frowns daintily. "Not yet. To be honest, I'm not one for dressing up. I find all the petticoats and corsets and everything . . . just so uncomfortable and, frankly, intimidating."

"My dear, I could help you find something," Jada says. "It doesn't have to be a chore."

"Really? I mean, I'd like that."

"I've often wondered," Conde Astón says, "how women manage with so many distractions. The hair and wardrobe and . . . not to be too indelicate, but—other *womanly concerns*. It would be difficult to go through life so encumbered."

Carilla's softness is chased away by a hard edge, and her focus on Astón is suddenly razor-sharp. "And yet, somehow, we've always managed," she says. "Managed well, in fact."

"Oh, certainly," Conde Astón says. "I meant no disrespect. But you have to permit that having so many extraneous things to worry about is difficult. It's why women are unsuited to certain types of work. Very few women attend the university, for instance. Fewer still become master carpenters, or captain merchant ships . . ." He grins slightly. "Or become Royal Guards. And when they do, they often find the challenge too much to bear."

The dining room is silent for a long moment, save for the scrape of the ambassador's fork against his plate. He eats blithely, as though unaware that Astón has taken a shot at me. Rosario, on the other hand, stops eating, rests his fork beside his plate, takes a deep breath.

I make my face as bland as I can, even as I watch for any

telltale movement, listen for any sound of warning. I'd love the luxury of imagining in great detail and at great length how it would feel to punch the high conde in the face. Instead, I must be fully alert to any possible danger to my prince.

Lady Jada can't help glancing at me. Carilla's face is made of ice and fury. Rosario is rigid in the seat before me.

But it is the ambassador who finally breaks the silence.

He dabs his lips with his napkin, sets it on the table, and says, "Knowing what I do of Joyan culture and custom, I must conclude that your words are meant to insult the empress's most infamous Guard recruit, even though you don't mention Red by name."

Conde Astón appears affronted. "I was merely making a general statement about women and their—"

The ambassador laughs, and it's so startling and delightful that I almost forget to keep my face bland.

"I don't understand what's so funny," Astón says.

"*You* are, Your Grace," says Ambassador Songbird. "You get away with deceptive, sideways insults because you are powerful, not because you are clever. You should spend some time in my homeland. Our council of Deciregi can teach you the art of deceiving without lying, of subterfuge with true grace."

"So you're saying Inviernos are deceivers?"

"Some of us are," the ambassador says, unabashed. "Just like Joyans. We merely go about it differently."

Conde Astón opens his mouth to protest, but Lady Carilla speaks first. "Excellency, I must admit that I find your candor refreshing."

"If not very diplomatic," Conde Astón says.

"Where I come from," Songbird says, "diplomacy is about truth. Surely you can agree that only truth can lay the groundwork for trust."

In response, Conde Astón shoves a forkful of roasted pepper into his mouth.

Rosario says, "Ambassador Songbird was handpicked for this post by Prince Storm himself, and over the years he has become a good friend to the family. My stepmother values his forthright council greatly."

The conde swallows. Smiles. Somehow, Rosario has walked into a trap. "So the rumors are true," Astón says. "Our foreign ambassador is acting as adviser to the empress."

"That's not what I—"

"Such an arrangement borders on treason," the conde says.

Rosario sputters.

The ambassador comes to his rescue. "Your empress is well known for taking in multiple viewpoints before making major decisions," he says. "I can assure you that *my* influence is minor. Besides, she only consults me on matters pertaining to Joyan-Invierno relations."

"Yes," Rosario says, his voiced tinged with relief. "That's what I meant."

Conde Astón's lips are still curved into a slight smile as he takes a sip of wine.

Servants sweep in to clear dishes and replace them with custard bowls, garnished with mint and orange peel. One reaches as if to set a bowl before Rosario, but I move my body

RAE·CARSON

to intercept him. Glaring, I hold my hand out for the bowl. The servant relinquishes it to me, bows in apology, and flees back to the kitchen.

I give the custard a thorough sniff before setting it before my prince, who shoots me a quick look of gratitude.

Lady Jada says, "Lady Red, will you and your fellow recruits be attending the Deliverance Gala? With so much of the Royal Guard traveling in state, you would be welcome as added security."

"We've not yet been given instructions about the gala, my lady," I tell her, moving back into place behind Rosario.

"I'm sure the palace watch will be sufficient for the task," Conde Astón says.

"I hear they aren't nearly as well trained or well vetted as the Royal Guard," Lady Carilla says. "I'd take a Royal Guard *recruit* over a palace watch *officer*, to be honest. It was much the same in Amalur."

"Yes, I've heard that you fostered with Queen Alodia for many years," Lady Jada says.

"It was a lovely and formative time," Carilla says. "I learned so much. And the queen's personal guard is formidable, just like our empress's."

"I disagree in part," says the conde. "Guard recruits are indeed well trained and vetted, but they aren't issued steel swords until their third year. They can't be expected to protect the prince without real weapons."

"I've heard," Carilla says, drawing out her words with slow precision, "that occasionally a recruit comes along who *doesn't need a weapon*."

Jada gives her a startled glance.

The ambassador sips his wine.

The High Conde of Ciénega del Sur places his napkin across the bowl before him and rises from his chair. His face is as hard as a granite block and his voice is dangerously low when he says, "Forgive me; I'm afraid I must excuse myself early. My son, Valentino, was recently injured, you see, and I must tend to him." He inclines his head toward the ambassador. "Thank you for including me and for this wonderful repast." To Prince Rosario, he says, "Your Highness."

He doesn't bother to acknowledge the women as he steps away from the table and strides from the dining room.

I watch him as he walks away: his long legs just like Valentino's, his huge feet, and—I gasp—his slight inward pronation.

Iván shoots me a look, and I indicate the conde's feet with a nod of my head, but it's too late. Astón is gone.

"Well," Lady Jada says, "this custard is sublime."

My mind is racing. Is it possible? Was Astón the man who ransacked Captain Bolivar's bedroom while Iván and I hid under the bed? Why would the most powerful conde in the empire sneak into the Guard barracks? Surely he has lackeys willing to risk themselves on his behalf.

Whoever it was wore Guard-issue boots. How would the conde get access to those boots? Or a key to the bedroom? What was he doing there? Maybe he was looking for something on behalf of Valentino, who was also sickened by poison. Perhaps he was removing evidence.

Or maybe it wasn't him at all. There are probably half a

dozen men on the palace grounds right this moment who have huge feet and walk on their inner arches.

The conversation moves back to the Deliverance Gala as the others finish their custard. Rosario assures everyone that the gala will be well attended as always, even with the empress away. The ambassador indicates his pleasure that more Inviernos than ever have received invitations to this year's event. Lady Carilla and Lady Jada agree on a time and place to meet for a shopping trip. No one mentions the recently departed conde.

Servants clear the empty custard bowls, and everyone chats a little longer over a final glass of blush-colored wine—a popular Ventierra vintage, Rosario proudly points out, from Hector's home countship.

Finally the monastery bells ring the eleventh hour, and Rosario stands. Everyone else follows suit. "Some administrative tasks call for my attention," he says. "The company tonight was so delightful that I'm afraid I put off doing them much longer than I meant to. Thank you so much, Ambassador Songbird, for a lovely evening."

The prince kisses Carilla on the cheek, clasps Lady Jada's hand warmly, then turns to the ambassador and grasps his shoulder. "I appreciated your support tonight," Rosario says.

"Always." Songbird gives him a slight bow. "Do you need an escort?"

"Not this time." To us he says, "Red, Iván, with me, please." With that, the prince skirts the table and exits the dining room, me and Iván at his heels.

He leads us quickly from the ambassador's quarters, but instead of turning left to return to the barracks, we turn right, toward the monastery. I'm desperate to find out what went so wrong that two first-year recruits served as actual Guards tonight. "Rosario—" I begin, but he hushes me.

"Hold your thoughts," he orders.

Suddenly, every shadow holds a dagger, and every whisper of sound is a footstep. I hate that we travel alone with our prince, weaponless, untrained. I peer in each doorway, and I note that Iván does the same. When we reach a branching corridor, I step in front of Rosario, forcing him to pause, while Iván checks it. "It's clear," he says, and we move on.

Finally we enter the sanctuary, with its beamed ceiling and long wooden benches and smoky air that smells of sacrament roses. People huddle on the benches despite the late hour, for the sanctuary is always open to those needing a quiet place to pray.

I study everyone with suspicion as Rosario leads us past the benches, beyond the altar, and into the archival wing, where the empire's oldest manuscripts are carefully stored. The chamber is cool, dark, and dry. Shelves reach to the ceiling, crammed with scrolls and parchment sheaths and musty vellum, all looming over a long stone table for study. Light pools around a single oil lamp in the middle of the table.

Rosario closes and bars the door behind us. "We can speak freely here," he says, taking a seat at the table's head. "I've arranged with Father Nicandro to be undisturbed."

He's silent, staring off into the gloom, as Iván and I take

seats beside him. I'm not sure where to start, or even if I should. Rosario has been so different the last two times I saw him, nothing at all like the smiling, mischievous boy I grew up with.

Iván is the one to break the silence. "Your Highness," he says. "What happened? Why didn't you have a proper Guard tonight?"

Rosario's lips press tight as he looks down at the table. His impossibly long lashes rest against soft cheeks, and I'm reminded that no matter how hard he pretends confidence and poise, he's only fifteen years old.

His finger traces an invisible line along the gray surface. "Fernando was hurt," he says.

"What?" I say. "I mean, is he all right? What happened?" I've known Fernando since I first came to this city. He's a child-hood friend of Hector's. One of Elisa's most trusted Guards. A friend to frightened little girls.

"It was my fault," the prince says. "I sent him alone to the kitchens to fetch some coconut milk. He wasn't wearing steel, just hardened leather. I should have thought . . . I should have . . ."

"Rosario?" I prompt.

His shoulders slump. "Fernando was ambushed in the hall on his way back. Three men, all wearing masks. He drew his sword to fight them off, but all they did was cut him—once across his arm—then they disappeared down the hall. He didn't give chase; his duty was to return to me and make sure I was safe. We alerted the palace watch, who found nothing and no one." Rosario takes a deep breath and adds, "By morning, the edges of Fernando's wound had swollen and . . . puckered . . . and he was running a terrible fever."

"Poison?" Iván says.

Rosario nods. "Doctor Enzo says he's seen it before. Not sweet dream; something else. Fernando is in the Wallows right now, beside Captain Bolivar. Enzo isn't sure if . . . Fernando is very sick."

First Captain Bolivar, then Fernando. Both close to Rosario. Both charged with keeping him safe.

I say, "Someone is picking off your closest supporters one by one."

"That's what I'm afraid of," Rosario says. "Several people in my spy network have gone missing too."

"Like the stable hand," Iván says.

"Yes. People loyal to me who have been with us since I was a little boy."

Something about that tickles my thoughts, like a scent brought by the breeze and then whisked away before it can be identified.

Iván rubs his jaw. He has the hands of an archer, just like Fernando, with long, slender fingers tipped by calluses. "Let's think about this," Iván says. "If someone is picking off your supporters, who will they target next? Maybe Lady Carilla? Everyone knows you've been spending time together."

Rosario shakes his head. "I'm worried it will be Red."

Iván's gaze snaps to mine. "That night in the barracks. When the Ciénega del Sur boys attacked you. Do you think someone planned that?"

RAE·CARSON

"Maybe? They blamed me for what happened to Valentino. But . . ."

Rosario leans forward. "I heard you got the best of them, that you weren't seriously wounded."

"Yes, but I think they would have hurt me badly if Iván and I had let them."

"Make no mistake," Iván says. "They tried to kill you."

"I'm not sure that's—"

Rosario says, "Is it possible someone put them up to it? Encouraged them?"

"It's possible," I concede. "Though I can't imagine who."

"Perhaps it was Conde Astón himself," Iván says. "He's their liege lord, right? He *hates* you, Red. The way he talked about you during dinner made me want to . . ."

I peer closer at him, as if I can make him finish his thought with the force of my will, but he clamps his mouth shut and looks away.

"Speaking of the high conde," I say. "Rosario, do you know if Astón ever took to the sand?"

"He did. As a young man, he served two years as a recruit under my grandfather, King Nicalao. He was never a serious candidate. Like a lot of inheriting noble sons, he did it to make connections and acquire extra training."

"So those could have been his boots after all."

"Red, what are you talking about?" Iván says.

"The man who walked in on us while we were searching Bolivar's quarters. I think it might have been Astón."

Rosario frowns. "Tell me about this."

So we do. We tell him about finding the tamarind candies, about hiding under the bed while someone searched the room, about trying and failing to get a message to him through the stable hand.

"And you think the person who walked in and ransacked the room was Conde Astón?" Rosario says.

I shrug. "Whoever it was had huge feet, a slightly inward-facing stride, and really old, dingy, Guard-issue boots."

"We have looked and looked," Iván says. "No one currently serving in the Guard meets that description. Come to think of it, Sergeant DeLuca would strip the hide off anyone who showed up for duty wearing boots in such bad shape."

Rosario is suddenly crestfallen. He rubs at the imaginary line on the table with his thumb, over and over, until I worry he'll rub his skin off.

"Rosario?"

"I was terrible in there!" he blurts. "At dinner. He made me so mad, and I just . . . froze. I couldn't think of a thing to say, and now it turns out he might be my greatest enemy."

"You did well!" I protest. "Truly. The conde is the one who made a fool of himself."

"If you say so."

"Which you probably remember did not go unnoticed by the ambassador?"

I'm relieved to see a slight grin. "It's true that Songbird put him in his place. And Carilla."

"I liked him," Iván says. "The ambassador, I mean."

"You seem surprised," I say.

RAE·CARSON

Iván doesn't respond.

Rosario stares at one of the shelves. Perhaps he feels the weight of history all around us, neatly piled and painstakingly cataloged. The archive is dry and cool, perfect for preserving ancient knowledge. Still, the priests are in a constant race against time, scribing copies of precious documents before they can disintegrate or fade or mold into oblivion.

"Do you have anything else to report?" he says at last.

"Just that we have a new swordmaster," I tell him.

"Master Santiago," Iván adds. "Do you know of him?"

The prince's eyes narrow. "He was the dowager queen's personal guard for many years. I don't know him well, but he is not Royal Guard."

"So, in your judgment, he should not be trusted?" I ask.

"Definitely not. Like I said, I don't know him well, but I did know Grandmamá, and she hated Elisa."

"How could she?" I say. "They hardly spoke."

"Maybe hate is too strong a word. She disapproved of her. Elisa was too foreign, too fat, too young. Grandmamá always hoped Papá would remarry, but she had her sights set on several other women, many of whom she foisted on him at every opportunity. A few even became his mistresses." Rosario frowns. "I was such a stupid little boy. Every time he got a new mistress, I toddled after her, hoping she would become my mother. How pathetic is that?"

"You ended up getting the best mother of all," I point out.

Rosario's face softens. "True. And Hector has been more of a father to me than the king ever was."

"Yes, well, that's not saying much," Iván says. "The list of things that were a better father to you than King Alejandro is very long. Like the plague, which at least shows up once in a while."

I round on Iván, ready to lay into him, but I hear Rosario chuckle.

"And the list of things less traitorous than your father is equally long," Rosario says. "Like a mosquito, which will stab you in the back only once."

Both boys are grinning ear to ear now, and I realize I'm on the outside of an old joke.

Suddenly they're both looking at me expectantly. Like I'm supposed to contribute something.

I say, "At least you both know who your father is! The list of degenerates who could be my father is longer than both your lists."

"My little sister has a good point," Rosario says, and a lump lodges in my throat because it feels so normal for him to call me that.

"We can at least be certain he was an Invierno, right?" Iván says.

"A worthless Invierno snake, you mean, who left my mother pregnant and alone," I say.

Iván says, "If we had a flagon of wine right now, I'd raise a toast to surviving terrible fathers."

"Hear, hear," Rosario says.

"I'd drink to that," I say.

"Anyway, *I* think Red's father was an animagus," Rosario

RAE·CARSON

says. "Red can sense Godstones, even better than a priest. Did you know that, Iván?"

"I've heard a little about it."

"Her affinity is so strong that . . . Red, is that your magic mark showing?"

My hand flies to my hairline before I can stop it. "I . . ."

"I thought you took some dye with you as one of your three items."

"It was vandalized."

Rosario's eyes widen. "Oh . . . well, I'll get you some more. I'll have it delivered to the barracks within two—"

"I don't need more dye. I'll be fine." I blink rapidly for a moment, letting my own words echo in my head. *I don't need more dye.*

Before he can respond, the monastery bells ring the half hour, and I nearly jump out of my seat. We must be directly beneath the bell tower, for it to clang so loudly. How do the priests ever sleep?

Rosario gives me a look of sympathy. He says, "Back to business, yes? I received a message by pigeon yesterday. The empress's procession has passed the oasis and is heading into the Hinder Mountains. They should reach Amalur in less than two weeks. Elisa is in good health. She sends her best wishes for Bolivar's recovery. Also . . ." He pauses before adding: "Mena lost her first tooth."

My smile falters as soon as it comes. Rosario is not smiling either.

"This is all good news, right?" Iván says.

"Yes, good news," Rosario says dully.

I know how he feels. Neither of us is there to exclaim over Ximena's missing tooth. Neither of us will be there when Elisa's baby is born.

"You don't seem pleased," Iván observes.

"It's just . . . when certain people are gone," Rosario says, "it feels like part of your very self is gone. Like an arm. Or a heart."

Iván looks back and forth between us. "The very best thing we can do in their absence is figure out what's happening and keep you safe."

"Agreed," I say. "Rosario, now that Fernando is injured, do you have anyone else to protect you?"

He nods. "I have three personal bodyguards remaining."

Iván frowns. "That means you only have two, since they must sleep in shifts."

"Yes."

"It's not enough," Iván says.

"No."

"I can talk to my brother, see if he can spare some of his own personal guard."

"Juan-Carlos needs his personal guard as much as I do."

"No!" I say, a little too fiercely. "No one needs a guard more than you. You're being targeted, little brother. They're chipping away at your defenses, bit by bit. Making you vulnerable, as if preparing for something. If we don't shore up your guard, Iván and I should quit the recruits to be at your side."

"Just say the word, Highness," Iván says, "and we'll both be there."

Rosario is shaking his head. "Bigger things are coming, and I need you both in the Royal Guard," he says. "Do you understand? I'm ordering you to do everything you can to not get cut."

"But—" Iván starts to protest.

"I'll talk to Juan-Carlos," Rosario says. "That was a good idea. I'm sure he can spare a man or two."

Iván slumps a little in relief.

"So what's our next move?" I ask no one in particular. "We still need to talk to Valentino, I suppose. To find out if he took sweet dream."

"Yes, we'll make that a priority," Iván says.

"The stable hand is gone," I remind them. "So how do we communicate when one of us has something to report?"

"An assistant cook has informed for us on occasion," Rosario says. "He's been doing the job for only a few years, but the spymaster trusts him. I'll have him identify himself to you, so be ready."

"Only a few years?" I say.

"Yes, why?"

"You said the spies who disappeared are all people who have been doing the job a long time."

The prince turns thoughtful. Light from the oil lamp sheens against his black hair, making it appear coppery.

Iván says, "The spies who disappeared . . . exactly how long had they been working as spies?"

Rosario considers this a moment. "Everyone who disappeared had been working for us at least nine years."

I say, "I don't understand how well-established spies were compromised but newer ones were not. That makes no sense."

"Unless . . ." Iván begins, "the person behind this is not familiar with current operations."

Rosario sits straight up. "You're saying it's someone who *used* to be familiar with them. Someone who was part of the king's inner circle nine years ago, before Elisa came to power."

"I don't know. Maybe? If so, the only person I can think of is Iván's father."

Iván glares at me. "Impossible."

"Are you *sure* he's not making a play for the throne *again*?"

"I'm sure. Last I heard, he was rotting in an Invierno mine." Then, softly, he mutters, "Please let him be rotting in an Invierno mine."

Rosario is shaking his head. "It's not Conde Eduardo. We've kept a very close watch on him over the years. We know where he is and what he's doing at all times."

"Then who?" I ask.

"I'll give this some thought. In the meantime, I need to get you back to the barracks before anyone gets suspicious."

"No," Iván says. "We need to get *you* safely back to *your* quarters. We'll find the barracks on our own."

Rosario nods once and rises from the table.

Someone bangs on the door.

"Who goes there?" Rosario says.

"Nicandro."

Rosario lifts the bar and opens the door. A small, hunched man in gray robes and a walking cane hurries inside and shuts it behind him. His dear, familiar face is grave, and he leans heavily on the cane with both hands. I haven't seen him since he presided over my failed adoption ceremony.

"Father," Rosario says. "We were about to . . . What's wrong?"

"Your Highness," he says, his voice thin with age. "I received news from Doctor Enzo. Captain Bolivar is dead."

17
Now

ROSARIO plunks back down in his seat and hunches over, hands on his head, as though pressed down by a crushing weight. More than anything I want to go to him, put my arms around his shoulders. But maybe that would be more of a comfort to me than to him.

I whisper, "I'm so, so sorry, little brother."

"Any word on Fernando?" Iván asks the priest.

"No change to his condition," Nicandro says. He turns to me, peering close. "Lady Red, I do not sense your Godstone, the one Elisa gave to you."

"I left it in the Guard barracks," I tell him.

"You should carry it with you at all times, my girl. It's special. More powerful than most. Elisa acquired it on the hidden isle, in a place of power, and she gave it to you for a reason."

"Yes, Holiness," I say, though I have no way to carry it.

He waves a hand in the air. "Stop with that holiness nonsense. There has never been formality between us." He turns to Rosario. "Sweet boy, I know how much you loved Bolivar. I regret that we will be unable to honor him in death right away; I think it's best that everyone still believes him missing. But I promise you that his body will be tended to with dignity and respect, and when your family returns from their travels, we will bury him in state, as he deserves."

"Thank you," Rosario chokes out.

"Does he have a family?" Iván asks. "Does he leave behind a widow or children? If so, we should—"

"The Royal Guard was his family," the priest says. "Now, come, all of you. Four trusted acolytes have volunteered to help escort you. They are not fighters, but they'll make a fine living shield for our prince."

Father Nicandro gestures us up and out of the archive, where three young men and one young woman in black robes wait, backs straight, arms crossed and muffled by their voluminous sleeves. The acolytes, Iván, and I all surround the prince, like he's the center of a meat pie, and begin our trek out of the monastery.

"Wait!" Father Nicandro says, and our strange little procession pauses. "I almost forgot."

He hurries back into the archive and returns a moment later carrying a book with a metal clasp. "Red, this is for you," he says, plopping it into my arms.

I run my hand across the cover. It's hardened leather, stamped with the rose and crown of the de Vega royal crest.

"What is it?" I ask.

"A copy of the *Articles of the Empire*. There's something

inside you should see. Or rather, there's something *not* inside you should see."

"What do you mean?" Bound books are valuable and rare. This is a royal gift, no matter what it contains.

"Just read it. If your heart is ready, you will see."

I have no idea what he's talking about. "I . . . thank you."

To Rosario he says, "I light a candle every night and pray for your safety. Be well, dear boy."

The barracks are silent with sleep when Iván and I finally make it back. Or so it seems. I store my book in the bedside table and shuck my boots. When next I look up, I'm surrounded by recruits. Aldo's head hangs over the top bunk. Itzal plunks down beside me. Pedrón and the Arturos stare at me with expectation.

"So," Itzal says. "What was it like? Did you see the prince?"

"I bet there were beautiful girls in beautiful gowns," Pedrón says dreamily.

Iván says, "You know we can't tell you anything."

"Not even a hint?" Aldo says. "Where did you go? Was it a grand ballroom?"

"I can tell you one thing," I say.

Everyone leans forward into my space.

"It was boring," I say, and they wilt with disappointment. "You just stand there, not able to say anything or eat anything. But you can't let your mind wander to pass the time, because you're watching everyone and everything for any possible threat."

RAE·CARSON

"Red's right," Iván says. "It was boring."

"You're lying," Itzal says, peering into my face, though I'm not sure what he thinks he'll see in this gloom.

Pedrón says, "Moneybags here just wants to hear about all the fine things. He says the ambassador has a flower vase that's worth three times my father's annual wage."

I lie down and push Itzal off the bed with my foot. "You'll find out yourself. It will be your turn soon enough. Now let me sleep."

The next morning at breakfast, someone I don't recognize mans the cauldron, and we line up so he can ladle porridge into our bowls. He is short and slight with sharp features, barely older than the recruits. When I reach the head of the line, he says, so softly that only I can hear, "My name is Luz-Daniel. Please come to me if you need anything."

I refuse to make eye contact as I whisper my thanks. This is Rosario's spy, who can get a message to the prince should the need arise.

The morning training session brings more practice with sword forms. And the morning after that. Our nightly class continues, and everyone's technique improves greatly. Even boys like Itzal, who came to the Guard with no training and hardly knowing left from right, can now be counted on to keep a strong grip while flowing through the poses like water.

Autumn begins to cool the air, bringing the occasional light rain, and we all become restless and frustrated with our routine: sword forms all morning, followed by fitness training in the afternoon, and more sword forms before bed. The boys are eager to learn how to fight, and I don't blame them one bit. We're ready. I know we are.

I'm equally frustrated by the fact that we've been given no opportunity to earn free time. I'm desperate to talk to Valentino. I'm harried by thoughts of Captain Bolivar's death, of Fernando fighting for his life. Every day that passes puts my prince in greater danger. One night, Iván suggests we sneak out, but once again, I refuse. We risked too much the first time we snuck down to the Wallows. We don't dare do it again. *Don't get cut*, Rosario said.

Finally, three weeks after the ambassador's soiree, we enter the training arena for our morning session, but instead of Master Santiago, Guardsman Bruno awaits us. He is swordless.

"Into formation!" he calls, and we scurry to grab our wooden swords but he stops us. "No weapons today."

Empty-handed, we line up in the staggered formation Master Santiago assigned us. Aldo gives me a questioning look. I shrug.

Guardsman Bruno paces before us, hands behind his back. "Swordmaster Santiago has other commitments today, so I will oversee your training. He assures me that you are not quite ready for swordwork yet. Instead, you will be given an introduction to close quarters combat."

Excited murmuring runs down the line. Finally we're going to learn something useful.

"I'm sure it has not escaped your notice that we haven't made any cuts in several weeks. Since the Ciénega del Sur boys did us the favor of disqualifying themselves, we were able to keep some of you on longer than we expected. That will change. I assure you, cuts are coming, so pay attention today and learn well."

Itzal groans softly. "It's me," he whispers. "I know it's going to be me."

"As Royal Guards," Bruno continues, "you may find yourself in a situation where swinging a sword is a terrible idea—when an attacker is too close to the empress, for example, or when you're in the middle of a crowd. We will teach you to disarm opponents, grapple an enemy into submission, and even de-escalate sensitive situations—all without ever raising a blade."

His bushy eyebrows knit together into a single caterpillar line, and he says, "Any volunteers?"

We are as silent and still as the grave, for no one wants to be made a spectacle of in front of everyone. A gust of wind kisses the arena sand, sending up a layer of dust.

"Recruit Red," Bruno says. "Thank you for volunteering."

I'm unable to resist giving him an angry glare as I step forward.

"Turn around and face your fellow recruits."

I do as ordered, and he steps up behind me. Maybe I imagine the warmth of his body permeating my skin, because he's not that close. Still, my limbs start to tingle, heat races up my neck, my heartbeat comes fast.

He's going to choke me from behind. But it will be a mere demonstration. Nothing to fear.

The recruits stare at us in anticipation.

"I'm going to reach for your neck," Bruno says. "I want you to try to escape my grip. Ready?"

I take a deep breath. "Ready."

My senses narrow to the presence at my back, the hands coming up to my throat, the thumbs pressing against my windpipe.

My body knows exactly what to do. I've practiced this maneuver with Hector and Rosario a thousand times. But Bruno is a stranger with strange hands and a strange smell and a strange grip, and I can't force my body to treat him like a friend.

I drop a shoulder and twist, forcing his grip to release, and I explode my opposite elbow upward, ramming him in the chin.

He flails backward.

I step in for the killing blow. His eyes are wide, his mouth open in surprise, and at the last second I pull my punch. Instead of a hard blow to the groin, I give his abdomen a light tap.

He blinks rapidly, opening his mouth wide to test his jaw.

"I didn't mean to hurt you!" I say. "Are you all right?"

He nods before finding his voice. "That was well done. Excessive, but well done."

A smattering of applause hits my back.

I breathe relief.

"Now what if I came at you with a forward choke hold?" He raises his hands to my throat again, except now he's facing me.

I'm less panicky, more calculated this time. I drop my head low so his thumbs can't maintain pressure on my neck, duck under, shoot back up, and send an elbow screaming down against his arm to open his torso to attack. I make as if to knee his groin, but I stop short. It's just a demonstration.

"That was acceptable," Bruno says. "We'll teach you two alternative escapes and work on your technique for the one you just performed—your ducking angle was off, and a trained warrior might have been able to reestablish his grip. Now please return to your place in line."

He's lucky I didn't use the escape that includes sticking my thumbs in my attacker's eye sockets.

"Red, that was great," Aldo whispers as I take up formation.

"Thank you." My mind has calmed, but my heart is still pounding, my skin sheening with far more sweat than the amount of exertion justified. The soldier sickness almost took over.

Bruno resumes pacing. "It takes six seconds for someone to choke you unconscious," he says. "You must not waste even a moment in panic or indecision. Therefore, we will practice escapes—and all their variations—until they are second nature.

"For example, in addition to the rear-choke-hold escape Red demonstrated, you have the option of repeated elbow strikes to the abdomen, a blow to the instep—and, for the strongest among you, a downward hook with your hands, which will force a release. We will teach you all of them, and drill them until you instinctively know which option to use in which situation. Everyone find a partner."

I look for Iván, but Aldo grabs my elbow, claiming me. "We've made good partners before," he points out.

I grin. "And we will again."

"Don't worry about who your partner is to begin with," Bruno says, noting our conversation. "We're going to rotate so that everyone gets practice against opponents of different sizes and strength."

Once everyone is paired, Bruno says, "We'll begin with a forward choke hold. I'll demonstrate with Recruit Itzal, and you will follow. I recognize that not everyone has had defense training. Don't worry; you'll all become adept soon enough. Those of you who learn this well will be given free time this afternoon."

I reach out, pretending to choke Aldo. We both grin.

"Now drop your chin to your chest and duck left," Bruno says. As Aldo easily escapes my grasp, I hear the Guardsman yell, "Your *other* left, Recruit Itzal!"

We take turns, and he makes us repeat it three more times before we switch partners, and then do it again. My third partner is Pedrón, and he comes at me faster than expected.

My reflexes kick in, and a split second later Pedrón is yelping as he hits the sand hard. Immediately, I reach down to help him—

"Recruit Red!"

I snap to attention. "Yes, sir!"

"We're supposed to be *drilling* them, not *killing* them!"

It's not really a question and I'm not sure if I'm supposed to respond, but I settle on a "Yes, sir!"

Bruno pauses to rub his face thoughtfully. "Of course, that's your training. It's the proper way to do it. We'll train all of the recruits to perform the same way . . . *eventually.*"

RAE·CARSON

My shoulders relax a bit; I'm not in trouble.

He scans the group. "How about this? Recruit Red, you take the army boys and the Basajuaños, they're all fairly advanced. If you're teaching them, you can't possibly hurt anyone. I hope. Start drilling them in the five basic escapes while I bring the others up to speed." When I hesitate, he asks, "You do know the five basic escapes?"

They were the first thing Hector ever taught me. "Yes, sir."

"Then what are you waiting for? Ask me when you need help with something. The rest of you partner up over here. Not you, Itzal—you're with me!"

Pedrón jumps up and gets back in place. "Can you show me that again, but slower?"

"Sure," I say. "Pair up with Arturo—the other Arturo, short Arturo."

I show him again, but slower.

I'm worried the other recruits will think I'm lording my training over them, but they're all competitive, they all want to be the best. By the end of the morning session, we're sweaty and sore, sand scraped and bruised, but we're all grinning.

Bruno orders us into line and inspects us. Half to himself, he says, "You performed better than I expected after speaking to Master Santiago. Maybe we should have started with the unarmed combat."

I exchange a glance with Iván. Hopefully one of us has done well enough to earn time off.

"Recruit Red," Bruno says.

"Yes, sir?"

"You may take the afternoon off. We'll see how much your group really knows." As relief surges through me, he looks over the rest of the recruits, the ones that he's been training. "Iván!"

"Yes, sir?"

"You did creditably well. You're free too. Now all of you, go get something to eat, and I expect to see everyone but Red and Iván back here before the next bell."

Finally, a spot of luck. Or maybe it wasn't luck at all. I wouldn't be surprised to learn that Rosario had engineered the whole thing. Iván meets my eyes on the way to the dining hall and we exchange a small nod.

It's time to go see Valentino.

"You're very good at unarmed combat," Iván observes as we walk together to the palace after lunch.

I'm not sure how to respond to that. "I had a good teacher."

"It's more than that," he says. "You react like your life depends on it. Every single time."

Sometimes life is a good teacher too.

Like many of the empire's most powerful nobles, Conde Astón keeps quarters in the Sky Wing, the finest part of the palace, where modern architecture promises fresh water plumbed from the underground river, glass-pane skylights, and high balconies overlooking interior gardens. The door to the Ciénega del Sur suite is not far from the royal apartments, where I lived before joining the Guard. Beside the door stands a spearman in full armor.

"We're here to see Valentino," I tell him.

"Lord Valentino is not receiving visitors," he says.

"He'll be happy to receive us," I say.

The spearman plants himself in front of the door to bar our path.

Iván steps forward. He's tall enough to look him dead in the eye; if it weren't for the spearman's pointed helmet, they'd be of height. Iván says, "Please tell Lord Valentino that Lady Red, ward of our beloved empress, and Lord Iván, brother of Lord-Conde Juan Carlos of the Quorum of Five, both wish a few moments of his time."

I give Iván a sharp look. We're recruits now, without title. But the spearman inclines his head slightly and says, "Wait right here," and disappears into the suite.

"It wasn't a lie," Iván whispers while we wait. "I mean, not exactly."

"Did I say anything?"

"You had that look."

The spearman returns. "Lord Valentino will see you now."

The parlor is dark with mahogany shelves, all filled with parchment and even several books. High clerestory windows fill the place with diffuse light, and a deep stone hearth—cool at the moment—gives off the sharp scent of pine ash.

A tapestry with the Ciénega del Sur crest hangs on the wall. It depicts a river flowing between two low mountains. In the center of the crest, where the river and the mountains come together, a sun rises. The design is so stylized that the sun looks like a crown resting on pillows.

Valentino sits at a writing desk, wearing blue silk robes with golden embroidery. His skin is sallow, and dark circles make hollows of his eyes. A walking cane topped with the head of a brass viper rests against the desk. When he sees us, his eyes light up and he struggles to his feet.

"Red! Iván! I'm so happy to see you," he says, reaching for his cane.

"No need to get up," Iván says.

"Oh, it's good for me, or so the family physician says. Come join me on the divan. I'll have my man fetch some . . . well, not wine, as I'm sure you can't stay away from the barracks long. How about some chilled coconut milk with honey?"

"That sounds wonderful," I say.

He lifts a bell from the desk and rings it, then makes his way slowly to the divan, which is a lavishly cushioned affair in deep, dusty purple. He plunks down and sinks into the cushions as though his short trek across the room was as tiring as a lap around the palace walls.

"As much as I'm glad for the company," Valentino says, "I'm sure you're not here to check on me."

His forthrightness makes me smile. "Checking on you is *part* of the reason we're here," I say. "Does your family physician expect you to make a full recovery?"

"He does. It's been slow; I was badly poisoned. But I expect I'll be able to join the army recruits in a few months. Because of my father's station . . ." Valentino pauses to stare at my hairline. The pause lengthens.

I stare back at him, saying nothing.

RAE·CARSON

Valentino blinks. "Er, because of my father's station, joining the army will come with an automatic officer's commission, so long as I survive their recruit training."

"You'll excel in the army," Iván says. "I have no doubt."

"Thank you."

I say, "I wish there was a way for you to come back to the Guard."

Valentino gives me a sad smile. "Me too. But once cut, you're cut forever. It won't be so bad in the army. Beto and the others joined up already, as soon as they left the Guard. They say it's a lot harder than Royal Guard training. The food isn't nearly as good, and none of their boots fit quite right, but . . ."

His voice trails away at the look on my face.

"Oh, Red, I'm so sorry about what happened to you," Valentino says. "I did *not* ask them to do that, and when they visited me, I gave them all a stern talking-to."

"They needed more than a stern talking-to," Iván grumbles.

"They did," Valentino agrees. "But I was bedridden at the time."

A servant hurries in, and Valentino orders three glasses of chilled coconut milk.

After he leaves, I say, "Valentino, I believe you when you say you didn't ask the Ciénega del Sur boys to attack me. But do you know if anyone else did?"

Valentino frowns. "Not that I know of. Though, to be honest, none of them is a particularly original thinker."

"We thought someone might have goaded them into it," Iván says.

I open my mouth and barely stop short of suggesting that maybe his own father is to blame. I don't want to put Valentino on the defensive too soon, because we have an even more important question yet to ask.

"You might be right," Valentino concedes. "Though I'm not sure it matters now."

Iván says, "It matters because if someone else was behind this, Red could be attacked again."

"Oh, that's a good point." Valentino takes a deep breath, releases it in a heavy sigh.

The servant returns with three glasses balanced on a silver tray, and he hands one to each of us. I give mine a subtle sniff—no telltale cinnamon scent. Still, I wait for Valentino to sip and swallow before following suit.

It's delicious. I swirl my glass around a moment before softly asking, "What was it like? To be poisoned, I mean?"

Valentino sips his milk then says, "It was the most awful thing I've ever experienced."

"We were really worried about you," Iván says.

"At first it was just like being drunk—all happy and dizzy and painless. Then it got harder to breathe, and my heart started beating faster than bees' wings. And that's all I remember until I woke up with the worst headache of my life and a belly that wouldn't keep down food or drink no matter what it was offered. The physician inserted a small tube directly into a vein and gave me water that way."

Iván's eyes widen. "I've never heard of that!"

"Doctor Enzo, the royal physician, published about it in the

Journal of Medical Anomalies. Our own physician said the technique saved my life."

"Enzo is brilliant," I say distantly, because I'm thinking about Captain Bolívar, and how even Doctor Enzo couldn't save him. Maybe he won't be able to save Fernando either.

"Valentino," Iván says, sitting forward on the divan. "We have to ask . . . how did you come to be poisoned? What poison was it? Who gave it to you?"

Valentino sets his glass on a side table and folds his hands together in his lap. "I thought you might ask."

When he doesn't offer more, I add, "We fear others in the Guard may be in danger. Anything you can tell us—"

He says, "It was an accident."

"Oh?" says Iván.

"It was sweet dream, that syrupy stuff coming from down south. Like duerma leaf except stronger."

Iván and I exchange a quick glance. This is exactly what we suspected.

"I thought it would help with the pain in my kidney."

I wince.

"Anyway, I won't tell you who I got it from."

"Why not?" I say, even as Iván says, "Please, Valentino."

Valentino shakes his head. "The person who gave it to me has apologized profusely for giving me the wrong dose and is making amends. I have accepted their apology. Therefore, I consider the matter closed."

We can't tell him about Captain Bolívar or Fernando—we can't tell anyone without possibly warning Rosario's enemies.

But we have to make him see the danger. I say, "What if—"

Valentino shakes his head. "It was an accident. It won't happen again. The Guard is safe."

"Assuming the person who gave you the sweet dream is telling the truth," Iván says.

"Everyone makes mistakes, Iván. And that's all it was. A mistake. This person promised to do better, and I believe them."

"I don't know that I could be so gracious in your shoes," Iván says.

I couldn't either. Valentino is better than I am. Too good to be the son of Conde Astón, at least. I mutter, "I can't believe you share blood with the high conde."

"What?" Valentino says, eyes widening. Iván shoots me a warning glare.

I blurt, "It's just that your father seems to hate the empress and all she stands for. He levels insults at every opportunity, and he never forgives a slight. He's not like you at all. You're so . . . honorable."

"Please forgive Red," Iván says. "She has a terrible habit of letting any old thought spill from her mouth."

I consider apologizing, but what is there to apologize for? I only spoke the truth.

Valentino has the grace to smile. "She is honest and blunt, just like the Invierno ambassador."

"She is."

"Red, you're not wrong," Valentino says, and suddenly his gaze seems far away. "I know my father's reputation. It's not unearned. In fact, we disagree on many things."

"Like whether or not Elisa is a good ruler?" I prompt.

Valentino doesn't rise to the bait. "Many things. Contentiously. It's why I went to the Guard. He got his peskiest son out of his hair, and I got to do something that would bring honor and reputation to my family that I felt good about. It seemed like such an elegant solution at the time."

"I'm sorry it didn't work out better," I tell him.

"Me too."

"Is there anything we can do for you?" Iván asks.

Valentino is so sophisticated and well-mannered, even when convalescing, that it's a bit of a surprise to see vulnerability flash across his face. "I would like it very much if you came to visit me again sometime," he says, unable to keep the wistfulness from his voice. "I've read through our entire library. It will be months before I can join the army." He stares off toward the writing desk. "Frankly, I'm bored."

I grasp his shoulder. He feels bony and frail. "We can definitely do that," I say.

He brightens. "That would be wonderful." His gaze shifts back to the writing desk.

"Did we interrupt some correspondence by coming here?" Iván asks.

"No. It's just . . ."

"Valentino?" I prompt.

He looks back and forth between Iván and me. Back to the writing desk. Back to me.

"If you decide you *want* to tell us who gave you the sweet

dream poison," Iván says carefully. "You know where to find us. But we won't press you."

"Thank you. I appreciate that."

Iván sets his glass on the side table and stands, and I follow his lead. "I wish we could stay longer, but Red and I have to get back to the barracks before our free time is up."

Valentino gains his feet with the help of his cane. "I understand. Do you mind seeing yourselves out? I've already done quite a bit of walking today."

"Of course," I say. Iván and I turn to go.

We are nearly to the door, when Valentino calls out, "Wait!"

We turn.

Valentino appears stricken. "There's something . . . Maybe this is a huge mistake, or maybe it's nothing . . ."

I peer closer. Stricken, yes, with a healthy pinch of fear for spice. "Valentino, are you in trouble?" I ask. "Do you need help?"

He waves off my concern. "I'm fine, I promise, but . . ." Using his cane for support, he makes his way to the writing desk, opens a drawer, pulls out a rolled-up piece of parchment. "I've been doing some work for my father during my convalescence. Mostly accounting and correspondence. I found this, and I haven't been able to get it out of my head. Maybe you'll know what to do with it." He holds it out for me to fetch.

I stride toward him and grab it.

"You didn't get that from me," Valentino says as I unfurl the parchment and read.

It's a list, neatly scripted in black ink.

Four barrels Ventierra white wine, two barrels barley, three barrels salt pork, eight live chickens, six barrels water . . .

"What is it?" Iván asks.

"A shipping manifest," I say. "For a ship called the *Kestrel*, which sailed to Brisadulce from the southern border. Looks like supplies for a long haul. Valentino, why . . . ?"

"Keep reading," Valentino says.

I continue to skim.

Three coils rope, one barrel pitch, one box iron nails . . .

Finally, near the end, something snags my attention:

Forty barrels date syrup

"This is odd," I mutter.

"So you see it too," Valentino says.

"What?" Iván demands, coming to read over my shoulder. "See what?"

I point. "Forty barrels date syrup."

"Why is that odd?" Iván asks. "I mean, that's a *lot* of date syrup, but . . ."

"Date palms grow around the edges of the great desert and in the oases. They don't grow down south in the jungles. The countships there—the Southern Reaches, Isla Oscura, Ciénega del Sur—they all harvest coconut palms."

Iván stares at the shipping manifest in my hand for the

space of several breaths. To Valentino, he says, "Is the *Kestrel* one of your father's ships?"

Valentino shakes his head. "It belongs to an independent merchant. However, my father has contracted with the ship on several occasions."

"And this caught your eye because you don't think it's really date syrup."

Still holding his cane, Valentino plunks down into the desk chair. His thumb caresses the brass of the viper's head, gently traces the curve of one shining fang. "My father has never shipped date syrup from anywhere. And forty barrels! I know the empress likes her sweets, but that's enough syrup for ten years' worth of deserts."

"Date syrup doesn't keep that long," I point out.

"Exactly," Valentino says.

"So what are you saying?" Iván asks him. "That your father is smuggling something else into the city?"

"All I'm saying is I don't think it's really date syrup, and . . . that's all. I've done my duty. I don't care to speculate what it might actually be." Valentino slumps over, putting his head in his hands.

Iván says, "But what if it's—"

I put a hand on Iván's arm, silencing him. "Thank you for bringing this to our attention, Valentino. I know this wasn't an easy choice for you."

"It could be nothing, right?" Valentino mutters. "It's probably nothing."

Iván is looking at me, and his eyes are wide with sure

knowledge, as he says, "Of course, Valentino. It's probably nothing."

The door to the parlor flies open. I spin to face whoever is coming, shoving the manifest behind my back.

It's Conde Astón, resplendent in royal-blue brocade. The golden medallion that marks his station as speaker of the chamber of condes hangs from his neck on a rope-thick chain.

"Hello, Papá," Valentino says smoothly.

The conde's face is emotionless, like he's made of marble. "You should have told me you were planning to receive visitors today," he says. "I would have had the receiving room set up with refreshments."

"Your son's hospitality was more than adequate, Your Grace," Iván says.

The conde's composure cracks just enough to let a bit of anger leak through. "Shouldn't you be in afternoon training? I thought it was a disqualifying offense to leave the Guard barracks without permission."

"We earned free time," I tell him. "Naturally, we wanted to see how our friend was doing."

"Naturally."

The parchment in my hand burns like fire. Surely he can tell I'm hiding something? Surely he's noticed how awkwardly my hand is being held behind my back?

"Well," Astón says after too long a pause. "I'm afraid my son needs his rest."

"Thank you for coming," Valentino says.

"We'll come again as soon as we can," Iván assures him.

"I'd like that. And Red, I'm sorry for—"

Astón interrupts: "What I meant was, you are both dismissed. I'd like to speak privately with my son now."

"Of course, Your Grace," I say hurriedly. "Please pardon the intrusion."

The conde steps aside, allowing us to pass him on our way to the door. As we do, I very carefully lower the shipping manifest to my side, keeping it out of sight.

The door slams—too loudly—at our backs.

Quickly I roll up the manifest and shove it in my pocket.

"I hate that we've just left Valentino alone with him," Iván says.

"Me too. Do you think he'll be punished for receiving us? It's not like he planned it or anything."

"If it were my father, I would have been punished."

"Oh." We leave the suite and step into the hallway. "I'm sorry."

We walk in silence for a while, passing squires with messages, servants with cleaning buckets, a minor conde surrounded by guards.

"The gala is more than a month away, and the palace is already filling up," Iván says.

"It's the busiest time of the year. I used to hide in my suite as much as possible until everyone went back home."

We leave the Sky Wing and angle toward the throne room. Beyond it is the central green, though it's usually muddy with traffic this time of year, and the entrance to the Guard barracks.

Just as we step outside into the sunshine, Iván yanks me

aside into the shade of a wide date palm. One of the sharp fronds needles into my shoulder.

"Careful!" I say.

"Sorry. I just wanted to see that manifest one more time before we go back to the barracks."

I pull it from my pocket and hand it to him. His eyes narrow as he reads. His long body is very close to me, shielding the parchment from any onlookers.

He says, "I don't know a lot about sailing. But the only thing on this manifest that looks like trading cargo is the forty barrels of date syrup. Everything else is standard sailing supplies for a large crew on a long haul."

"Yes."

"Red." He looks me dead in the eye. "I don't think those barrels are full of date syrup."

"No."

"They're full of sweet dream syrup."

"Yes."

"Enough to poison an army."

"Or a gala full of nobles."

He gasps. "You think poisoned food will be served up at the Deliverance Gala?"

"I don't know. I do know that the gala would be a really good time for a coup."

"We need to let the prince know about this."

"And we need to do it right now. Let's go find that assistant cook."

We have nothing to write with. So I pull the last shards of my dye pot from my drawer. One curved shard still shelters a small dollop of dye, with just enough moisture that I'm able to dip my finger and make a large X on the manifest, beside the line item for date syrup. After it dries, I fold it up small and tight and shove it into my pocket.

At dinner, we are served caramelized onions and garlic-spiced lentils on a bed of spinach.

Normally, my mouth would be watering with anticipation over such a meal. Instead, my stomach roils as I stand in line, waiting my turn, my palm turning damp with sweat as it clutches my plate and the folded manifest along with it.

I reach the head of the line. The assistant cook gestures for me to hand him my plate, and I stretch my arm out carefully, hoping beyond hope he'll see the parchment poking out from under the plate's edge.

"Here you go, girl," he says, and sometime between a tong full of spinach and a ladle full of lentils, the parchment disappears, so smoothly that I barely feel it slide out of my fingers.

I'm so relieved as I find a seat that when Pedrón insists on sitting beside me, I actually smile at him.

"How did afternoon training go?" I ask him.

"Not well," he says. "Itzal is right. He's going to get cut unless he gets some extra help. I could use some help too."

"We'll practice those escapes in our class tonight. You're big enough that I can teach you different techniques that wouldn't work for me or Itzal, more than just the five basic escapes."

RAE·CARSON

Pedrón beams. "I am big." He waggles an eyebrow. "I'm big *everywhere.*"

"Gross." I grab my bowl, rise from my seat, and go find Aldo to sit beside. Aldo has never once been gross with me.

We practice escapes in our unsanctioned class and Pedrón is right; Itzal is hopeless. He might be the clumsiest person I've ever seen. But that doesn't stop him from trying. If anyone can succeed in the Guard on sheer determination, it's him.

After the oil lamps are blown out and everyone settles into their cots, I lie awake, worried for Fernando, hoping Rosario will receive and understand our message, thinking about the upcoming Deliverance Gala. Finally I give up on sleeping, and I grab the book Father Nicandro gave me and sneak into the latrine. By torchlight, I read.

The *Articles of the Empire* is a massive document, detailing all sorts of matters pertaining to governance, specifically laying out the powers and rights of the chamber of condes, the Quorum of Five, and the imperial throne. Thirty pages alone are devoted to the proper procedure for raising or lowering taxes. If this tome doesn't put me to sleep, nothing will.

Finally I reach article fifty-seven, section eight, which outlines inheritance law. A single paragraph addresses the adoption of non-genealogical children as inheritors of land, wealth, and power. Taking on wards from other families is such a common practice among the nobility—including among the three queens of the empire—that it's no wonder some enterprising conde insisted this clause be included. I read it carefully. Then I read it again.

There's nothing here I don't know. All adoptions resulting in inheritance of rulership must be approved by a vocal majority of the chamber of condes. So what? What did Father Nicandro want me to see?

No, there's something *not* here that he wanted me to see.

I read it again, understanding dawning. I read it yet again to be sure. I read it five more times.

My pulse quickens. My face feels warm. Hope is unfurling inside me, even as I try to tamp it down. Hope is frightening. Hope is risky.

The seed of a precious idea has formed, but I dare not consider it too deeply. I slam the book shut and return to my bunk. I have other things to worry about. Like keeping my prince alive until the empress returns.

18

Then

WAR was coming.

Mula didn't know what that meant when the cook had first said it, but she soon learned. Over the next few months, thousands of Inviernos marched through the free villages on the way to the great desert, cutting a swath through the forest as they went, turning the trading square to trampled mud. Once the spring thaw hit, the air began to stink of feces. Soon after, six villagers died of sour gut.

The army was ravenous, demanding more stew and ale than Orlín the innkeeper could provide. Everyone in the village reported missing livestock—horses, goats, chickens, pigs. People were going to starve come winter, for true.

"It's all because of that new queen rising in the west," the cook told the girl one day as he was sinking his fist into a batch of bread dough. He sneered out the word "west" like it was the most contemptible place in the world. "I just hope the White Hairs kill her quick, get this blasted war over with before the land is dead and our village starved."

"For true," Mula said. She hoped the White Hairs killed the new queen quick too. Because Orlín was selling her blood every day now. Sometimes more than once a day. Her thumbs and fingertips were crisscrossed with cuts that didn't have time to heal before the next dagger came along. She walked around in a dizzy haze, so tired and thirsty she thought she might die of it.

Then one time, a sorcerer came to the inn with a hollow bone needle and a bleeding tube. He took so much blood that she toppled over and crashed onto the floor, knocking the needle from her vein, soaking the rushes with crimson.

She woke in the kitchen, the cook standing over her. "Poor little thing. That lump on your forehead is something else. Here, drink this." He tipped up her head and set a mug of warm mare's milk to her lips, which she lapped up obediently.

"Orlín is a greedy goat," the cook said. "Little girls your age ought to grow faster than a summer sequoia, but not you. You're tiny as a sprout, and you're going to stay that way if he keeps taking your lifeblood. Take this." He shoved a heel of bread into her hand. "Eat every bit of it, hear?"

"Hear," she whispered, and forced the bread into her mouth, even though the lump on her forehead throbbed so hard it was making her tummy squishy.

During the next few months, the cook kept her busy in the kitchen or the smokehouse as much as possible to keep her out of sight. He even sent her to the creek for water or to the market for supplies. He gave her extra mare's milk and the occasional strip of jerky—all under Orlín's nose.

RAE·CARSON

The innkeeper still sold her blood, but thanks to the cook, she occasionally skipped a day or two, and she had a little extra food and drink besides. She grew a tiny bit, just enough that her pants barely reached her ankles, and her pinky toe wore a hole in her right shoe.

The flood of White Hairs through their village shrunk to a trickle. Mula grew a little more; her shoes became unwearable, and she could no longer pull her pants over her bony hips. Even though Orlín had made a small fortune selling her blood, he refused to buy her new shoes or new clothes. Instead, he gave her two stained, tattered burlap sacks and told her to make a shift out of them, which she did.

With summer came word that the queen in the west had won, against all odds, and the few surviving sorcerers were trudging home, tails tucked between their legs like whipped mongrels. Mula wasn't very good at sleeping. So she often lay awake at night wondering about the western queen, marveling that any person in the world could defeat an army led by blood sorcerers with magic stones.

The end of summer brought chilly nights. The White Hairs stopped coming at all, and somehow, Orlín seemed to think this was her fault. He cuffed her more often, tied her nighttime bonds tighter, made her fetch water when the air crackled with cold and the creek iced over—even though she had no shoes and only a burlap shift to wear.

It was going to be the worst winter many of them had ever known, everyone said so. A girl like Mula, with her bare feet and fleshless limbs and a sleeping roll in the back storeroom as far away from the hearth as it could be, might not even survive such a winter.

One day in autumn, after the poplar tree had coated the inn's roof with dry leaves and all the merlins had flown west to warmer weather, Mula felt it again. That little jump in her chest, followed by a steady buzzing in her limbs. It meant a sorcerer was approaching.

She was in the common room, gathering filthy rushes to replace them, and she paused, eyes darting around in panic. Orlín was there, serving mugs of ale from a tray; he would notice if she fled to the outhouse or into the kitchen. She was trapped.

The brass bell on the door rattled. Four people walked in, and Mula gasped. The tallest was clearly an Invierno, with long, slender limbs, eyes like emeralds, and badly dyed black hair that was growing out yellow-white at the roots. His three companions were Joyan, with hair of true black and deep brown eyes and dusky skin. One man wore an eye patch. The other two were women—one tall for a Joyan, the other shorter and generously plump.

It was the plump woman Mula couldn't stop staring at. She was young, with shining black braids wrapping her head like a crown. She wore the clothing of desert nomads: an undyed linen shirt tucked into a utility belt, all over woolen pants and camel-hair boots. The fabric may have been undyed, but it was still the prettiest fabric Mula had ever seen, with a fine, soft weave and decorative brown stitching at the hem. The plump woman was a fancy lady, no doubt about it.

But the thing that made Mula stare, that stopped her in her tracks, was the fact that the itching in the girl's throat, the buzzing in her limbs, the feeling of something inside her yearning to burst free—it all came from *her*, the short Joyan woman.

As the group settled at a table and called for stew, Mula realized she was sensing something from the Invierno too, just a little. But it was nothing like the riot of feeling inside her every time she looked at the woman with the crown of braids. She was a sorcerer, just like the White Hairs. She didn't have an amulet around her neck or a magic staff, but she was hiding a sparkle stone somewhere. Mula would bet her evening bread crust on it.

"Mula!" Orlín yelled. "Venison stew for our guests. And be quick about it, or you'll feel the back of my hand."

Mula dropped the rushes. As she fled to the kitchen, she felt the strangers' eyes boring into her back. Quickly she ladled dogmeat stew into four bowls, balanced them on her forearm, and returned to the common room.

She slipped the first three bowls onto the table with practiced ease. But as she neared the plump woman, something leaped inside her, and the fourth bowl met the table too hard and fast. Dogmeat stew sloshed over the side, onto the planking.

Mula stared at the mess in horror. "Lady," she whispered. "Please don't tell that I spilled."

The plump woman regarded her thoughtfully. She was probably wondering how much blood she could take, wondering how much it would cost. Mula ought to be afraid of her, but she wasn't, because her hidden sparkle stone felt different. Louder. Joyous. Like it was greeting her.

Finally the woman said, "I see no spill."

Mula flashed her a quick grin. Then she dashed back to the kitchen.

Beside the hearth, Orlín was head-to-head with the cook. "They're fine lords and ladies, mark my word," Orlín was saying. "Finest I've ever seen."

"It's the second group this week with Joyans and Inviernos traveling together," the cook observed.

"These are strange times," said Orlín.

"Will you be wanting real venison for them?"

"Don't bother." Orlín spotted Mula, hovering near the door. "Girl, when the newcomers are done with their stew, show them to their rooms. Give them the dormers, hear?"

"Hear."

"And as soon as you get a chance, find out what's inside those travel packs. They might be traders. Rich traders."

"You want me to steal something?" Mula hated stealing, but she did it once in a while on Orlín's orders. She could be quiet as a rabbit in a burrow, when she needed to be.

"Not yet. Just tell me what's inside."

Mula nodded and backed out the door before Orlín could think up some other awful task for her.

The girl did exactly as asked. Once the strange group had finished their stew, she led them upstairs to the dormer rooms. She lingered while they settled in, hoping to get a glimpse inside their packs.

The tall woman approached her. "Do you need something from us?" she asked with an arch look.

"What's inside those packs?" Mula asked. "Are you traders?"

The two women exchanged a glance.

"Just supplies," said the plump woman.

"Orlín thinks you might be traders."

"Orlín?"

"Man who owns this inn and everything in it."

"Ah."

"Yes, traders," the tall woman said. "Spices. If they sell well, we might come back with more."

The plump woman stepped forward, cocked her head to study the little girl. "Did the innkeeper put you up to asking?"

Mula should lie. She knew she should. But Mula was terrible at lying, and these people had kindness in their eyes, so she nodded once, quick, then looked away, unable to meet their gazes.

The plump woman said, "You may tell your innkeeper that we carry marjoram and sage. Now please allow us some privacy."

Mula turned to go. She knew what sage was, but she'd never heard of the other one. She practiced the word in her head.

Mula wasn't sure what made her turn back around, pin the plump woman with a look and say, "Orlín says you might be fancy lords and ladies. He's got a very bad want for seeing inside your packs."

In the ensuing silence, the girl's heart was fierce in her chest. What had she just done? If Orlín found out . . .

"But please don't say I told!" she added, then she fled, pounding back down the stairs in her bare feet.

Orlín was waiting for her in the common room. "Well? What did you find out?"

"Traders," Mula said, breathless. "They have spices. Sage and merry jam."

"Marjoram?"

She nodded.

"Did you see? Or did they tell you?"

"They told."

Orlín frowned. "When they leave their rooms tomorrow, I want you to get inside and have a look around."

"You think they're lying?"

"Joyans are known for it."

"They have an Invierno with them," Mula pointed out.

"They do indeed." Orlín tapped a fingertip to his lip. "Which makes me think they are definitely not traders." He crouched down before her, grasped her shoulders, pinned her with a gaze. "You must find out what's in those packs," he said. "You will not eat until you find out, hear?"

Mula's lower lip trembled. "Hear," she whispered.

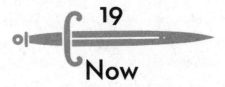

19
Now

THE next morning, Master Santiago is back, and we return to endless practice of forms. Our forms are perfect. I have no idea why he refuses to progress our training, why he constantly belittles and berates us. At lunch, I sit beside Aldo, Iván, and Pedrón as usual. Across the room, the Arturos and their fellow Basajuaños are deep in quiet conversation with some of the second years.

"What do you think they're talking about?" Aldo says.

"No idea," I say.

We find out that night, during our unsanctioned class. I instruct everyone to grab their wooden practice swords, but Tall Arturo says, "Wait. We need to talk." He gestures for us to gather into a cluster in the center of the arena. "Might as well sit down for this," he says.

Short Arturo adds, "And speak quietly so no one lingering on the walls can hear."

Iván and I exchange a startled glance as we comply. Soon, we're all cross-legged in the sand, sitting in a tight circle.

Evening paints the sky pink and coral. Two palace guards make their rounds nearby; their silhouettes seem to float along the arena wall, black against the sunset.

"What's going on?" I whisper.

Short Arturo gives Tall Arturo a nod of encouragement. Tall Arturo takes a deep breath and says, "We've been talking to the second years. They had a very different first year of recruitment than we've had."

"What do you mean?" says Pedrón, though I have a guess where this is going.

"First of all, they were trained by Captain Bolivar," Tall Arturo says. "I know Sergeant DeLuca said the captain was busy doing something else, but it's highly irregular. The captain of the Royal Guard oversees training every year. *Every year.* The second years have no idea where he is or why he's been absent so long."

I sense Iván stiffen in the space beside me. I resist the urge to look at him.

"I've been wondering about him," says Itzal. "I was looking forward to meeting the captain. Supposedly he's one of the empress's most trusted men. And a gifted instructor besides."

"Maybe he's away on a special mission for the empress," Pedrón says.

"It's been almost two months," Tall Arturo points out.

The truth is like a silent scream in my head. *He's dead. Dead, dead, dead.* It goes against everything in me to allow the deception to continue. Maybe these boys, who've sworn to protect the empress even if it costs them their lives, deserve to know the truth. It's not like Prince Rosario specifically ordered us to keep his death a secret. . . .

"There's more," says Short Arturo. "By this time last year, the second years were practicing real swordwork, not just forms. They were learning blocks and parries and even a few attacks."

"Maybe we're just terrible compared to them," Itzal says.

"No, *you're* just terrible compared to them," Pedrón says.

Itzal sighs. "I don't deny it. I'm going to get cut for sure."

"We're not terrible compared to them," Short Arturo says. "Everyone says we're the most promising class in a decade. Iván and Red have had extensive training. Pedrón and the former army recruits are here specifically because they were too good for the army."

"Damn right we were," Pedrón says, and his friends echo him with, "Damn right!"

"Aldo is surprising everyone," Short Arturo continues. "We Basajuan boys grew up on the Invierne border, so we've been adept with slingshots and bows and traps since we could walk." He pauses to let it all sink in. "There is absolutely no reason for Master Santiago to delay our training."

"I'm the one holding everyone back," Itzal says, hanging his head.

"No!" I say. "If that were true, they'd just cut you. You've survived this long for a reason. We all have. Pedrón, what does your brother say?"

"I haven't talked to him. The third and fourth years don't stay in the barracks. They're out on maneuvers." Pedrón is dragging his fingers through the sand, unable to sit still. "I know I'm not as smart as the rest of you," he says. "But it sure sounds like the swordmaster is delaying our training on purpose."

The Arturos are nodding. Tall Arturo says, "The second years think it's very strange that Sergeant DeLuca brought in an outsider for training. And then to see him teach us nothing but forms, forms, forms, for weeks on end . . . I mean, I'm glad we're strengthening our arms and wrists and shoulders or whatever, but this is getting ridiculous."

I can't resist piping in with, "Our forms are excellent now. Even Itzal's. I don't see how they can get any better."

Aldo speaks up for the first time. "So what does all this mean?" he asks, and his voice carries a note of challenge.

"We're not sure," Tall Arturo says. "And we don't want to alarm you . . ."

". . . or overreact," says Short Arturo. "But . . ."

"There's no reason to keep Guard recruits ignorant and incompetent, unless . . ."

". . . you want them to remain ignorant and incompetent."

"In short," Tall Arturo says, "we're a little bit concerned for our prince."

Silence greets this pronouncement. Distant wagon wheels roll across cobblestone. The sun sinks behind the outer wall and the sea cliffs, leaving the arena in shadow.

Softly, Iván says, "I think we should tell them. He would want us to use our own judgment, right?"

The Arturos exchange a startled glance.

"What? Tell them what?" Pedrón demands. "Who wants you to use judgment?"

I ignore them all, staring at Iván. His face is a tad apologetic as he leans down and whispers in my ear, "We don't have to tell them everything. But they deserve to know about the captain. We don't have orders for secrecy, right?"

I'm so relieved he feels this way. "I agree," I tell him.

"Red? Iván? What are you whispering about?" Aldo says.

"You must swear to tell no one what we're about to tell you," I say.

"On my honor as a Royal Guard," Pedrón says.

"On my honor as a Royal Guard!" everyone echoes.

I say, "The Arturos are right to be suspicious. I'm afraid Iván and I must inform you all that Captain Bolívar is dead."

"*What?*" says Tall Arturo.

"No!" says Itzal.

"How?" says Aldo.

I'm not sure how many details to reveal. Before I can decide, Iván says, "We're not sure. But there's a good chance he was assassinated."

Pedrón tosses a handful of sand at me. "Why didn't you say anything? Why would you keep that a secret?"

"It's not her fault!" Iván says. "We thought it was the sergeant's place to tell everyone. Or Guardsman Bruno's. We just followed their lead by keeping quiet."

"Oh," Pedrón says, somewhat sheepish. "That makes sense."

It *does* make sense. I never would have thought up such a perfect response.

Aldo says, "Where did you find the captain? How do you know what happened to him?"

Iván gives me a questioning look, and I shake my head slightly.

"We weren't given those details," Iván says smoothly. "I mean, we're just recruits."

"But you *are* friends with the prince, right?" Aldo presses. "Is he the one who told you?"

"Yes. The other night at the soiree."

Aldo looks down at his hands, frowning. I know how he feels. Right now, it feels like all of us have failed.

"This is serious," Itzal says. "Getting Bolivar out of the way made it possible for Sergeant DeLuca to take over training."

"Right," says Tall Arturo. "And Master Santiago wouldn't have been brought in at all if the captain were still here."

"It's all connected," says Itzal.

"That's why we're worried for our prince," says Short Arturo. "Especially now that we know Bolivar is dead. It sure seems like sabotage."

"So what do we do?" Pedrón asks.

"We're just recruits," Aldo says. "First years."

"We should tell someone," says Pedrón.

"We don't know who to trust!" says Itzal.

"There has to be *something* we can do, right?" says Short Arturo.

Everyone starts talking over each other. Their voices get louder and louder, edged with panic. Soon the whole palace will hear us arguing.

RAE·CARSON

"Stop it!" I yell.

Suddenly everyone is looking to me. What would Rosario have me do? Tell them to go to bed and not worry about it? Carry on as though nothing has happened? Pretending has never been my strong suit.

I say, "Harsh winds."

"Rough seas," say Aldo and Iván.

"Still hearts!" says everyone else.

We repeat the Guard motto, in unison this time.

Into the ensuing calm, I say, "We train."

Pedrón smiles.

"How?" says Itzal. "More forms and escapes?"

"Short Arturo is right," I say.

"Just call me Arturito," he says. "Or Rito."

"Rito, then. You're right. We're the most promising class in a decade. All of us bring something. I don't have a lot of experience with a sword, but I can teach dodging and close quarters combat. Iván is a wonder at footwork."

Iván points to Aldo. "He showed us how the forms work. I bet he can teach us how to parry and how to turn those forms into attacks."

Aldo hesitates, not meeting anyone's gaze. "I guess can do that," he says. "I mean, I'm not just here in the Guard because I'm better looking than the rest of you."

Rito rolls his eyes.

"My boys and me," Pedrón says, "we learned some exercises as army recruits that made us strong."

"Good!" I say. "That's good, Pedrón. Exactly what we need."

"We Basajuaños can teach everyone basic archery," says Rito.

"And *I*," Itzal says, "am a magnificent encourager."

I grin at him. "Everyone can help in some way."

"We don't have real swords," Andrés points out.

"We don't need real swords to train," I insist. But we will need them if we ever have to fight. That's a problem we'll have to solve another day.

Iván says, "We can do this."

"We can do this," Aldo agrees.

"If the Guard has been compromised," Tall Arturo says, "or if someone comes for our prince, we'll be ready."

I jump to my feet. "Let's start right now."

The others follow. "Start with what?" Itzal asks.

"Grab your wooden swords," I say. "Let's learn some basic parrying. Aldo, can you help us out tonight?"

He grins. Whatever hesitation he had, I can tell he's fully committed now. "Of course. You're not really training for combat until you've felt the impact of your opponent's sword shiver down your spine."

We spend the next half hour on parrying angles. Aldo is a good teacher. Just like he did on that first day, he shows us how the forms interact, how they've prepared us to defend and counterattack. Even better, he shows us how to anticipate the direction of a swipe by watching someone's shoulders and how to ground ourselves so we don't get knocked down. The wooden swords clattering against each other sound like a group of furious carpenters building something in the arena.

RAE·CARSON

During a pause to wipe the sweat from my forehead, it occurs to me that we *are* building something in this arena.

"There's a lot to learn," Aldo says as he adjusts Itzal's wrist to strengthen the boy's grip. "As you get better, I'll show you how to make sure you don't leave yourself open to a follow-up attack, and how to use your parry to knock an opponent off balance. But for now, I want you all to focus on your stance, your grips, and your angles."

We are exhausted by the time the torches are snuffed. My muscles burn with the satisfaction of having worked hard. As we pass under the portcullis and return to the barracks, Iván whispers in my ear, "I hope we did the right thing by telling them."

"Me too."

We settle into a routine: useless forms in the morning with Master Santiago. Fitness exercises or chores in the afternoon. Our unsanctioned class at night before lights out.

After three days of parrying, we all agree to switch to archery for a few days, to keep ourselves fresh and give our bodies a chance to recover. I expect Iván to be good with a bow. When he misses the target over and over, I give him an arch look.

"What?" he says, looking offended. "I'm allowed to be bad at something."

"But your fingers . . . those calluses . . ."

"These?" He holds them up in the fading light. "Red, I play the vihuela."

"Oh." I blink up at him. In spite of sharing Traitors' Corner, in spite of conspiring together on behalf of our prince, there's still so much I don't know about him.

"Or rather, I used to play the viheula. I haven't picked one up since I joined the Guard. My brother talked me out of bringing it as one of my three items. He said I play so badly I'd end up murdered in my sleep by the other recruits."

I can tell he regrets the joke as soon as it leaves his mouth, remembering the night that Beto and his duckling friends literally tried to do that to me.

"Sorry," he says.

I lift my chin toward his bow and quiver. "You should be sorry. You're terrible."

"You're not much better!"

I shrug. "Once everyone realized I would never have the height for archery, Hector focused on teaching me how to beat larger opponents. We always thought the biggest danger for me was going to be attacks at close quarters. Rosario is competent with a bow, though. And Mara can put an arrow through the eye of a soaring pigeon."

Iván frowns. "That might be the level of competence we need. And we might need it soon."

I'm afraid he's right.

A few days later, we switch to close quarters combat, and I start teaching everyone how to use elbows, knees, and palms to evade a weapon and subdue an attacker. After that, one of Pedrón's friends introduces us to basic shield work.

"It's easy to overuse a shield," he says. "To rely on it too much.

So we'll go easy until we're all adept at basic swordsmanship. We will learn it, though, and learn it well. Solid shield work is one of the most effective ways to keep our empress safe."

True to his word, Itzal encourages us all relentlessly. Whenever someone performs a new skill correctly for the first time, Itzal is there with a smile and a back slap and a "Good job!"

Midway through the second week, we enter the arena to find a handful of second years already there, waiting for us. The sand is wet from a recent rain burst, and their footsteps crunch as they approach.

"Uh-oh," says Aldo.

One steps ahead of the others. He's broad shouldered, with a deep cleft in his chin. "I'm Tanix," he says. "Squad leader for the second years."

"What do you want, Tanix?" I say. There are only five of them, and there are thirteen of us. We can take them, if it comes to that.

"We've been keeping an eye on you," the squad leader says.

"Keep watching," Itzal says. "Maybe you'll learn something."

"No call for that," Tall Arturo says, putting a hand on Itzal's shoulder. "He's here at my invitation."

"What? Why?" says Pedrón.

Tanix lifts his chin and says haughtily, "We'd like to join your class. We think we can help you."

Aldo says, "We're doing just fine."

"Wait," Iván says. "Let's stop and think." His voice is calm and steady—in fact, I can't remember him *ever* raising it—but there's something about it that makes people stand at attention. Something about him. He says, "Are we Royal Guard?"

Several murmurs of assent.

"Are we *all* Royal Guard, sworn to protect Empress Elisa, her family, and her interests?"

"We are," Tanix says. "Every one."

"Tanix and the second years can help us," Tall Arturo insists. "And we can help them. Their training has been stalled for weeks too, and no one knows why."

I say, "This isn't all of you."

"No," Tanix says. "Not everyone could be convinced that we need to team up. We're all in danger of getting cut, you see. The better your class does, the higher the chance they'll get rid of some of us."

"The other way around holds too," Itzal says.

"Yes," Tanix acknowledges.

"Making us all compete against each other is the best way to keep us divided," I point out. "Keep us weak."

"Red has a point," Itzal says.

"But that's how it's always been done, right?" says Pedrón. "After four years, only the best remain in the Guard."

"Maybe things need to change," I mutter.

"You're saying people should stay in the Guard who aren't the best?" Pedrón says.

"No. I just think there has to be a better way. And now, this year, when everything is weird and our prince might be in trouble, we have to stick together more than usual."

"Hear, hear," says Iván.

"Let's vote on it," I say. "All first years in favor of welcoming the second years to our unofficial class, raise your hand."

Arturo's hand shoots into the air. Other hands follow quickly, even Pedrón's.

"It's unanimous," Itzal says, grinning now. "Welcome to the class, Tanix."

Tanix and the second years fail to hide how pleased they are.

After a few minutes of wrangling, we settle on a plan for the next few weeks, which will rotate us through swordsmanship with occasional shield work, archery, hand-to-hand combat, and fitness training. None of us is an expert at anything, but everyone knows something. It will have to be enough.

Two weeks after the second years join us, Luz-Daniel, the assistant cook, slips me a note while he ladles refried beans into my bowl. I slide the note into my pocket. Reading it will have to wait until I can break away from the crowd.

As we're leaving for our afternoon fitness session, I say to anyone who is listening, "I need to use the latrine. See you all out there."

"I'll guard the door for you," Aldo says. My fellow recruits have been taking turns at this, allowing me peace and privacy for tending to my personal needs.

"Thanks, Aldo."

While Aldo stands in the doorway with his back to me, I pull the note from my pocket and read.

Three barrels date syrup destroyed. Searching for others.
From Amalur: continued health. Baby soon.
Keep training.

Relief hits me like a brick, and I almost loose a sob. Rosario understood my note. He's taking action. Elisa and the baby are fine. The prince knows about our training and approves.

But my relief is short-lived, because when I read the note a second time, I realize that thirty-seven barrels remain unaccounted for. Enough to poison an army.

"Red? We'd better hurry," Aldo says from the door.

"Coming." I toss the note into the latrine and cover it with mulch, then hurry to rejoin Aldo at the door. "Let's go." As we jog through the tunnel toward the arena, I add, "Aldo, you were great last night. Your parrying reflexes are incredible. I'm learning a lot from you."

He beams. "And you're learning fast. Which is good."

"The two of us are on the small side. We have to work harder than everyone else."

"Yes," he says solemnly. "In addition, I bear the great burden of beauty."

"But you soldier on."

"By the grace of God."

We are the last of the recruits to arrive, and we barely have time to take up our positions before Bruno enters, followed by two other Guards.

"Good afternoon, first years. Today, you'll be running the walls. This time, you'll carry packs filled with sand."

RAE·CARSON

We know better than to groan aloud, but I sense some of the boys around me drooping. It's a very hot day, the worst kind of day for running.

"But first, I'm afraid we have to announce a cut. We've put it off as long as possible, but the time has come."

Everyone around me is frozen in place. A muffled din of voices filters toward us from the nearby stables. The sun beats on my scalp. I can hardly breathe. *Don't get cut*, Rosario said. If I'm kicked out of the Guard, I will have failed him.

Guardsman Bruno says, "Itzal, you are dismissed from training. The empress thanks you for your service."

I'm dizzy with relief. Then sick with disappointment. Itzal is clumsy, yes. Slow to learn anything physical. But he's intelligent and earnest. I'll never forget the day I received my uniform, when Itzal stood before me to create a privacy barrier.

Itzal's head is down, his shoulders rounded with defeat. "I knew it," he mutters.

I'm hardly aware of what I'm doing when I break formation and go to him. "Itzal," I say, wrapping my arms around his shoulders. "You will be missed."

Suddenly we're surrounded by recruits, and Itzal is forced to suffer patting on the back and hugs and even a robust hair ruffle from Pedrón.

"Good job, Itzal," someone says.

"Stay strong," says another.

"We won't forget you."

"Still hearts, my brother."

Itzal's eyes are filled with tears as he breaks away, but his head is high, his back straight, as he begins walking toward the barracks to retrieve his things.

"Wait," Guardsman Bruno calls out. "I'm not finished. The rest of you, back into formation!"

We hurry to comply. Itzal stops where he is and stands tall, though his expression is perplexed.

"Itzal, you have other qualities that have been noted by your teachers," Bruno says. "And it's clear you've earned the respect and affection of your brothers. Er, and sister."

Itzal does not respond. He simply waits, calm and poised.

"One of our stewards is soon to retire," Bruno says. "It's exceedingly rare for us to offer a staff training position to someone who hasn't made it beyond the first year of recruitment, but we feel an exception is in order. Recruit Itzal, are you willing to accept an apprenticeship with the quartermaster? It will entail bookkeeping, supply chain, and inventory management."

"Absolutely yes sir thank you sir with pleasure yes."

Bruno cracks a small smile. "In that case, gather your things and report to the central storeroom at once." He pauses. "And now the empress thanks you for your *continued* service."

"Yes, sir!"

Aldo starts clapping, and I join him. Soon, everyone takes up the applause, and Itzal flashes us a quick grin as he steps under the portcullis.

"Light feet, recruits!" Bruno yells. "Ten times around the palace tonight. The first five finishers get dessert."

The Guards hand us packs, which we hitch over our

shoulders. Guardsman Bruno gives the signal. As one, we rush for the wall.

I usually finish well, in spite of my shorter legs. Even with the added burden of the pack, I have a good chance at the top five. I'm not sure it's worth making the effort on such a hot day for a mere dessert, though. Then again, finishing well will shore up my case to survive the next cut.

The key to endurance running is to occupy your thoughts with something else, so I ignore the weight bouncing against my back, pick up my pace, and think of Itzal. I'm glad he found a permanent place with the Guard. I'll miss him in training, but at least he'll stick around. In fact, next time I see him, I'll make sure he knows he's still welcome in our nightly class.

After the third lap, I let myself fall behind a little, just enough so Iván can catch up. When he does, I whisper about the note I received.

"Still thirty-seven barrels unaccounted for," he whispers back.

As winter approaches, an unseasonable heat wave turns the arena sand into scorching lava that we feel even through our boots. My nose reddens and peels, then reddens again before it can heal. We are forced to launder dust and sweat from our uniforms every single evening, giving us less time for our unsanctioned class.

But we keep at it, training every night before bed. Tanix and his small group of second years maintain perfect attendance, and their addition is a boon; one is a natural at sword and shield, another knows some grappling throws that are especially useful for taking down a larger opponent. Itzal joins us when the quartermaster allows; a few weeks later, he shows up with one of the cooks and an apprentice blacksmith.

"We are all Guards, even if some of us aren't fighters," he says proudly. "And we are all willing to take up arms on behalf of our empress, should the need arise."

The rest of the class votes to let them stay.

The palace becomes dense with bodies and riotous with noise, for people are arriving from all over the empire for the annual Deliverance Gala. The courtyard plaza is packed with supply wagons and nobles in their carriages, all surrounded by personal guards and servants, camels and horses. Some settle into townhomes just outside the walls, along the famous Avenida de la Serpiente. But plenty of others keep quarters in the palace itself, and out of necessity, our afternoon fitness training is replaced by running errands and messages between them all.

"That happened to us too," Tanix tells us one night. "We acted as pages to every conde and condesa in the empire for three weeks. Pay attention. It's good experience. As Royal Guard, you'll be expected to know every corridor and corner and courtyard of this palace so well you could navigate it blindfolded."

Three days before the gala, I get another message from Rosario.

Four more barrels destroyed.
Fernando not fit for duty but recovering.

Thirty-three barrels still unaccounted for. And while I'm delighted that Fernando is recovering, he won't be able to protect the prince throughout Deliverance Week.

The morning before the gala, we have taken our places in the sand and we are performing Eastern Wind when the monastery bells ring out, so startling and crisp and strange that I drop my sword.

The other boys laugh at me. I smile back sheepishly, telling my heart to calm down, the firing nerves in my limbs to settle. I realize that I haven't had a startle moment like that in a long time. Weeks, for certain. Months, perhaps.

Guard training has changed me.

The bells continue to sing as I retrieve my sword and dust off sand from its wooden blade. The sound is a raucous tumble of joy, so much louder and stronger than its usual marking of time or its weekly call to prayer.

Master Santiago pauses, looking toward the bell tower, his eyes narrowed.

Guardsman Bruno suddenly appears through the portcullis, running toward us, a huge grin spreading beneath his giant nose. "It's a prince!" he calls out. "The empress has given birth to a prince! Alive and healthy. She has named him Alejandro Hector né Riqueza de Ventierra."

Cheers erupt from every direction—the palace watchtower, the nearby blacksmith, the entry courtyard, the stables—as word spreads about why those bells are ringing.

Iván is the first to cry out, "Long live Prince Alejandro!"

and we quickly take up the cry. Within moments, the entire palace rings with the cheer.

"Long live Prince Alejandro! Long live Prince Alejandro!"

If Elisa were here right now, nothing in the world could stop me from running to her. I want to see that baby more than anything. Kiss his tiny forehead. Tell him how glad I am that he's here.

Then again, maybe I don't have a right to any of these things. Maybe this joy is not mine to hold. I'm not his sister.

Gradually the cheering dies down. The monastery bells cease, though I know they'll take up again tomorrow and probably every day for a week, as is the tradition when a royal heir is born.

As the noise subsides, an odd muffled sound turns my head. To my right, Aldo is bent over slightly. It takes me a second to understand. He is quietly weeping.

He notices me noticing him and he peers at me through teary, long-lashed eyes. He blinks. Wipes his eyes. Composes himself. "Good news, right?" he says through a timorous smile.

"The best news," I tell him.

I reach out to pat his shoulder, but he flinches from my touch, and I let my hand drop.

RAE·CARSON

20

Then

"GO on then," Orlín said, raising his hand to strike her.

Mula flinched and darted out of the kitchen doorway, where the innkeeper had been lying in wait for her. It had been a whole day, and she still hadn't spied out their guests' supplies.

Reluctantly, she dragged herself back up the stairs to the dormer rooms. The scents of fresh-baked bread and leek soup and dogmeat stew followed her from the kitchen, tortured her, as she crept toward one of the doors.

She was a hollow girl, she'd known it for some time, but there was nothing like hunger to remind a body. It felt as though emptiness clawed at her, threatening to eat her away.

The two men had left in the morning, Orlín had assured her. The south-facing room should be empty. Mula put her ear to the door and listened. Nothing.

The door pushed open easily. She peeked inside. Relief flooded her, for the room was empty save for two cots and a single bulging travel pack. She closed the door silently behind her and tiptoed forward.

The pack was made of thick leather, with a flap that tied it closed. She fumbled with the knot, flipped it open.

The most amazing smell she had ever smelled walloped her in the face. Saliva swamped her mouth.

She reached inside, rummaged through, until she found it. Dried leaves wrapped around something glorious, something magical. She peeled them back and drew in breath.

It was dried meat. Nothing more. But it smelled better than any dried meat she'd ever had. She couldn't help herself. Her hands brought the meat to her mouth of their own accord. She bit down. Flavor exploded on her tongue.

It was venison, still a little tender, smoked and salted, cured with a bit of sugar and something else she couldn't identify. She could eat this forever. Every day for the rest of her—

A rough hand gripped her shoulder, spun her around. She almost choked on the venison.

"Hello, little thief," said the Joyan man with the eye patch.

Mula couldn't say anything back. Her mouth was too full.

He snatched the rest of the meat from her hand. "Come with me," he said, and he dragged her across the hallway to the other room.

The two women were inside, sitting on their cots, the Invierno standing over them. "Look what I just found," said the eye-patch man, thrusting the girl forward. She tumbled to her knees, scurried across the floor to the wall, where she huddled as small and tight as she could get. "She was after this." He held up the packet of meat.

The girl could finally swallow. She said, "I'm sorry! I didn't mean to steal! It was a black thought, and I tried to make it go away, but it smelled so—"

The plump woman reached for her, but Mula flinched away, knocking her head against the wall.

"I'm not going to hurt you!" the fine lady said. "Here. Have more." She grabbed some meat from the pack, tossed it at Mula.

The girl snatched it from the air, shoved it into her mouth quick. The taste made her want to weep.

"Look at me," the fine lady said, and Mula tried, but it was terrifying, looking into those deep brown eyes that were trying to see inside her. "If you weren't there to steal, why were you in that room?"

Mula froze.

"Did the innkeeper put you up to it?"

Mula said nothing. The fine lady grabbed another piece of meat and tossed it to her.

The girl snatched it from the air, shoved it into her mouth.

"Mula? Is that your name?"

The girl shrugged, chewing as fast as she could. This was the most food she'd eaten at one time in as long as she could remember.

"Please answer my question. It's an easy one, yes?"

Mula said, "I wanted to know what merry jam smelled like." There. A partial truth. Not so bad to say.

Gently, the tall woman said, "But did Orlín put you up to it?"

They weren't going to let it go. "No. I did it my own self." But her words were shivery and she couldn't make herself look the fine lady in the eye, no matter how hard she tried. The lie echoed in the room around her. Shame clogged her throat.

The Invierno had been silent until now. He leaned forward and said, "God hates liars."

Yes, Mula agreed silently. *And me most especially.*

The fine lady rose from the cot and began to pace in the tiny room, turning and turning and turning, a thumbnail between her teeth. Finally she whirled, faced the eye-patch man. "We have to leave. We can't risk staying."

"No!" Mula said, scrambling to her feet. "He'll say it's my fault! He'll . . . If you stay, you can bleed me. Right now. For free."

"What?" said the tall woman.

Before Mula could explain, the eye-patch man grabbed her shoulder. "You're staying right here until we're packed up, with everything accounted for."

"Careful, Belén," said the tall woman. "She's just a little girl."

"I'm not! I'm big!" said Mula, squirming, but the eye-patch man held her fast.

They gathered and sorted and organized with incredible efficiency. Within moments, they were cloaked and booted, packs slung over their shoulders. Together, they hurried down the stairs, Mula trapped in the middle like a sausage in a blanket.

The common room had filled with villagers coming in for their evening ale. The air was wet and hot with hard-worked bodies. Two men Mula recognized from the market stood in the corner, playing their vihuelas. A few people clapped along.

Orlín wove through the crowd toward them, a wide, false

grin on his face. Mula knew that grin. It meant he was on the edge of rage. He just needed a little push.

"Some ale for you all?" he asked cheerfully, but his eyes roved their full packs. "I also have dandelion wine in the cellar, which we save for our higher class of customer."

"We're leaving," said the fine lady.

Mula didn't see the blow coming, but suddenly, she was on the floor, blood leaking into her eye from a gash on her forehead. The room swam. She clutched for the nearest bench, trying to make sense of the world.

"What did you do?" Orlín advanced on her. "Were you caught stealing again, you filthy little rat—"

The music ceased. The laughter was whisked away as if by a wind. Stools scraped. Embers popped in the hearth.

"Leave her be," said a quiet, deadly voice.

Mula peered at the innkeeper, blinking. It took a moment to parse what she was seeing: the tall woman, her lips at Orlín's ear, her dagger at Orlín's throat.

The plump woman in fancy braids looked on, horrified. She whispered, "Oh, Mara, what have you done?"

The knob in Orlín's throat bobbed against the dagger. "It's the height of rudeness," he said calmly, "to threaten a man in his own home."

"It's worse to beat an innocent child," said the tall woman named Mara.

"The mule is mine," the innkeeper said. "I can do whatever I wish with it. Do you tell the cook to be gentle with the turnips?"

Mara pressed the dagger into his skin. Blood welled at the tip.

Mula wanted to run, as far and fast as she could. She'd seen enough common-room brawls to know it was always the littlest ones who got hurt. The weakest. The ones who tried to hide under the table. The ones who couldn't get away because their heads were pounding and their vision was blurry.

Besides, Mula knew something no one else did. The fancy braided lady had a sparkle stone. If she wanted to, she could burn the whole place down.

The silence grew long.

Finally the plump lady said, "Mula! How much did this man pay for you?"

The girl had no idea. The day she was sold to Orlín was one of the gaps in her memory. She thought hard. Did she imagine that she remembered the glint of copper as it clinked into the monster lady's hand?

Just a few coppers, then. She was sure of it. Pride made her say, "Three . . . three silvers."

The fancy lady turned to Orlín. "I'll buy her from you."

Mula gasped. Everyone in the common room began to murmur.

Carefully, the woman named Mara lowered her dagger. A slow smile spread across Orlín's face.

He said, "I fed the mule, raised it, clothed it. I can't let it go for less than eight silvers."

The fancy lady frowned. "I need to do some trading to come up with that much coin. How about I give you three silvers now, to feed her and care for her tonight, and seven more when I fetch her in the morning?"

Ten silvers! It was an unheard-of price for a slave, even one who could be bled for a few coppers once in a while.

"Deal!" Orlín said.

They spat into their hands and shook on it.

The fancy lady crouched down and peered into the girl's face. Even though the room was spinning, the girl saw gentleness in her eyes.

"You bought me," Mula said, her voice full of wonder. "You bought me!"

"No! I didn't buy . . . just . . . stay strong. I'll be back for you in the morning."

The fancy lady and her companions swept out of the common room, into the cold night. Mula stared after them. Light filled her soul. The vihuelas picked up where they left off, and it felt like they were singing just for her.

Finally she could bear it no longer, and she yelled to anyone who might listen, "Did you see that? A fine lady bought me! I'm going to be the slave of a fine lady!"

Mula did not sleep one bit that night. She gave up eventually, sat on her bedroll, brought her knees to her chest, and went over that moment again and again in her head. A pair of kind eyes looking deep inside her, really seeing her, telling her to stay strong. *I'll be back for you in the morning.*

Orlín did not keep his word, refusing to feed her breakfast. Then he demanded that she remove the shift she was wearing.

She didn't care. As soon as it was light, she bounced naked out the door to wait on the stoop. She saw them in the distance, at the edge of the trading square. They were checking over the horses, strapping packs to their saddles, talking among themselves.

Fear shot through her like an arrow. Maybe they had forgotten about her. Or maybe it had all been a lie, and they didn't intend to take her with them at all. *Joyans are known for lying*, Orlín always said.

Her legs twitched to run after them, to beg them to take her away, and she was just about to give in when the fine lady and her companions began walking toward her.

"Where are your clothes?" the lady demanded.

"You bought me," Mula said. "You didn't buy my clothes."

The fine lady took a deep breath. She sent the eye-patch man into the inn to settle their agreement with Orlín.

The tall woman, Mara, said, "I'll go fetch her something to wear," and she hurried off.

The Invierno man stared down at the girl, and Mula stared right back. She'd once killed a man who looked very much like him.

He'd cut the false black out of his hair, and now it was close shorn and yellow-white. "Are you a . . ." She almost said "White Hair," but then she remembered the Invierno word. "An animagus?" He had a sparkle stone too, she was almost sure of it, but it didn't sing to her the same way as the one the fine lady was hiding. "You look like an animagus. But your hair is ugly."

The Invierno bristled. "I am a pr—"

"Storm!" the fine lady snapped. More gently, she said to Mula, "Storm is my dear friend, and you will mind him always."

"Oh, yes," Mula said. "I will mind perfectly. You are going to be so glad you bought me."

The woman just stared down at her. She obviously didn't believe the girl.

"I can cook a little!" she said, quick before the lady could have any regrets. "I can clean, scrub laundry. I'm good at changing rushes, fetching water. I'm big, so I can carry a lot of firewood."

"How old are you?" the fine lady asked.

Mula shrugged.

"Do you have a name besides Mula? I don't want to call you that. No one should call anyone that."

"Sometimes Orlín calls me Rat."

"What about before you were with Orlín? You had a mother, yes? What did she call you?"

Mula was sad to disappoint her new master so soon, but she said the truth anyway: "I don't remember."

The fine lady frowned deeply. "A little girl ought to have a proper name."

"Like what?"

"How about you name yourself?"

Mula's mouth dropped open. "For true?"

"For true."

"Anything?"

"Anything you want."

The Invierno called Storm leaned forward. "A name is a grave matter."

Mula nodded. "I will think hard about it."

The fine lady smiled. She had a beautiful smile, soft and kind and wise. "Just let me know when you've decided."

Mara returned with a blouse for her, which fell all the way to her knees. They lifted her onto one of the horses—a giant near-black creature that danced in place—and the girl was too filled with wonder and amazement to be even a little bit scared.

They rode east, away from the village.

The girl dared to ask, "Where are we going? Joya d'Arena is west. . . ."

"A very good friend of mine is missing," said the fine lady. "We have to find him. His name is Hector, and you will like him very much."

"I'm big," the girl said solemnly. "I can help."

"I'm sure you can," said Mara, riding beside them.

"By the time we find him," the fine lady said, "we can introduce you using your new name."

She was going to have a name! A true name. A perfect name. Something a little bit Joyan, but a little bit Invierno too, just like her. It would be the most beautiful name she could think of. The *strongest* name she could think of.

Mountain jays called after them, and a crisp breeze whisked the clouds through a cornflower sky, heralding a crystal-sharp winter. The girl who would never be called Mula again felt the hollow space inside her filling up, with hope and warmth and maybe even her very own self.

RAE·CARSON

21
Now

THE day before the gala dawns bright and hot, and as usual we are training with Master Santiago. Guardsman Bruno observes us this morning, perhaps to discover why our training is taking so long.

Master Santiago has become extraordinarily creative in his ability to find fault with our forms. I make a game of anticipating what imagined flaw he'll focus on next—maybe the way Arturo grunts.

Santiago opens his mouth to berate someone, but Sergeant DeLuca barrels through the portcullis and into the arena.

"Sergeant," says Master Santiago. "What a pleasant surprise. Are you here to inspect these wretched recruits? They persist in evading proficiency, but they are not as shameful as they were."

"Not at this time," the sergeant says. "I'm here for two quick pieces of official business, and then you can resume your training."

Santiago bows his head and steps back, ceding the arena floor. "The class is yours, Sergeant."

Guardsman Bruno peers at his superior, eyes narrowed. Something about this isn't part of the usual routine. Well, nothing about our class is part of the usual routine. But DeLuca seems as pleased as a well-brushed pony, and for some reason, this fills me with dread.

DeLuca says, "The time has come for the first years to choose your squad leader. It should be someone with proven competence, with the ability to inspire and make good decisions. Someone who has helped make the rest of you better, someone you trust to lead you for the next three years."

No one says anything, but it feels like a ripple passes through our group. We've known this was coming. I've already decided to vote for Iván, whose quiet intelligence has made us pay attention more than once. He's had just as much training as I've had, but he's so much smoother when talking to people.

"So consider who you will elect while we take care of the second item of business," he says.

Something about the way he says it causes everyone to go very still.

He folds his hands behind his back. "I've received disturbing reports about the behavior of some of our recruits," he says. "As a result, I'm afraid I have no choice but to make another cut today."

Guardsman Bruno's mouth parts in surprise.

I can't imagine what the sergeant is talking about. Since Valentino's ducklings were cut, everyone has been on their best behavior. We're doing everything they ask of us. And *more*.

Beside me, Aldo shifts in place. I hope it's not him. He's the smallest and youngest of us, true. But also the cleverest and quickest.

"Recruit Red, step forward," DeLuca barks, so much louder than necessary, and my stomach drops into my toes. "Pack your things and go. Her Imperial Majesty thanks you for your service."

"What?" says Iván.

I try to step forward, but my legs won't budge. I can't even look at anyone. I don't want them to see my face.

"What reports are you talking about?" says Guardsman Bruno.

DeLuca rounds on Bruno. "I do not have to explain myself."

Bruno doesn't back down. "I thought my input on the recruits meant something. I'm usually consulted on these decisions."

"This ruling was handled by those above your rank and station," DeLuca counters. "And above mine. But if you want to do this here, we'll do it here. If you want to embarrass your recruits, fine. The fact is, it has come to our attention that having a young lady in the Guard is an insurmountable distraction."

I can barely hear his words for the blood rushing past my ears.

Bruno inhales deeply, considering his next words. Finally: "Red is one of the best in this class. And this whole class is better than average."

"You're out of line, Guardsman," DeLuca says coldly. "And you're wrong. For blessed sakes, man, the recruits are still practicing their *forms.* We've never have a class take so long to make so little progress."

"Sir—" Bruno begins.

"Guardsman," DeLuca interrupts, "if you contradict me one more time, the only thing you'll change my mind about is your fitness for duty. Report to my office after class today."

Bruno snaps to attention. "Yes, sir."

DeLuca addresses the recruits, though he avoids looking at me. He says, "You don't understand this now, but one day it will be clear to you. One cannot expect boys your age to learn and grow when there is such a lovely young woman in your midst. It's our job as your teachers and mentors to shelter you from distractions as you mature into the young men we expect and know you can be."

I finally find my voice. "I am not a distraction."

"What?" DeLuca says, apparently surprised that I'm still here.

My face is hot with fury. My fists shiver with an overwhelming need to bash something. "I am not a distraction. I am a Guard recruit, just like the others."

"Dear girl," says DeLuca. His indulgent smile makes my skin crawl. "It's meant as a compliment. Of course you're not like the others. You're beautiful and charming. Most young ladies in the palace wish they had half your qualities. You should be proud."

"Red is not a distraction," Iván says.

"She's an asset," says Arturo.

"You can't tell us to pick our squad leader and then kick her out!" says Pedrón.

DeLuca turns on them with the same open fury that he

showed Bruno. "You are all speaking out of turn, and you'll run the walls tonight after dinner. It will give you time to consider your words, and how you've let this young lady manipulate and deceive you. You wanted proof that she's a distraction—well, there it is! Your training would be much farther along by now if she had never taken to the sand."

I stare daggers at him, my fists clenched at my sides. He would never dare cut me for such a ridiculous reason if Elisa were around. I can't believe he dares it now. Something happened. Or someone got to him. And the only person I can think of with the power to make him cut me, the ward of the empress, is Conde Astón of Ciénega del Sur.

It hits me all of a sudden: He wants me out of the way for the Deliverance Gala. He wants to make sure Rosario is as exposed as possible.

I'm already cut. The worst thing that could possibly happen to me has happened. So I have no hesitation saying, "You are going to regret this, DeLuca. You have my word on it."

If my threat lands, he gives no indication. "Gather your things and go."

Suddenly I'm surrounded by recruits. "We won't forget you, Red," someone says. "This is wrong," says another. Hands pat my shoulders. One grabs my hand and squeezes.

All at once, the space around me is taken up with Iván. He leans down and whispers in my ear, "Get to Rosario. We'll figure this out."

"Get back in line right now," DeLuca says. "Or there will be further cuts!"

Before Iván can step away, I grab his collar and whisper back, "Make sure no one eats or drinks tomorrow. Especially during the annual Deliverance toast."

Hands grab me. My eyes are locked with Iván's as DeLuca drags me away.

Iván nods once, slightly.

DeLuca shoves me through the portcullis. "Guardsman Bruno," he says. "Escort this civilian out of the barracks by the quickest route possible."

Bruno watches over me as I gather my baby rattle, my Godstone, and Father Nicandro's book from the drawer. I leave the broken shards of my dye pot where they are. They're useless now.

"Ready," I tell him.

"You must change out of your uniform too."

I stare at him.

"I'm sorry, Red," he says. "I don't agree with DeLuca's decision, but . . ."

"But you have to follow orders."

He nods.

"Can you at least give me a little privacy?"

"Don't make me regret this."

He turns his back, and I quickly shuck shirt, vest, belt, boots, and pants, and re-don the desert garb I wore the day I first took to the sand.

I stare at Bruno's back a moment, wondering if there's something else I ought to do while his back is turned, something sneaky that might help me. . . .

But of course I can't think of a single thing.

I shove the Godstone and the baby rattle into my pocket, then grab the *Articles*. "Now I'm ready."

Bruno looks me up and down. His gaze lingers on my bound book, but he chooses not to make an issue of it. "Follow me."

He leads me through the tunnel, past the latrine, to the side gate where they take deliveries for the barracks. When he opens the pass-through door, I step into the alley between the barracks and the stables. The sun is cruel on my face.

"Farewell, Red," Bruno says. "I wish you every blessing." Then he ducks back inside. I hear the heavy bar slam down, closing off the barracks to me. The guards standing at this entrance couldn't let me back in even if they wanted to.

Now what?

The alley is busy with gala traffic. It feels like everyone is staring at me, the girl who just exited the barracks empty-handed. I'm well known here, the former ward of the empress, the half-human hybrid. And now that my hair has grown back to my shoulders, my white streak has surely grown to my ear.

Get to Rosario, Iván said.

I hurry through the plaza to the main entrance of the Sky Wing, where I'm stopped by a pair of unfamiliar guards.

"I'm the ward of the empress," I tell them. "Lady Red Sparkle Stone. I live here."

One snickers at my name. Someone is always ready to snicker at my name. But the other says, "Do you have a pass signed by Sergeant DeLuca of the Royal Guard?"

"No."

"Then you don't live here, at least not until after Deliverance Week is over. We have strict orders to let no one into the Sky Wing without a written pass from Sergeant DeLuca."

Someone wanted to be sure I was unable to get in to warn Rosario.

"Thank you, gentlemen," I tell the guards. Glumly I add, "Happy Deliverance Day."

There has to be another way inside.

I could access the monarch's quarters through a secret entrance in the city, but I'd still have to traverse several corridors of the Sky Wing to get from there to Rosario's suite. If they caught me, I'd see the inside of the prison tower before I ever saw Rosario.

The monastery bells ring the hour. Which gives me an idea. The sanctuary is always open to the public, night or day, all year round. I'll start there.

I hurry through the plaza, dodging carriages and supply wagons and teams of horses. A few merchants have set up stalls on the outskirts, those who could acquire a coveted palace vendor license. They do quick business this time of year, with so many visitors in need of extra items. I pass a saddler, a counter full of steaming meat pies, even a jeweler.

Halfway past the jeweler, I pause. I dig into my pocket and fish out the baby rattle.

"Lady Red," the merchant says, trying not to stare at my white mark. I don't recognize him, but it's not unusual for people to recognize me. "I thought you were . . . er, how can I help you?"

RAE·CARSON

Carefully, so that I don't drop anything, I find the tiny latch at the base of the rattle and flick it open, just like Rosario showed me months ago. The ball of the rattle dislodges from the base with a pop, and I upend the contents into my palm.

Four gemstones wink up at me, small but lovely. A sapphire of royal blue, an emerald with one noticeable inclusion but still beautiful. A tiny ruby with a slight pink cast. A golden tiger's-eye. "How much will you give me for these?"

The merchant's eyes widen. He lowers his head to peer closely at my palm. "Hmmm," he says. "Interesting. I don't know. . . . Maybe that one . . ."

"Sir?" I prompt.

"I don't have enough coin on hand to purchase them all," he says. "But I can give you three gold crowns and eight silvers for the tigereye and the emerald."

I don't know much about gemstones, but that price hardly seems fair. Alas, I'm in too much of a hurry to haggle much. "Throw in that silk amulet bag," I say, pointing to a tiny bag of blue silk embroidered with green vines and leaves. "And you have a deal." It hangs on a silken tie and closes tight with matching drawstrings. Ladies wear them to keep locks of their children's hair close to their hearts, or fill them with their favorite scent. It will be perfect for carrying my Godstone.

"Deal," says the merchant, and we make the exchange.

I slip the Godstone into my new amulet pouch as I move to the next stall, a weapons seller with several items on display, including a crossbow, a few swords, and several daggers. Showpieces for noble scions. Most of the daggers are fairly useless, with their ornate hilts and tiny blades, best for breaking seals on correspondence.

"Let me see that sword," I say to the merchant, a younger man with day-old stubble and a blacksmith's apron.

He hands me the one I indicate. It's smaller than the others, but it comes with a belted scabbard, and when I hold it out straight, the light hits the steel blade with perfect evenness and clarity. "A nice piece," I tell him.

"I made it myself!" he beams. "That's Basajuan steel too, so you'll never have to worry about it shattering."

"How much?"

"Five golden crowns."

I set the sword back on the counter, disappointed. "I don't have that much."

"Well, make me an offer I can't refuse," he says.

I fish out my baby rattle again, and retrieve the ruby. "Three crowns and this ruby."

"Done!" he says, so quickly that I'm sure I've overpaid.

But if danger is coming for Rosario, no price is too high. Now I have a sword, a safe way to carry my Godstone, and enough silver to eat for several weeks. Buoyed by my success, I head toward the monastery entrance.

Five paces away, I stop short. My throat itches. My limbs twitch. There's a buzzing inside me, like something is about to burst from my skin. I look around frantically, because I know this feeling.

An animagus is nearby. In the palace complex. During Deliverance Week.

"Out of the way!" someone calls, and I realize I've blocked his horse cart. I step aside, still studying my surroundings, racking my memory for anyone who might have brought an animagus along with them. Ambassador Songbird does not have a sorcerer among his staff. None of the condes or condesas I know of keep one for an adviser. The only animagus who is allowed unfettered access to the palace is Storm, Elisa's brother-in-law, and he is far, far away.

I hurry into the monastery, more desperate than ever to reach Rosario.

22

Now

THE sanctuary is more crowded than usual, with stable boys in work frocks sitting side by side with noble ladies in fine silks. The altar reeks of burned blood and rose petals, for many choose to perform the Sacrament of Pain during Deliverance Week.

I search the faces, my gaze lingering on anyone in priest's robes, hoping to see Father Nicandro. But he is not here.

I'm almost to the archival room when a priest steps in front of me, blocking my way. "Can I help you, child?" he says.

I don't recognize him, so I have no idea if I can trust this man, but time is short and I'm desperate, so I say, "Where is Father Nicandro?"

"Father Nicandro is unavailable at the moment." Meaning, *He's the head priest and you seem like no one, so go away.* "Perhaps—"

"Tell him Lady Red Sparkle Stone is here to see him on a matter of grave urgency."

He opens his mouth, closes it. Ponders the white streak in my hair. "Very well," he says. "Have a seat on the bench." He turns before I can reply.

I adjust my new sword and sit. The bench grows hard beneath my rear. It feels as though an eternity passes, though I'm sure it's only a few moments, before Nicandro comes shuffling my way, aided by his cane.

"Red," he says, voice low. "I did not expect to see you. Please come. Hurry."

He guides me past the archives and into a private prayer chapel. Candles line the walls. Kneeling cushions litter the floors. The arched ceiling is low, trapping heat and the scent of the rose petals that are scattered everywhere. This is where the priests themselves come to pray, when they need a respite from their flock. For now, at least, we are alone.

"Now tell me," says Nicandro.

"I was cut from the Guard for being a 'distraction' to the boys."

The priest frowns. "That reeks of political maneuvering."

"Yes. Someone got to Sergeant DeLuca, convinced him that cutting me was a good idea. Rosario's supporters have been eliminated one by one. I fear for him."

"I'll get a message to him at once."

"Thank you."

"Wait here." He turns to leave.

"One more thing."

"Yes?"

"There's an animagus in the city. Maybe right here in the palace."

Father Nicandro's eyes narrow. "I thought I might have sensed something earlier this morning, but then it was gone, like a breeze."

"I'm certain of it."

"I believe you, dear girl. Unlike you, I can only sense Godstones when they are drawing magic. You've always been more sensitive than I, and I'm an old man besides."

"Do you know of anyone attending the gala who would retain the services of a sorcerer?"

"I do not. Is your Godstone with you?"

I reach for my amulet and lift it toward him.

"Good. Keep it safe. It may keep you safe."

"How will my Godstone help?"

"I don't know that it will . . . though in the past, the empress achieved some immunity to the magic of others with her own Godstone. In any case, now is not the time to discuss the finer points of theology." His shoulders slouch, and he suddenly seems ten years older. But when I peer into his face, his eyes are full of fire. "I'll get a message to the prince as quickly as possible."

Getting a response from the prince could take hours, so I pick one of the largest cushions and settle in for a long wait. After a few minutes, though, I'm twitching to move around, to do something. So I stand, kick all the cushions to the side of the room to clear a space, and draw my new sword.

I haven't worked with a real sword in months, and it feels foreign and cold in my hand as I start moving through the forms. But my wrist and forearm adjust. I'm stronger now, thanks to endless practice with Master Santiago, and the sword is so well balanced that by the time I hit Bulwark, I'm grinning. I feel so fluid. So powerful.

I whip the sword through the air, performing some swipes

that Iván taught us during our nightly class. Then a few thrusts. Careful of my footwork, I move through some parrying positions I learned from Aldo. The sword sings.

My blood is warm, my forehead damp with sweat, by the time Rosario himself enters, accompanied by two fully armored guards.

"Little sister," he says.

"You shouldn't have come yourself!" I tell him. "It's not safe for you to . . ." The look on his face silences me.

"I just . . . wanted to see you."

I sheath my sword and wrap my arms around him, hugging him close. "It's good to see you too, little brother."

He clings a little tighter than usual, then disengages, saying, "Nice sword."

"I thought it might come in handy."

"Father Nicandro says you were cut from the Guard."

"Yes," I say, avoiding his gaze. His two accompanying guards wear breastplates trimmed in blue steel, marking them as knights of the Eastern Reaches. "I'm glad Juan-Carlos was able to lend you some men."

"Efren and Iago have proven themselves invaluable," Rosario says. "I'm so grateful to them and to Juan-Carlos. You may speak freely in front of them." He sighs deeply. "I really wish you hadn't been cut."

"I'm so sorry. I know I failed—"

"It wasn't your fault! I'm more concerned that DeLuca was convinced to cut you at all, because it means someone beside the empress has undue influence on him."

"That's what I'm worried about too."

"Do you still think he's the traitor?"

I shake my head. "Or at least he's not *the* traitor. He gives orders like a man who's been taking orders, and he talked about how the command came from someone who was 'above his rank and station.'"

"That's what happens when you teach blind obedience," Rosario says. "Sometimes it doesn't matter who the orders come from anymore."

"But he's not innocent. He still had—*has*—a part in this. Someone gave the intruder a key to Bolivar's quarters, right?"

"Right." His face falls, and he stares off at nothing in particular. He has the longest, prettiest eyelashes I've ever seen, and even though he's grown tall and lanky, those long-lashed eyes make him seem as vulnerable as a babe. "Red," he says. "What do I do?"

"Oh, Rosario, I wish I knew."

"We only found seven of those barrels."

"What about the ship itself? The *Kestrel*?"

"Now *that* was interesting."

"What do you mean?"

"The ship is long gone, left port more than a week ago. But we tracked down its records . . . it belongs to one of my father's former mistresses."

"That *is* interesting."

"I have no idea what it means, though."

"Rosario, maybe you shouldn't attend the gala. If anything happens, it will be then."

He straightens, trying to look royal. "I have to. It's my responsibility. I have to give the annual blessing, show myself around, assure everyone that all is normal. People come from all over the empire to be in the same room with their empress. There'll be no empress this year, of course, but at least we can give them a prince."

I'm shaking my head. "It's not worth it. Not if your safety is at risk. Rosario, I sensed an *animagus* nearby."

He draws in breath, but collects himself quickly. "If I don't go, our adversaries will use my absence to their advantage. 'See how he doesn't take his responsibilities seriously?' they'll say. 'See what a coward he is?'" When I don't respond, he adds, "Besides, I have Efren and Iago to keep me safe."

"And me."

He brightens. "And you. I'll give orders that you're to be allowed full palace access. Want to stay in my room tonight? You can have the floor."

I'm so relieved to have somewhere to go. "Yes, please."

Even though I'm snugged up in the space between the wall and Rosario's bed, nested into the softest pillows and the most luxurious quilt in the whole empire, I can't make myself sleep.

I roll everything around in my head: my failed adoption. Captain Bolivar dead, possibly poisoned by the most powerful conde in the empire. Fernando ill, unable to protect Rosario. Barrels of dream syrup hidden somewhere here in the capital. Training for Royal Guard recruits inexplicably stalled. I wish I knew what it all meant.

One thing is certain, Efren and Iago and I cannot protect the prince all by ourselves. He needs a small army if he's going to get through the gala alive.

Sunrise brings warmth and light into Rosario's suite. I stand and stretch, glad the long night is over, and look down at my sleeping prince. He always sleeps spread-eagle, taking up his entire giant bed with his gangly limbs. His mouth is open, and a puddle of drool soaks his pillow.

I try to be silent as I fold up my quilt, but he stirs anyway and sits up in bed. "That's the best I've slept in a long time," he says, following it with a huge yawn.

"Rosario."

He's suddenly trying very hard not to laugh. "Now that your hair is shorter," he says, "your sleephead is spectacular."

I'd love nothing more than to pretend nothing is wrong and joke around the way we always do. Instead I place the folded quilt across the foot of his bed and say, "We need more protection for you."

"Every fighting man in the Royal Guard will be at the gala. I'll be fine."

"The Royal Guard that Sergeant DeLuca is currently in charge of? *That* Royal Guard?"

He frowns.

"You know we can't trust him."

"What do you suggest?"

"Send me to retrieve the recruits. They're not fully fledged Guards, but we've been training so hard. Surely they're better than nothing."

RAE·CARSON

He considers this. "First-year recruits aren't even issued swords."

"No, but they have bodies. Bodies that can be barriers between you and an enemy."

"I *hate* that idea." He runs a hand through his mussed hair. "Using the recruits as human shields."

"They took an oath to die for you."

"For Elisa, you mean."

"Elisa won't be empress forever. When she steps down, they'll be your Guard. Everyone who takes to the sand understands this."

"I'll think about it."

"Don't think too long. In the meantime, be careful what you eat or drink."

His smile is sad and resigned. "I already took the liberty of securing some trail food—jerky, a canteen of water, some dried coconut. It's all I plan to eat today."

"Gross," I say.

He nods. "It's going to be the worst Deliverance Day ever."

Rosario spends the morning suffering a final fitting for his formal gala outfit, which I'm happy to see includes a layer of light armor beneath a silk jacket. Early in the afternoon, he settles into the receiving room of his suite, where he endures visits from the seneschal, the mayordomo, and an unending stream of lords and ladies who have come a very long way just to say hello. He is polite and gracious to everyone.

Efren and Iago search every single person who enters the

receiving room for weapons, no matter their station. Even so, I glare at anyone who dares come too close to the prince, all the while keeping my hand ready on my scabbard.

Finally Rosario's receiving schedule is complete for the day. He breathes deep, scrapes his chair back, and puts his feet up on the desk. "It's getting harder and harder to smile at everyone."

"You'll have to do even more of it tonight."

"Promise you'll dance with me at least once," he says. "I'll need a break from everyone else."

"I won't be dressed for dancing," I say, indicating my desert garb.

"I don't care. I just want . . . Red, are you all right?"

My chest is buzzing, my breath coming in gasps. The magic squirming beneath the earth sings to me, yearning to break free. All it needs is a little blood. . . .

Blood welled up on her thumb, dripped to the floor in time with her heartbeat. The girl tried to wrench her hand away, but the White Hair gripped her arm too tight. The amulet hanging from his neck began to glow with blue fire. Its heat warmed her face. . . .

"Red?"

I lurch back into myself. "I'm sorry. I . . . the animagus. He's nearby."

"You did that thing where you . . . go away."

My heart is racing. "Sensing the animagus triggered a memory. Rosario, please let me go call up the recruits on your behalf."

One of the guards, either Iago or Efren, says, "A rogue animagus is a serious matter, Your Highness."

Rosario looks to me. His borrowed guards. Back to me. "Fine," he says at last. "Do it."

I'm dizzy with relief. "Thank you. I need a letter from you authorizing my entry to the barracks and officially calling the recruits into service."

"Bring them back as quick as you can. I'll be heading to the ballroom soon. Meet me there."

As soon as the ink is dry, we roll up the parchment, seal it with red wax, and stamp it with Rosario's signet ring. With a final admonishment to the guards to keep him safe, I dash from the suite, down the stairs of the Sky Wing, and into the impossibly busy plaza.

I dodge carriages and horses, pages and hostlers. By the time I reach the Guard barracks, my camel-hair boots are covered in dust and manure. Two Guards stand at attention, holding spears and shields.

Their steel helmets cover everything but their eyes and mouths. I peer closer. I'm almost certain I don't recognize them. After months of training, moving through the barracks, three meals per day in the mess, surely I've chanced upon every member of the Guard by now?

"The Royal Guard barracks are off-limits to the public, by order of Her Imperial Majesty," says one.

"I have authorization," I say, waving my rolled parchment with its red wax seal.

"Who are you?" asks the other.

Not only do I not recognize them, they don't recognize me. I say, "It doesn't matter. What matters is that I'm here on the orders of Prince Rosario himself. Do inspect the seal. But I suggest you allow Sergeant DeLuca or Guardsman Bruno to break it."

The first Guard holds out his hand. I give him the parchment. He examines it closely, grunting. Then he hands it back. "You may pass," he says with obvious reluctance.

I dash into the tunnel before he can change his mind.

The sun is not yet touching the rooftops of the Sky Wing, which means the first-year recruits will probably be in the training arena for their afternoon fitness regimen. The barracks are eerily silent as I traverse the long corridor. I've been absent only one day, but my heart squeezes to see the familiar rock walls, to peek inside the bunk room and spy Traitors' Corner at the far end, to pass the mess hall and smell a batch of fresh bread rising in preparation for dinner. When did I become so attached to this place?

I encounter no one—no Guards, no servants. Which is odd. I slow my pace, listening.

Laughter, in the distance. Outside, maybe. It pulls me forward, and finally I break into the sunshine of the sandy training arena.

All the first-year recruits are there, jogging in place with high knees to a count given by Guardsman Bruno. "High, two, three, four!" he urges. "I want to see those knees almost hit your chins!"

RAE·CARSON

I step forward, and Bruno fumbles his count. He goes silent. One by one, the boys stop jogging in place. They turn to see what he's staring at.

Iván's face lights up.

"It's Red!" someone says, and all of a sudden I'm surrounded by sweating bodies and grinning faces. "What are you doing here?" "Are you reinstated?" "We're going to have a gala celebration of our own tonight." "You should join us, Red."

Then Guardsman Bruno is there too, and he reaches through the mob, grabs my shoulder.

"You're not supposed to be here, girl," he says.

I hold up Rosario's letter. "I have authorization, sir. His Imperial Highness is officially drafting all first-year recruits into service for the evening. He has sent me to fetch them."

The air goes taut with silence. Bruno takes the letter, breaks the seal, reads.

I hold my breath. If he's not loyal to the prince, he might try to stop us.

"Well," he says at last. "Everything looks in order." He rolls the letter back up, hands it back to me. "Lady Red, the first-year recruit class is yours."

"Thank you, sir."

Guardsman Bruno wears a slight smile as he turns his back on us and exits the arena, leaving us all alone.

"Whoa," says Pedrón. "What just happened?"

"I think we're Royal Guards now," says Rito. "Real Royal Guards."

"At least temporarily," I say. Two palace watch soldiers pass by along the arena wall. "Let's get back to the bunk room. I'll explain everything there, in private."

"Wait!" says Aldo. "There's something we need to do first."

Everyone snaps to attention at his voice.

A brass half-moon is now pinned to the shoulder of his uniform. At my questioning look, he says, "Yesterday after you left, the recruits voted me squad leader."

"Aldo, that's wonderful!" I say. "Congratulations."

He beams. "Thank you."

"If the two of you hadn't agreed to start the practice group, we wouldn't have any useful training by now," Pedrón says.

"But it was close," Rito explains. "A tie vote between him and Iván. Sergeant DeLuca had to break the tie."

Something about that makes me twitch. But I say, "Well, you couldn't go wrong with either."

"Anyway, once I knew I was squad leader," Aldo says, "I arranged for a little surprise for everyone to celebrate Deliverance Day. Bruno helped me. He said we'd earned it. Seems like I ought to give it to you all now, before we head off for duty. Is that all right with you, Red? Do we have a few minutes to spare?"

"I think so, yes."

Aldo grins. "Follow me!" As we exit the arena, he says, "I'm really glad to see you, Red."

"Nice sword," says Pedrón. "Can I hold it?"

"No! Get your own."

"Where did you go after you left?" Iván asked.

"To the monastery. To . . ." I almost say "to pray," but that would be a bold-faced lie. "To find some peace."

RAE·CARSON

He gives me a strange look.

Aldo leads us to the latrine and gestures for us to go inside.

"Really?" says Pedrón. "The latrine?"

"Sorry, but yes," Aldo says with a sheepish grin. "There wasn't enough space in the bunk room."

We file in. The smell is terrible, way worse than usual, as though the latrine hasn't been maintained all day.

"Aldo, what are you talking about?" Rito says. "There's nothing—"

The door slams shut behind us. The bar latch thuds down, locking us in.

23
Now

I'M attacking the door, pounding with hands and feet, yelling for Aldo, even as my mind parses what just happened.

"Aldo, this isn't funny!" Pedrón calls out.

"Yes, this is a very bad time for a prank," yells Arturo.

"It's not a prank," Iván says darkly.

"Aldo!" I'm practically screaming. "What are you doing?"

Something heavy scrapes across the stone floor outside, plunks against the door.

"What was that?" asks Luca.

I step back from the door. I don't realize tears are streaming down my face until a drop of wetness hits my collarbone. "He's blocking us in," I say. "He's probably dragging cots and nightstands over, anything he can find. He has betrayed us."

"Why?" says Rito.

"Why?" I echo, louder, my mouth to the door. "Aldo, why are you doing this?"

Finally a muffled voice reaches us. "All you had to do was

eat breakfast today. But no, you just had to tell everyone not to eat or drink. So I had to improvise."

I whirl on Iván. "Everyone heeded your warning?"

"Most of them."

"I'm *really* hungry," Pedrón says.

"What about the rest of the Guard? Second years? Bruno's people? The barracks were oddly quiet when I got here."

"I don't know," Iván says. "I suspect that whoever heard the rumor had a choice, and some people made the choice to eat and drink and some didn't."

"The Guards at the entrance," I say. "I didn't recognize them."

"You think they've been replaced?" Iván says.

"They've definitely been replaced," I say. "But I don't know what Aldo has to do with it."

Arturo is looking back and forth between us. "You're saying the rest of the Guard might be poisoned? That's why we've seen hardly anyone since lunch? I thought they'd left for the gala already."

I turn back to the door and pound on it. "Aldo! This is your last chance. Let us out!"

"I can't," comes the muffled voice. "I'm sorry, Red. I really wish I didn't have to do this. You're my friends. If you just stay there and don't make trouble, I promise this will all be over in a few hours and no one will get hurt. You're all going to stay in the Guard."

"You tried to poison us," I say. "You don't poison your friends!"

"It wasn't going to be enough to kill you," he protests. "Just knock you out. Like Valentino."

Several of us gasp.

"Why did you poison Valentino?"

"He was too good. A favorite. Either you or I would have been cut if I hadn't eliminated him. I did it to save us both."

My ears ring, my face is hot as a desert, and my toe hurts from kicking the door. I *liked* Aldo. I thought he was my friend.

If I could get to him right now, I would stab him in the heart.

"We're finally called up to do something real," Rito says, staring at the door. "Something important, and we're trapped."

"Someone will come along," Arturo says. "They'll notice the door to the latrine is blocked and let us out, right?"

"Not if everyone has been knocked out by poison," Rito says.

Iván gives me a questioning look. I nod agreement. Softly, so Aldo can't hear through the door, he says, "We're not trapped."

"What do you mean?" says Pedrón.

I whisper, "When we're certain Aldo has left, we'll show you."

Pedrón raises an eyebrow. Then he pounds on the door, yelling, "Aldo!"

No answer.

He tries again. Still no response.

"Pedrón, keep making noise," I command quietly. "Everyone else, come this way."

Pedrón does his job with enthusiasm, yelling and kicking. The others follow me toward the sconce in the wall. I give it a

RAE·CARSON

yank, and the section of wall slides away. "Inside, quick," I say.

Iván grabs the torch and leads the way. The rest follow, their gazes rapt, their mouths hanging open.

"All right, Pedrón, your turn."

He gives the door one last kick and follows everyone else into the secret tunnel. I'm the last to enter. I flip the lever so the door closes behind us.

"Now what?" Rito whispers. They're all in a single-file line in the tight corridor. Pedrón's shoulders brush the walls. If not for Iván's torch, it would be too dark to see any of them.

"We have to reach the prince," I say. "We move fast and quiet; some of these walls are thin. The passage will take us beneath the Sky Wing, near the entrance to the catacombs. Hopefully, we'll be able to reach the prince from there. Iván, do you remember the way?"

"I think so."

"Then lead on."

"Wait . . . you've both been here before?" Rito says.

"Long story. Let's get our prince through this gala alive, and then we'll tell you."

The storage room is too small for all of us, so several stay behind in the secret passage while Iván and I peek into the corridor.

I've barely cracked the door open before I yank it shut. A group of men marches by, blocking our way. I glimpse rawhide armor and daggers and the kind of thick-soled sandals worn by people of the southern countships.

"I heard marching," Iván whispers. "And armor."

"I didn't recognize a single crest," I whisper back.

"What should we do?"

"What's going on?" Pedrón whispers from inside the corridor.

"The only way out from here is blocked by soldiers I've never seen before," I say. "Wait here. After they pass by, I'm going to get a closer look."

Iván says, "Red, are you sure—"

"I'm the only one not wearing a recruit uniform," I say. "If I get caught, I'll just say I'm delivering a message." I wave Rosario's note in front of his face.

He frowns. "Be careful."

I wait for the sound of marching to fade. Then I crack open the door and slip through into the corridor. I follow the oddly dressed soldiers, sticking close to the wall.

The sound of marching ceases abruptly. I freeze, trying to disappear into the sandstone.

"All right, boys," comes a gruff voice. "No one gets into the Sky Wing. We hold this intersection no matter what. When the bells signal, we attack. Do our jobs right, and there's a fat purse waiting for us, hear?"

"Hear!" a dozen voices echo.

I know this accent. These men are from the southeastern part of the empire. Maybe even the free villages. Which means they're probably mercenaries.

I tiptoe back to the storeroom and slip inside.

"The way is blocked," I tell the recruits. "Mercenaries. They said something about holding the intersection until the bell signal."

"We were right," Iván says. "It's a coup."

"That's the only way back to the upper levels," I say. "The empress had any branching corridors blocked off years ago."

"Does that mean we're trapped down here?" Rito says. "We *have* to reach the prince. Somehow."

"Let's fight our way through," Pedrón says. "We're Royal Guards, right? The best of the best."

"They have weapons and armor," I say. "We don't."

"Then we go through the catacombs," Iván says. "And up through the Wallows."

"We can *do* that?" says one of the Basajuaños.

"That's why Elisa blocked off this passage," I say. "It might be the most important corridor in the whole palace."

"Making it easier to guard also turned it into a potential trap," Iván points out.

"It will take more than an hour to exit through the secret hideout and circle back," I say.

"Then we'd better get started," Iván says.

"What secret hideout?" Pedrón says.

"You'll see soon enough," I say. "Follow my lead. Remember: fast and quiet."

I exit the storeroom, all the first-year recruits on my heels. We jog down the corridor on light feet, in the opposite direction from the mercenaries.

At the entrance to the catacombs, we stop short. A Guard lies on the floor, arm extended at an odd angle, blood pooling beneath his head on the stone floor. The mercenaries took the time to scout the whole corridor before taking up position at the intersection.

"Holy God," whispers Rito. "This is serious."

If the killing has already begun, Rosario is in grave danger. "Hurry!" I urge. "We'll come back for him later." I step over the body and start toward the stairs.

"Wait," Iván says in a sharp whisper. "Somebody grab his sword. And any other weapon he has."

Iván would have been a great squad leader. No wonder DeLuca didn't let him win.

Pedrón is nearest to the body. He drops to the floor and searches it. "The sword's gone. And all his pockets are turned inside out."

"Then the looting's already started," I say. "Let's go!" I take the stairs into the catacombs at an unwise pace.

The boys gasp when we reach the Hall of Skulls. They gape in wonder when I finger the latch that pivots the stone casket aside, revealing the dark well that will lead us to the underground village.

Iván goes first, and I usher everyone down into the spiral staircase, intending to take up the rear. Rito is the last one. He stares down into the darkness, eyes wide, limbs frozen.

"Arturito?"

"We're going to get killed tonight, aren't we?"

"I'm hoping we'll at least reach the prince first."

His eyes dart around as if looking for escape, and I realize this is one of those times when a less candid person would tell him something comforting and false.

"Will it hurt?" he whispers.

I find something true to say. "If we survive this, and we keep our prince safe, no one will dare cut us from the Guard. We'll be heroes."

He perks up a little. "You think so?"

"Heroes know how to weather a storm, right? What do we have when the winds are harsh and the seas are rough?"

He nods. "Still hearts."

"Now *go*."

We catch up to the rest. The tide is in, and we soak our boots wading through ankle-high salt water. Our footsteps squish as we climb the narrow stairs. Pedrón and Iván must duck their heads to avoid the low ceiling.

The boys want nothing more than to stand and gawk when they see the underground village. Light streams down from fissures above, and the whole place sparkles. The rushing river hugging the cavern's far edge creates a light breeze.

A fire pit still smolders, and a few villagers are smoking fish on a rack beside it. But the village is mostly empty. The entire remaining Guard was called up for the gala. I wonder if any of them are still alive.

"How have I never heard of this place?" Pedrón whispers.

"You do know what 'secret' means, right?" I say.

"I mean, how do you keep a place like this a secret? It's a whole village!"

"Only the empress's inner circle knows about it," I say. "And the villagers who live here get to do business without guild

fees and regulations in exchange for their silence. Now, hurry."
I grab the rope ladder that hangs down the wall and start to
pull myself up. "Only one at a time on the ladder," I call down.

I reach the landing and its resident hut and step inside
to find yet another ladder along the back wall, leading to a
trapdoor.

Everyone is strong and fast. Within minutes we are through
the trapdoor and gathered inside a typical Wallows hovel with
a dirt floor, driftwood walls, and a palm-thatch roof.

"Now what?" says Arturo, breathing hard.

"Is this the Wallows?" asks Rito. "I hear it's the most dangerous quarter of the city."

"I grew up on the border of the Wallows and the Fishers'
Quarter," Pedrón says. "It's not so bad. Just keep your eyes
down and don't make trouble."

"We have to run for the palace," I say. "The road zags all
through the Wallows and then curves around the palace outskirts, so we'll have to run fast to make it to the prince before
the Deliverance blessing begins. But we've all run the walls,
and this is nothing compared to ten laps around the palace
grounds, right?"

"Right!" they answer in unison.

"We're prepared for this, right?"

"Right!"

"Let's go."

We set off at a fast jog. The streets of the Wallows are
narrow, crooked, and steep, lined by ramshackle huts pressed
together so tightly it seems as though you could remove one

plank and bring the whole neighborhood down. The gutters smell of rotting fish and refuse. At least the streets have gutters now, thanks to a huge project undertaken by Elisa in the third year of her reign.

We pass a woman beating dust from a rug. Her skin is like leather, and her feet are bare. A man in ragged pants repairs the thatching on his roof. Three children—two boys and a girl—kick a ball through an alleyway; the ball is made of old linen scraps rolled together and tied.

Everyone ceases what they're doing to stare as we run by. Some of them, the lucky ones, will get a Deliverance Day gift from a loved one today. An extra helping of fish, maybe, or a doll made of sticks and scraps. But no one here in the Wallows cares about the palace gala that is the entire focus of our rushed journey. They'll never see the inside of a ballroom, never eat date and honey scones, never wear silk.

We turn a corner and lurch to a stop. A damaged cart blocks our path. It rests at an odd angle, one cartwheel shattered. Coconuts have tumbled into the alley. The coconut seller waves his hat at several children who dart in to steal them.

Iván says, "There's no way around."

He's right. And we'll lose precious time backtracking.

"We'll have to climb over."

Pedrón is the first to clamber up. The coconut seller waves his arms and screams obscenities at him as more coconuts tumble to the ground in his wake. Pedrón reaches down to help the others up. Several coconuts are squashed, their filmy milk soaking everything. I'm the last to climb over. I fish out one of the silver coins I got from trading my baby rattle gemstones and hand it to the seller.

"Happy Deliverance Day," I say. It feels less happy every time I say it. He grabs the coin, but I feel his cold anger on my back as we sprint away from him, down the alley.

The palace complex looms over us, perched on the highest hill of the city. Traffic thickens as we approach—carts and carriages, people on foot, children playing in the streets. It's a holiday for most citizens of Brisadulce, and many people are trekking through the city streets to gather with friends and family. We are forced to slow our pace.

"We're not going to get there in time," says Iván as he dodges a cart horse.

"Just keep pushing forward," I say.

The line of carriages along the Avenida de la Serpiente is at a near stop, for each carriage must be checked by the palace watch before dropping off passengers or entering the plaza. We don't have time to wait our turn.

"Get to the front of the line!" I yell over the cacophony of wheels and horses and bellowing carriage drivers.

Arturo leads the recruits now, and he shifts to the side of the road in an attempt to skirt some of the larger carriages. The other Basajuan boys are close on his heels, followed by Pedrón and the army recruits, and finally Iván and me.

Townhomes line the Avenida this close to the palace— luxurious, multistory stone edifices with silken banners draped from window casings, proudly displaying house sigils to all the passersby. A flurry of activity draws my attention to one.

RAE·CARSON

"That's a lot of guards for one townhome," Iván observes.

He's right. Soldiers scurry in and out of the front door, many hefting bulging burlap sacks. They're dressed in the colors of the palace watch, except . . .

"Look at their shoes," I say.

They all wear those hefty sandals, the same ones the mercenaries in the Sky Wing were wearing.

"Isn't that the mayor's house?" Iván says.

"He and Lady Jada live there. They're important allies of the empress." I still remember the man who stood and proclaimed in favor of my adoption.

"I think it's being looted," Pedrón says.

"We have to hurry," I say, and I press forward. It goes against everything in me to pass by, to do nothing, but reaching Rosario must be our priority.

As we near the gate, it becomes clear that the mayor's home isn't the only one. I recognize the sigil of Lord Liano of Altapalma, then that of Lady Pilar of Lagunas Azules. Both friends of the empress. Both with an inordinate number of foot soldiers wearing not-quite-right uniforms. It's a subtle thing. There's no yelling, no clashing of weapons. Anyone not paying close attention would never know that a takeover is happening right under our noses.

"Red," Pedrón says at my back. "There may be hostages inside those townhomes."

"That's because they plan to take the whole city," I tell him. "But there's nothing we can do about it now. And none of it will matter if we don't save the prince."

Iván grabs Pedrón by the collar. "We're the Royal Guard, not the City Guard. Our only job is to protect the prince. Got it?"

Pedrón swallows hard, but his back straightens with resolve. "Yes, sir."

Ahead, Arturo has reached the gate, a giant arched portcullis with speared points that could crush a person's head if it was ever lowered quickly.

"Do you think they'll just let us in?" Iván asks. He's as breathless as I am. Even though we're well practiced running the walls, running uphill has made my thighs burn and my lungs ache.

"No. I don't know. I still have Rosario's letter. Maybe we can talk our way in?"

"What if we can't?"

"We *have* to. We don't have time to figure out something else."

Iván and I sprint to catch up, dodging horses, ignoring the angry shouts of people accusing us of skipping the line.

". . . out on maneuvers," Arturo is saying to one of the palace watch officers. "We've just returned and are ready to report to the barracks."

"You're not reporting to the gala for duty?" the watch officer asks.

"No, we're just first-year recruits. See? We don't even have weapons."

"She does," says the officer as I come up behind Arturo. He indicates the small sword hanging from my hip.

RAE·CARSON

"She's the only one," Arturo says. "Because she's our squad leader."

"It's barely more than a toy," I tell him. "A sign of my station more than a real weapon."

The watch officer considers. My face flames. I just told a huge lie, straight out.

"Fine, go ahead," he says, waving us through.

We dash into the plaza and step off to the side, out of the way of traffic.

"That was easier than I expected," Arturo says.

"Too easy," says Iván.

"They didn't bother searching us for hidden weapons," Pedrón says. "Don't they always search for weapons on Deliverance Day?"

"Lords and ladies are allowed some small personal weapons," I say. "You can even buy them here in the market stalls. But that was still too easy."

"They aren't even asking for invitations," Arturo says. "I listened very closely. Two carriages ahead of us were allowed to drop off their passengers without any questions at all."

"They want everyone here," I say. "As many people as possible."

"Why?" says Pedrón.

"I have no idea." My brain races through the possibilities, none of them good. "But I don't like it."

"To the ballroom, yes?" Rito says.

"Yes. But first . . ." I put my hand on Rito's shoulder and look him dead in the eye. "I need you to do something heroic."

"Just me?" he says, his voice edging higher.

"I overheard those mercenaries saying they would attack when the bells ring. They're waiting for a signal. If they never hear the signal—"

"Then they won't attack," Pedrón finishes.

"Exactly. Rito, I need you to return to the barracks and find anyone who is not poisoned. Itzal, maybe. Tanix and the second years. Check the kitchens and the storerooms too. Surely some of them heard the rumor and refrained from eating or drinking today. Find them all, and get them to the bell tower. Make sure that signal never happens. Can you do that?"

"What if I can't find anyone?"

"Use your best judgment. Stop that signal if possible, but don't get yourself killed for no reason. Lay low until this is all over if you have to. Don't do anything dangerous alone."

He straightens. "All right, Red. I'll find everyone I can. If there's any way to stop that signal, we'll do it."

"Good man. The rest of us will make for the ballroom."

We say our goodbyes to Rito. Arturo wraps him in a tight hug and kisses the top of his head. "Be careful, Rito," he says.

Rito lays his palm against Arturo's cheek. Then, with a nod to the rest of us, he dashes away toward the barracks.

The way to the grand ballroom is across the plaza and through a wide tunnel. The tunnel is jammed with lords and ladies in their Deliverance garb, all awaiting entrance. The sun is low, but the air is still hot and dusty. Several people fan themselves as they wait. Serving staff with trays skirt the crowd, offering cold water and hors d'oeuvres.

"I wonder if that food is poisoned," Pedrón says, staring mournfully at a tray of tiny meat pies garnished with parsley.

"If we stand in line, we'll never get in before opening ceremonies," Arturo says.

Iván leans down and whispers in my ear, "Do you know of another way in?"

Only through the Sky Wing, which is swarming with mercenaries. If I lead a bunch of unarmed recruits that way, not only will we never reach Rosario, we'll never reach tomorrow.

"I'm thinking," I tell him.

In very short order, I realize I don't have any ideas.

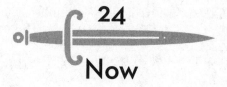

24
Now

"IT doesn't have to be complicated," Pedrón says. "Let's just shove our way in."

We can do that? Obviously, I am the wrong size to think of some solutions.

"They're nobles," Pedrón explains. "They'll be angry and make all kinds of threats, but they won't push back."

"It's better than any plan I have," I say.

"Maybe if we yell 'Make way for the empress,' they'll get out of our way faster," Iván suggests.

Pedrón nods enthusiastically. "That's really smart," he says, and starts heading for the door.

I grab him and pull him back. "We can't yell that. It will draw all the mercenaries and everyone else who's part of the plot to come and stop us. We need to delay that as long as possible to give us the best chance of reaching Rosario."

"So what's the plan?" Iván asks. He bounces on his feet. We're all anxious.

I take a deep breath and motion for everyone to come in

close. "Pedrón, you, Luca, and Andrés are the biggest. You form a wedge and lead the way. Iván, Arturo, and I will be right behind them. The rest of you crowd in behind us."

Everyone nods, so I continue.

"We don't know what we'll find when we get inside. If we get separated, everyone make their own way to Rosario. We'll surround the steps at the bottom of the dais, so no one can attack him."

Iván adds, "But if trouble starts, you find the nearest mercenary or fake Guardsman, anyone we don't know and trust, and you take their weapon."

He means "Dispatch them," but there's no need for me to clarify. By the looks on their faces, everyone understands. I might be the only one here who has ever had to kill someone, and even *I* don't feel prepared.

I'm suddenly as scared for all of them as I am for Rosario. The prince is so determined to be brave, to go through with the ceremony; I've no doubt he'll proceed even though we're not there to protect him. And once he begins, he'll be completely exposed.

"Everyone knows what to do," I say, shoving Pedrón toward the door. I try not to let anyone hear the words catching in my throat. "Let's go!"

Crushed in the middle of this mob, I can't see a thing as we surge forward, but I hear all the protests and ultimatums that Pedrón predicted. I hold on to Pedrón's belt as I'm jostled and stepped on. But we do not wait our turn, we do not care if anyone complains to the Guard, and we do not stop shoving.

The moment we are through the door, we get separated. The army boys surge ahead, leaving me behind. I reach after Iván, but I get bumped aside by a group of southerners who followed us through the door.

I spot the tops of Iván's and Pedrón's heads, and start weaving my way toward them, but I'm not moving fast enough.

The ballroom is massive, even longer than our training arena. The air is rich with flower scent, for rose garlands sweep from crystal chandeliers, running the entire length of the hall. Candelabras are aflame in high balconies, and vases overflow with night bloomers just now opening their glowing stamens to mark the night. Tables clothed in bright silk line the walls, laden with silver platters heaped with appetizers. Men in Royal Guard uniforms stand along the wall at regular intervals, but I don't recognize a single one. They are all imposters.

I've attended galas over the years as the empress's ward, but never have I seen such a crowd. There must be a thousand people here, all milling about in their annual finery, laughing and chatting and displaying themselves just so. Servants dart everywhere, clearing empty platters and picking up spilled crumbs. We weave through them all, trying to avoid the gazes of the imposter Guards, trying to reach the Hand of God, where Rosario will officially open the festivities.

The viheulas and dulciáns in the corner go silent. A hush descends.

I hear the prince before I see him. His voice rings out. "Lift up your heads in honor of our Deliverance."

We are too late.

He begins reciting the Deliverance prayer.

"In you our ancestors put their trust,
They cried out and you delivered them."

I lose track of Iván and the others as I push through a thick forest of silk and satin. Someone grunts; I've stepped on their foot. A large man tries to block my way. I bump the back of his knee so it buckles and slide past him as he teeters off balance.

I can see the prince now. Rosario sits exposed and alone, cupped in the Hand of God, a giant sculpture carved centuries ago by the great artist Lutián of the Rocks. Sitting in the Hand is an annual tradition, to remind us all that God's righteous right hand delivered our ancestors from annihilation.

"Yea, from the dying world they were saved;
In you they trusted and were not put to shame.
Bless us, O God, as we remember your hand;
Your righteous right hand endures forever."

"Selah!" the crowd responds in unison. I'm almost there. I scan the high balconies for crossbowmen as Rosario steps down from the Hand with the help of Efren and Iago, and returns to the dais.

The people in front of me have closed ranks, making it impossible to proceed. I spy a possible route to the right, nearer the wall, where fewer people congregate. I edge in that direction, leading with my shoulder.

My sense of urgency fades a little, because now that I'm close enough to see the dais, it's clear Rosario is surrounded by friends. Lady Carilla has taken Rosario's arm, and she gazes up at him adoringly. Beside them, Lord-Conde Tristán of the Quorum of Five is holding hands with his lover, Iladro. Iván's brother Juan-Carlos is there too, whispering something to Songbird, the elegantly attired Invierno ambassador. Father Nicandro stands before them all, leaning on his cane. The priest wears a robe of pure white to mark the occasion.

Conde Astón has a place on the dais as well; as speaker of the chamber of condes, it's his right. But he stands off to the side, creating a cushion of rejection between him and the others.

Several attendees shift. A path clears, and I dart forward.

A heavy hand descends on my shoulder, grabs me, yanks me backward. A vambraced arm wraps my neck. My back is pulled against an armored body, and hot breath fogs my ear. "Going somewhere, little mule?" says a low male voice.

It's Beto, one of the boys who attacked me. Now an imposter Guard.

Of course he would be.

I dip my left shoulder, preparing to drop and twist free, but a sharp point sticks into my side.

"Don't even think about it," says another male voice. Sancho.

Valentino said these rejected recruits joined the army. So does this mean the army has been compromised? Maybe they're mercenaries.

RAE·CARSON

It doesn't matter. All they are is an obstacle.

"Just wait," Beto says, twisting my arm up behind my back and turning me toward the stage. "You're going to love this."

Sancho grins wolfishly and presses his knife harder into my side.

I scan the crowd, looking for my fellow recruits—Iván or Pedrón, anyone who can help—but the crush of people is too thick.

The air turns taut and prickly, as though a massive thunderstorm is gathering. My limbs start to tingle; a knot forms in my gut. It's the Invierno sorcerer. He's here, and he's reaching for his well of magic.

Rosario raises his hand to signal the musicians to begin playing. His hand freezes midair.

The crowd collectively gasps, then goes eerily still.

The tip of Sancho's knife is cutting my skin. Blood seeps down my side, thick and warm against my skin. But I can't flinch away from it. I can't move at all.

We stand in silence—no rustling of fabric, no murmured conversation, no creak of armor. I try to twitch my finger, but I can't. Like everyone else, I'm frozen in place, an invisible barrier clenching tight around my body.

A white-haired Invierno steps forward from his hiding place behind the Hand. An animagus. He's a head taller than almost everyone else in the room, with limbs so thin and cheeks so gaunt he is like a skeleton with skin. The whites of his eyes are bloodshot, shadowed by dark circles. He is not well.

The sorcerer mounts the dais. The Godstone at the tip of

his staff glows with blue fire. When he speaks, his voice sounds magnified, either by the shape of the room or by some sorcery I am unfamiliar with. "Lucero-Elisa, Queen of Joya d'Arena, Empress of the United Joyan Empire, Bearer of the Godstone, the Sorcerer-Queen . . . the Queen of Joya . . ."

He stumbles over his words, pauses, and then smiles.

"Empress Elisa sends her blessings."

I want to shout, to call him a liar, but I can do nothing except move my eyes. On scattered faces all around me, I see the stricken look of people who have had their worst fears realized.

"On behalf of the empress Elisa and the ambassador of Invierne, I welcome you. Today we celebrate a new Deliverance. Beginning today, your young empire and the ancient empire of Invierne will be forever joined as one."

Rosario's eyes widen in protest, but he can do nothing. He can't even speak.

"Let all those who would oppose this union consider the wisdom of their choices."

A stream of fire bursts from the sorcerer's staff, exploding against a serving table. Dishes clatter to the floor. Flames lick the banners hanging from the wall.

Either the sorcerer is not powerful enough, or he is well and truly ill, for he is unable to hold everyone frozen while performing fire magic. A murmur of fear and despair passes through the crowd. My limbs release; the dagger at my side shifts slightly in surprise, and I don't even think, I just react. My heel crashes down on Beto's instep. Bones crunch. He screams.

Movement around us as others are released. Panic.

I drop to the floor before Sancho can gut me with his dagger. When I shoot up, my palm smashes into his chin. His head snaps back, cracking against the wall; then he slides down, head at an odd angle, as he crumples to the floor.

The crowd is too thick, too frantic, for me to draw my sword, so I grab Sancho's dagger and thrust it deep into Beto's neck. He topples over, blood spilling everywhere.

Too late, I realize my mistake.

Blood soaking into the earth will make the animagus stronger.

A woman screams as another banner goes up in flames. Everyone mills about, trying to get away. Tristán and Juan-Carlos have drawn their swords; they close ranks before the prince and Carilla and Iladro. I press forward, trying to get to them, using knees and elbows, but I keep getting pushed back by the panicked crowd.

A great *boom* reverberates through the ballroom, and I startle so badly that I trip over someone's gown and almost fall to my knees. The double doors have been slammed shut, closing us in. "We're trapped!" someone yells.

My heart feels like it's leapfrogging out of my chest. I don't have time to panic. I don't have time to stop and do the breathing exercises Hector taught me. I have to be fine right now. *Still hearts*, I tells myself. *Still hearts, still hearts.*

People pound on the door with their fists. The fire spreads to another table.

"Silence!" the Invierno yells, and the air goes taut once again.

This time I'm frozen midstep, my knee raised. Ahead of me,

close but so, so far away, Father Nicandro turns his head to look at the sorcerer.

The priest can move. Not much, but it gives me hope.

I remember what he said about my Godstone. My instinct is to grab it, but of course I can't.

Instead, I do exactly what Elisa taught me: I hold an image of the Godstone in my head, and focus on it. I pretend my feet are one with the earth. I reach down mentally, grasping for the well of power, the magic that lives beneath the skin of the world.

My step lands. It's working. I concentrate harder.

"The empress Elisa will be merciful to those who obey her," the sorcerer intones. "But she is not here today. I am. And I have no mercy for the disobedient."

I'm not too terrified for my prince, nor too caught up in my efforts to shake the freezing spell, that I don't recognize a bit of terrible theater when I hear it. "No mercy for the disobedient?" This is a staged crisis. And someone wanted as many people as possible to witness it.

Someone wants everyone to blame Elisa.

The sorcerer raises his staff again. This time, he aims for the crowd.

I'm able to take another step, but I won't reach him in time. A stream of flame, as swift and white-hot as lightning, shoots from the staff, crashes into a huddled group. The brightness sears my eyes. The scent of burning hair and flesh chokes me. I recognize the mayor and Lady Jada just before their agonized faces are melted away.

My vision clears, revealing Father Nicandro hobbling

toward the sorcerer, raising his cane as though to wallop the animagus in the back. The priest has shaken off the spell, and if he can do it, so can I.

Just a few more steps. I clench my teeth, continuing to draw on the well of power even as I begin to draw my sword.

The sorcerer is about to attack the crowd again, but Nicandro's cane whacks him in the back. He whirls on the priest, spins his staff in the air, sends it crashing into Father Nicandro's temple. The priest drops his cane, crumples to the floor. His wide-open eyes stare lifelessly at my feet.

The animagus turns on Rosario.

I'm almost there, but I'm moving too slow, as though wading through date syrup. My legs are lead. My sword arm is weighed down by a millstone.

Rosario and Carilla stare wide-eyed, unable to react as the animagus raises his staff. His Godstone is suddenly brighter than the sun.

A body flies up the steps out of nowhere. I catch a spark of steel, a flash of purple fabric, as someone throws himself at the sorcerer, whisks a dagger across his throat.

The animagus chokes, head lolling, then plops to the ground in a heap of robes. His Godstone winks out.

It's as though a switch has been flipped, for everyone is released, suddenly able to move. One woman collapses to the floor, quietly sobbing. Flames continue to lick at the food tables.

A boy in golden armor and a purple cape stands over the body of the Invierno. His dagger drips with blood.

It's Aldo.

25
Now

EVERYONE looks on in panic and confusion. I push through the crowd, and finally break into the open just in front of the dais. Aldo looks down at me, notes my sword. Smiles triumphantly.

Then he lifts his head and smiles at the crowd.

He raises the bloody knife in the air.

People cheer.

This theater is not yet over, but for a split second I'm too confused to act.

Conde Astón, however, is not. He walks across the dais and places a hand on Aldo's shoulder. In a loud, clear voice, the speaker of the chamber of condes says, "Thank you, my prince. You saved us all."

Confused murmuring comes from all sides. *My prince?*

The reaction is perhaps not quite as universal as he hopes. Many people are still crying, from fear or injuries. Some call for help. Groups have organized to put out the fires. Fists still beat against the doors.

This does not slow down Conde Astón.

"I see an introduction is in order," he says, smiling magnanimously to the still-terrified crowd. "It pleases me greatly to present Prince Alejandro né Basajuan de Vega, son of our late king, Alejandro de Vega, nephew to Queen Cosmé of Basajuan."

I stare at the boy who used to be my bunkmate.

"Prince Alejandro is the true heir to the imperial throne," Astón says, his voice booming through the chamber.

Aldo. Alejandro. He's the son of one of the king's many mistresses. Rosario's secret half-brother. I should have realized. Those same delicate features. Those same impossible eyelashes.

The bastard prince eyes me as I skirt the bodies of Father Nicandro and the animagus, to take my place before *my* prince.

"Red?" Rosario whispers. "What's happening?"

Nothing good. It appears as though Aldo has saved us all, but I'm not so sure. The drama has yet to play out.

It occurs to me that in all the chaos, I have not heard the monastery bells ring out any kind of signal. It gives me hope.

Lord-Conde Tristán says, "His Imperial Highness Prince Rosario is the true heir, named so by Empress Elisa herself, ratified by the chamber of condes."

"The empress is a traitor!" shouts a high female voice. A figure comes forward, the crowd parting for her in a way it never would for me. She's the most beautiful woman I've ever seen, with golden skin and eyes like honey, only a shade or two darker than my own. I have seen her once before. Standing next to Lady Malka, on the day that my adoption was rejected. She wears a sleeveless gossamer gown the color of champagne. Her armbands and bracelets drip with jewels.

"Hello, Mamá," says Aldo.

"Condesa Ariña!" says Conde Astón. "It's a delight to see you here."

She inclines her head slightly. "Thank you for commuting my exile," she says. "I have yearned for my friends here in the capital."

"You suffered long enough," the conde says. "The chamber was only too happy to grant your request."

I'm not sure what to do. This is some form of treachery; I'm certain of it. But I can't just start attacking people. Or maybe I should.

Others push through the crowd. Relief fills me to see Iván's face, then Pedrón's. Valentino is inching forward as well. He still looks wan, but he no longer uses a cane. He has eyes for no one but his father.

The weeping and the cries for help subside. Smoke obscures the ceiling, but the flames have been suppressed.

"Many of you are already acquainted with Condesa Ariña," Conde Astón says. "The longtime paramour of King Alejandro, and the choice for many of us to become our next queen." To the beautiful woman, he says, "If we had known that you had borne his child, a prince, we never would have allowed the usurper to exile you. Please accept my apologies on behalf of the kingdom and all who are loyal to the memory of our true king."

"This is an outrage," yells Conde Tristán. "Rosario is the true heir, beloved by all. This boy is a stranger! He could be an urchin from the streets of the Wallows, for all we know."

"Oh, I have proof of my son's lineage," says Condesa Ariña, and she holds aloft an item for all to see. It's a baby rattle, golden just like the one Rosario gave me. Except the one she displays is engraved with the de Vega seal.

Some people gasp. Others hold their tongues.

"A gift from his father, upon news of his birth," Ariña says. "We kept my darling boy hidden, until such time as we married and I became Alejandro's queen. But the usurper changed everything. She stole the throne for herself. Threw me out of the capital. Forced us all to accept treaties with our greatest enemies."

Rosario finds his voice. "You were exiled because you conspired to betray my father. You were stripped of title, your sister Cosmé made heir to your lands and titles. You got exactly what you deserved."

Condesa Ariña smiles. "I'm sure that's what you've been told. But as you say, my sister retained my lands and titles. She is now queen of Basajuan. That means my son, Alejandro, is not only your half-brother, he is nephew to Queen Cosmé. His claim to the imperial throne is even greater than yours."

Even though such a claim is ridiculous, everyone in the ballroom is rapt. This was the plan all along. Discredit Elisa and Rosario. Infiltrate the Royal Guard. Lock down the palace with mercenaries. Present Aldo as a heroic, patriotic alternative.

I have no idea what to do. I've been training to guard someone's life, not shore up their political support.

"Empress Elisa invited that animagus here," Conde Astón says. "You heard him. They were longtime friends. And now innocent people lie charred on the floor of this very ballroom."

"You lie!" Rosario protests.

"Even *I* have never seen him before," Ambassador Songbird says.

"We are so lucky Prince Alejandro was here to save us," Conde Astón continues, unabashed. "The Inviernos bring nothing but duplicity and death. How many of you lost fathers, brothers, sons to the Inviernos in the war? There can be no treaty with duplicity. There can be no peace with treason."

"Enough of this!" Rosario shouts. "Red, seize the pretender."

I react instantly, leaping toward Aldo, my sword raised high.

Aldo is already spinning on me, drawing his own sword. Steel clangs against steel as he parries neatly.

He thrusts for my belly, but I twist my abdomen, and his blade sails past. With a flick of my wrist, I knock the blade aside and move inside his guard, priming my fist to bludgeon his face.

"Stop, or Rosario dies!" someone yells.

I freeze. Someone has Rosario pinned, a knife to his throat. Efren and Iago, the prince's borrowed guards, are dead at his feet.

Aldo's grin of triumph falters as he lifts his blade, presses the tip to my heart. "Surrender, Red," he says. "You are my friend. Truly. And I want you as part of my own Royal Guard. As I told all of you, when I locked you up for your own safety, you can still be in the Guard."

I gape at him. Does he really believe there can be friendship between us, after what he's done?

RAE·CARSON

From the corner of my eye, I see Valentino edging closer. Aldo notices, but does nothing. After all, Valentino is weak. The son of his greatest ally.

On the dais, the knife presses deeper into Rosario's throat. I have to do something. I can't watch him die. But there's no way I'll reach him before that blade slits his throat.

"Well, Red, what's it going to be?" Aldo says. To Condesa Ariña, he says, "Mamá, please relieve her of her sword."

Ariña steps forward, and I allow her to take my weapon. It clatters as she drops it to the ground, then kicks it aside.

Beside Rosario, Carilla lifts her hand to her hair. It's a slow, subtle gesture.

"Why did you join the Guard?" I say, buying time.

"I needed a way inside. Also I really wanted to meet you and Iván, and all the empire's brightest sons."

"Why did you pretend to be our friend?"

"I didn't pretend! You *are* my. . . I knew that once you realized I was the true heir, you would . . ." He glances toward his mother.

"What were the barrels of sweet dream syrup for?"

"You're trying to get me to say something unwise in front of everyone, aren't you?" He puts pressure on the blade. The tip parts my skin, bringing searing pain.

Carilla pulls a hairpin from her hair, which loosens it, toppling her black curls to her shoulders. The pin is half the length of my forearm.

"Aldo," I say to keep his attention on me. "I'm going to kill you now."

Carilla spins, thrusts the hairpin up, under the chin of Rosario's captor and deep into his brain.

I throw myself backward, turn in midair to land on my hands while my feet arc out and sweep Aldo's legs out from beneath him. He rolls away and is back on his feet before I can blink.

He whips his sword around. "I should have been ready for that move, after seeing you fight Valentino."

Carilla has a dagger in her hand now; where it came from I have no idea.

Tristán and Juan-Carlos advance on Condesa Ariña. Aldo sees his mother is in danger and yells, "Guards! Seize them! Kill anyone who dares raise a weapon to your prince!"

Three imposter Guards rush forward. Tristán and Juan-Carlos are forced to retreat back, toward Rosario and Carilla.

Conde Astón starts to duck behind the Hand, but suddenly Valentino is there, blocking his way. "If you try to hide from this war you've started, I will kill you myself," the boy says to his father.

Aldo whips his sword toward my head, and I duck, dancing out of the way. But several false Guards have made it through the crowd and are suddenly at my back, giving me no quarter. As one, they lift their swords, aiming for my throat. Aldo says, "If you will not join me, there is only one choice left to you. Do you want it in the heart, the throat, or the head?"

I'm trapped. My prince is trapped. Nothing to do now but die fighting.

Rosario, I'm sorry I couldn't save you.

I take a deep breath. If I'm very fast and very lucky, I can take out one or two before a sword pierces my throat.

The guard closest to my side grunts. He topples over, a cheese knife sticking out of his back. It's Pedrón.

Before anyone can react, Pedrón punches another guard in the face, felling him with a single blow. Aldo is swinging at me again, but Pedrón has opened up some space for me to maneuver, and I dodge, rolling out of the way.

The sword of a fallen Guard lies at my nose. I grab it, leaping to my feet.

The Guards are occupied now, for my fellow recruits have engaged them, weaponless though they are. I catch a glimpse of Iván dodging a downward stroke like someone who has practiced the move a thousand times. He dashes past his opponent's guard, then rams an elbow into his kidney, exactly the way I did with Valentino months before. The imposter Guard drops to his knees, and Iván easily disarms him.

The rest of the crowd has pressed itself into the walls, as far away from swinging blades as they can get. Tristán and Juan-Carlos have killed their initial attackers and have leaped from the dais. Tristán holds a sword to Ariña's throat. Juan-Carlos and Carilla crouch before the prince, ready to engage anyone who approaches.

Aldo circles me, his sword at the ready. "I *know* how well trained the first years really are," he says. "But they're outnumbered. You can't win this fight."

"But we can still fight this fight," I say. "And you will still die."

"You would never kill one of your friends," he says, but for the first time, fear flashes in Aldo's eyes. Fear can make adversaries even more dangerous. He advances on me.

His right shoulder lifts, and I ready my own sword to parry . . . but it's a decoy move, meant to lure me into position.

I register my mistake a split second before a second blade, a small dagger, arcs toward my belly. I dodge, but I'm not fast enough; the tip swipes my shirt, slices it. Blood wells, and a blink later, pain screams through my abdomen.

I'm wounded but not gravely. If I had not dodged, Aldo would have carved me open.

I resist the urge to clutch my side, to keep my lifeblood from dripping to the floor, before I remember that it doesn't matter anymore; the sorcerer is dead.

So I focus on Aldo instead, who is circling again, just out of reach. He means to wear me down, frustrate me into making another mistake.

I won't make another mistake.

Just like Hector taught me, I feel the solid earth beneath my feet, breathe deep through my nose. My sword is an extension of my arm, which must be mighty and fast.

Aldo attacks with a flurry of swipes, but I counter them all. I am speed and light. I am power. He dances back, attacks again. I defend only, letting him bring the fight to me. He's the one who will wear down, the one who will make a mistake.

But the chaos of battle is always the greatest enemy, and something impacts my shoulder, sending me reeling toward Aldo. He reacts instantly to the opportunity, lifting the point of his blade to skewer my gut. I barely knock his blade aside with my own as the momentum carries me past him, exposing my back.

I fall on purpose, rolling away and flipping to my feet. I lift my sword just in time to block his downward, arcing blow. The impact rings in my ears, shudders all the way down through my hips.

"You don't have enough training in how to attack," Aldo says. His breath comes in gasps now.

He'll get no retort from me, because Elisa's voice in my head is the only one that matters. *There is nothing more dangerous than an opponent who thinks.*

Aldo advances, lifts a shoulder. . . .

I am the opponent who thinks. I dodge the opposite direction of his feint. His dagger finds air.

He spins, trying to dance away, but I'm wise to this now too, and I swipe low with my sword—*Slit the Rope*—right across his hamstrings.

He shrieks, crumples to the ground, rolls around in agony.

"Alejandro!" his mother screams.

I kick his sword out of the way and raise my arm for the killing blow, but something stays my hand.

What would Hector do? Kill Aldo? Or hold him for questioning? There's still so much we don't know.

When I don't allow my blow to fall, his mother rushes to his side, crouches down. Tears stream from her cheeks.

"Mamá," Aldo gasps out. "They hate me. Why do they hate me?"

Still not sure what to do, I take a moment to take stock.

Tristán is still on his feet, though his left arm hangs limp from its socket. Juan-Carlos seems uninjured, but his chest heaves, and bodies litter the ground, attesting to his effort. Carilla whirls, a hairpin in one hand, a dagger in the other. She is like a dust devil, small and fast and wondrous as she forces back anyone who dares to approach her prince.

Rosario himself has drawn his ceremonial sword, and a cut on one cheek indicates that someone got past Carilla and the condes before being dispatched. Behind them all are Iladro and Ambassador Songbird, huddled together, trying to stay low.

Valentino hovers over his father. He has taken up someone's fallen sword and holds it to Conde Astón's throat. Valentino is not yet in fighting form, but at least he has eliminated his father as a threat to the rest of us.

Clusters of combat are all around me. The air smells of blood and rings with battle cries. A quick head count indicates we've probably lost at least one recruit, though I can't tell who. The scuffles are getting closer, though. We're being gradually forced to retreat, herded toward the prince.

Aldo was right. We're going to lose. Soon we'll be corralled, with nowhere to go.

I turn to Aldo. Maybe if I kill him, his men will stop fighting. Or maybe the men are Astón's. Or are they the condesa's? Which one should I kill?

Maybe I'll kill them all. Aldo raised a weapon before the prince, which means I can kill him with impunity. But the others . . . executing nobles without a trial is something I could hang for. But if I don't, we'll all die anyway.

I raise my sword, ready to bring it down on Ariña's neck.

The doors to the ballroom fly open. Someone shrieks. Nobles flee the ballroom like a receding tide, emptying the space. Others pour in, taking their place. They are armed with wooden swords and kitchen knives, pitchforks and blacksmith tongs. It's Itzal and Tanix, along with the stable hands, the cooks, the stewards, and anyone else they could find.

Arturo is backing toward me, chased down by two imposter Guards. They swing their swords and he's dodging as best he can, but he's starting to slow with fatigue. I step in front of him, parrying with my sword. The impact wrenches my shoulder.

"Get back, Arturo. Find a weapon if you can. Help protect the prince."

He scurries back as I parry another blow, then another. If we make it out of this alive, I'm going to make sure we recruits practice defending against two attackers at once.

They come at me from opposite directions; dodging one blow will send me right into the other. So I drop to my belly, roll away as their swords barely miss impacting each other.

I leap to my feet, guard up, only to find they have both been dispatched. A stable boy stands over one with a bloodied pitchfork. Itzal has walloped the other's head with the pommel of his wooden sword.

"We took the bell tower," Itzal says. He breathes heavily, and a bruise is beginning to purple his left cheek. "You could see the whole ballroom light up like a torch from there."

The sorcerer's fire was supposed to be the signal to ring the bells.

Itzal adds, "Rito is there with Guardsman Bruno and a few of the second years, holding it."

"Guardsman Bruno helped!"

"He's the only fighting Guard who heeded the warning. The rest are passed out in their quarters, some in the mess. Sergeant DeLuca fell asleep in the officers' latrine, pants around his ankles."

"The *sergeant* was poisoned?"

"The barracks were ransacked for uniforms. Red, it's awful over there."

The clashes around us are dying down. We're going to be victorious after all.

"Itzal, great work. You and Rito, you saved us."

He grins. "I think we all saved each other."

Only a few small pockets of fighting remain, and our Guards, our real Guards, seem to have them well in hand.

"It's not over yet," says someone at my shoulder. Iván is propping up his brother, Juan-Carlos, who has sustained an injury to his knee. "We saw all those mercenaries in the Sky Wing, remember?"

"Right," I say. "And others were looting estates outside the palace."

"What do we do?" Itzal asks.

I have no idea. I'm about to say as much when Rosario steps down from the dais, Carilla once again like a burr in his side.

The prince crouches before the sobbing Ariña, tilts her chin up. "Who hired the mercenaries? Was it you?"

Ariña says nothing.

"How you answer me right now will determine whether your son lives or dies," Rosario says.

Ariña swallows. Then she says, "Me. And Conde Astón. It was both of us."

"Ariña!" Astón exclaims.

"How do we get them to lay down arms?" Rosario presses.

"Tell them . . . tell them the deal is off. No payment is forthcoming. We were going to pay them with dream syrup. Fighting men will do anything for dream syrup, you know. It's hidden in the empress's quarters. Take it out. Burn it."

Of course. King Alejandro's former mistress would definitely know secret ways into the Sky Wing. And Rosario would never think to search there.

"And this creature?" Rosario says, nudging the dead sorcerer with his boot. "Did you hire him too?"

"He was . . . a pet of sorts. Addicted to the dream syrup. He played his part, freezing everyone but my son. He did not know he would die today, though."

"Thank you," Rosario says. "If everything you say proves true, I will ensure that your son is not executed."

The prince stands, strides toward Conde Astón. Valentino still holds a blade to his throat, but it wavers. Tears stream down the boy's face.

"You, on the other hand, will most certainly be executed," Rosario says to the high conde. "And the *Scriptura Sancta* tells us that the sins of the father shall be visited upon the children, from generation to generation."

Rosario pauses to glance at Valentino.

In a softer voice, he adds, "But I don't believe that. I believe that children should *never* pay for their father's sins. Surrender now, Astón. Get word to the mercenaries to lay down their arms, that payment will not be forthcoming. If you convince them, I swear by God's righteous right hand that your family name will *not* be stricken from history, and your son Valentino will be named your heir by royal decree and declared a loyal subject, respected and beloved, until he passes the name to his own heirs."

Conde Astón blinks. "I have two older sons," he says.

"And they will all live and keep your name. But Valentino is the one who has proven himself. He will be lord of Ciénega del Sur."

Conde Astón looks to Ariña. Then to the boy who holds a sword to his throat. His hand goes up to cup Valentino's cheek. "My son," he says.

Valentino's eyes are wet with tears. "Why did you do this, Papá? *Why?*"

"To make a better future for you. For all of us."

"You were wrong."

"It doesn't matter now." To Rosario, he says. "I will do it. By God's righteous right hand."

Rosario steps aside. "Then go. Spread your message. Your three sons' lives and futures depend on you keeping your word."

Astón rises, dusts himself off, and flees the ballroom.

"What if he escapes?" I ask, staring after him. "What if he never comes back?"

"He will," says Valentino, wiping his cheeks. "My father is

many things. But most of all, he is proud. He will not let his family name be extinguished."

Next Rosario turns to Aldo, who lies gasping on the floor, blood pooling beneath his legs. "You stupid, stupid boy," he says.

Aldo sneers at him. "You would not be saying that if our plan had succeeded."

Rosario shakes his head in disbelief. "Do you have any idea how happy Red and I would have been to learn we have a brother? All you had to do was come to me, tell me who you were. You could have been a prince of the empire. I would have shared everything with you."

"It's my birthright," Aldo gasps out. "I was born for it. I deserve—"

"No," Rosario says. "One of the most important things I learned from my stepmother is that no one *deserves* to rule. Anyone who believes otherwise will make a truly terrible monarch. You made your choices. So be it."

"That's not . . ." Aldo pleads, transfigured into a small child, heartbroken and lost.

But Rosario has already turned his back.

"Conde Juan-Carlos, are you well enough to take these pieces of trash to the prison tower?" Rosario says, indicating Aldo and his mother.

"With pleasure, Your Highness," he says, retrieving Father Nicandro's cane. "May my brother accompany me? I seem to have misplaced a kneecap and could use a little help."

"Of course. You," Rosario says, indicating Itzal. "Fetch

Doctor Enzo and all his staff. We have lots of wounded. And you—it's Pedrón, right?"

"Yes, Your Highness." Pedrón's right arm hangs limp from his shoulder; I can't tell if it's out of its socket or broken or worse.

"Inform the monastery that their head priest has fallen."

"Yes, Your Highness."

Rosario crouches beside Father Nicandro's broken body. He reaches down and brushes his eyelids closed. "Rest well, old friend. You will lie in state, with my true family."

He looks up at me. "Red?"

He is my brother, but he is also my liege. I snap to attention, the way I've been taught. "Your Highness?"

"I need you to . . . please just stay by my side while we clean up this mess."

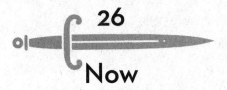

26

Now

THE next few days are a blur. Rosario reinstates me to the Guard, but instead of training, we are tasked with cleaning up. In the ballroom, we find two of the Basajuan boys. The Arturos insist on carrying their bodies out to the desert and burying them in the sand. "From sand we come, to sand we return," they intone.

Only eleven first-year recruits remain.

Next, we retrieve the remaining barrels of dream syrup and destroy them. Pedrón's right arm was badly injured, and he is forced to carry it in a sling. Doctor Enzo says his upper arm was broken in three places, that it might take a year of care to rehabilitate. Still, Pedrón does the work of ten men, lifting and dragging and tossing with his left arm.

Condes Tristán and Juan-Carlos lead the effort to root out any remaining mercenaries. The General opens an investigation into his army's recruitment practices to make sure no one like Beto or Sancho remains, who might have been compromised by Conde Astón and Condesa Ariña.

Conde Astón makes good on his word. After he releases the mercenaries from service, and returns to the palace, Rosario holds him in the tower, in a cell far, far away from either Aldo or Aldo's mother. Rosario tells me that Astón answers questions openly and without reserve, even confesses to poisoning Captain Bolivar and searching his quarters. His execution will wait until the empress returns, so that she and Lord-Commander Dante can question him themselves.

Sergeant DeLuca is also held for questioning. He maintains his innocence, insists that he was acting in good faith, and that if he betrayed his empress at all, he did so because he was deceived by Conde Astón into believing a traitor had infiltrated the first-year recruits. The conde himself verifies the sergeant's story, confirming that he manipulated DeLuca, playing on his deep desire to win the notice of the empress, along with his intolerance for all things Invierno. The sergeant had no idea who Aldo was, or about their greater plan. He assumed *I* was the traitor.

Soon after, Sergeant DeLuca is found hanging in his tower cell, his face swollen and blue, his Guard-issue belt cutting into the skin of his neck.

His loss makes me ill. I disliked him, almost as much as he disliked me, but he was still a Royal Guard, and he didn't need to kill himself. He was a fool, not a traitor, and Elisa would have been merciful. I'm sure of it.

A few days later, I'm in the barracks, running errands for Guardsman Bruno, who is in charge of everyone who remains, when Rosario sends for me. I meet him in his receiving room. He sits behind his desk, regal in satin, a small golden diadem circling his head. As always, Lady Carilla stands at his shoulder. It's the first I've seen her since the chaos ended.

"You're a warrior," I say to her, and it sounds more accusatory than I intend. "Trained for it, just like me. Except I think you're better."

Carilla smiles. It's a smile that says, "Much better," but without rubbing my nose in it. I appreciate her restraint. "You know I fostered in Amalur, yes?"

"Of course. With Queen Alodia."

"That's where I trained."

I blink, understanding dawning. "You were trained to be a guardian, by the warrior priests at the Monastery-at-Amalur."

"Yes."

"Elisa had a guardian for many years," Rosario says. "She thought I ought to have one too. Anyway, that's not why I called you here. You're a hero, Red. You saved me. You saved the *empire.*"

"It would have been really embarrassing if Elisa and Hector returned and we had misplaced it for them."

Rosario's look becomes pointed. Like that of a prince instead of a brother. "I do not consider this a humorous matter."

"It was a group effort," I say quickly. "Iván . . ." I have no idea what I want to say about Iván. There's too much, and yet all of it seems inadequate.

"I have already met privately with Iván," the prince says.

"But it's not just him. Every single first-year recruit helped, even some who got cut, like Itzal and Valentino. With the exception of DeLuca and Aldo, your Guard remained true down to the last nonfighting man."

He nods. "I'm glad to know it."

"Some died in the process. If a single one of them had failed, if a single one of them had not answered the call to duty, we could have—*would* have—lost."

"Their contributions are noted and will be recognized. And yet, from my position here, sitting at this desk instead of lying dead on the floor of the ballroom, it appears to me that our entire victory hinged on one moment: when you came to me and asked to activate the Guard recruits. Activating recruits is unprecedented. You pushed beyond tradition and expectation to come up with an idea that could help us, and you pestered me until I gave you permission. Without that one decision, you and I and many others would most certainly be dead by now. And the country would be in the midst of a civil war."

There is nothing I can say in response to this, so I bow my head. "Your Highness."

He taps his finger on the desk and stares at me thoughtfully. "Elisa will return in a month or so. I expect she'll offer you a boon. I wanted to give you time to consider. Think about what you'll ask of her."

I inhale sharply through my nose.

"Red?"

I hate asking for anything, but . . . "I already know."

"Really? I mean, tell me. What do you want?"

I grin, my heart swelling with hope. "Everything. Rosario. I want *everything*."

He raises a questioning eyebrow, and I tell him my plan.

We return to training. Master Santiago meets us in the sand one morning, and his face is dejected, his eyes clouded.

"I must explain a thing to you," he says, pacing along our staggered line. "Sergeant DeLuca hired me to advance your training. He told me to make you strong, but also to withhold knowledge of true swordsmanship. He said there was a spy among the first-year recruits, and he didn't want to enhance the skills of an enemy until we could suss him out."

He whips his sword around, making it sing through the air. "Ah, but he lied. *He* was the real traitor, or rather, the real traitor's fool. I guess that makes me the fool's fool. But had I known . . . I never would have . . . I am dreadful with words; truly, my words are a foul cacophony of noise, unfit for decent ears, and anyway, who wants to learn the three basic stances from which to launch an attack?"

"Hear! Hear!" says Pedrón, raising a wooden sword in his left hand.

"Hear! Hear!" we echo.

And with that, our official sword training finally begins.

Two months later, Empress Elisa returns. We know it because the monastery bells sing a welcoming hymn, and we are relieved of training for an entire afternoon in celebration.

I'm desperate to see everyone—Elisa, Hector, Mena, Mara, the new baby—but no one sends for me or comes to see me. Maybe they don't want to. Iván believes they must stay away to avoid the appearance of bias or favoritism while they sort out everything that happened. I hope he's right.

Lord-Commander Dante returns, though, and he thanks us for our service, informs us that investigations are under way so that he and Elisa can come to a full understanding of what transpired and why.

We break into cheers when he promotes Guardsman Bruno to the rank of sergeant. And we break into even louder cheers when he announces that we have proven ourselves, and no more cuts will be forthcoming.

I look around at my fellow recruits, my heart full. Iván, Pedrón, the Arturos . . . I wasn't ready to say goodbye to any of them. And now we'll all be together for our second year.

The desert blooms with spring, scenting the air with creosote and lavender, sending orange bougainvillea and purple wisteria creeping up the castle walls.

A month after the empress's return, we are ordered to report the following morning to the audience hall. All of us are named in the summons: me and the other first years, Tanix and the second years who helped us, Sergeant Bruno, Itzal and the stewards, stable hands, cooks and blacksmiths, Carilla, Valentino.

Bruno gives us extra time that evening to launder our clothes, telling us we must look our very best.

I finally dye the white streak in my hair, using dye that Rosario himself ordered specially for me. Iván helps, scrubbing it into my hair while I hold my head over the drain in the laundry room.

"It's taking really well," he assures me, which I appreciate, because I haven't seen a mirror in months.

I don't sleep a wink that night. Strangely, I miss Aldo. I miss whispering with him at night, even the way his occasional turning caused the bunk to creak, reminding me he was there. I miss seeing his face looking down at me in the morning.

Being a Royal Guard is dangerous work. I knew when I took to the sand that if I made it through recruitment, I would eventually lose friends to death. I didn't anticipate that I'd lose one to betrayal, or that the loss would ache just as fiercely.

He's not who I thought he was, I remind myself. *He was never a true friend.*

But even if I make peace with Aldo's loss, I know it won't help me sleep. Nothing will help me sleep. The soldier sickness will be with me always, no matter how much time passes, no matter how many victories are won.

So I make my bed on the floor and nest myself into the corner. I clutch my Godstone to my chest and make the choice to be at peace with myself.

The next morning we march, bathed and laundered and looking our very best, straight from the barracks and into the audience hall. My heart races, and my throat feels tight.

We are met at the door by Carilla and Valentino. *Conde* Valentino, I remind myself, for he has taken over rulership of Ciénega del Sur. His father still rots in the prison tower, awaiting his execution.

The double doors swing open, and we gasp. The entire court is in attendance.

Silence greets us as we enter and begin our walk down the aisle toward the throne and dais. Then the muttering starts.

They're staring at my hair, at my dyed white streak, which is no longer white but rather bright, bright red like a ruby. For no matter what happens today, I am Red. Red Sparkle Stone, citizen of Joya d'Arena and descendant of Invierne, by birth and by choice, and my name is beautiful and perfect, as it has always been.

Elisa sits on the throne, wearing her crown of shattered Godstones, and how she manages to look as regal as ever while holding a swaddled baby is a wonder. Hector stands at her right shoulder, and when he notes my red streak, a hint of a smile quirks his lips. Rosario stands at the empress's left shoulder, holding tight to Ximena's hand. The little princess grins, showing off a huge gap in her teeth.

Mara and the Quorum of Five stand behind them, looking on like indulgent parents.

I yearn to run to them all, but I don't dare. I'm just a Guard recruit.

We reach the end of our march. The audience hall rests in silence.

The empress stands. It's like a thunderclap when, as one, every single recruit, noble, and servant drops to their knees.

Elisa hands the baby to her husband.

"Rise, Royal Guard, recruits, stewards, courtiers, and staff," she says.

We obey.

"Traitors rose among your ranks. They threatened this empire. Took Joyan lives to further their own selfish causes. Yet you stayed true. More than that, you dedicated yourselves to exposing these traitors. You prepared yourselves beyond the scope of your expectations and training. And when my heir and our empire were at their most vulnerable, you risked life and limb to save us all. Therefore, it is my great pleasure to bestow upon each and every one of you the imperial medal of honor for acts of extreme loyalty."

The audience cheers.

I feel a little dizzy. All my friends are being honored. *All* of them.

When the cheers die down, Elisa continues. "You must forgive me, for this is the largest conferring of the medal of honor in the history of Joya d'Arena. Such a pinning ceremony would last until the night. Lord-Commander Dante will dispense medals at a later time. But, for now . . ."

She pauses. Looks at me. Smiles a smile that makes my heart ache.

"Recruit Red, Recruit Iván, please step forward."

We do. My legs are shaking. My fingers are numb. I'm not sure why. I know what I want. It shouldn't be so terrifying to ask for it.

"We conducted a thorough investigation of events. It became clear that the two of you displayed incredible leadership, uniting recruits, pursuing inquiries about a potential traitor, ensuring that Prince Rosario had a protective fighting force with which to defend this empire. Therefore, it pleases me to bestow upon you both the very highest honor in the empire, the Queen's Star for acts of honor and bravery in circumstances of extreme danger."

Once again the audience erupts into cheers, and no one cheers louder than the Royal Guard at our backs.

Lord-Commander Dante hands Elisa the medals. She steps forward to pin them herself, first to the collar of Iván's shirt, and then to mine. The empress and I are face-to-face when she whispers, "I like your hair."

She returns to the throne and sits. "Now, Recruit Iván, ask a boon, and if it is both reasonable and within my power, I shall grant it."

Iván bows. "I wish no boon save this," he says. "Simply a declaration, signed by Your Majesty's own hand, that all past sins perpetrated by any previous rulers of the countship of the Eastern Reaches have been redeemed through blood and sacrifice, and that it shall forever remain a beloved and loyal vassal of this empire."

Elisa inclines her head. "It shall be done. And you, Recruit Red? What boon will you ask? If it is both reasonable and within my power, I shall grant it."

This is what I've been waiting for.

I open my mouth, but nothing comes out. Rosario catches my eye, gives me a slight nod.

I try again. "If it please Your Majesty," I begin, my voice reed-thin. "I ask that you reconsider the adoption petition we put forth together in this very throne room almost a year ago."

The audience murmurs. Elisa frowns. "The chamber already voted. What has been done by the chamber cannot be undone by me."

"The chamber voted to deny adoption with inheritance," I clarify. "As delineated in article fifty-seven, section eight, of the *Articles of the Empire*. However, the *Articles* do not address adoption with*out* inheritance."

My heart is racing now. It feels as though all the air has been sucked out of the audience hall.

Elisa nods, considering. She says, "And of course, all powers not specifically delineated by the *Articles* remain with the crown."

"Yes, Your Majesty," I squeak out.

"So you're saying . . ." Do I imagine that her voice wavers a little? Beside her, Hector, Rosario, and Mara . . . they're all still as statues, barely breathing, waiting to hear what comes next.

The empress's thoughtful gaze deepens. Adopting me without making me an heir confers little political advantage. She will do it only if she wants me. Just me.

Hector reaches down for his wife's shoulder, squeezes.

Elisa says, "You're saying you would like to become our daughter, even if it means relinquishing all claim to the rights and powers of the throne. Even if it means you will be struck from the line of succession, your title of princess an honorific only?"

I can hardly get the words out. "Yes, Your Majesty. More than anything."

The audience murmurs again, but this time there is a more favorable tone to it. Murmurs definitely have tones. Or do I imagine the sense of approval emanating at my back?

In a stronger voice, I add, "And truth be told, being an inheriting princess wouldn't work for me. You see, I want to remain in your Guard."

Elisa launches to her feet. Her chin quivers. She gestures for Hector, Rosario, and Ximena to accompany her, and together they rush down the steps.

"My Red," she says, opening her arms wide, and I go to her like it's the most natural thing in the world.

Her arms wrap me tight. Then Hector's and Rosario's. Tinier arms clutch my waist.

"My sky," Hector says. "I'm so proud of you."

"Welcome to the family, little sister," says Rosario.

"I knew you would be my sistew," says Mena. "I *knew* it!"

"Look," Elisa says, brushing aside the swaddling from the sleeping face of the infant in Hector's arms. "It's time to meet your baby brother."

I sit on the arena wall, my legs dangling over the side. Iván sits beside me. Pedrón is a few paces away, collecting bets from the Arturos. Tall Arturo is our squad leader now. Iván and I split most of the vote, allowing Arturo to overtake us both. Which is perfectly fine with all of us; he'll be a great leader.

Below us is an assembly of children, ranging from ages twelve to eighteen. This year, there are nearly forty, in various styles and quality of dress. They've taken to the sand in hopes of making it through recruitment training and becoming Royal Guards.

Two of them are girls.

I'm unsurprised when Prince Hector strides toward us; he often attends recruitment day. Everyone begins snapping to attention, accosting him with a chorus of "Good morning, Your Highness," but he waves us at ease. "Placing bets, I take it?" he says to me.

"We would never," I say, even though I'm the worst liar who ever lived.

He grins. Then he leans down and kisses the top of my head.

"Papá!" I whisper in protest. "Not in front of *everyone*."

"They're used to it," he says. "You've already been my girl for eight years." To everyone else he says, "Enjoy the show," and he strides away to join another group of onlookers.

"That tall fellow looks promising," Iván says, pointing to a boy whose incredible height makes him a head taller than the next tallest recruit. "Who'd you bet on?"

"Her." I point. "Carilla. She's going to surprise everyone."

He snorts. "She's already a favorite. Everyone knows she's Rosario's guardian."

"But now that the secret is out, she might as well train publicly."

"Actually, I bet on her too."

I smile up at him, marveling that I ever thought him horrible.

"We've come a long way," he says, as if discerning my thoughts.

"Even made some friends."

"Not us, though."

"Of course not. We'll never be friends."

He fails to hide his smile, looking down at the recruits in the sand as they're paired off for sparring. The morning sun peeks through the palace towers, bathing the stone walls in light and heat. "Well, Princess," he says. "How does it feel to be the first girl to survive a year of recruit training?"

"Not as good as it's going to feel to become the first lady-commander."

His lips twitch. "You'll have a good shot at it, your mother being the empress, your father being a former lord-commander."

I raise an eyebrow at him. "My parents will be harder on me than anyone. That's how they are."

Iván's gaze moves toward my father, who is chatting easily with a group of nobles who've come to watch the spectacle. "He's the kind of father who'll always show up, isn't he?"

"Yes."

"And you don't hate it."

"No."

He bumps my shoulder with his own. "Just the same, I might give you some competition for that commander position."

"Good! Though, before we think about that too much . . ."

"We have to survive year two."

"We will," I tell him with conviction. "All of us, together."

Author's Note

POST-traumatic stress disorder affects approximately 3.5 percent of adults in the United States in any given year. Like all mental illnesses, it rarely affects two people in the exact same way. I wrote Red's experience with PTSD to reflect my own: her sleeping challenges, a socially embarrassing startle reflex, the inability to perceive love from others (even when it's obvious to everyone else), haunting but imperfect memories of traumatic events.

I'm only an authority on my own experience. So, if you suspect that you or someone you love suffers from PTSD, I strongly recommend talking to a mental health professional. Treatment for PTSD has come a long way, and great help exists. I'm rooting for you.

In writing Red's story, I'm indebted to the following saintly humans:

My husband, C.C. Finlay, who read multiple drafts and understood when I had to occasionally step away and hide in a cool, dark, safe place.

My whole team at Greenwillow and HarperCollins, but especially my editor, Martha Mihalick, and my publisher, Virginia Duncan, for saying yes to this book so quickly and without hesitation, and then waiting patiently while I took my damn time.

Dr. Erin Murrah-Mandril, assistant professor of English and core faculty member for the Center for Mexican American Studies at the University of Texas at Arlington, who applied her vast knowledge and reading experience to the text.

Shenira Becker, PsyD, who read with an eye toward the experience of trauma and its aftermath.

Early readers Melanie Castillo, Kristine Piedad, and Greg van Eekhout, who all gave editorial feedback based on their own knowledge and perspectives.

And last but never least, all my incredible readers who contacted me over the years to demand Red's story. This one is for you.